ADVANCE PRAISE FOR

Three Holidays and a Wedding

"Uzma Jalaluddin and Marissa Stapley have joined forces to create the quintessential holiday rom-com. Set in December of 2000, when Ramadan, Hanukkah, and Christmas all fell at the same time, *Three Holidays and a Wedding* combines two budding romances, a massive snowstorm, unlikely friends, meddling family members, and one magical small town for the most festive book you'll read this year. It's a hopeful story about having the courage to open yourself to others and the journey to finding where you belong."

—Carley Fortune, author of *Every Summer After*

"A sweet and touching celebration of friendship, family, faith, and of course, love, *Three Holidays and a Wedding* will delight readers seeking to lose themselves in the romance and magic of the season. Marissa Stapley and Uzma Jalaluddin have penned a new festive classic."

—Lily Chu, author of *The Stand-In*

"The perfect cozy read that turns winter travel chaos into triple-holiday magic! Complete with a holiday movie, wedding gone awry, and small-town festivities, Uzma Jalaluddin and Marissa Stapley create a sparkling world readers will never want to leave."

—Amy E. Reichert, author of *Once Upon a December*

"*Three Holidays and a Wedding* is the most delightful holiday rom-com. Marissa Stapley and Uzma Jalaluddin have written a charming novel that explores love, happiness, and honesty with sweet and hilarious characters that will steal your heart. I devoured it!"

—Jennifer Close, author of *Marrying the Ketchups*

"From its very first pages, *Three Holidays and a Wedding* whisked me away and dropped me down, gently, into a festive fairy tale. This sweet, sparkling novel is as fun and surprising as a perfect snow day. Uzma Jalaluddin and Marissa Stapley have proven that wherever you may find yourself, community is the people you love."

—Lauren Fox, author of *Send for Me*

Three Holidays
and a Wedding

Uzma Jalaluddin and
Marissa Stapley

G. P. Putnam's Sons * New York

PUTNAM
— EST. 1838 —

G. P. PUTNAM'S SONS
Publishers Since 1838
An imprint of Penguin Random House LLC
penguinrandomhouse.com

Trade paperback ISBN: 9780593543917
eBook ISBN: 9780593543924

Printed in the United States of America
1st Printing

Book design by Elke Sigal

For our families

. . . and for anyone who has ever wondered
where they belong during the holidays

The sun's light looks a little different on this wall than it does on that wall, and a lot different on this other one, but it's still one light.

—RUMI

Three Holidays
and a Wedding

Once upon a time—*the year 2000, to be precise—Christmas, Hanukkah, and Ramadan all fell within days of one another.*

Store shelves were emptied of baking ingredients. Travel agents frantically worked overtime to book tickets home. Toys and gifts were sold in record numbers.

All around the world, there was a sense of fated, feted felicitations.

And in a crowded airport in Denver, Colorado, a group of strangers were about to board a plane. Little did they know that their lives would never be the same again . . . or that holiday miracles can happen anywhere, to anyone, no matter what they celebrate . . .

ONE

Anna

December 20, 2000
Denver, Colorado

5 days until Christmas
2 days until Hanukkah begins
The 25th day of Ramadan

Anna Gibson awoke to the sound of sleigh bells ringing. She opened her eyes to see her boyfriend of six months, Nicholas Vandergrey, standing beside the bed, his blond curls still mussed from sleep. He was wearing the deep blue bathrobe she liked because it matched his eyes and a Santa hat at a jaunty angle—and he was holding a ribbon of sleigh bells.

"Good morning, most perfect woman in the world," he said, smiling down at her. "It's time for you to wake up." He shook the bells, and she tried not to wince at the jangling sound. "You have to get out of bed and start this day, because it's going to end with you landing in Toronto and joining the Vandergreys for *the best Christmas of your life*." He knelt down beside the bed and stared deep into her eyes. "I love you, Anna."

Anna found herself hoping she had remembered to remove last night's mascara as she said, "I love you, too, Nick."

"I can't wait for what's in store over the next week. I have so many Christmas surprises for you."

"And I have so many surprises for *you*," she said, sitting up in bed. "It really is going to be the perfect Christmas." She felt a small twinge as she said the word "Christmas." She couldn't help it. This year, Christmas and Hanukkah fell at the same time, which brought memories of a childhood long past, when her family celebrated both holidays, no matter where they landed on the calendar. The best years were when they aligned, like this one.

Except she had a new life now. A perfect life. With Nick.

"You okay there, Anna?"

"Oh, I'm fine. Just"—she smiled at him and told a tiny lie—"happy."

There is only one happiness in this life. To love, and be loved. Anna heard her father's encouraging voice in her head, the way she often did. Jack Gibson had always been a big proponent of useful aphorisms—and now that he was gone, Anna was grateful for these sayings because it often felt like she still had him guiding her.

She now smiled a genuine smile. She was twenty-seven years old and on her way to a happy ending. Plus, it was *wonderful*, she decided, that two of her most beloved holidays were falling at the same time. She had read in the *Denver Post* the day before that it was Ramadan, too; this was why the stores and airports were busier than ever this year. The increased demand on travel from this rare tri-holiday season was the reason she hadn't been able to get on the same flight as Nick, whose mother, Alicia, had booked his ticket home ages ago. As much as she had wanted to fly with her boyfriend, catching a slightly later flight gave her time to stop into the office and approve one last thing as deputy photo editor of *Denver Decor* magazine—*and* squeeze in a hair appointment before heading to Toronto. "There's just so much festive joy and celebration floating around," Anna said to Nick. "We're bound to have the best holiday season of our lives, aren't we?"

"Guaranteed," Nick said. "Now, come on, sleepyhead. I made you some coffee. But it's in the kitchen, meaning you have to get out of bed to enjoy it." He winked. "I'm going to hit the shower."

Anna waited until the bathroom door closed before she fell back on the pillow and rolled onto her side to look at the small framed photo beside the bed, taken the night they met. It was six months earlier, at the Denver Botanic Gardens. Anna's boss, Janey Sawchuk, had come down with the flu that night and had called Anna in a panic. *Someone* from *Denver Decor* simply had to attend the Habitat for Humanity Under the Stars fundraiser, Janey insisted. Anna had plans with friends that night, but she couldn't say no to her boss if she wanted to keep her job; Janey had a reputation for firing people on a whim.

The night of the gala, Anna had dutifully dashed off to the mall to grab the closest approximation to a gala-appropriate dress on her limited budget. She had borrowed teetering golden sling-backs from Karina, the style editor. Gia, Janey's long-suffering assistant, had a deft hand with hair and makeup. Soon, her work friends had transformed Anna from harried office worker to upscale gala attendee. "Please make a good impression, Anna," Janey had instructed. "Nicholas Vandergrey of

Vandergrey Industries is sitting at your table—and if you play your cards right, they'll advertise."

At the time, all Anna had known about the Vandergrey family was that they owned one of the biggest household cleaning product companies in the world. A quick Google search told her that the company had originated in Toronto, so Anna, who had been born in Toronto, left for the gala confident that she had at least one icebreaker in her back pocket.

She had assumed Nicholas Vandergrey would be a gray-haired man in a business suit and had not realized there was a Nicholas Vandergrey *Junior*—who preferred to be called Nick, and was quite charming, in addition to looking very much like Scott Foley. Okay, so it was Scott *Speedman* who was her ultimate *Felicity* actor crush—but after a few glasses of champagne she had forgotten all about that. She might have even blurted out, "Has anyone ever said you look like—"

"Scott Foley?" Nick had replied. "I get that a lot. Has anyone ever told *you* you're a dead ringer for Audrey Hepburn? I swear, you might just be the most perfect woman I have ever seen in my life."

That was the first time he had called her "perfect"—but it wouldn't be the last. After six months, even if she knew deep down inside she was nowhere close to perfect, she had almost started to believe him.

She snuggled further down into Nick's thousand-thread-count sheets and tried hard not to think about the things she had never gotten around to telling him. The way she had been derailed by her grief over her father's sudden death two years ago. But the mess she had previously made of her life because of grief had no place in her busy schedule today. At the gala, when Nick had asked what she had been doing before starting at *Denver Decor*, she had told him she had decided to be impulsive and go traveling—which *was* technically true. What she hadn't told him was that she had given zero notice to her job at Colorado Interiors, then only made it as far as Paris before falling into a depression so deep she had only seen the inside of a Latin Quarter hotel room and the underside of a duvet cover for almost a month. Eventually, she ran out of money and maxed out her credit card on a plane ticket home.

"I'm so glad you went traveling and found yourself in Europe," Nick had told her once. "Because the self you found is absolutely right for me."

If only you knew, she would sometimes think. But it was too late to tell him now. She needed to leave the past behind—which was an easy thing to do when Nick knew so very little about who she had been before they met. The night of the gala, they had bonded over both being Torontonians at heart. "Up until a few years ago, my dad and I always went back there for a few days over the holidays," she had told him, feeling the pull of nostalgia.

"Why did you stop going?" Nick had asked. There must have been other people at the table, but Anna didn't remember who— she and Nick had been completely wrapped up in each other.

"My dad passed away last year," Anna had told him. Nick had told her how deeply sorry he was for her loss. But he had not asked for details, and this became a pattern. Anna had learned that Nick did not like to dwell on unpleasantness. He felt life was for living, and the past was the past. Which was true, wasn't it? It was a better way to live than wallowing in loneliness and misery.

"What if I promise, here and now, to take you to Toronto during the holidays?" he had asked Anna that night at the gala. She had nearly melted into a puddle on the ballroom floor— and then he had asked her to dance.

When she had relayed the story to her work friends the next day, their reactions were divided. "This is *magical*," Gia had declared, swooning onto the couch in Karina's crowded-with-fashion-samples office. But Karina had been more cynical. "I could swear I saw a photo of him in the society pages just last month, out on the town with his girlfriend, Elsa Miller. The *model*."

"Well, he didn't mention any models last night," Anna had replied, her expression dreamy. It was clear she had fallen head over borrowed heels. Karina had patted her on the shoulder and said, "I love seeing you so happy—but keep your eyes open." So, Anna dutifully made a weak attempt to look into Nick's past relationships by going through newspaper back issues and asking around. Except she felt like she was testing her luck. If she looked too deeply into him, he might do the same to her—and not like what he found. So, Anna had decided to stop digging and take Nick at his word. From day one, Nick was fully committed to her. He was the perfect boyfriend, and she was the perfect girlfriend—and they were going to have a perfect life together. Which now included the most perfect Christmas ever.

Anna hopped out of bed and crossed the room to where Nick's packed suitcase sat open. It was a marvel of rolled-up socks, neatly folded boxers and undershirts, an array of silk pajamas, ties in several colors. A heavy garment bag beside the suitcase contained his suits and tuxedo, the sort of attire that was required for a Vandergrey family Christmas. Anna knew it was all going to be dazzling—and very expensive. She felt queasy when she thought of the state of her already pathetic bank account after she bought several expensive new outfits and a thoughtful, tasteful gift for each of his family members. Growing up, she hadn't been deprived of anything, but her family's celebration of both Christmas and Hanukkah had been homespun rather than all store-bought. Anna, Jack, and Anna's stepmom, Beth, had always exchanged at least one handmade gift—which, Jack always said, were the gifts that came from the heart.

Even though Anna sensed handmade gifts were not the Vandergrey style, she hadn't been able to resist making Nick just one special thing—to show him how much she cared about him and invite him into her holiday world. This gift wasn't one Anna necessarily wanted Nick opening in front of his family. It was humble and personal: a handmade photo album chronicling their relationship so far. It had only been six months, but there were still many photos to fit in the little album. So many that Anna had had a delightfully hard time choosing among the snaps of their weekend in New York City, their ski trip to Vail, charity balls, picnics, and dinner dates. Now, as she flipped quickly through the album, smiling back at her own grinning face, the cache of memories made her feel secure and confident in her relationship. She was nervous about meeting his family, but it was all going to work out. She carefully moved aside a pair of socks so she could slide the album into Nick's suitcase, where he would find it later as a surprise.

Anna was the one who was surprised, though: a tiny jewelry box was tucked in among Nick's clothes.

She shouldn't look at what was inside; she knew that. But suddenly Anna felt consumed by the desire to know what the box contained. She had bought Nick solid gold cuff links in the shape of little stars, a loving reminder of their meeting at the Gala Under the Stars—but if Nick had bought her something far more extravagant, she would need to get him something else, too. She didn't want to be caught unawares, embarrassed in front of his family. There was so much riding on this. Just a tiny peek, she told herself. Just so she could make sure this was going to be the most magical Christmas ever and she was not going to disappoint Nick in any way.

She flipped open the box—and gasped.

It was a square-cut diamond on a yellow gold band—just like the one Brad Pitt had once given to Gwyneth Paltrow.

An engagement ring.

For her.

Anna stared down at it and tried to slow her racing thoughts.

Nick was planning to propose over Christmas. It was *so* romantic!

It was also . . . so *soon*.

She heard the shower turn off and quickly replaced the ring in the suitcase. Then she dashed across the room and hopped back into bed, mind still reeling. She had thought about marrying Nick, many times—of course she had. You didn't meet a Prince Charming and not fantasize repeatedly about walking off into the sunset together. But she had always assumed they'd date at least a year before getting engaged.

Was it terribly romantic that he wanted things to move fast? Or was it terri-*fying*?

The bathroom door opened. Anna stared up at the ceiling, trying to get her breathing to return to normal.

Nick entered the room in a towel and stopped when he saw her. "Hey. Don't you need to get to the office, then to the airport? Today has to go like clockwork, don't forget."

"Right, yes, of course," Anna said, hopping out of bed and planting a kiss on his cheek as she headed into the kitchen for her coffee.

After showering, Anna dressed in the outfit she had planned for this very eventful day as she listened to Nick in the kitchen, singing along to a Michael Bublé Christmas album piping through the many speakers in his apartment. She surveyed herself in the mirror. Her outfit was not practical for winter weather but could go seamlessly from day to night, and airport to gala: a blue silk strapless cocktail minidress paired with an oversized blazer she could shrug off and replace with the pashmina she had rolled into her handbag.

She double-checked that her own luggage was as perfectly packed as Nick's. It was a small carry-on bag—which she and Nick had agreed was the right choice to ensure she could get out of the airport as quickly as possible. They were heading straight to a champagne reception his family was hosting in a private room at the Ritz. After that, it was off to Roy Thomson Hall for box seats at a seasonal symphony performance with a select group of family and friends. Anna couldn't remember if they were eating dinner before the symphony or after—but she knew it was all on the schedule, printed and placed in her suitcase by Nick so she wouldn't get confused about the swarm of activities his family had planned.

Normally, a holiday during the winter months required packing winter gear like parkas or boots, but Nick had explained there wouldn't be time for any outdoor activities. "Not even skating at Nathan Phillips Square?" Anna had asked, thinking back to another fond memory from her days in Toronto as a child.

Nick had tilted his head quizzically, as if the thought of going skating at Toronto's city hall had never occurred to him. Anna had decided not to pursue it—and did not suggest tobogganing on the Christie Pits slope or a wintry walk through High Park, either.

"Okay, babe, I'm heading out."

Anna walked with Nick to the door of his spacious condo, one that overlooked downtown Denver on one side and the Rockies on the other, to give him a kiss before he left for the airport. She could still see the engagement ring in her mind's eye, sparkling, beautiful . . . and overwhelming. She looked up into his eyes and wondered when it would happen. Would he propose to her in a stolen moment that was just the two of them? Or would he do it on Christmas morning, in front of the tree . . . and his entire family?

She stood on her tiptoes to kiss him goodbye.

"Mmm," she murmured. He tasted like the expensive toothpaste he ordered from Italy. But he pulled away from her and frowned.

"Coffee breath," he said with a shrug. "Hope you didn't pack your toothbrush already." Then he put his hands on her shoulders and held her firmly. "Okay, so remember. *Clock-*

work. I'll see you later at Pearson." This was Toronto's main airport.

"Of course. Got it. I have the schedule," Anna said, lowering her head as she spoke because she now felt self-conscious about the coffee breath. But as she ducked her head, she nestled into his chest for a moment and listened to the beating of his heart. This was going to be the best Christmas. She just had to get through one morning of work, grab a taxi to the airport, fly to Toronto—and then the fairy-tale holiday season would begin. She looked up at Nick again and smiled. "Everything is going to be perfect."

"It has to be," Nick said, patting her on the head, then releasing her. "Now, one last thing. I have a surprise for you before I go."

Anna felt light-headed. It was happening already. If this was going to be the big moment, maybe that was a relief—because, she realized, her hands suddenly slick with sweat, she didn't know what she was going to say. Maybe she could ask for a little time to think. Maybe they could have some time to talk about it. "There is no more lovely, friendly, and charming relationship, communion, or company than a good marriage," Anna had watched her dad write in a wedding card to a pair of friends once, quoting Martin Luther. Marriage was a serious thing; she had been raised to believe this. It was not something to be taken lightly—or said yes to on a whim. She loved Nick and felt almost sure she wanted to spend her life with him. But her heart was now beating so fast she was near panic.

Nick was down on one knee. Anna squeezed her eyes shut.

Then she realized he was touching her feet. She opened her eyes and saw that he was taking shoes from a shoebox. And not just any shoebox: this one bore the distinctive Manolo Blahnik name.

"A present already?" she managed through her breathless relief. "But it's not even Christmas morning yet . . ."

Dismay rushed in. She had messed things up already. *Her* pre-Christmas gift, the little photo album she'd made for him, tucked into his suitcase, was a sweet idea—but in comparison to a pair of Manolos, the photos were just embarrassing. "I don't know what to say . . ."

"You could start with 'thank you.'" He placed the first shoe on her foot, then the second. They were blue satin pumps and matched the color of her cocktail dress exactly; each toe sported a light silver crystal square buckle; the heel was a high stiletto.

"They're gorgeous! Thank you!"

"Now you really are going to look absolutely perfect."

Anna bit her lip. She had no room for these in her suitcase, and had been planning to wear shoes with a lower heel that were easier to walk in. She had so many places she needed to go today. But how could you say no to Manolos? She'd just channel her inner Carrie Bradshaw.

She kicked out one of her feet. "Perfect fit."

"Perfect *everything*." He checked his watch. "And on that note, I should go so I don't miss my flight. See you tonight—but call me when you get to the airport and let me know everything's on track. Don't forget, my mother is a very exacting woman. Nothing can go wrong."

Anna's smile faltered, but Nick didn't notice. The door clicked shut and he was gone.

TWO

Maryam

December 20
Denver International Airport

"Maryam. Maryam *beti*. Look around. The most perfect time of year, *nah?*" Dadu said.

Beside her grandfather, Maryam Aziz nodded but didn't look up. She was too intent on herding—there really was no other word to describe it—her parents and grandfather through Denver International Airport while maneuvering the leaning stack of suitcases piled on their overstuffed luggage cart.

Dadu, Maryam's paternal grandfather, reverted to a happy child during the holidays. A slightly wizened, five-foot-seven child, with a pot belly and a lined but beaming face. He was dressed now in a festive bright red cardigan, green corduroy pants, and shiny brown patent leather loafers. The woolen scarf around his neck was decorated with smiling snowmen and the words "Merry Christmas" embroidered in bright green at the edge—a gift from their next-door neighbor Mrs. Lyman.

Maryam suspected the widowed seventy-five-year-old grand-mother had a small crush on her dadu. The irony, of course, was that neither their Muslim family nor Jewish Mrs. Lyman actually celebrated Christmas.

But this year was different. This year Christmas, Hanukkah, and Eid—the celebration at the end of the Muslim month of Ramadan—would all fall within days of one another for the first time in over three decades. As a result, the decorations, songs, and general good cheer hit Maryam a little differently; she was almost thirty-one years old, and this was the first time she had felt included in the various holiday traditions she had witnessed her entire life. Her grandfather, meanwhile, had been absolutely giddy at the tri-holiday convergence, and made sure to gift the entire neighborhood and his friends from the mosque with brightly wrapped boxes of Indian *mithai* sweets and candy canes before they left for Toronto for her younger sister Saima's wedding.

"*Beti*, you're not looking! See the tree? And they are playing your favorite holiday song." Sure enough, the strains of "All I Want for Christmas Is My Two Front Teeth" could be heard faintly above the sounds of thousands of frazzled passengers. Maryam flushed.

"I liked that song when I was six, Dadu," she muttered, but obliged him by admiring the thirty-foot tree in the middle of the departures lounge. It was decorated with white fairy lights and giant red, silver, and gold ornaments. A serene angel, garlanded in lace, a delicate halo of gold adorning her dark brown hair, graced the top of the tree.

"She looks like your dadi-ma," her grandfather said, referring to his late wife. They were silent for a moment, both lost in memories. Her grandmother had passed away a few years ago. This was the first trip Dadu had taken since, adding to the pressure Maryam carried today.

Not that she needed any more pressure. With a quick glance to make sure her parents, Ghulam and Azizah, were following, she cut a path through the packed crowd.

"So much happiness," Dadu sighed. "Plus, a wedding as well! How blessed we are, yes?"

Maryam pushed the luggage cart and tried not to panic. When her younger sister, Saima, resident family nomad, had impulsively announced her engagement to a virtual stranger named Miraj Sulaiman six weeks ago, followed by the happy couple's intention to tie the knot during the last ten nights of Ramadan, her parents had predictably freaked out. While Maryam worried over her sister's hasty decision to marry, her parents, once they were assured that Miraj was also a medical doctor and the son of a prominent Toronto family, were more concerned about the logistics of the wedding.

"You can't get married during Ramadan," Azizah said. "Ramadan is for fasting, family, and prayer, not parties, dancing, and shopping!"

"We're getting married on December 25, and that's final," Saima said firmly. She had called them from Sierra Leone, where she was completing her two-year tour with Doctors Without Borders. Leave it to her sister to find true love in the middle of a war zone. "It's the only time that works for both of us. Besides, Muslims get married on Christmas all the time! Even Maryam—" she started, but came to an abrupt halt.

"Muslims marry on Christmas because it's *convenient*. Everyone is at home anyway. Nobody gets married during Ramadan!" Azizah said, ignoring Saima's comment. "I absolutely forbid it."

"Miraj and I are heading back to Sierra Leone in January. I'm sure you wouldn't want us to travel without a *nikah*. What would people say?"

Maryam had to hand it to her baby sister: hitting their parents with the double whammy of sacrificing-doctor and *log kya kahenge*, what would people say—as in, every *desi* parent's horror over becoming the next item on the community rumor mill—was pure genius.

"This wedding *will not* happen during Ramadan—" Azizah repeated.

"Fine. If you don't care to come to my wedding, we'll just get married in Sierra Leone. There's a mosque near my hostel, I can arrange a *nikah* tomorrow—" Saima started, causing her mother to squawk in outrage.

"Should I call my good friend Shah Rukh Khan to mediate this discussion?" Dadu offered. In another life, Dadu, aka Mohamed Ali Mumtaz Aziz, had been a hotshot Bollywood director for some of the biggest blockbuster hits of the '70s and '80s. Which he managed to bring up in every single conversation.

Still, Azizah wasn't going to give up without a fight, even if it had been a while since their family had a reason to celebrate. Maryam knew she was partly to blame for why *log kya kahenge* was so effective on her scandal-shy parents.

"*Beta*, be reasonable. Ramadan is only six weeks away. How can you organize a wedding while you are in Sierra Leone treating patients? And you know December is the busiest time of year at the pharmacy; plus, we will all be fasting . . ." Her mother trailed off into meaningful silence, and Maryam recognized her cue. Everyone in the family knew how this conversation would end: with Maryam stepping in to solve all the problems, as usual.

"Don't worry about anything, Saima," she said. "I can coordinate the wedding details from Colorado."

"But nobody gets married in Ramadan," her mother tried one last time.

"It will be a small *nikah*, only close family and friends," Maryam assured her. "The important thing is that Saima found someone who makes her happy." She paused, wondering if now was the time to press the point. "You *are* happy? This feels rushed."

"Relax, Bor-yam, I'm happy. I promise," Saima laughed. Maryam stiffened at the nickname but didn't push back. Also as per usual.

"Maryam *beta*, I will ask A. R. Rahman if he can DJ the wedding—it's the least he can do after I jump-started his career," Dadu said, referencing the world-famous Grammy- and Oscar-winning composer best known for his '90s Bollywood bangers.

Maryam smiled at her grandfather and patted him on the shoulder. "I can handle this on my own," she said. "In fact, I think organizing Saima's Ramadan wedding will be fun!"

Famous last words, Maryam thought sourly now as she inched past a large travel party heading to Disney World, complete with matching T-shirts and Mickey Mouse hats. While Saima was thankfully not a bridezilla, coordinating with Miraj's family in Toronto had turned out to be a nightmare.

So far, Saima's future in-laws hadn't lived up to a single Canadian stereotype: they didn't punctuate their conversations with "eh," they disdained Tim Hortons, and they had no desire to be friendly to their brand-new American family. In fact, for the first two weeks following her sister's engagement, she couldn't even reach them on the phone.

When Maryam finally got hold of Miraj's mother, the woman's first order of business was to emphasize how important their family of doctors were in the Toronto Muslim community, followed by a third-degree interrogation about the Aziz family. After Maryam admitted to being a pharmacist, Saima's future mother-in-law reassured her it was never too late to return to school, especially since it was *much* easier to get into medical school in the United States. Apparently, they were *far* more selective in Canada.

Then she dumped all the wedding planning on Maryam, reasoning that since she was still single at nearly thirty-one ("Do they not have any suitable boys in Colorado, and is that why your sister went husband-hunting in Sierra Leone?"), she had nothing better to do.

And Maryam had thought Canadians were supposed to be *nice*.

By the time she arrived at the airport, Maryam had had just about enough of her family, Miraj's family, and the world in general. The only person who hadn't been irritating her was Dadu, and even he was testing her patience at the moment.

She gave the precariously loaded luggage trolley, piled high with half a dozen carry-on bags, an extra hard push in her frustration. Her family were overpackers in the best of circumstances, and for a whirlwind wedding with three formal events—*mehndi, nikah, walima*—plus the gifts they had bought for Miraj's family, they had outdone themselves. They had paid extra when they checked in their luggage, but still had plenty to carry on.

Why did Saima do this to us? she thought again, after she pulled Dadu back from tripping over a stroller while making funny faces at a toddler.

Maryam wasn't normally resentful. Usually she was calm, patient, and responsible. Dadu called her "the Unflappable Maryam Aziz." It was just that at this moment, she longed to flap away somewhere quiet, such as a cabin in the woods, or a deserted island in the South Pacific, or even a tiny town in the middle of nowhere.

Anywhere but Denver International Airport, five days before Christmas, in the middle of a tri-holiday maelstrom, while she was fasting. She hadn't eaten since five that morning, and her stomach felt cramped with hunger. With the two-hour time difference, by the time they arrived in Toronto, she would have gone without food and water for over fourteen hours. Nothing she wasn't used to, of course—she had started fasting at the age of ten—but she could have used a shot of caffeine right now. In an IV drip, preferably.

Their little party was also attracting more than their fair share of attention, she noticed. She could feel curious, interested, bored, and occasionally hostile eyes resting on her hijab, and on her father's long salt-and-pepper beard.

She had started to wear the hijab last year. While her mother only occasionally drew a *dupatta* shawl over her head, and Saima didn't observe the head covering at all, Maryam had felt strongly compelled to start wearing the traditional head covering, and she was still getting used to the unwelcome extra attention it caused.

A young white woman passed them, the heels of her sky-high, expensive blue satin stilettos clicking as she pulled a chic cream-colored suitcase behind her. Her caramel-highlighted brown hair was perfectly blown out, the edges carefully curled so they framed her face. The high cheekbones of her triangular face emphasized large brown eyes, a ski-slope button nose, and a wide smiling mouth. She jostled the leaning tower of suitcases in her haste, forcing Maryam to reach out a hand to steady them, glaring at the oblivious woman's back.

"Come along, Maryam *beta*, our flight leaves soon," Ghulam called. "I have been watching the Weather Network, and they are calling for snow in Toronto."

"We're flying to Canada. Isn't it always snowing there?" Maryam grumbled, but she leaned her shoulder into the luggage cart and followed.

She spotted brunette Barbie again at the security line; the other woman sailed through without any "random" security checks or secondary screening. Meanwhile, the security officer spent a good three minutes comparing the admittedly unflattering picture in her American passport to her face, and she could hear the entire line audibly groan when she started piling luggage onto the scanner bed.

In contrast, the young woman was already halfway across the departures lounge, chatting intensely on a little flip phone. People with cell phones were so annoying. Maryam was positive they were a passing fad, and renewed her vow to never buy one.

When the Aziz family entourage finally made it to their gate, Maryam collapsed onto a seat, feeling as if she had run a marathon. She was pretty sure she had sweat through her white blouse, too. She idly scanned the crowd—and her gaze snagged on a familiar face. Maryam did a double take. It couldn't be. Heart pounding, she chanced another quick peek at the young man seated a few rows away.

Sharp jaw, large brown eyes, dark curly hair flopping over his forehead, and dressed in a travel-sensible black hoodie and blue jeans, Saif Rasool looked impossibly handsome. She hadn't seen him in nearly five years, since he had moved to California after law school. The son of her mother's best friend, he was also her forever-unrequited childhood crush, so of course it made sense that she would bump into him now.

Not that it mattered—Saif likely couldn't pick her out of the crowd. She was just another one of the daughters of his parents' friends he nodded at vaguely during *dawaats*, dinner parties. Whereas she had been in love with him, on and off, since she was twelve years old.

In all the times Maryam had fantasized about casually bumping into Saif outside of their family orbit, she was always effortlessly chic, her makeup on point, hijab tied just so—not in her current sweaty, cranky, caffeine-deprived state. In an effort not to draw his attention, Maryam carefully maneuvered so that only her side profile faced Saif, and cast her gaze behind her, straight at beaming brunette Barbie.

Clearly, God was testing her.

"You sure have a lot of bags," the young woman remarked, not bothering to keep her voice down as she slid her phone back into an expensive-looking handbag, all friendly smiles and dimples. Maryam bet this woman wouldn't turn a perfectly curled hair if she bumped into her childhood crush at the airport. Who was she kidding? She bet all of brunette Barbie's childhood crushes serenaded her via acoustic guitar, like Adam Sandler in *The Wedding Singer*, professing their lifelong adoration.

"My family considers the two-bag limit more of a suggestion than a hard-and-fast rule," Maryam replied.

The pretty woman laughed loudly. From the corner of her eye, Maryam could have sworn Saif looked up.

"Would you mind keeping your voice down?" Maryam hissed.

"Why?" her unwitting conversational partner asked, brows furrowed.

"Because . . . because . . . my grandfather is sensitive to high-pitched noises!" Maryam said in a rush.

The woman was unfazed. "Is that your grandfather talking over there? He's so cute! My grandfathers both passed away when I was little, and I didn't get to know them at all. Hi, I'm Anna," she added, extending her hand.

"Maryam." The women shook hands, and though Maryam hated making small talk, this conversation was a good distraction from wondering whether Saif had noticed her yet, and if she should hide behind the Christmas tree until their flight departed.

"I saw you and your family in the departures lounge. Your parents?" Anna asked, nodding at Ghulam and Azizah seated behind Maryam. She glanced again at the luggage piled around Maryam. "And those must be all the bodies you're smuggling across the border, right?"

Anna laughed that musical laugh again, and Maryam looked around uneasily. A few of the other passengers had looked up at the words "smuggling" and "bodies." Barbie really didn't seem to get it.

"That's not funny," Maryam said. "You do realize we're traveling while brown and Muslim, right? You could get us into trouble with that sort of talk."

Instantly, Anna clapped a hand to her mouth, her pretty brown eyes rounding in embarrassment. "I'm so sorry!"

Maryam stood up. She needed to take a breather, get some space from Saif and from Anna, too. It was also probably time for her diabetic grandfather to have a snack before his blood sugar dipped.

When Maryam returned a few minutes later with a fruit smoothie, she stopped in her tracks. Instead of Anna disappearing, as Maryam had hoped, she was cheerfully chatting to Maryam's parents and Dadu.

"Yes, first time flying to Toronto. Our daughter is getting married to a surgeon," Azizah boasted.

Anna, noticing Maryam's approach, grinned at her. "You didn't tell me!" she said, beaming. "I'm flying to Toronto to meet my boyfriend's family. I guess we're both taking a huge plunge!"

"I'm not getting married," Maryam said, handing the snack to her grandfather.

"Our younger daughter, Saima, is the *dulan*, the bride. She's a doctor, too! She and Miraj both work for Doctors Without Borders," Azizah explained proudly. Maryam felt her chest expand at this descriptor—she really was so damn proud of her little sister. Even though Saima's impulsiveness was hard to deal with, the thought of seeing her sister again filled her with joy. They were close, and when Saima was at home, they spent a lot of time together. It had been too long since her last visit.

"If you're all flying into Toronto together, where is your sister?" Anna asked, turning to her.

Maryam glanced at her watch. Saima's connecting flight should have landed by now. The plan had been to meet at Denver International and fly to Toronto together. Saima had insisted on stepping foot on Canadian soil with her family.

An announcement interrupted her response: "Flight AC7164 with nonstop service from Denver International to Pearson International in Toronto, this is a special announcement. The inbound flight has been delayed due to weather. The new departure time is fifteen hundred hours."

Maryam looked at her parents. Since they had elected to fast today, despite the difficulty of doing so while traveling, this new delay meant they would have to break their fast in the air, and not in Toronto, as they had originally planned.

"I'll go pick up some meals," Maryam said, resigned. "I'm sure Saima is calling Miraj from a pay phone. I'll look for her, too." At least this additional errand would be another distraction from Saif. But when she glanced over, she saw he had disappeared. With any luck, by the time she returned, Anna would be gone, too.

While in line for takeout, Maryam caught sight of her sister at the duty-free shop, rubbing perfume on her wrists. She waved, and her little sister ran to her, clasping her tightly in a hug. She smelled strongly of some heavy floral fragrance, and

Maryam wrinkled her nose, even as she held on tightly to her sister. Laughing, Saima released her, sticking her wrist under Maryam's nose.

"It's called Happy, don't you love it? So sweet and floral!" Saima said.

Maryam recoiled at the scent, which was even stronger now that they were facing each other.

Her sister laughed. "Right, I forgot. Bor-yam can't stand to smell the roses."

That nickname again. Bor-yam—boring Maryam. "Actually, I'm allergic to roses, not to enjoying things . . ." Maryam started.

Saima grinned and Maryam stopped, realizing she was being teased. Saima was four years younger, but aside from a similar arch to their full dark brows, they looked nothing alike. Where Maryam was the tallest person in their family at five foot eight, Saima was a petite five foot two. Maryam's complexion was light tan year-round, whereas Saima's skin was a few shades darker, her face rounded, a contrast to Maryam's pointed chin, thin lips, and large dark eyes. Saima had full lips and smaller eyes that perpetually sparkled with mirth and mischief. Dadu called the sisters his "Grumpy/Sunshine," and though Maryam had tried to tell him that term was a popular romance trope that did not apply to siblings, she had to admit it also captured their sisterly dynamic. Maryam had spent most of their childhood feeling both exasperation and deep affection for Saima, usually at the same time. For a trained medical doctor who worked in some of the most conflict-ridden places on earth, her sister often treated her family with a flippant manner that bordered on immaturity. Maryam had been surprised to hear from her sister's medical school classmates that Saima was often praised for her steadiness during emergencies.

"How is the wedding planning going? What are you wearing? Oh God, I hope you talked Mom out of that hideous orange sari. I know we're Hyderabadi and addicted to bling and bright colors, but there is a *limit*," Saima chatted happily, barely stopping to take a breath. Sort of like the overfriendly Anna, Maryam thought as she listened to her sister prattle. Within fifteen minutes, their to-go bags were ready, and the sisters returned to their gate, where her family waited to greet their returning daughter.

Azizah clutched at Saima as if she would never let go of her younger child, Ghulam wiped tears of happiness from his eyes, and Dadu beamed at them all.

"It is so wonderful to have the entire family together again after so long," he said happily.

Maryam looked up and caught Anna, now seated a few rows over, watching her family with a wistful expression on her face.

"Where are your seats?" Saima asked, pulling out her plane ticket. Maryam proudly showed her the four seats she had booked in Economy Plus.

Her sister made a face. "I bought my ticket too late—I'm at the back of the plane. Plus, I'm stuck with an aisle seat. Aisle seats are the worst." Saima looked hopefully at Maryam, but before she could say anything, their father broke in.

"The *dulan* can't be stuck at the back of the plane. You will take my seat, *beta*—your sister made sure our seats have extra leg room so we can be comfortable and avoid leg cramps on the flight," Ghulam said gallantly.

Maryam sighed. "Dad, that's okay. I'll switch seats with her. I prefer aisle seats anyway."

Her sister grinned, reaching across to give her a side hug. "I missed you all so much! Can you believe I'm getting *married* in five *days* in *Canada*?"

The passengers started to board, and Maryam helped her parents and Dadu collect their carry-on luggage and food, before waiting for her group to be called—last, of course.

Anna stood a few feet away, talking on her flip phone again. She looked far less cheerful and perky than she had earlier. Maryam didn't mean to eavesdrop, but it was clear Anna was having an intense discussion.

"No, I completely understand. It all has to run like clockwork. Which is exactly why I only packed a carry-on, as we discussed. To be prepared for *any* eventuality. Like this one. I know, but—" Her brows were furrowed with concern. "Yes, but I can't really do anything about a plane delay. I'm sure your mother is upset, but none of this is my fault!" Her voice rose, and then, as if remembering she was in public, she seemed to struggle to rein in her emotions. "The minute we land, I'll grab the first cab I see. I'll meet you there. I'll probably only be a tiny bit late for the cocktail party, no one will notice." Another pause, then: "Okay, so your mother will notice, but no one else. I really should go. Love you. Bye." Anna hung up, and Maryam caught her eye.

"Your boyfriend sounds like a real stickler for time," she said, sympathetic.

Anna stiffened. "Actually, he can't wait to see me. I think it's sweet." She marched ahead and joined the queue to board the plane without a backward glance.

Realizing she must have hit a sore spot, Maryam made sure to wait a few minutes for Anna to get ahead of her before joining the line. It didn't matter, in any case; it was unlikely they would ever meet again. In a few short hours, her family would arrive in Toronto, ready to launch her baby sister's wedding and then celebrate Eid. A wave of excitement caused her lips to lift in a smile—her first genuine one since she had woken up before dawn. This really was the most wonderful time of year, and she couldn't wait for all the joy and adventure waiting around the corner.

THREE

Anna

December 20
Denver International Airport

"Okay, so where were we?" Anna tucked an errant lock of hair behind her ear—hair she had just that morning paid a small fortune to have layered and highlighted to perfection. Style inspiration: Rachel Green, from season six of *Friends*. She smiled up at the tall, sandy-haired flight attendant who was explaining that she was going to have to hand over her suitcase to him, even though she had managed to bring her miniscule suitcase all the way to the very front of the line. She was so close, she could see the plane just beyond the gates. Anna gently interrupted his passive-aggressive yet still cheerful monologue.

"But it's carry-on size," she said, maintaining her smile and spinning the cream leather case 360 degrees on its little tan wheels. "And it's ten pounds underweight. You won't even notice it's there." Anna prepared to step forward and board the plane. *With* her precious case containing her capsule wardrobe for four days of upscale holiday celebrations and all the expensive gifts for the Vandergreys: a cashmere scarf for Nick's father, a custom flask for his brother, a statement collar necklace for his mother, chandelier earrings and butterfly brooches for his sisters.

"I'm afraid that's not going to be possible."

"Please. I've gone full-on Mary Poppins here. You don't understand how much I've managed to fit into this bag. I *need* to carry it on." But the flight attendant was still standing in her way, and he wasn't smiling anymore.

"I'm sorry, miss, but there simply isn't room on board for one more piece of carry-on. Not even . . ." He glanced down at the case and did not, in Anna's opinion, give it the respect it was due when he finished his sentence with "*that.*" Anna could hear some throat-clearing behind her and knew the other passengers were getting impatient.

"But I don't have time to wait at baggage claim when we arrive in Toronto."

"Miss—"

"*Please.* My boyfriend's mother is already having a meltdown about the plane delay because she is a *very exacting woman*—and to top it all off, my boss is now waiting for me to fax her a magazine layout change approval as soon as I land, and . . ." Anna trailed off, desperate for a convincing closing argument. It was all true: despite the fact that she had gone into the office that morning to approve the photo layouts for the New Year issue of *Denver Decor,* Janey had changed her mind about the

Malone Mansion spread layout when Anna was halfway to the airport. It had been all Anna could do not to tell Janey that she quit, that Janey could keep her job, with all the hoops she made Anna jump through and unreasonable requests she made—but Anna *needed* the job. She had debts to repay, and she had to keep on being able to pretend she was the perfect woman Nick believed her to be.

"I had a plan, don't you see?"

His voice was as ice-cold as the snow falling outside now. "You're going to delay the flight even more. Please hand me your bag and move along."

Anna felt anxiety stirring like a flock of birds in her chest, ready to take flight along with the plane. She lifted the case into her arms and held it as if it were a small child. "I'll keep it on my lap."

"It is against safety protocols to keep a case of that size on your lap, and there is *no more room on the plane for a carry-on*. Unless you'd like to take a different flight—which I do not recommend, because there's already a lot of snow out there and the flight crew has let me know we need to get moving immediately—please give me your suitcase *now*, and I will check it for you"—he said this as if he was doing her some sort of favor—"and you will see it when you arrive in Toronto in about five hours, if we're lucky."

"*If* we're lucky? What's that supposed to mean?!" Anna was a nervous flier already and his grim words had not instilled much confidence. But there was no way she was forgoing this flight because of fear. She needed to get to her seat and pop the Dramamine tablet she had determined would make her drowsy enough that her in-flight nerves wouldn't be an issue, but not so sleepy that she'd be bleary-eyed for the Vandergreys' cocktail party. *"Fine,"* she said under her breath, handing over her case. She stepped forward to board, reflexively lifting her hand to touch the plane's smooth white door exterior for luck.

The little ritual calmed her somewhat. She settled into her aisle seat on the cramped plane. Her seatmate hadn't arrived yet, so she still had an unobstructed view of the feather-like snowflakes falling outside. As she watched them, she felt her anxious thoughts and feelings begin to retreat. The world looked like a Christmas movie set: a world where, despite a few hiccups, everything was going to work out and a happy ending was guaranteed.

And, Anna told herself, determined to remain positive, she now had a few hours of uninterrupted time to indulge in a favorite pastime: reading magazines about home decor and movie stars, people with perfect lives that were nothing at all like hers. The ideal escape from worrying about the delay and the blizzard. She riffled through her handbag, in which she had packed all the magazines she hadn't had time to read this month, everything from *People* to *Architectural Digest*.

As she flipped through *People*, her roving gaze landed on a small piece with the headline "Happily Ever After." The accompanying photo showed two actors—the gorgeous and talented Hollywood "It girl" Tenisha Barlowe and a handsome actor Anna hadn't heard of, Chase Taylor. The two were locked in an embrace in a romantic-looking, snowy, small-town setting.

Tenisha Barlowe gets cozy with rumored boyfriend **Chase Taylor**

on the set of *Two Nights at Christmas*, the big-budget sequel to cult favorite *One Night at Christmas*. Hollywood and the rest of the world are completely abuzz over *Two Nights*—and rightly so! Never before has a story that started on the Heartline Channel ended with Nora Ephron penning the sequel for Universal Studios.

"We're trying to keep the spirit of the original movie, while of course putting our own spin on the story and the cinematography," sources close to the famed screenwriter said recently, speaking from the undisclosed location (rumored to be in Canada) where the movie is now being shot. Production in upstate New York had to be shut down last month when the set was overrun by fans and paparazzi, causing extensive delays and disruptions. While the shoot is now rumored to be woefully behind schedule, things are said to be back on track for a Christmas 2001 release.

Anna sighed happily as she read. Even though she knew it couldn't possibly be anything other than a film set, just looking at the stills for *Two Nights at Christmas*, she couldn't help but wish it was a town she could visit. It wasn't that she didn't want to celebrate Christmas in Toronto with Nick and his family. But it all just felt like so *much*. Plus, there was that engagement ring sparkling in her mind's eye to consider. She looked down at the happy couple on the magazine page. *You love Nick*, she reminded herself. *You're just having cold feet.*

Anna's thoughts were interrupted by the sound of a throat clearing beside her.

"Excuse me? I think you're in my seat."

Anna looked up to see the young woman she had met in the airport earlier, the one with the intense, wide-set brown eyes framed by thick, dark lashes. A soft-looking navy blue cotton scarf completely covered her hair. Her small Cupid's bow mouth was turned down in a frown.

"Maryam! Hi!" Anna knew she hadn't been at her best with Maryam earlier, when she'd just finished having a tense conversation with Nick. She felt guilty about this and hoped she could make up for it now. "What a lucky coincidence, we're seatmates!"

"Yeah. Lucky," Maryam said, but Anna got the sense she didn't really feel that way at all. "So . . . my seat?"

Anna put away her magazine and fumbled in her handbag for her plane ticket. When she double-checked, she realized that she was indeed in the wrong spot.

"I'm so sorry," she said. "I hate it when people do that. You'd think I'd know the difference between A and B. I'd much rather have the window, wouldn't you? Sure you want to switch?"

"Completely sure."

Anna smiled at Maryam as she settled into the correct seat, but Maryam's smile didn't reach her captivating eyes. Back inside the airport, she had seemed to be the one at the center of her cheerful, chaotic family. In charge of everyone— and unflappable as she somehow managed it all with ease. In fact, Anna had felt a pang when she observed Maryam and wondered what it would be like to be surrounded by so many loved ones.

Maryam took a book out of her bag—*The Tipping Point*, by Malcolm Gladwell—and buried her nose in it. Anna thought about trying to start a conversation but decided to wait a bit. For now, she'd go back to her reading. This time, she chose *House Beautiful*—and was caught by surprise when an envelope addressed to her fell out of it.

She retrieved the envelope from the small square of floor at her feet. She knew that handwriting well. The letter was from her stepmother, Beth, and it must have gotten stuck among her unread magazines.

Ex-stepmother, Anna reminded herself, frowning down at the envelope. She knew what was inside: it was a "Happy Holiday Missive," the annual letter Beth and Anna used to love compiling together. Sending out the letter had been Beth and Anna's way of beginning to feel like a real family—and this had been so meaningful for Anna. Her mother had died of pre-eclampsia when she was an infant and, until Beth, Anna had always felt like her family life was missing a wheel. Back then, Beth had made it a point to make Anna feel loved, secure—the center of a family, albeit a small one.

She lifted the envelope and tested its weight. It was thicker than usual, and this was upsetting. Was Beth's life even more full and rewarding now that Anna's dad was gone? The yearly letter, sent out to family and friends, had always included a few color-copied photos of the highlights of the year (their adventurous family road trips to Salt Lake City, Wyoming, Montana; Anna's school photos; funny snapshots of their twin cats, Brenda and Brandon). It also always included sunny little slivers of news (Beth's decision to leave the interior design firm she worked at and go freelance; Anna's youthful fascination with design and decor, inspired by Beth's career, on display in images of the two of them working on home projects together; Beth's dad's move from corporate to family law; Anna's school photos; celebrations of graduations throughout the years).

Now Anna clocked the new return address in Highlands Ranch. "Unbelievable," she muttered. It was bad enough that Beth had remarried a few months ago, so quickly after Anna's father's sudden death from a heart attack two years ago—but now she was sending out her own Happy Holiday Missive from her new life. As if her old life had never existed. As if a person could just step gracefully into a new existence and forget about the past altogether.

Anna shoved the letter into the seat pocket in front of her, behind the airsickness bag—where she intended for it to stay, unopened, until a flight attendant threw it out after Anna was long gone, off to her happy holiday ending with Nick in Toronto. There would be no looking back—and definitely not at Beth, who had hurt her deeply.

She flipped open *Architectural Digest* instead. But while she had previously been excited about poring over what were projected to be 2001's hottest home design trends, she could no longer concentrate.

"It's coming down pretty hard out there, isn't it?" she ventured.

Maryam kept her eyes on her book for an awkwardly long time before turning her head toward Anna. "Yep. It's snowing," she said. "We do tend to get a lot of snow in Colorado."

"True. Right. But I don't think I've ever seen *this* much."

"Hmm" was all Maryam said, shooting Anna that polite but distant smile before returning to her book. Anna went back to her own magazine, skimming an article about a potential new trend in see-through furniture, then flipping the page and staring forlornly at the Pantone color for 2001. It was a jaunty and invigorating shade of magenta that should not have made anyone feel as sad as Anna was feeling now. Especially on the heels of the shade from the year before, which had been a drab, dull blue that had perfectly encapsulated Anna's drab, dull feelings all year. Until she met Nick, she reminded herself. She willed the bright swatch of color on the page before her to help her feel positive.

Anna checked her watch. The plane would leave soon. In just under five hours, she'd be safely in Toronto, with Nick. Perhaps, she thought hopefully, because her bag had been checked in last, that meant it would be unloaded off the plane first.

Anna turned to the window and watched the baggage car now making its way through the snowfall. She could see her suitcase, right there on top of the pile, until—Anna jolted forward, bumping her arm into Maryam's and nearly knocking her book out of her hands. Her bag had just tumbled off the pile of luggage and into a snowbank! "Sorry, Maryam—it's just, I think they dropped my bag out there!"

"Oh, that's too bad. But I'm sure it's fine," Maryam said wearily, just as a striking young woman with dark hair flowing in waves down her back approached in the aisle.

"Maryam, did our meals get switched?"

"I don't think so, Saima, why?"

"I'm sure this is a shrimp burrito. I know I ordered vegetarian. Can you check to see if you have mine?"

Maryam dug through her bag and determined that she did

not have the missing burrito, while Anna pressed her nose against the glass and saw nothing of any use, just swirls of white snow and flashing lights. She reached deep into her own bag, looking for the little enamel pill case containing the Dramamine tablet. Her fingers closed around it just as the flight attendant, the same sandy-haired guy who'd taken her suitcase from her, stepped to the front of the plane and began the always overly cheery explanation of what you were supposed to do if the plane crashed—sorry, *emergency landed*—and death was imminent—sorry, *you needed to exit the plane*. Anna always hated this part. It made her heart race and her palms instantly sweat, which was what happened now, causing the pill case to drop out of her hands and roll onto the floor.

"Hi, excuse me," she said to Maryam, disturbing her again as she leaned over. "But I just dropped something . . ."

Maryam didn't budge. She had her eyes tightly shut, Anna realized.

"You can't be asleep, you were reading ten seconds ago," Anna said under her breath. Maryam's eyes flew open.

"Excuse me?"

"Do you mind? I dropped my pill case, and I need—"

"I was not *pretending to be asleep*. I was praying, okay?"

"Oh! I'm sorry! I didn't mean to interrupt your praying. But I really need—"

The plane abruptly started to taxi and Anna watched as the pill case wobbled in the aisle, then rolled all the way under Maryam's seat. Anna undid her seat belt, her pride completely nonexistent now. She needed to fall asleep, damn it, and if she had to dive under a stranger's legs to get sweet oblivion, so be it.

"Miss?"

Anna looked up into the eyes of Mr. Sandy Hair.

"Seat belts on," he said in his irritatingly bright *everything is going to be fine if you just do what I say* voice. "Perhaps you missed what the pilot just announced because you were doing . . . whatever it is you're doing there. But air traffic control has just decided that because of the blizzard we need to get going, so we'll be taking off any minute."

Anna leaned up and snapped her seat belt around her waist as the attendant moved on. She couldn't help but notice Maryam wasn't focused on her book anymore. She had a look of sheer alarm on her face.

"I'm sure it will be fine," Anna offered, trying to ignore how shaky her own voice sounded. "Pilots fly through blizzards all the time, right?"

Maryam picked up her book from her lap. "Of course it's going to be fine," she said, cool as a cucumber once more as the plane gathered speed on the runway. "Who said I thought it wasn't going to be fine?"

What was that weird noise, though? Were engines supposed to sound like that? The plane's wheels left the ground and the aircraft began its sharp ascent into the sky. Anna's palms were now so sweaty they left marks on her dress when she wiped her hands across her thighs. *Taking off is the hardest part*, she told herself, *and it will be over soon*. But the ascent seemed to go on for an interminably long time, with all sorts of veers, zigs, zags, and what felt at one point like a half somersault. Or maybe that was just her stomach. If only she had the Dramamine. Anna retrieved her bag from under the seat in front of her, daring the flight attendant to come after her again.

She dug through it and found the little bottle of lilac perfume oil from The Body Shop. It was a scent that always relaxed her, and reminded her of the richly scented bush in the backyard of the house she'd grown up in.

"Hope you don't mind the smell of lilac," Anna said nonchalantly as she began to screw open the lid.

"Actually, I really do," Maryam replied.

Seriously? Who hates the smell of lilacs? "Fine, *sorry*," Anna said—but just then, and presumably because of the rising air pressure, the lid exploded from the bottle, spraying the oil all over Anna and Maryam, and releasing a scent that even Anna had to admit was aggressively strong rather than gently soothing. She and Maryam both started to cough.

"I'm—" Anna began when she had recovered, but her seatmate shook her head.

"I know, you're *sorry*. Can we just . . . can nothing else happen for the rest of this flight, please? I'm just going to read my book and—" She coughed again. "Soon we'll be in Toronto."

Anna sighed. Five hours was a long time to sit beside someone who hated you. As her ears popped from the same mounting air pressure that had unleashed her perfume oil, Anna rooted through her bag again until she found the bag of round, white, long-lasting mints she'd packed for the flight. She opened the bag noisily, popped one in her mouth, and tilted them toward Maryam, a peace offering. "Want one?"

After a long pause, Maryam finally looked up from her book again. "No," she said. "Thank you."

"Oh, shoot. Right. I'm sorry! Again! I totally forgot. It's

Eid! You're probably fasting, right? I've fasted before, for Yom Kippur. It was actually really—"

She had been about to say it had actually been really special, that Beth had told her it was a time to slow down and think about the year that had passed, to set intentions to be and do better, and that this yearly ritual had always stayed with her—but Maryam interrupted.

"It's not *Eid*," she said, her tone more irritated than ever. "It's Ramadan. Eid is the holiday at the end of the month of fasting. Now, if you don't mind—" She held up her book. "I *really* just . . ."

The plane gave an alarming shudder and Anna nearly choked on her mint. When it was safely out of her windpipe, she started crunching on it to get rid of it, her heart racing at an alarming pace. "Just the fact that I'm eating these mints around you is a problem, though, right?" she said nervously, unable to stop herself from talking even though she knew Maryam wanted to be left alone. "Like, even smelling any kind of food breaks your fast, right? I had a Muslim roommate in college, and her cousin told me that, I'm sure of it. I was eating pizza in front of him. He was so annoyed. He said that particles of food might enter your body through your nostrils." Anna crunched harder, mortified, determined to get the mint down so Maryam wouldn't hate her even more than she already did. But the strong mint taste combined with the lilac oil she had just spilled everywhere made her sneeze, which made some more of the mint go down her windpipe, which made her cough again—which *then* made Mr. Sandy Hair come rushing over to see what drama she was causing now.

"I'm fine, really," she insisted until he moved along. By now, Maryam was pretending to read again, probably out of self-preservation. "Maryam, I really am . . ."

Maryam put down her book and looked down at her lap for a moment, her shoulders shaking slightly. Alarmed she had pushed her seatmate to tears of frustration, Anna was about to apologize again, or offer to sit on the floor of the plane, when Maryam looked over and Anna saw that she was laughing. "Let me guess," she managed. "You're sorry? It's *really* okay. I'm notoriously grouchy while fasting—ask anyone in my family. And just so you know, it's fine if I smell someone eating a breath mint. Your friend's cousin was probably pulling your leg, maybe because he really wanted to eat pizza. But some things, like smelling food, just can't be avoided."

"Okay. Well, that's a relief. Because I also have a muffin in my bag."

Maryam smiled. "And I have a burrito, which I will be eating in approximately"—she checked her watch—"two hours and three minutes, at sunset. Listen, we've gotten off on the wrong foot. Traveling with my family is a little stressful."

Just then, her father stood up from his seat in the front of the plane, and called, "Maryam, did you remember to pack the snow boots?" Without missing a beat, Maryam answered, "They're in the checked luggage, don't worry!" before turning back to Anna and rolling her eyes. "But I shouldn't be snapping at you. Please, accept my apology."

Anna was touched—but something was bugging her, still. She was remembering a bit of information her college roommate Nadia had shared with her one year during Ramadan. "Wait. Isn't it true you're not supposed to think negative thoughts about people while fasting for Ramadan? Like, you're actually not allowed? So, really, you're just being nice to me now because of that, right?"

Maryam rolled her eyes. "Honestly, you're impossible," she said—but she laughed again and Anna did, too, relieved that things had thawed between them. Especially since the plane had now hit a patch of turbulence that was becoming increasingly difficult to ignore. What a relief to have someone to talk to.

"Whoa," Anna said as the plane bumped along. "This is starting to feel more like a bus ride than a plane ride."

"Yeah. And it's really snowing hard," Maryam said, looking with concern out the window at the snow falling in thick white sheets. "You'd think we'd be above the clouds by now."

Just then, the loudspeaker crackled to life and the pilot's smooth voice filled the plane. He sounded like Matthew McConaughey, all relaxed Southern charm. "Ladies and gentlemen, this is your captain speaking. As you can tell, we've hit some rough air. We're just going to be navigating our way through that, so you may notice some bumps and pressure changes. Should be all clear in about ten, fifteen minutes. In the meantime, cabin crew, please ensure the cabin is secure and all passenger seat belts are on. Thanks, y'all." The loudspeaker clicked off.

"Do they get training for that, do you think?" Anna asked Maryam.

"To fly a plane? I certainly hope so!"

"No, I mean to talk that way, even in a crisis. Like everything is going to be all right. I've often thought I'd love a pilot to be the one to deliver bad news. You know? Tell you you're being dumped or losing your job—but don't worry, just keep your seat belt on, hang tight, it'll all be fine! They always sound so reassuring."

Maryam smiled and nodded—but then her smile became an expression of terror as the plane seemed to lose altitude and fall for a few seconds. There went Anna's pill container, cartwheeling down the aisle. Not that Dramamine would have helped much at this point anyway.

"This is intense," Anna muttered, rubbing her sweaty palms on her thighs again and looking over at Maryam. "Hey . . ."

Maryam had her eyes closed and her fists clenched. Her shoulders were rigid, like she was trying not to cry. "Maryam . . ." Anna's own fear took a backseat as she touched Maryam's trembling arm. "I'm sure it's just what the pilot said, turbulence that will be over in a few minutes." Anna wasn't positive she believed this, but she really wanted to help Maryam. She hated seeing someone so scared. "I've been through way worse. Last year, when I was flying home from Paris, the turbulence was so bad food was flying all over the place. And look, I'm still here."

Maryam tentatively opened one eyelid, then the other. "I really don't want *this* to be the way I go," she said.

"You mean stuck in a blizzard on a flight to Toronto beside a person who just exploded your least favorite scent all over you? Who *wouldn't* want to die that way?" She tried to laugh. Then she heard her dad's voice. *A little help is worth more than a lot of sympathy.* "I promise, this is not the end," she said, fighting back her own fear to reassure her new friend. She glanced at her watch as the plane bumped frantically through the turbulent air. "The pilot said ten, fifteen minutes, and it's been three now, so we're . . . almost halfway to the end of this?"

Maryam nodded. "You're right," she said. "We're going to be fine."

"You bet we are! *I'm* going to make it to Toronto to meet my boyfriend's family and have the best Christmas ever, and you and your family are going to your sister's wedding!"

Suddenly, Maryam looked more dejected than she had the moment before, when she had been fearing death. "My sister's wedding, in the middle of Ramadan."

"Doesn't really sound like you're looking forward to it much," Anna said, gripping her armrest against a particularly violent lurch.

Maryam winced and shook her head. "Not really, if I'm being honest. It's just a lot to deal with at this time of year. And I'm not sure my sister has really thought this through. Marriage is a huge commitment."

"I totally agree," Anna said.

"You have to be really sure."

"Absolutely."

"And does a really sure person plan a last-minute wedding in the middle of our most important holiday?"

Lurch, lurch, lurch. Anna tried to think of something supportive to say, but the shuddering of the plane was a total distraction.

Even if the right words didn't come to her, Anna was proud of herself, she realized. Sure, she was scared—but there was a clarity to her fear. As the plane careened and floundered, something felt like it had started to shift inside her. It was as if none of the things that had worried her so much as she was boarding the flight could touch her anymore. She didn't care that her suitcase was probably stuck in a snowbank at Denver International. She didn't care that she might not make it to the Vander-greys' Christmas cocktails or any of the other fancy events her boyfriend's family had planned. And she especially didn't care that she might never get to wear the engagement ring she had found in Nick's luggage that morning.

The truth was, she was relieved.

"Oh no," she said as she truly came to understand the seriousness of this. She was actually thinking she would rather get in a plane crash than have Nick propose to her. If her moments on earth were numbered, she needed to find a way to work through this. She turned to Maryam as the plane took a sudden nosedive and said, "I think my entire life is a lie—"

Just as Maryam said, "I'm so tired of being someone I'm not."

The two young women's eyes were wide as they stared at each other. The plane lurched hard, once, twice. "What are we supposed to do?" Anna asked Maryam, her voice strangled by fear. "Assume the crash position? To be honest, I never pay attention when the flight attendant explains the emergency protocols, it's too terrifying . . ."

"What if we just kept talking?" Maryam suggested.

"Distract each other. Okay. So tell me more. Why exactly do you feel like you're pretending to be someone you're not?"

"I'm so tired of taking care of everything," Maryam said. "Everyone relies on me for everything. Instead of being upset with my sister about upending Ramadan this year, my parents are secretly delighted she's marrying a fellow doctor, even though she's off traveling the world and never home. Why should they care? I'm the dutiful one, the one who decided to become a pharmacist to keep the family business going. You'd think that would make them happy. But it doesn't feel like enough." Her eyes were filling with tears. "And my sister calls me Bor-yam."

"'Bor-yam'?"

"Yes. Boring Maryam. That's my nickname. But the *worst part* is they're right! I *am* boring! I bore my-*self* sometimes! For the record, being a pharmacist is possibly the most boring job in the world!" Anna thought about the way she had felt the night before, back at her apartment, as she had carefully chopped one tiny Dramamine tablet in half. It hadn't been the most interesting task.

"What would you do instead, if you could do anything at all? Sky's the limit," Anna asked, curious now.

"I'd be a writer." Maryam responded so quickly, Anna could tell she really meant it. "I'd have a fascinating, interesting, creative life and not have to worry about anyone but myself. Please, don't get me wrong, I love my family, but I don't want to carry around every single detail about everyone else's life inside my head because they all think I'm too boring to have my own dreams! But there is zero money and zero future in writing. Ask my parents." She took a deep breath. "Do you know what I also want? To be seen for who I really am by a certain someone. But he, like everyone else, only sees one thing when he looks at me: Bor-yam!"

"Who is this certain someone?" Anna said, her voice hoarse. Her knuckles paled as she gripped the armrest while the plane gave a particularly pronounced shudder.

"His name is Saif," Maryam said. "He's probably on this plane, sitting in the front with the rest of my family. I've had a crush on him since I was old enough to talk. But I'm sure he's never noticed me once in his life."

"Oh, Maryam. I'm positive that's not the case. I mean, *I* noticed you at the airport!"

"Oh, please—you only noticed me because of my hijab and because we were making such a scene, and so different from you."

"That's not true," Anna said, and meant it. "I noticed you because you're gorgeous, poised, and seemed in charge of everything—so calm and collected. And also, totally surrounded by family. In the middle of this circle of people who needed you."

"What about you, don't you have a family who needs you?"

"I'm an only child. My mom died when I was too young to remember her, and my dad"—she swallowed hard here, trying to keep it together, because even if she was about to die, she didn't want it to be while she was a sobbing mess with mascara running down her face—"passed away two years ago, from a heart attack." She wasn't able to help it, though; a tear slid down her cheek. "Then this year, my ex-stepmother, Beth, got remarried and . . ." She wiped her eyes and kept talking as the plane made a strange whining sound and she realized a potential crash probably was really on the table here and if she didn't get this all out now, she might not ever get the chance. "She has a new husband and another stepdaughter now, and I don't have any family left at all. Like, truly. I'm an only child, and so were both my parents. I suppose I have some second or third cousins somewhere, but we're not in touch. So, I'm heading to Toronto to spend the holidays with my boyfriend's family. We've been dating for six months and he's the perfect guy: good looks, good job, good family, good everything. Except I'm realizing now that being with him has made me realize how very *un*-perfect I am. I've started feeling like I'm playacting a role in my own life. Like my life is a movie. Ideal job—except my boss is a tyrant. Ideal boyfriend—except I'm not sure Nick knows the real me. But maybe that's *great*, right? Who doesn't want a perfect-looking life and a happy-looking ending? Does it even matter if any of it's real? Is anyone being honest about who they are and how happy their life really is?" Anna shook her head, trying to dislodge all these swirling, complicated thoughts so she could breathe properly again. "I suspect Nick is going to propose on Christmas Eve because that would be the fairy-tale way to do it. And I'll say yes, because *who* would say no to a fairy-tale ending? It's just that it doesn't feel right."

"I had no idea, Anna," Maryam said softly.

Anna wiped away another tear. "And all I can think about is how something will be missing as I celebrate Christmas with his family. It won't be like my past, like *my* family did it. Beth is Jewish, so we celebrated Hanukkah, too, from when I was seven onward. It started to feel like part of who I was. And this year, with Hanukkah falling at the same time as Christmas, it feels really special. And I miss . . . well, *everything*. It's hard, feeling like you don't have any family at all. Like your past is all just . . . gone. I've been trying to put my past behind me, but it isn't working."

"Tell me about your holiday celebrations as a kid," Maryam said as the plane continued to behave like it was a ship in a stormy sea, not an air vessel cruising at high altitudes. Anna felt a wave inside her as well—but instead of fear, it was gratitude toward Maryam, a woman she hardly knew but who wanted to talk to her and distract her from her abject terror. This was the only person she had been able to really tell her truth to in a very long time. A person who was asking her about something she had tried to pretend did not exist in her life, for two lonely years.

Anna closed her eyes, but instead of seeing visions of the plane crashing into the mountains, she could see the twinkling lights on the Christmas tree she and her dad would cut down together at a farm every year. Her dad never rushed her choice—even though one year that meant he got frostbite on one of his hands, a fact he tried to hide from her until she saw the bandage. "Totally worth it to make my little Anna Banana happy," he had said.

In addition to the Christmas tree lights, Anna could see the soft candle glimmers in her mind's eye. Those were coming from the brass menorah that always sat in the center of their dining room table during the eight nights of Hanukkah, a menorah that had been passed down to Beth by her own mother—a woman who had died when Beth was young, too. This shared sadness had bonded them close, carried them through some of their rockier early days, when Anna had worried there might not be room for her in her father's new marriage. "No matter when Hanukkah fell, we'd always try to get our tree up at the same time. Then there'd be extra lights. Extra sparkle. We'd wait to decorate the tree until closer to Christmas, but always turn on our Christmas tree lights, light the menorah, say the prayers—and then Beth and I would make Christmas cookies together. Or Nutella rugelach, which is truly the best thing in the world. And latkes, she makes—made—the *best* latkes." She smiled and continued. "We'd walk to the carol service at church on Christmas Eve. At the end, the lights in the sanctuary would be dimmed, and everyone would get to take a candle—total fire hazard, I guess, but nothing bad ever happened—to hold. The choir would sing 'Silent Night' while everyone filed out of the church holding their light. We'd walk home with our candles, and I would always think about how light and goodness were so important to both holidays. I'd look down at my candle and feel like maybe it could light up the world."

Maryam clutched her arm and Anna jolted back to reality. "I think it stopped!" she said. "I think we're going to *live!*"

Anna waited a beat and realized Maryam was right: the plane was now sailing gracefully through the air as if that had always been the case. There was a crackle on the intercom, and the pilot's calm voice was in their ears again.

"Ladies and gents, thank you for your patience as we flew through that patch of bad weather. We're out of it now, but for the continued safety of the flight and crew, air traffic control has let us know the best thing to do is divert our flight path. So, we won't be landing in Toronto—we'll now be landing in Ottawa in just under an hour. Should be clear sailing there." The "Fasten seat belts" light dinged off, and Anna breathed a sigh of relief.

Beside her, Maryam undid her seat belt as well and stood up to stretch her legs, leaning against her seat. Anna smiled at her. It was over. They had survived. Except now they were about to make an unscheduled landing in the wrong city, in the middle of a blizzard—meaning there was a very high chance all her careful Christmas plans were about to collapse like a house of cards.

When she glanced at Maryam to commiserate—what would happen to her sister's wedding plans now?—she noticed the other woman standing stock-still. Then her seatmate emitted a high-pitched squeak and, without another word, walked quickly down the center aisle of the plane. What had just happened? Anna looked around, wondering what had caught Maryam's horrified gaze, and noted the sole passenger seated behind them: a handsome young man with floppy hair and kind eyes, a large sleep mask dangling from his neck. He was cute, but surely not worth a mild panic attack?

"Hi," the man said, his voice warm velvet in Anna's ears. "That was some crazy turbulence, right? My name is Saif."

FOUR

Maryam

December 20

No, no, no, no, no, Maryam thought as she blindly moved up the aisle of the plane, desperate to escape. Saif Rasool had been sitting behind her the entire time. Her lifelong crush had likely heard every word she said!

This was like the plot of a bad movie.

No, it was like the inciting incident in a romantic comedy—except, in Maryam's case, all she would get was lifelong embarrassment. Plus, never being able to show her face at another family *dawaat* again.

Oh God—what if Saif told his parents? Who would then immediately tell her parents? Who would then tell Saima and Dadu, who would then respectively laugh and come out of Bollywood retirement to make a film based on this story? She would forever be teased about spilling her secrets to an overly perky stranger just because she was afraid of flying and was desperately unhappy and living a lie and . . .

Maryam stopped.

Was she unhappy? Was she living a lie? Was any of what she had blurted to Anna actually . . . true?

In her rush to escape from Saif, she had glossed over the rest of her confessions, including her secret dream, the one she hadn't thought about in years, to be a writer. Not a contemplating-life-from-a-drafty-attic type of writer, but an actual type-one-hundred-thousand-words, get-an-agent, *look, Mom, I got a book deal* writer.

She shook her head. She was sleep-deprived, stressed, and had just survived one—no, *three*—near-death experiences: first the lilac-scented oil explosion, followed by the scotch mint uprising, and then turbulence so bad she vowed to drive back to Colorado. This was merely some sort of psychic-dissonance response; she was reverting to a simpler time in her life when she had a mild—practically nonexistent!—crush on Saif, and when she might have toyed—for the briefest instant!—with the idea of disappointing her family by pursuing a job in the arts.

If that's true, why did you immediately run away when you spotted Saif seated behind you? a voice whispered mockingly. *And when you told Anna you wanted to be a writer, why did it feel like . . . the truth?*

Maryam pushed the thought firmly from her mind. This was all just wedding-related stress. It didn't mean anything. She needed to rejoin her family at the front of the plane. They needed her. Once she saw her parents and sister again, she would remember who she was—not who some tiny, random part of her wished she could be.

Except her family didn't seem to need her at all. When she joined them in Economy Plus, Saima, her parents, and

Dadu were eating their *iftar* dinner. They looked up at her in surprise.

"Everything okay, Maryam *beta*?" Dadu asked.

"I'm fine. Never better. All good. Just wanted to make sure you were okay and . . ." Her stomach gurgled, and she checked the time. It was half past five; she should have broken her fast ten minutes ago. The day was catching up with her, and she felt a wave of hunger hit hard.

"Drink some *pani*," Azizah said, handing her a bottle of water. "We were worried about you. The turbulence was so bad, *nah?* Saima started crying!"

"*Mom*," Saima muttered, embarrassed. "I just felt bad I sent her back there all alone. I forgot how much Maryam hates flying."

Maryam did hate flying—planes were chaotic spaces— but strangely, she hadn't felt alone beside Anna. Maybe it was because Anna Gibson had been so chaotic herself, but also a friendly and calming presence. When the turbulence had gotten really scary, it was comforting to have Anna seated next to her.

Ghulam stood up from his aisle seat and insisted Maryam take his place, while Dadu handed her a burrito and urged her to eat. Maryam felt better after a hurried *bismillah* and a sip of lukewarm water. She really was a grumpy faster, as she had told Anna, and yet every time she broke her fast after a long day without food or water, the feeling of relief and gratitude that washed over her felt like a hard-won, necessary reminder of her many blessings. She devoured the burrito in a few bites, and Saima passed her a thermos filled with hot tea bought in the airport lounge. She sipped slowly and felt her body calm. This was where she belonged, surrounded by family, by the people who truly mattered, taking care of them while they in turn took care of her.

With a pang, she remembered Anna's confession about how alone she felt after the loss of her father, and her current estrangement from her stepmother. Anna looked so capable, cheerful, and put together—the same way she had described Maryam, she recalled grimly. Well, maybe not "cheerful." But Anna was on her way to visit her boyfriend and his family. They would be kind and welcoming; they would sit her down when she was clearly upset, pass her some water, and talk about trivial things until she had eaten something.

"Did you know Saif Rasool was on this flight?" Maryam asked now, picking a piece of chocolate from the box her sister offered—another duty-free purchase, she assumed.

Azizah smiled fondly. "Such a nice boy. His parents raised him well, even if he did become a"—her mother lowered her voice and looked around quickly, to make sure there were no eavesdroppers—"*lawyer.* Shukriya was so disappointed when he was accepted into Columbia Law."

"Yes, that must have been devastating," Maryam said dryly. Her parents considered the science professions the only truly acceptable career options for their children, with engineering and technology a distant second.

"He greeted us when you went to pick up the food," Azizah said. "His parents are already in Toronto visiting his *phupho,*" she explained, referring to his paternal aunt. "Farah is also on the plane, along with her parents," she said, mentioning another close family friend.

"I haven't seen Farah in years. She's a teacher now, right?"

"A *physics* teacher, at the science charter school that opened up in the old neighborhood," Azizah corrected.

Of course.

The pilot announced that they would be starting their descent, and Maryam was gripped with a sudden panic. There was no way she could go back to her seat. She couldn't face Saif or Anna. Now that she had eaten something, she was starting to feel embarrassed by how much she had revealed to a complete stranger.

As if picking up on her mood, Dadu rose and insisted she stay where she was while he took her seat at the back for the landing. Relieved, Maryam didn't argue. Her grandfather could always sense when she was distressed, even as a child, and he never asked questions until she was ready to talk. Striving for casual, she turned to her sister to continue their conversation.

"I didn't think you were still close with Farah," Maryam said to Saima. The two women were around the same age. Her sister shrugged.

"Maybe she wanted to visit Toronto and this was a good excuse," she said, not very interested. Farah had always been a pleasant, if bland, social acquaintance—conventionally pretty, always turned out in the latest Pakistani fashions, her shiny dark hair cut into a sleek bob. The women had drifted apart as adults, as often happened, but Maryam was touched that the younger woman had felt compelled to attend her sister's wedding.

Which was scheduled to start in just two days, in Toronto—first with the *mehndi* party, followed by the *nikah* ceremony two days later, and finally the *walima* reception the next day. Except their plane was not landing in Toronto. Where the heck was Ottawa?

She must have spoken out loud because an older white man seated across the aisle leaned over. "Ottawa is the capital of Canada," he explained. "It's about four hundred kilometers away from Toronto."

The four Americans looked blankly at the older man, who sighed. "That's around two hundred fifty miles," he said kindly. "Five-hour drive in good weather. But you're not going anywhere tonight. Apparently, the Toronto mayor, Mel Lastman, is calling in the army to help deal with the snow. I heard the flight attendant call this the Storm of the Century."

"Doesn't Canada have one of those every few weeks in the winter?" Maryam asked.

The older man shrugged. "That was some nasty turbulence we flew through. In fact, we didn't even make it to Ottawa." He nodded out the window. "We're circling Rockport Airport. I used to fly in when the cheap flights landed here."

"Where is Rockport?" Saima asked.

"Regional airport, serves the town of Snow Falls." He laughed at Maryam's incredulous expression. "It really is called Snow Falls. Tiny town, more of a village. It's seventy kilometers . . . forty *miles* from Ottawa. My guess is we'll be stuck overnight, but should be on our way tomorrow morning, or the next day at the latest."

"No!" Saima burst out. She had been quiet all this time, and Maryam could see that she was pale, one hand gripping the armrest tightly. "We're supposed to be in Toronto tonight. My *mehndi* party is the day after tomorrow, and I have dinner plans with Miraj's friends from school, and I haven't even met my in-laws yet, and the *nikah* is in *five days* . . ."

"My sister is getting married," Maryam explained to the older man with a smile. She turned to her sister. "We'll rent a car and try to make it to Toronto tonight. Even if it takes double the time, we can do it," Maryam said, trying to sound more confident than she felt.

"I hope your wedding deposits are refundable," the older man said before settling back in his seat for the landing.

Once the plane was on the ground and taxiing, an announcement over the PA confirmed everything the older man had said, and the wedding party sat back, absorbing the news. Maryam gathered their bags and helped her parents. At least one good thing had come out of this experience: she hadn't thought about Saif once in the past hour.

But she did wonder how Anna was holding up. If her plan worked and she managed to snag a rental car, she likely would never see Anna Gibson again. The thought didn't make her happy, for some reason.

*U*nfortunately, they weren't the only ones with plans to hightail it out of Snow Town, or Iceberg, or whatever this podunk place was called. The line in front of the rental agency was already ten people deep by the time Maryam, her family, and all their bags shuffled through the beige-carpeted arrivals lounge of Rockport Airport. From the harried expressions of the three airport staff, Maryam deduced this flyover village hadn't had this much excitement in years.

"Maryam, look outside!" Dadu said, excitedly pulling on his granddaughter's sleeve. It was dark; the sun set early in December, but the tall lampposts shone a spotlight on the snow falling steadily, a veritable stream of white fluff that didn't look like it would stop anytime soon. As they watched, the snow started falling harder, as if it were taunting them. A few propeller planes on the runway already boasted a deep blanket of snow on each wing, wheels half buried.

"Three feet already," Dadu said. "How glorious!"

Saima looked from the line at the car rental agency to the snow outside and dropped her luggage. "My wedding is ruined!" she wailed.

Instantly, Azizah, Ghulam, and Dadu surrounded Saima, patting her on the shoulder, offering tissues and more *chai*. Her mother looked at Maryam with a plaintive expression: *Do something!*

Except the man at the rental agency shook his head when Maryam finally reached the counter. "Miss, the roads are impassable. Even the snowplows aren't heading out until the snow eases some."

"Don't you have an SUV we can rent? Jeep? Humvee? I'll pay double. Triple!" Maryam said, desperate. Behind her, she could hear her sister sobbing loudly, attracting a crowd. "My sister is getting married in Toronto," she added.

The man—a boy, really, barely out of his teens—shrugged sympathetically. "You'd need a car with a plow attached, and snow chains on the tires besides, and even then you wouldn't get far. We got a bunch of movie folk snowed in just the same as you, and if movie folk can't get out, no one can. They're calling it the Storm of the Century. Trust me, Toronto isn't going anywhere," he said, pronouncing it *Toronna*. He looked over her shoulder. "Next!"

Dejected, Maryam headed back to her family. Her sister had stopped wailing, but her tears fell as steadily as the snow outside.

"I'm not leaving the airport," Saima said after Maryam conveyed the bad news. "We'll spend the night here. That way we can get the first flight out."

If you didn't want your wedding to be waylaid by a snowstorm, maybe you shouldn't have insisted on getting married in December. In Canada, Maryam thought, but wisely kept silent.

Then again, it was Ramadan, the month of miracles. At this point Maryam would take the miracle of getting a good night's sleep over almost anything else. After glancing at her parents and Dadu, she could tell the feeling was mutual. It was nearly seven p.m., and she felt dead on her feet. This day refused to end.

"Saima, don't you want to get a good night's rest so you can look fresh tomorrow when you meet your in-laws for the first time?" Maryam wheedled. "I doubt the airport will even be open overnight. Let's see what they're offering in terms of accommodation."

Her sister considered her words and reluctantly nodded. "But we come back here right after *suhoor*," she said, referring to the predawn morning meal that kicked off their fasting day.

This time Ghulam went to the counter for the hotel and meal vouchers, returning with a wry smile on his face. "Snow Falls Inn," he announced.

Maryam sighed. What she wouldn't give for a Marriott, preferably one with a twenty-four-hour concierge lounge. Who knew what horrors awaited them in this tiny Canadian hamlet. Plus, they would probably be the only Muslim and non-white people in the entire village. The good citizens of Snow Falls had probably never even heard of Ramadan. How were they going to find something to eat at five a.m., for *suhoor*?

Just for one night, she reminded herself. She would scrounge something from a vending machine, and they would be out of here on the first flight.

Before they boarded the yellow school bus commandeered to ferry stranded airport passengers to Snow Falls Inn, Maryam dug out boots and heavy snow jackets from their luggage, for once grateful for her family's overpacking tendencies. With a pang, she wondered where Anna was, and if she had packed wisely. Or if her luggage had managed to get on the plane after all, she thought, recalling that Anna had noticed her suitcase on the tarmac back in Denver. Those heels were pretty, but completely impractical in this weather. She looked around but didn't see Anna.

Maryam boarded the bus with her family, the rumble of the engine lulling her even as the musty pleather seats recalled her long-ago school days. Beside her, Saima sniffled quietly. Maryam squeezed her hand. "It will be all right," she whispered.

"You don't know that," Saima said. "You're always trying to make everything better, but you don't control the weather. You don't control the planes. This is a disaster."

"Things will be better tomorrow, *Inshallah,*" Maryam said. God willing. "Make *dua*. Whatever is meant to be, right?" As a child, she had been taught to pray for what she wanted, but also to accept what was written for her, both the good and bad. While her adult belief in fate and predestination had become more nuanced, it seemed appropriate to remind her sister that, at this moment, there was very little they could do. "Just think how funny this story will be to your grandchildren," Maryam added. "Especially since they'll have no idea what snow is, because of climate change."

Saima pushed her. "You're always so paranoid. What's climate change?" she grumbled, but smiled slightly.

The bus rumbled to a halt, and Maryam wiped the fogged-up window and peered out at a deserted, silent side street, every surface piled high with snow. When she stepped onto the sidewalk, her foot sank into powdery snow nearly to her knees. At least the blizzard-like conditions had eased, so there was some visibility. Maryam tried to make out the details of the looming three-story inn. She linked arms with Dadu, who was clearly delighted by their wintry surroundings.

"A white Christmas!" he exclaimed. "Just like in the movies." He started to tunelessly sing the holiday anthem. *"I'm sleeping in a white Christmas,"* he sang. *"Just like the amazing ones in the fort."*

"I don't think that's how the song goes," Maryam said, amused.

"You don't know the backstory of the song, *beti*," her grandfather explained. "You see, every piece of art that endures has a strong origin story. This song is about a soldier dreaming of the snow forts he used to make before he joined the army." Maryam didn't have the heart to correct her grandfather, especially when he got a familiar faraway look in his eyes. "I used to sing this to your dadi-ma. I only wish she were here. Every Christmas we would watch the holiday movies, too," he said, his face falling. Her grandmother had passed away three years ago, after nearly fifty years of marriage, and Dadu still mourned the loss keenly.

"I bet she loved the romantic ones," Maryam said softly.

"What is a movie without love?" Dadu asked rhetorically. As a former Bollywood director, he loved a good romantic story line. "This town would have been the perfect backdrop for one of my films," he added.

"The hero and heroine running through the snow toward each other?" Maryam asked, teasing him about an old Bollywood trope.

Dadu smiled at her, and they shuffled carefully through the snow to the main entrance, carrying their bags. Snow Falls Inn was an imposing building constructed in the Second Empire style, with a pitched mansard roof, dormer windows, and massive bay windows out front. Slim white columns stood sentry in front of a recessed entry with oversized wooden doors closed tight against the chill. Stained glass windows streamed cheery light from inside the establishment, and with its elegant stone face, the hotel looked like it would be more at home on the streets of Paris—perhaps minus the garish holiday lights, in varying shades—than in this quiet Ontario village. With a quick glance to make sure the rest of her family was following, she pulled the heavy wooden door open.

A blast of warmth instantly extinguished the chill from her hands and face. Inside, she found her grandfather a seat before making her way to the lobby. The inn had a grand reception area decorated with a riot of color, with a fireplace so large she could have stepped inside without stooping. It was piled high with logs, the fire banked. Behind the reception desk, two middle-aged white women cheerfully checked in other stranded passengers. One of the women, dressed in a bright red Christmas sweater with three green dinosaurs in matching Santa hats, made Maryam smile. Her smile faded when the young man currently being served turned around and she recognized Saif's impossibly handsome face. She looked around for a pillar to hide behind, or maybe a swimming pool to dive into.

"Maryam?" Saif said, his deep voice making her shiver despite the warmth from the fireplace.

"Where?" she said, and then flushed bright red. Had she really responded with "where" to her *own name*? Dear God, please let her Ramadan miracle be a giant pit opening in front of her so she could disappear.

Saif laughed, his eyes crinkling in the corners. "I know, right? I can't believe we're stuck here, either," he said, kindly reframing her inane remark. "I was looking forward to catching up with my cousins in Toronto, and of course attending your sister's wedding. Guess we're all stranded for the night."

"Yup. Guess so," she stammered. Part of her was surprised that Saif recognized her. She knew she looked different now that she wore the hijab, and it had been years since they had last met. For his part, Saif had only grown more attractive. He had always been tall, but his six-foot frame had filled out over the past five years; he had put in some serious time on the weight bench. The last time she had seen him, he had been lanky; now his broad shoulders, powerful arms, and trim waist were emphasized by his well-fitting hoodie and jeans. But it was more than that—Saif seemed comfortable in his own skin. The lazy smile he threw her now did something to her stomach. She caught a whiff of his aftershave as he took one step closer—something woodsy with a hint of citrus—and she resisted the urge to inhale deeply.

"I like your hijab," he said, his tone low and teasing. "The dark blue suits your eyes."

Maryam's eyes flew to his face in surprise, and thankfully one of the women at reception beckoned her forward, and she beat a hasty retreat, muttering excuses.

"Good evening, love, how are you tonight?" the woman behind the reception desk asked in a rolling Aussie accent. Her name tag read "Kath," and she was tanned despite the frigid weather, dressed in a black blazer and sensible blue khakis.

Maryam, still reeling from her embarrassing encounter with Saif, gave her a strained smile as she handed her the hotel vouchers from the airport.

"You'll have to double up, love. Plenty of stranded passengers; plus, the . . . business folk had dibs on the renovated suites." Kath winked, and Maryam wondered what sort of business she meant. Kath reached across her partner's desk for the room cards.

"You lot must be especially tired. Ramadan, isn't it?" the woman in the Christmas sweater, whose name tag read "Deb," asked conversationally, and Maryam blinked in surprise.

"Ye-es," she said. "We were supposed to fly to Toronto for my sister's wedding. She's getting married in a few days."

"Bad luck, then," Kath said sympathetically. "Let us know if you need anything," she added, passing Maryam the room cards. "We're new owners, took possession last year when Deb's grandmother left us the inn in her will. Kind old lady, she knew we needed a fresh start together." The loving smile she threw her business partner left no doubt that the two women also enjoyed a more intimate relationship. "She knew Snow Falls would be a welcoming place. Decided to try our hand at the hospitality business. We've been fixing the old place up, but it takes time."

Kath winked at Maryam and turned to the next person in line.

Saif was chatting with her family when she returned, and she avoided his gaze as she passed out the key cards. Dadu agreed to bunk with her parents, while Saima and Maryam would share a room. To Maryam's dismay, Saif offered to help carry the suitcases to their rooms. Stupid polite brown-boy genes, Maryam thought. She walked ahead, but Saif quickly caught up.

"Crazy turbulence on the flight," he remarked as they maneuvered down the narrow carpeted hallway.

Not trusting herself to speak, Maryam nodded. Her parents, Dadu, and Saima walked slowly, caught up in conversation with the other guests; she wished they would hurry up. She didn't want to be alone with Saif—who knew what fresh humiliation this conversation would bring?

"Yup. It really was so loud on the plane. So very, very loud, I couldn't hear a thing," he added.

He was trying to tell her something, she realized with

growing embarrassment. Which could only mean one thing. "You heard me," she said flatly. She had been pretty sure, but Saif's clumsy reassurances to the contrary only served to confirm her fears. A new wave of humiliation warmed her cheeks.

"It's no big deal," he said easily. "Nothing I haven't heard before."

"Do you often witness near-death confessions about lifelong regrets and crushes?" Maryam asked.

Saif seemed surprised at her sarcasm but quickly recovered. "I mean, I am a lawyer. People tell me things."

"Aren't you in-house counsel for an insurance company? Besides, I thought you didn't hear anything because the plane was *so loud*. But just in case a few stray words might have slipped through, I hope you understand that was not meant for your ears," she said, her face still flaming. She couldn't even look at him.

"It's fine, Maryam," Saif said, and the kindness and pity in his voice was almost too much to bear.

"This is me," she said, reaching for the suitcases in his hands. He had pushed up the sleeves of his hoodie, and her gaze lingered on his forearms, which were ropy with muscle now. He noticed and smiled indulgently.

And in that moment, Maryam started to feel the first prickle of annoyance. He was enjoying this. He thought her humiliation was *funny*, a little boost to his already healthy ego. Saif had turned into a man comfortable not only with his new, hot body, but also with its effect on others. She narrowed her eyes and held out her hand for the suitcases.

"I don't need your help," she said shortly.

Saif leaned forward, and that woodsy-citrus scent hit her

again, making her light-headed. "The storm might have unearthed all sorts of secrets, but don't worry, Maryam, they'll
stay buried with me," he whispered. He straightened and gave
her another lingering smile. "Good night," he said softly, and
disappeared down the hall, toward his second-floor room.

FIVE

Anna

December 20
Snow Falls, Ontario

Nick, there's nothing I can do about this. I'll call you back as soon as I get to the hotel."

"*Fine.*"

"I'm sorry." Anna felt a pang at how angry Nick sounded—as if he couldn't really believe she was stranded at an airport rather than on her way to him. But he was already gone. She sighed, then dialed Janey's number and attempted to explain the situation again.

"Surely you can at least find a fax machine?" Janey asked, her tone clipped and cool.

"I . . ." Anna looked around the almost-deserted airport. ". . . will try," she concluded. The fact that Janey had decided the next issue of *Denver Decor* lived and died on the Malone Mansion spread having a new photo layout was a problem Anna didn't know how to solve. She would, though. She had to. Because she simply could not get fired. She had to get rid of her debt before Nick ever found out about it. Never mind that he could probably pay off everything she owed without even noticing the money was gone—that wasn't the point. He'd see her differently, for who she really was: a very unperfect person.

Anna rushed through the nearly empty airport, toward the area where she had been told a school bus was waiting to take the stranded travelers to an inn in a town nearby.

But the bus was gone. There were only banks of snow and one lone taxi idling in the snow-frosted night. The driver appeared to be asleep, his toque pulled down low over his eyes.

Anna tapped on the glass. "Hello?"

The driver unrolled his window and mumbled a bleary-eyed greeting.

"Can you drive me to . . . the nearest town?"

"Sure. That'd be Snow Falls, get in," he mumbled. Anna weighed the potential dangers of getting in a car with someone who didn't appear to be fully awake against the discomfort and loneliness of sleeping in the airport—and chose the former. She had to get out of this airport.

"No luggage?"

Anna held up her handbag and shook her head. "Traveling light." She tried not to think of her lost suitcase, and all the expensive clothes and gifts inside, as the taxi maneuvered away from the airport and through the snowy night. What few cars there were drove slowly, like whales in a large pod moving toward the same goal. Anna felt her nerves begin to calm—until she heard her phone ringing in her handbag.

"Janey, I'm on fumes here," she said—which was true; her phone battery was close to dead. But it wasn't Janey; it was Nick.

"I'm about to leave for dinner without you. Have you made any progress on getting out of there?"

"Babe, I told you, I just need to get to a hotel, check in, and—"

"A *hotel*? Don't you know that if you leave the airport they take you off standby?"

Anna sighed. "There are no flights going out tonight to be on standby *for*—"

"And in the morning? What about those flights?"

"You want me to sleep at the airport?" Anna looked out the window—and saw a sign come into view: "Welcome to Snow Falls, Your Happy Holiday Town!"

"Mother doesn't understand why you aren't here—"

"Has she looked at the news? This storm is all across the eastern seaboard and apparently it's just getting started."

"Anna . . . are you catastrophizing?"

When they first met, it was one of the things she loved about Nick: that he was always trying to convince her that her problems weren't really problems at all. But today—and a few times recently—it had felt instead like Nick wasn't listening to her when she tried to tell him how she felt. Now he continued, in an oh-so-calm voice, "Surely there has to be a way for you to get a flight out of there rather than checking into a hotel. You just need to take a few deep breaths and think of a—"

He was cut off mid-sentence. Anna took her phone away from her ear and shook it. The battery had died.

The taxi driver was looking over his shoulder at her expectantly. "Here we are, Snow Falls," he said. Anna could just make out rows of low brick buildings, all shops and restaurants strung with holiday lights, through the thickly falling snow. She paid the driver and stepped out of the taxi into knee-deep snow. She looked in horror at her brand-new, completely impractical shoes.

"Shoot—wait!" She had just realized that she couldn't see a hotel anywhere, had no idea where she was—and couldn't walk more than half a block in three feet of snow, wearing stilettos. But the taxi was already fishtailing on the slippery road as it moved away from her. She felt a surge of frustration with Nick and Janey. If they had stopped pestering her, she would have been able to focus on figuring out how to get herself to the hotel with all the other stranded passengers. Now she was lost.

She took in her surroundings as best she could in the snow. Holiday lights in varying shades of gold, green, and red twinkled at her through the snowflakes. All at once, a sense of peace stole over her. Her phone was dead, and she could no longer receive frantic calls from her boyfriend or her boss. She was lost, yes—but this town was adorable. It didn't feel real, more like some sort of holiday fantasy world come to life. She had the sudden sense that anything was possible—even the happiest ending you could imagine. The one Anna had been longing for. *True happiness. No pretending.*

It had been a long while since Anna had experienced such lightness of spirit. She lifted her face up to meet the snow—then impulsively stuck out her tongue and felt a snowflake, crisp and cold, land and melt there. Its brief, sharp tang was reminiscent of her best childhood moments. She made a wish. *For the happiest ending possible.*

Just then, the door to a restaurant opened in front of her and voices spilled into the cold night air.

"It's a big game tonight between two division rivals," came the familiar voice of sportscaster Harry Neale.

"That's right," Bob Cole chimed in. "Here come the Leafs versus the Senators . . ."

Anna followed the sound, picking her way carefully across the slippery sidewalk until she reached the door to a sports bar called It's the Most Wonderful Time for a Beer.

The place was busy, but one of the bartenders had seen her come in and waved her over to an empty seat in front of him at the bar. Anna plunked her elbows on the smooth walnut surface, letting the warmth in the room filter through her all the way to her feet in the ruined Manolos.

Shelves behind the bar were lined with bottles of peppermint schnapps, winter spiced rum, Irish cream—all the drinks Anna remembered being served at holiday cocktail parties in her childhood home in years gone by. On a screen above the bottles, the Toronto Maple Leafs and the Ottawa Senators were playing a hockey game. The patrons at the bar were clearly divided, half of them in blue-and-white Leafs regalia and half of them in Senators red and black. But all of them were smiling and chatting despite their competing team allegiances. Anna couldn't help but smile to herself, thinking of how excited her dad used to get about Maple Leafs games. After their move from Toronto, she was happy in Denver, which quickly felt like home—but she had loved their Toronto visits, and knew he always had, too. Maple Leafs games had been a part of that.

As Anna watched the players passing the puck back and forth, she remembered suggesting to Nick that they try to attend a Leafs game as part of their holiday visit. Nick had thought she was joking. "My perfect Anna at a hockey game," he had said with a laugh—and then he had moved on to talking about something else, and she hadn't had the chance to explain that her dad used to take her to hockey games all the time, and she was a fan.

As Anna settled in, brushing the snow off her blazer, Jonas Höglund scored on an assist from Mats Sundin. One of the bartenders, a tall, bespectacled man wearing a Leafs jersey, turned to her. "Mulled wine or hot apple cider is always on the house when the Leafs score."

"Hot apple cider would be lovely. But could I please pay you for it?" As she pulled her wallet out of her handbag, the bartender held up his hands in good-natured protest.

"No way. It's bad luck to take payment after the Leafs score."

"Not sure how this place stays in business, Don," said a woman to Anna's right. She was, somewhat confusingly, wearing a Maple Leafs jersey *and* a Senators toque. Just then, Marián Hossa scored for the Senators and the woman said, "Oh, darn!" before letting out a jubilant *whoop* and "Go, Hossa!"

The bartender was in front of Anna again. "Mulled wine or apple cider on the house when the Sens score," he said with a grin.

"Wait a second, weren't you wearing a Leafs jersey just a second ago . . . ?" Anna asked. The bartender just shrugged, then topped up Anna's steaming, fragrant mug before making his way down the bar, handing out free drinks.

"They're twins. That was Ron," a voice beside her said—a deep voice that was warm and inviting, much like the cider. She turned her head. The man next to her had a chocolate brown beard, black-rimmed glasses, and a Maple Leafs toque pulled down low over dark hair. His chestnut-brown eyes were warm and kind, and crinkled at the side when he smiled at her—which he was doing now. She had the sudden feeling she knew him, that they had met somewhere before. "The other one is Don."

"Thanks for clearing that up," she said. On the screen above, a Senators player came close to scoring, a Leafs player blocked him, they engaged in a wrestling match across the ice, and the bar erupted in *oohs* and *aahs*, which Anna joined in on. When the moment passed, she saw her barstool neighbor was looking at her closely.

"You don't look like you'd be a hockey fan."

"And why not?" she said, tilting her head. "Leafs fans can't wear cocktail dresses to sports bars? I'm in blue, after all."

"True, but didn't anyone tell you it's winter out there? The time of year when people wear parkas, boots . . . hats and mitts? That kind of thing?"

Anna blew on the cider, then took a sip. It was spicy and fortifying. "I'm not supposed to be here," she said. "I thought I was going to a gala tonight."

He tilted his head, quizzical. "In Snow Falls?"

"Toronto. But my plane got diverted." She turned her head and their eyes collided again. Once more, she felt a jolt of recognition. "So now, here I am," she said, not quite sure why her heart was racing around in her chest as fast as a puck on ice.

"Here you are," he echoed. "Of all the festive sports bars in all the world—"

"This has *got* to be the only one, right?"

Another smile. "Probably. I saw you outside, catching snowflakes on your tongue. I thought I'd imagined it, a woman dressed for a party, in the middle of this town . . . walking into this bar . . ." He turned his sweet, crinkly-eyed gaze to the screens above just as Mats Sundin nearly scored on a breakaway.

Anna clapped her hands. "*So* close. Oh, he's my favorite!"

"Mine, too. Although I think Gary Roberts might end up being a contender for favorite, now that he's signed."

"So much character," Anna agreed, sipping her cider.

"Maybe we'll finally have a shot at the Stanley Cup, right? Who knows, could happen . . ."

Anna sighed along with him, a sigh that was familiar to Maple Leafs fans everywhere: the wistful *hey, it could happen . . . but probably not* sigh. "Maybe," they both said at the same time. Then they exchanged a rueful glance and laughed at themselves. The Leafs hadn't won a Stanley Cup—or even come close—in thirty-three long years.

"Champions keep playing until they get it right. At least that's what my dad always used to say."

A cheer rang out—but it was for the wrong side now. The Sens had scored again.

"Well, the Leafs really seem to be taking a while to get it right, then."

"Cider refill?" The bartending twin with the Senators jersey was back.

Anna shook her head. "I've barely made a dent in my first glass. But I hope it's not bad luck to say no? Congratulations on the goal."

The bartender laughed. "My brother's the superstitious one. I know what really wins hockey games is skill." He shot his twin a pointed look—and the Leafs fan twin shook his fist in mock anger. Anna turned her attention back to the screen—just in time to see the Leafs take an unfortunate penalty.

"I can't watch," said the handsome stranger beside her. "Talk to me. Put me out of my misery."

"Okay, so . . . you're from Toronto?"

"Born and raised."

"What are you doing here in Snow Falls?"

"I'm here for work," he said, and suddenly his tone seemed evasive.

"What do you do?"

"That's not interesting. Tell me about you. So, you were on your way to Toronto for a gala and got diverted by the storm?"

"Exactly. Well, sort of exactly. I was heading to Toronto for the holidays, not just a gala. But our plane ended up landing here instead because of all the snow. It was a bit scary, actually."

"You're all staying over at the Snow Falls Inn, right? News travels fast in this little town. Although . . ." He seemed thoughtful for a moment. "The people who live here are also surprisingly good at keeping secrets."

There was something mysterious about him, something that made her want to know more, but he kept asking her questions about herself. "You're part of that group from the diverted plane then?" he prompted.

"I think I'm *supposed* to be staying there—but I missed the bus and I'm not quite sure where the inn is. Actually—" She glanced behind her, out the window. "I really *should* be out there looking for it . . ."

"Nothing in this town is far. Two lefts and a right once you leave here—but I'm staying there, too. I can walk you over, once the game is through."

"We-ell." It had been such a long time since she'd sat and enjoyed a Maple Leafs game. And as pressing as the need for a place to stay was, she found she didn't really want to leave the cozy bar yet.

"Don't you want to stay and see just how badly the Leafs can lose this thing?"

Anna felt another wave of déjà vu as she looked at his understatedly handsome face. "Have we met somewhere before?" she found herself asking.

His eyes skated away from hers, back up to the game on the screen. "Hmm, I don't think so. What's your name?"

"Anna Gibson." She extended her hand and he turned toward her again. "Pleased to meet you. I was born in Toronto, but moved to Denver when I was seven. Who knows, maybe we met a very long time ago."

"Josh Tannenbaum," he said, still holding her hand in his. His skin was smooth and warm. He released her hand just as the Leafs scored and the bar erupted in a cacophony of cheers, with Anna and Josh joining the ruckus of hoots and hollers.

Now the Leafs fan twin was standing before them with a carafe of mulled wine. "Ready for the strong stuff?"

Anna shook her head, and Josh covered his mulled wine cup with his hand, too. "Early start tomorrow," he said. "I'm at my limit. But maybe some poutine?"

The Leafs were now shorthanded, and doing pitifully on the power play.

"Josh, tell me about you," Anna said, soon munching happily on a plate of gravy- and cheese-curd-covered french fries. "What do you do that's brought you to Snow Falls? Are you stranded, too?"

He glanced down at the bar for a split second, but then his warm brown eyes were on hers again. "Nope," he said. "I'm here by choice. But it's very boring. Tell me, what *you* do?"

"I hate my job, actually," Anna found herself admitting. "Sorry, that's really negative. But it's true. I had this experience today on the plane that reminded me of how short life is."

"Flying through a blizzard? Thinking the plane was about to crash? Been there." Josh laughed. "I think the last time I was on a turbulent flight I told myself I was going to climb Kilimanjaro if I made it through."

"And? Did you?"

"No. Sadly, I just haven't had the time."

"Ah, I see. Lack of time is the *one* thing stopping you from climbing Kilimanjaro?"

"We-ell, that, and I'm afraid of heights." He shrugged and she laughed. "How about you? What did you decide to do with your life during your frightening moments in the not-so-friendly skies?"

Anna thought for a long moment. "It's not so much that I decided to *do* anything—just that maybe I had a realization: I'm living the life I thought I wanted—but it might not be what I actually want. That realization might have been even scarier than thinking the plane might crash." She pushed the plate of food away and looked up at Josh again. He was watching her intently. "Sorry. This is really my day for oversharing with strangers. It's just . . . I feel like I know you. Like we've met before." She tilted her head as she regarded him. "It's kind of weird, actually."

"I'm just one of those people with a familiar face. I get that all the time. Now, what you just said—" He stopped talking and looked up at Tie Domi and Chris Neil locked in a violent embrace, each trying to get the jersey off the other—but she could tell he didn't really see it, that his mind was somewhere else. "I understand that. I've been feeling that way about my life, too. I worked really hard toward something I thought I wanted, and it was not an easy path. I got a bit diverted at one point but then got back on track. Now everything is coming together for me. It's just that having what I thought I wanted, it's not . . . easy." He sighed. "But that's ridiculous, right?" He gestured toward the screen, where the Leafs players were now battling frantically to score another goal. "I mean, let's just say the Leafs ever make it to the Stanley Cup finals—they aren't going to decide it's not as much fun as they thought, right? That it's too overwhelming. It's *work*. They'd just have to accept that. But I . . ." He shook his head. "Sorry. Now I'm the one unloading on someone I just met. You're easy to talk to, Anna."

"So are you." They held gazes for a moment, and Anna felt a confusing flutter in her chest. She found herself wishing she could remove his glasses and get a really good look at his appealing brown eyes—but you could not touch the face of a stranger you just met in a bar. Especially when you had a boyfriend anxiously waiting for you in Toronto. "Let's face it," she said, trying to cover up how flustered she felt. "The Leafs are never going to be in the Stanley Cup finals—so your analogy doesn't hold water, I'm afraid."

He rewarded her with a deep rumble of a laugh that was as warm as a fire on a cold winter's night. She looked down into her cider glass, the steam now curling into the air in a lazy ribbon as it cooled, then back up at him. She couldn't deny it: there was something about him that made her want to know him. It seemed all her feelings were closer to the surface since the near-death experience on the plane. She was living in the moment. Was that so bad?

"Everything you've ever wanted is on the other side of fear," she found herself saying.

He smiled. "Who are you, Yoda?"

Anna laughed. "My dad was. He was always saying stuff like that, giving me little bon mots to help me get through life."

"You have great timing. How could you know that was exactly what I needed to hear?"

"Just lucky, I guess," Anna said, watching as a bar patron asked for the check, then paid with a handwritten IOU. "Gotta love small towns," she murmured.

"And this is an especially lovable one."

She turned to him. "You seem very at home here."

"This is my second time in Snow Falls. I was here years ago."

"For your uninteresting job?"

He looked at her for a beat, as if gauging whether he could trust her. "Yes, for my job." He sipped his mulled wine and looked away.

She tilted her head as she regarded him. "Josh, are you a spy?"

He nearly spit out his drink "A spy? What would give you that idea?"

"You just seem . . . a bit mysterious, that's all. Plus, I read somewhere that they choose spies partially based on who has the most forgettable looks—the kind of person you could *swear* you'd met before."

"Really? Forgettable?" He laughed. She blushed.

"Hey! Wait! The *article* said forgettable! *I'm* not saying you're forgettable. I think you're—" She had been about to say "quite cute," but she cut herself off and looked down into her cider mug. Had the bartender inadvertently given her the strong stuff? No. Her head was clear as a bell. And in this state of clarity, she had been about to tell a guy she'd just met at a bar that she thought he was cute—when meanwhile, Nick was about to ask her to marry him. "I guess you just seem like a regular guy," she continued. "But there's something about you that tells me you're not."

"So, you immediately went to 'this guy is a spy.'"

She laughed again. "Hey, I have a wild imagination, what can I say?"

"I promise you," he said, and now his expression was surprisingly intense, "I really am just a regular guy." He leaned back a bit and gestured at himself. "Look at me! Leafs jersey and toque, sitting in a sports bar, watching the game in small-town Ontario. What could be more regular than that? *You*, on the other hand . . ."

He trailed off, and she waited, expectant, suddenly very curious to know what he had to say about her. "You don't look like a regular girl." They stared at each other for a long moment. It felt like all the noise in the bar fell away.

Then a buzzer sounded on the TV for the end of the game. It had concluded in a draw and there would now be overtime.

The twin bartenders were walking up and down the bar, offering more free refills of cider or wine. When they got to Anna, she shook her head. "That's it for me, but thank you." She held out cash, but the twins shook their heads and said in unison, "No way, bad luck!"

"Wait, I thought only one of you believed in bad luck?"

"Not when it's a tie!" said the Senators-jersey-wearing twin. "When it's a tie, anything is possible!"

Anna put her wallet away and looked at Josh. "Thanks for keeping me company, but I'd better be going. It's been quite a day, and I still have to figure out where I'm staying. I don't think I have overtime in me tonight."

"Me, neither. I'll read about it in the paper in the morning. But I meant what I said earlier. Let me walk you to the inn. I couldn't stand the idea of you getting lost in the snow. And . . ." He took a black parka from the back of his barstool and held it out to her. "Wear this? Please? I also couldn't live with myself if you turned into an icicle on the way there."

Anna protested, but he wouldn't hear of it. She slid on his jacket and felt immediately warm and cozy. She couldn't help but notice how nice the jacket smelled, too. Subtle and expensive, a blend of amber and bergamot that did not seem like something a regular guy would wear.

They made their way to the front door and outside into the snowy night—but Anna stopped on the sidewalk when she realized how much the volume of accumulated snow had already increased. "These stupid shoes," she muttered. "I think I need to call a taxi, I'm sorry."

"You're not going to find a taxi at this hour in Snow Falls. Most people walk home from the bar—or snowshoe or cross-country ski," he said—just as two bar patrons shushed past gaily on skis. "I do know of a rickshaw, however."

"A rickshaw?"

"Okay, not really a rickshaw, but I could carry you? Really, what are your options, other than frostbitten toes?"

She was about to decline—but she knew he was right. With the shoes she was wearing, frostbite was a legitimate concern. The snow fell gently into the short waves of hair that hugged the back of his neck as she stared up at him, knowing she probably *should* say no—she didn't really know this guy at all, no matter what the excitement of a long, unpredictable day was making her feel. But when he kept smiling that sweet, generous smile, she found herself saying, "Yes, please."

"Okay, ready?" He swept her up into his muscular arms and carried her like he was a firefighter rescuing her from a burning building. She could feel his firm chest against the side of her body, smell his cologne and the cinnamon-and-clove spiciness of his breath.

"You know, this is probably the most ridiculous thing I've ever done," she said as he carried her through the snowy night.

"It *is* ridiculous to wear shoes like that in the middle of winter," he said. "I agree." She playfully punched his arm and he looked down at her. Their faces were very close. "But admit it, it's also fun. Didn't you say thinking you were about to die in a plane crash made you want to make some changes in your life? Shouldn't those changes include more spontaneous fun?"

"How can I argue with that?" She looked up at the swirling snowflakes as he carried her through Snow Falls. Two lefts, a right, and in no time at all they arrived at a stately three-story gray brick stone inn. It was covered in scaffolding on one side, but was still utterly charming—aside from the fact that it was strung with chaotic strings of Christmas lights in every shade. Anna had the urge to immediately find the owner and give them some holiday decorating tips. *Less is more*, she would say. *One or two colors tops, but multicolored is a bit busy for the classic style of this building.*

A hand-painted sign to the right of the short stone staircase Josh was carrying her up proclaimed this to be the Snow Falls Inn—except one of the *n*'s was covered in snow, so it said "Snow Falls In."

Josh set her down in front of the tall oak door, festooned with not one but three different wreaths. "There, door-to-door service."

"Thank you, Josh."

He smiled down at her. "I had a really fun time watching the game with you, Anna."

"I did, too. Thanks for getting me here safely."

As fluffy white flakes fell gently around them, Anna felt like they were suspended in a snow globe. "So," he finally said. "Do you still think I'm . . . what was the word you used? 'Forgettable'?"

"Carrying me through the snow definitely makes you *un*-forgettable in my book." She found herself unable to look away from his gaze.

"That's a relief," he said softly, eyes on hers as he reached out to brush snow from her hair. His hand grazed her shoulder, and his gentle touch made her body feel like a lit sparkler in the darkness. Then he cleared his throat. "Better get you inside where it's warm." He turned away and pushed open the heavy

front door, holding it open for her. "Welcome to Snow Falls
Inn," he said with a smile. Beyond the reception area, a massive
fireplace was lit up with a welcoming fire and was surrounded
by comfy-looking couches and chairs. It all would have looked
like something from the pages of a decor magazine—had every
surface not been festooned with Christmas ornaments in every
color, shape, and size.

Anna began to shrug off Josh's parka, just as she saw Mr.
Dadu, Maryam's kindly grandfather, sitting comfortably in a
cozy chair near the crackling fireplace. He gave her a friendly
wave and she waved back.

"I'm sure Deb and Kath, the owners, will take good care of
you," Josh said.

His glasses were covered in melting snowflakes. She hoped
he would take them off to clean them, so she could get a better
look at him—she had the sudden urge to memorize his face in
case she didn't see him again. But he left them on. She handed
him his parka. "Thank you, Josh."

Something was different about him now, she noticed. His
demeanor had suddenly changed. He glanced from side to side,
as if looking for someone—or trying to hide from someone.

Maybe he really *was* a spy.

"I should go," he said. "Good night, Anna. Again, I really
enjoyed our evening."

"Good night, Josh," she said, and tried to ignore the pang she
felt at the idea that she might never see him again. "I did, too."

"Safe travels tomorrow." He waved goodbye and headed for
the stairs.

She watched him go, then turned and approached the

reception desk. A smiling woman with a loud Christmas sweater—whom Anna was immediately certain was behind the loud light display outside and the questionable Christmas-decor decisions inside—greeted her.

"The good news is, we *do* have a room left," she said in an Australian accent. She handed Anna a key chain shaped like a holly sprig. "I was told there was going to be one last straggler, and I was starting to think about sending out a search party! Unfortunately, your room is one of the ones that isn't quite done yet. This place is a work in progress, and we've got a large . . . er, corporate party booked on the other side of the hotel, the side that's all renovated." She tilted her head in the direction Josh had headed off in. "The bed's comfortable, though. And we looked into the mold on the ceiling—I can confirm it's the non-toxic kind! Just don't . . . touch it. Ever. Promise?"

None of this sounded promising, but a comfortable bed to sleep away this long day was all she needed, really. The woman handed her a bottle of water and a granola bar—one of those hippie ones that was full of good-for-you things but always tasted like sawdust. Anna took it gratefully, not sure how easy it was going to be to get breakfast in the morning. "Oh, wait," she said, remembering Janey's urgent layout request. "Do you have a computer with email, or a fax machine?"

"So sorry, love, no internet here, and the phone lines have been knocked out by the storm. That means our fax machine isn't working. Hoping phones'll be back up and running in the morning."

"Thanks anyway."

Upstairs, Anna found her room, turned on the light, and looked around. Unfortunately, the cheerful woman at the desk had oversold it. The ceiling was water-stained—and covered in patterns of mold that resembled those inkblot tests. Anna could see a man with an axe and a fish with two heads. The overhead lighting was dim and flickering. She turned on a bedside lamp, hoping the softer light might improve things—but no such luck. The new lighting angles picked up more strange stains on the walls, and peeling wallpaper. Anna sighed.

It wasn't that she was like Nick and had grown up wealthy, used to only high-class accommodations. She hadn't. Her dad had been a lawyer, but had made the switch to family law and opened his own office in Golden after he met Beth. After a while, his generous nature had landed him so much pro bono work he never quite seemed to break even. But Beth was an interior designer, and she was the one who had influenced Anna's tastes for fine surroundings—even if those fine surroundings were simply a matter of resourcefulness. She—and Anna alongside her—had always loved the challenge of taking something that already existed and turning it into something even better. Anna and Beth had come up with a game inspired by the show *This Old House* on PBS, which they had watched obsessively. They made up their own pretend show, *New Room, No Budget*: Anna and Beth would make believe they were on a reality show, really play up the drama for the nonexistent cameras in whichever room in their house they had chosen to transform that day. *Use what you have, do what you can* had been one of Beth's mottos. Many days, by the time Anna's dad got home from work, the house would have been transformed into something that looked completely new and different—no matter that Anna and Beth hadn't spent a cent.

Anna sighed and pushed away the memories. Even an

enthusiastic round of *New Room, No Budget* wouldn't help *this* room. There was no way to turn this place into something brand-new because all she had on hand, she found as she dumped her handbag onto the bed, was an almost-empty Body Shop perfume oil bottle, a half-eaten bag of scotch mints, a smooshed muffin, a bunch of magazines, her makeup bag, and a pashmina. She rooted through the pile, searching for the charger for her flip phone, but came up empty-handed. She had packed it into her suitcase, she realized, figuring she wouldn't need it until she was in Toronto with Nick. She picked up the room phone— but as Kath had said, there was no service. Just as she had when her phone died, Anna felt something like relief flood through her.

She unrolled her pashmina, draped it over the foot of the bed, then peeled off her dress and tights and slipped between the sheets—and was pleasantly surprised to discover the mattress was not lumpy and mildew-smelling, as she had been certain it would be. Instead, the sheets were crisp, white, and smelled as if they had been dried on a line in the middle of spring. The mattress was the perfect balance of firm yet yielding. This bed would never have made it into an episode of *New Room, No Budget* because it was obviously very expensive.

She settled her head on a pillow that was magically the ideal height and texture for her and fell fast asleep dreaming of how it felt to be carried through the snow by a kind, handsome stranger.

SIX

Maryam

December 21

4 days until Christmas
1 day until Hanukkah begins
The 26th day of Ramadan

*S*uhoor was a disaster. Maryam had been so exhausted the night before, and so flustered after her run-in with Saif, she had forgotten to ask Deb and Kath, their friendly Tasmanian innkeepers, for help sourcing *suhoor*, the early-morning meal that would sustain them during a full day of fasting. Naturally, no one else had thought to ask, either, which meant that at four this morning Maryam had to go on the hunt for enough food to feed the wedding party—their own family, plus Saif and Farah.

Just once, Maryam wished she could be the one who got to throw up her hands, plop down on the ground, and insist that someone else carry this burden.

By five a.m., she had managed to scrounge up a half dozen granola bars, a bag of dates, some apples, a few packets of hot chocolate powder, plus what Saima had scavenged from the vending machine: ketchup-flavored potato chips (why, Canada?) and Coffee Crisp chocolate bars, which, okay, were delicious.

"The Prophet Muhammad, peace be upon him, would fast an entire day in the hot desert sun after eating only two dates and drinking water," Ghulam said to Maryam in the lobby, surveying her efforts. "In contrast, this is a feast."

Her grandfather didn't fast, due to his diabetes—Muslims with chronic health conditions weren't required to abstain from food or drink—but he had woken up early to "join in the fun" this morning. She still gave him more dates, granola bars, and fruit than anyone else, and he settled on a comfortable armchair in front of the fireplace. His sleep had been erratic these past few years since her dadi-ma's death, and she knew Dadu needed to be around people. She wouldn't be surprised if he stayed in the airy foyer all day, chatting with whoever walked past. The wedding party was quiet as they ate in the central lobby of the inn. It was early enough that no one else was up, not even Deb and Kath. Maryam made a mental note to make arrangements for *iftar*, the evening meal, before catching herself.

We won't be here at sunset, she reminded herself, *because we are getting out of Snow Falls* today. *Just as soon as the snow stops.* Maryam tried to catch Saima's eye, but her sister sullenly drank the *chai* Maryam had brewed using their in-room percolator.

Saif Rasool stood at the outer edges of the group. He smiled at her, holding up his granola bar in a mock salute. Maryam looked away, face burning, her humiliation still fresh in her mind. *If it hadn't been for Anna, none of this*—

She paused. If it hadn't been for Anna's comforting presence on the flight, she might have had a full-blown panic attack, like she used to in college before an exam, and which had been happening to her more frequently lately. If it hadn't been for Anna's relentlessly cheerful chatter, she might have made a bigger fool of herself in front of Saif by truly freaking out.

Instead, he simply knew all her deepest secrets . . . and thought they were *hilarious*. Despite herself, she wondered where her seatmate was. She hoped Anna had found her way to a safe hotel, and was faring better than they were.

Maryam drank the last of her water—she made sure to drink at least two cups during *suhoor*—and rose, calling for the entire group's attention. "We'll pray *fajr* in a few minutes," she announced, referring to the predawn prayer. "We can use the tablecloths as prayer mats."

A few people discreetly left to make *wudu*, the purification ritual performed before prayer, and Saima took the opportunity to sidle up to her.

"The plan is to leave right after *salat*, right?" her sister asked, and Maryam hesitated.

"I checked the weather this morning . . ." Maryam started.

"Please. We have to be in Toronto today," she said, and Maryam could tell her sister was keeping a lid on her boiling frustration with effort.

"I know, but it hasn't stopped snowing," Maryam said patiently. She had kept an eye on the storm on the small twenty-four-inch television in their room, and the situation didn't look promising. The Weather Network newscasters had used the word "Snowmageddon" too many times for Maryam to discount the severity of the situation. It was a small miracle this tiny town still had power.

"We have to try," Saima urged, and her voice finally

cracked, a tear making its slow trek down her cheek. "You promised we would leave today." She wiped her eyes, just as Maryam realized they had an audience—her parents, Farah, even Saif, had noticed Saima's breakdown.

Maryam sighed. Her sister might not be making much sense, but she was right—a promise was a promise. "After *fajr* we'll try to find a way back to the airport," she said, just as their mother walked over and put an arm around Saima, leaving Maryam to prepare their makeshift prayer area alone.

She spread the tablecloths on the ground by herself while the rest of the party huddled around Saima—everyone except for Saif, who grasped the other end of the long rectangular cloth she was struggling to lay in a straight line.

"Thanks," she muttered.

He smiled at her. "You're doing the heavy lifting by trying to keep us organized," he said, reaching for the second tablecloth. "I'm only following your lead. Is your sister okay?"

"Her name is Saima," Maryam answered, reaching down for the other end of the tablecloth.

He seemed surprised at her gruff tone and turned to face her. "I know her name, Maryam. We grew up together."

"We attended the same parties and events, but we didn't grow up together. We barely know each other," Maryam countered.

Saif leaned close. "I know you," he said, voice low and meaningful, and she tried not to shiver at this intimacy. An intimacy he wasn't entitled to, she reminded herself.

"Only because you eavesdropped on a conversation that was never meant for your ears," she said.

"You weren't trying to keep your voice down," he said. "I might have overheard a few things, but does it really matter? We've known each other since we were kids."

Maryam stopped fiddling with the tablecloth. "Why couldn't you just pretend you hadn't heard a thing?"

Saif said nothing, sharp brown eyes intent on her face. "What's really bothering you?" he asked, and he sounded so gentle, so sure, that she had a sudden urge to lay her head on his broad shoulder and just . . . breathe.

"You know all this *stuff* about me!" she burst out. "The scales aren't balanced!" She instantly felt childish and waited for him to make fun of her. Except he didn't.

"You're right," Saif said quietly. "I'll tell you something about myself. Something no one else knows."

Maryam didn't want to be curious, but she couldn't help herself. She had spent too many years wondering about Saif. She watched him now, and his eyes, fringed with sooty dark lashes, turned light brown as he looked at her. His thick hair was slightly mussed, and she wondered how much sleep he had gotten last night, and whether he had thought about her at all. The idea made her feel restless, and she shifted under his gaze as he smiled slightly, attention focused entirely on her. He had always been intense, but to have that intensity leveled in her direction felt . . . dangerous.

He leaned close; even at this early hour, he smelled so good. "I'm not happy, either," he whispered.

He gently tugged on his end of the tablecloth, pulling her a half step closer, and she had to remind herself: Saif was toying with her, like a cat with a mouse. He was a charmer she hadn't seen in over five years, and he couldn't be trusted. As if reading her mind, her father came up to them, protective.

"Everyone is ready for *fajr* prayer," Ghulam said, giving Saif a hard look. Silently, Maryam joined her sister and mother in line for the communal *salat*, Saif's words echoing in her mind.

I'm not happy, either.

Did he mean it? Did it even matter? They barely knew each other, no matter what Saif had implied. She could wish things were different, but they weren't. And her family needed her now.

Dadu led the prayer, and afterward, the group sat quietly, making personal *duas* and enjoying the peace. Saima gestured to Maryam.

"I tried to call a cab," she said, keeping her voice low. "But the phones aren't working. The airport is maybe ten miles away. How do you feel about walking?"

Maryam stared at her sister. "You want Mom and Dad to walk ten miles through this snow? You want Dadu wading through drifts taller than him?"

Beside her, Saima vibrated with nervous energy. "This is why I wanted to stay at the airport overnight!" She scrambled to her feet and stalked to the main entrance of the inn, unbolting the main door and pushing it open. Or, rather, attempting to push it open. The door wouldn't budge. She dug her shoulder into the solid wood, then turned around and put her back into it. Maryam wasn't sure if she should laugh or try to help her.

"Saima, allow me," Saif said, coming to her aid. He gave the door a mighty push, biceps flexing impressively beneath his thin shirt. The door opened about two feet—and a heap of snow tumbled inside the foyer. Saima, Maryam, and Saif jerked back, then cautiously peered through the small gap outside, at the now alien landscape.

It had snowed heavily last night, but it had been too dark to fully make out the geography; plus, they had been too tired to pay attention. Now, as the sky lightened on the horizon, a thread of pink ribboning across the sky, they stared at their snowy prison in silence.

The cars in the parking lot were nothing more than buried white lumps, streets indistinguishable from sidewalk, pitched roofs decorated with a thick layer of fluffy white. A massive pine tree in front of the inn, branches bent low, resembled a lady in a ruffled white dress. And everywhere there was a blanketed stillness, as if the rest of the world had decided to sit this significant weather event out.

"Snowmageddon"? Try "apocalypse in a picturesque snow globe," Maryam thought. *It feels like the morning after the end of the world.* Saif and Maryam looked at each other. Beside them, Saima choked back a sob, turned around, and walked swiftly in the direction of their room.

"Do you need to go after her?" Saif asked.

Maryam shook her head. "She needs to scream first. Then I'll think of a plan." She turned to Saif, who seemed relaxed despite the chill temperature. He gazed outside, where the sun was slowly starting its ascent, coloring the sky a streaky pink and orange. It promised to be a beautiful day-after-the-apocalypse.

"It's so strange. I've been having dreams about a place like this," he said, voice husky against the still darkness. "A quiet town, away from everyone, a deep blanket of snow. Like when we were kids. Remember?"

A sudden memory sprang unbidden to her mind: She was about ten years old and their families had rented a cabin one weekend during the Christmas holidays. A novel experience for all—both sets of parents had immigrated from India, and had never grown up camping or cottaging, particularly during the winter. But her father had thought it would be fun, and Saif's father had agreed, and they had found a place near a small frozen lake with four bedrooms and a single bathroom. Maryam had built a snow family, while Saima had insisted on a parade of snow cats, snow dogs, and even a snow parrot, aided by Saif's older brother Raihan, before being ambushed by Saif, intent on starting a snowball fight. They had roasted halal marshmallows, once their fathers had figured out how to start a fire in the small wood-burning fireplace, and their mothers had prepared a feast of naan, fragrant rice *pilau* with fresh peas, baked tandoori chicken, plus savory *haleem*, a meat stew prepared with lentils, wheat, and barley, topped with fried onions and fresh coriander, and wedges of lime to squeeze over the top, her favorite dish. In the morning Ghulam and Saif's father had prepared eggs and pancakes for the two families, and the children had gone sledding for hours, returning tired and content. In the years that followed, the two families spoke often about returning to that magical cottage by the frozen lake, but had never found the time.

"You smashed Saima's snow cat," Maryam said.

Saif raised an eyebrow. "You sat on my snowman."

"Don't you mean snow blob?" Maryam teased.

"Hey, snow blobs have feelings, too."

They smiled at each other, and for a moment, Maryam grew wistful. If only she hadn't fallen deeply in crush with him at age twelve and become completely tongue-tied anytime they were in the same room together. If only they had kept in touch as adults. Maybe things would have been different now. But they weren't.

She really should go check on Saima. Instead, Maryam rested her head against the doorjamb and tried to resist the urge to reach out and touch his arm. He had really nice forearms. When he had strained against the door, his shirt had ridden up, revealing a flat stomach, the shadow of abs, a dusting of dark hair. Saif wasn't just cute, she thought. He was sexy. The thought brought her up short as she realized who he reminded her of, and she straightened, suddenly businesslike.

"Well, unless you have access to a private jet or helicopter to swoop in and save my sister's wedding, I should go help Saima figure this out."

"No private jet or helicopter, sadly. My clients are usually insuring their first home—not buying their first plane." His eyes twinkled with amusement, but this time Maryam recognized it for the danger sign it was. She had succumbed to a dangerously charming man once before and had no intention of doing so again.

"Tell Saima I'm sure things will work out. I'll see you at *iftar*, Maryam Aziz," he said, turning for the stairs.

Ghulam caught her eye, motioning for her to join him in the alcove where the extra firewood was stored. Her mother was there, too, and as Maryam approached, she noted the worried looks on her parents' faces.

"I'll find Saima and try to calm her down," Maryam reassured them, but Azizah only took her arm while her father shifted on his feet, looking uncomfortable.

"We noticed you speaking with Saif last night and again today," her mother started, and Maryam immediately wanted to sink into the floor.

"I really should get back to my room," she said, edging away. "Saima is really upset."

Except it was her father who seemed upset right now. "*Beta*, I know that Saif is a good-looking man—"

Oh God, please make him stop, Maryam thought, desperate for some divine intervention.

"—but we have heard a few things about him," Ghulam continued.

"From his own *mother*," Azizah said. "He doesn't visit very often, even though they are aging. And Shukriya told me herself that he has a *girlfriend*," she said, whispering now. Her words hit Maryam like a blow, and she took a step back, staring at the stairs across the room, where Saif had only moments ago disappeared. He had a girlfriend? Not that he had been flirting with her, of course. Any attention he might have been paying her had been all in her head.

"Be careful, *beta*," her father said. "We don't want you to get hurt again."

Maryam nodded her head. "You don't have to worry about me," she told her parents. "I should get back to the room. I'm pretty tired."

*M*aryam woke at noon, groggy and blinking against the gloom of the blackout curtains. She hadn't paid a lot of attention to her surroundings, other than to note the shabby-chic vibe of Snow Falls Inn that she suspected was not intentional.

She was sharing a queen bed with her sister. A pretty antique-veneer bureau had a wood-paneled twenty-four-inch tube television perched on top, where she had watched the Weather Network foretell doom last night. An elegant Queen Anne chair was positioned in front of the windows, upholstered in gray damask stripes, but the floor was covered in hideous red-and-brown carpeting.

The en suite bathroom was currently occupied, and Maryam was relieved to have a few minutes alone. They had been up late, repeatedly testing the phones to see if they worked before falling into an exhausted sleep. It seemed like they were stuck in Snow Falls for at least another day. A dull headache now started behind her eyes.

Maryam lay back and contemplated the plaster ceiling of the room, a swirling design in an infinite pattern, with no beginning and no end. Her life had started to feel like that, lately—a never-ending whirl of problem-solving and disasters. She was tired of fighting fires.

Saima emerged from the bathroom, clad only in her knee-length nightshirt, curly hair loose around her shoulders. Silently, she started to dress. "I'm going to the lobby to see if the phones are working yet, and try to call Miraj," she said stiffly. "I'm pretty sure we've lost the deposit for the *mehndi* hall." The *mehndi*, which had been scheduled for tomorrow, was meant to kick off the wedding festivities with a ladies-only dance party. Maryam had been looking forward to the *mehndi* the most; she had even secretly prepared a choreographed dance for the occasion.

Maryam waited until Saima left the room before getting out of bed and taking a quick shower in the tiny en suite. She had finished tying her navy blue hijab when there was a knock at the door. Saima must have forgotten her key card.

Opening the door, she was surprised to see Saif on the other side.

"What do you—" she started, but he muttered a hurried "Sorry" before diving into the closet behind her and shutting the door.

"What the hell?" Maryam said out loud.

"Hey, Maryam, have you seen Saif?" Farah, her family friend, called out, rounding the corner. She had been running and was out of breath.

Maryam resisted the urge to look at the closet behind her. "Who?" she asked, trying to buy time.

"Saif. Remember him? He was walking down the hallway in this direction." Farah lowered her voice. "Our parents are trying to set us up. They don't care about the rumors. I thought since we're all stuck together in this weird inn, we might as well have the conversation, you know?"

Inwardly, Maryam wanted to scream. Of course, this was why Farah had joined the wedding party. It was practically an expectation that a *desi* wedding should beget more weddings. She wondered if Farah knew that Saif had a girlfriend in California. Or that he was a disappointment to his family.

But of course Farah knew. She was intelligent, and had an engaging, friendly presence that likely resonated with her middle school physics students. Maryam bet she was great at designing hands-on experiments involving light or speed or . . .

"Prisms," Maryam blurted.

Farah gave her a strange look. "No," she said patiently. "Saif. Have you seen him?"

Maryam crossed her arms and tried desperately not to think closet-y thoughts. Her hand crept to her mouth. "Mmm. Saif. Yes. Saif Rasool."

Farah leaned forward eagerly. "That's his name. He turned the corner just here. Listen, I saw the two of you flirting this morning, so I hope you won't take this the wrong way, but I really need to speak with him."

"Flirting!" Maryam exclaimed, flustered now. "We weren't flirting. I was just asking if he had a plane. Or, you know, a he-licopter I could borrow."

Farah sighed. "You're so weird. If you happen to see him, could you pass along a message?" She glanced significantly at the closet behind Maryam and raised her voice slightly. "Tell him that while I think he's a *really* nice guy, and my parents are, like, *totally* into him, I'm sort of dating the gym teacher at my school. So it would be SUPER AWESOME," Farah said, prac-tically yelling, "if he could just act like a jerk or whatever during the wedding? So I'll have an easier time convincing my parents we aren't meant to be?"

Maryam bit back her smile. "Sure," she said. "If I happen to bump into him, I'll pass along the message."

Farah squeezed Maryam's hand. "Thanks. Bummer about the wedding. Maybe something good will come out of all this. *Desi* weddings lead to more weddings, right? It's practically the law." She winked and disappeared around the corner.

Maryam opened the closet door and raised an eyebrow at a sheepish-looking Saif. "I hope you heard all that because it would be really embarrassing for both of us if I had to repeat it. What was the plan here, exactly?"

Saif emerged, blinking in the light of the room. "I thought she was trying to . . . um . . ."

Maryam's eyebrow climbed higher. "Let you down easy? I mean, we all have a fear of rejection, but this might be taking things too far. Have you considered therapy to deal with this phobia?"

Saif flushed, his ears turning a bright pink. "My parents told me Farah was looking forward to meeting at the wedding. She tried to corner me in the airport last night, and then again this morning at *suhoor*. When I spotted her walking down the hall, I might have panicked."

Maryam grinned at him. "Jumping into random closets is definitely the best way to avoid a setup. It beats having an actual conversation."

"You're hilarious." Saif was dressed in a white collared shirt and slim-fit black pants; she decided she liked him better in a hoodie and jeans, when his good looks were more manageable. Right now, it was hard to ignore how devastatingly handsome he was. Her smile faded, thinking about the conversation with her parents this morning. Saif had a girlfriend, and yet he had been flirting with Maryam this morning, according to Farah, and possibly was doing it again right now. And she was letting him.

She held the door open for him to leave, but Saif didn't move.

"Thanks," he said gruffly. "My parents have been trying to force the marriage issue. I prefer to do things on my own, without all that pressure. You know?"

"I think the people you need to have this conversation with are your mom and dad," she said firmly, trying not to let her eyes linger on the way his shirt framed his shoulders. "We don't even know each other. Remember?"

Saif nodded, embarrassment clear on his face. "It's just that . . ." He trailed off, and there was that searching look again, his gaze moving from her eyes to her lips, and for a moment Maryam wondered if Farah had been right. And the follow-up question: Was she flirting back?

"Do you ever wonder if this is all there is?" he said, the words sounding as if they were being pulled out of him.

Maryam looked into his beautiful brown eyes, and then away, nodding slightly.

Saif continued. "Every day I feel like I'm just going through the motions. I did what I was expected to do, and now my reward is, what? To repeat the same day, over and over, for the rest of my life?"

Saif's words reflected her own thoughts so well, Maryam had to catch her breath. Strangely, as she mulled over Saif's confession, she thought about her father.

Ghulam Aziz had moved to the United States from Hyderabad, India, as a twenty-two-year-old graduate student with plans to return home and open a fleet of successful drugstores. Instead, he had fallen in love with Azizah, the American-born daughter of a family friend, and she had agreed to marry him, even though her married name would be Azizah Aziz.

They had settled in the outer suburbs of Denver, where Ghulam had opened one independent pharmacy. When teenage Saima had confided in Maryam about her dream of working with Doctors Without Borders, twenty-one-year-old Maryam had applied to the local pharmacy college, and then loudly declared her enthusiasm for carrying on the family business. She had worked alongside her father ever since her graduation, over five years ago. This was what family did for one another: they sacrificed their sleep, time, and energy to make one another's dreams come true. Except disquieting thoughts had been hard to ignore lately.

Something had happened on the plane. A tiny cloud of unhappiness had been shaken loose, and with it the questions she had buried—*Who am I? Who do I want to be? Am I happy?*—had come roaring to the forefront. Sitting behind her on the plane, Saif had been a captive listener, but maybe he hadn't found her words hilarious, as she had initially assumed. Maybe he had found them relatable.

As if reading her mind, Saif said, "We grew up with the same pressures and expectations. I don't regret becoming a lawyer, but sometimes I wonder if there's anything . . . more."

She used to walk around with a notebook, when she was younger. A cheap spiral-bound thing, somewhere to jot down her scraps of story ideas, character sketches, even the funny conversations she heard on her way to school. When she had shared some of her half-finished stories with Saima, her sister had told her they were really good, that she should polish them up, try to get them published. Maryam never had. Because she had been too afraid, and then too busy with school, and then distracted by other things. It had been easier to think about a charming smile and an easy compliment rather than running after a hazy dream she had no idea how to pursue. Later, when her life had taken an unexpected turn, she had been too broken to return to writing.

Except now, a tiny, uncertain flame of . . . *want* had been lit, and after only a few hours, it was proving difficult to ignore.

But she would. She didn't have time for this—not for charming men who lied, not for failed dreams that fizzled. She didn't have *time*. Saima's wedding festivities—*desi* weddings were multiday affairs—were supposed to start tomorrow. Her family was counting on her. She wasn't some tragic heroine from one of Dadu's Bollywood weepies, pressured and cajoled into a life she never wanted. Her choices had been her own—both the good and the bad—and she owned them. Maybe this was what happiness looked like for her: a small life with a few lost dreams. That wasn't so bad, really.

Maryam straightened and held the door open wide, her dismissal unmistakable this time. "Don't make me lie for you again," she said to Saif, her voice cold and resolute.

After a final searching glance, he left.

SEVEN

Anna

December 21

Voices outside her door woke Anna at—she checked the clock radio beside the bed—10:27 a.m. The two-hour time difference between Denver and Ottawa had caused her to sleep late. She lay still, blinking up at the stained ceiling as her eyes adjusted and she remembered everything that had happened the day before. The perilous plane ride, the arrival in Snow Falls, the festive sports bar. The mysterious Josh Tannenbaum, the way he had carried her in his arms through the snow . . .

But *Nick*, she reminded herself. He was probably worried sick about her. At the moment, he would be attending a brunch at an exclusive Forest Hill restaurant without her, one of the many events that had been rigorously planned. Then there was her boss, Janey, who was doubtless livid at this point. Anna reached her hand across the end table, searching for the room phone to check if the lines were back up—but when she lifted the receiver, it was only dead air. Still no service.

Anna stood and walked barefoot across the cold, weirdly damp carpet until she reached the window. She yanked on the heavy curtains—which also had a slightly moist feel that made her shiver—and opened them to reveal a world so filled with snow, at first she didn't realize the hulking lumps scattered in rows were cars in the inn's small parking lot. There was condensation on the inside of the glass, dripping down the wall, too—which would explain the clammy feeling everywhere. *Snow falls in*, she thought, and grimaced. If the amount of snow out there was any indication, it didn't look like she would be getting out of this town anytime soon, either. She couldn't even determine which part of the winter wonderland outside was the road that led to the airport.

She dressed quickly. In the bathroom, she splashed cool water on her face and sighed at her rumpled clothes. The cocktail dress, tights, and blazer had seemed a practical enough choice—but that was before she had ended up stranded with no luggage. She was going to have to remedy her no-proper-clothes, bare-minimum-of-toiletries situation—and she was especially going to have to remedy the fact that her phone was dead, she had no charger, and she had important calls to make and an entire life to deal with. She checked her watch. *No time like the present*, she decided. The Forest Hill brunch would be ending soon, and Nick and his family would be heading off to a tony Christmas market to do a little last-minute shopping. She needed to figure out a way to get to Toronto as soon as possible.

Downstairs, the reception area was quiet, the front desk empty. Anna leaned over the counter and picked up the phone—but the receiver was silent, just as the one in her room had been. She turned away and headed into the large lounge area of the vast lobby, where she plunked down on the ottoman closest to the crackling fireplace. From her bag, she retrieved the granola bar Kath had given her the night before and nibbled on it as she stared into the flames, trying to figure out a plan.

"I'd be looking quite sad, too, if *that* was all I was getting for breakfast."

"Mr. Dadu!"

"Good morning." The patriarch was sitting to the right of the fire, tending to it with a brass poker. "Just enjoying some peace and quiet." There was a plate beside him with some dates, granola bars, and apple slices.

"Where is everyone?"

"They've gone back to bed after waking at dawn for their *suhoor*," he explained, then leaned in, eyebrows raised. "Earlier, I saw a film crew leaving. Apparently, this town is referred to as Hollywood North *North*—lots of films shot here—very exciting."

"Really?" Anna said with interest. "Do you know the movie they're working on?"

He shook his head. "No, but I could swear I saw the famous director Katrina Wakes in a hat and sunglasses."

"*Wow.*"

Mr. Dadu lifted his plate of food and offered some to her.

"No, no, that's for you," Anna protested.

"But you look hungry," he said.

She looked down at her half-eaten granola bar. This was true.

"Please," he pressed. "They think I'm an invalid about to expire any second—but it's just diabetes. They won't even let me fast and feed me a steady stream of food all day while they abstain." He looked wistful for a moment, then extended the plate to her again. "I miss fasting with everyone else."

"Do you miss not being able to have *water*?"

He laughed. "I miss all of it. Now come, join me. I swear, you aren't depriving me," Mr. Dadu insisted. "I can eat what I want all day."

As they ate, Anna asked him to tell her what it was he missed about fasting. He told her about the sense of closeness when the *ummah*—community—of Muslims fasted at the same time, and also about the different intentions you might set when you're fasting, like generosity or kindness. "I give to charity to make up for not fasting, but it's just not the same," he explained.

"I used to fast once a year, on Yom Kippur with my step-mom." She paused and tried to remember the exact words Beth had shared when she asked a young Anna if she'd like to try fasting with her for the holiday she observed. "Beth described it as . . . a day to be quiet, and search your soul for the things that need forgiving, and the things you want to go forward into the new year doing better at. Like maybe being more honest, or more generous, or more grateful. I remember it was always a cozy, quiet day for us. We both liked to keep busy—but that day, we never did. We just . . . were."

"Sounds like you and your stepmother had some special times together."

"Ex-stepmother," Anna mumbled, staring into the fire.

Then she turned her gaze to Mr. Dadu again. "Lately, all I seem to do is worry. I never let my mind slow down. I remember how everything would come into focus when I fasted with Beth. It seemed I could see exactly who I was. I miss it."

"My Maryam is like that, too, you know. You two have a lot in common."

"We do? It feels like we're complete opposites."

"It takes time to get to know the real Maryam. She's always such a busy bee. Essential. So important to the inner workings of this family—possibly even more important than she realizes. She can be quite sweet and cuddly once you get to know her. But"—he smiled ruefully—"she has a stinger. Always has. Her dadi-ma was like that, too. Positively relentless, that woman, and drove me to distraction sometimes. But oh, how I miss her."

Anna smiled. She imagined Maryam would not like being compared to a bumblebee, even a sweet and cuddly one, but sensed the description was quite accurate.

"Perhaps you should find Maryam and spend some time with her today," Mr. Dadu suggested.

"Maryam clearly has a lot going on. She doesn't need me bothering her."

"Maryam is always so busy with us. What she *needs* is a friend—someone she can really talk to. *About* us. About the way she is always contorting herself into what she thinks everyone else wants her to be."

Anna was surprised by his words. This was almost exactly what Maryam had said to her on the plane. But Maryam had been convinced her family didn't understand her. Her grandfather clearly did, though.

Mr. Dadu put down the poker and dusted off his hands. "I

have a feeling about you two. Unlikely friends—it's a well-known film trope, you see. Speaking of, I plan to watch a stack of Bollywood movies for the rest of the morning. Care to join me and while away the time?" He patted a stack of VHS tapes on a small table beside him and pointed to the television. "I never travel without my own entertainment."

"That sounds like fun," Anna said, "but . . ." She frowned. "I have so much I need to take care of today."

"What could possibly be so urgent in a town like Snow Falls?"

She pointed to her cocktail dress and impractical shoes. "I'm afraid a snowy town like this is going to require more than the clothes I have on. And you're right, nothing in Snow Falls is urgent—it's my life *outside* this town that requires attention." She started to explain more about her to-do list to Mr. Dadu, but he just shook his head.

"None of those are problems you can attend to right now. Have you seen it out there? It's . . . What are they calling it? Snowmageddon. The best thing for you to do is stay here where it's warm and cozy. In fact, Miss Anna, maybe *you* should commit to a fast."

"Oh, wow," Anna said thoughtfully. "I haven't done that since Beth and I used to . . ." She frowned, pushed the memory of fasting for Yom Kippur with her now ex-stepmother away, and waved a wedge of apple at him. "Besides, I'm eating right now!"

"Not from food. I am suggesting you fast from worrying so much. Who knows how long you will be here in Snow Falls, but maybe you can make a deal with yourself that as long as you are here, you try to let things go—save them for later.

Tomorrow. The day after, even. Maybe, if you give your worries a little time, they will start to shrink." He winked at her, then hummed along to the festive song playing in the lobby. "It is a trick I employ all the time."

Anna thought about what he said. Her mind was always pulled in so many directions—except for those moments on the plane yesterday when, instead of agonizing over who she was supposed to be and what she was supposed to do, she had focused on nothing but the deepest truths inside her. Despite her fear, she had felt centered. It had been freeing. And come to think of it, it had felt very similar to the sensation she had experienced every year on Yom Kippur. "I'll try it," she said to Mr. Dadu.

"Good. Now, how about we relax and watch some excellent films?" He clicked the television on—and the screen filled with a snowy scene, and two actors gazing into each other's eyes.

"What luck!" Mr. Dadu exclaimed, delighted. "This is one of my favorites. *One Night at Christmas*—have you seen it?"

"No, I don't think so," Anna said.

"Bollywood can wait—we absolutely must watch this!"

In the film, a couple walked together through the streets of a town at night. "All this looks a little familiar," Anna said. "That town . . ."

"Oh, all the towns in Christmas movies look the same. That's the best part. With this movie, the best is also the acting."

"The acting? But it's a cheesy Heartline Channel holiday movie."

"So you would think—except *One Night at Christmas*

is special. It features one of the most underrated actors in Hollywood—Chase Taylor. The poor man was cast in a terrible movie called *Captain Eagleman*—honestly, someone needs to speak to his agent about that—and it nearly torpedoed his career. But then he and Tenisha Barlowe—that's her—appeared together in *Moonshine*." Mr. Dadu pointed at the screen, to the striking woman who was now looking deeply into Chase Taylor's eyes as the snow fell around them. "She is an absolute gem of an actress. The movie was a little high-minded and artsy for me—no dancing." He winked. "But I saw the appeal. Maryam loved it. And it got a lot of critical acclaim."

"*Right*, I was reading about this on the plane. And the fact that they're apparently a couple is really buzzy, too, right?"

"Exactly. It is so Bollywood, but in real life! They met on the set of a romantic holiday movie and now look at them!" He turned back toward the screen. "Okay, so the story line is that Jane—played by Tenisha—comes back to her hometown after having her heart broken. Tyler—played by Chase—is her high school boyfriend, only he stood her up at prom. He had his reasons, of course. But I will not spoil it for you. All you need to know is that this is one of the most romantic Christmas movies of all time." He rubbed his hands together in delight.

Anna leaned in, watching as Tyler and Jane were interrupted by a horse and carriage running loose through the town just as they were about to kiss. Soon, she was swept up in the story—and she had to admit, both Chase Taylor and Tenisha Barlowe were fine actors, adding a surprising layer of depth to the simple story. She squinted at the screen as the camera zoomed in on Chase. He was handsome and clean-shaven, with warm brown eyes and a nice smile. "He looks so familiar to me—I must have seen him in something else," she remarked at one point.

"I hope for your sake you never had to endure *Captain Eagleman*." Mr. Dadu shuddered and Anna couldn't help but laugh, but then his expression turned serious. "*Moonshine*, though, that one I hope you did see. Mr. Taylor penned the script for the film and then asked his 'friend'"—at this, he waggled his eyebrows—"Miss Barlowe to play the lead role. It won the People's Choice Award at TIFF! And Toronto is where Mr. Taylor is from—what a feather in his cap!"

"Oh, right, I think my office friends were talking about that one, but Nick, my boyfriend, wasn't interested, so we didn't see it. About a struggling artist living in LA . . . ?"

"Yes! But the Oscar buzz fizzled. It did not gain nominations for best picture or screenplay. Mr. Taylor didn't write another film, but returned his focus to acting. Now that *Two Nights at Christmas* is being made, Barlowe and Taylor are going to be reunited on-screen—and possibly in real life, too!" He gestured at the movie currently playing on the screen. "But you cannot possibly enjoy the sequel until you see this one!"

"Wow, you sure do know a lot about the film world."

"Other than my dear, departed wife, the cinema is my greatest love," Mr. Dadu said with a happy sigh.

Later, as the credits rolled, Anna found she felt deeply relaxed—and very satisfied.

"Nothing like a happy ending, right?" Mr. Dadu said, brushing away a small tear of joy. Heartline was running a Christmas movie marathon, and another movie started right away. But

Anna had seen Kath heading back to her post at the front desk. "I know I said I wasn't going to worry," Anna said to Mr. Dadu. "But I *do* still need to find a toothbrush and see about the phones. I'll be right back."

Anna rushed to the front of the lobby, hoping for good news.

"My dear, it looks like you're here another day at least," Kath said. "The airport is still completely shut down."

Anna glanced at her watch and felt a flutter of dismay.

"How about the phones?"

"Sorry, love. Not yet. There's a pay phone in town that always seems to work when heavy snow knocks the rest out, though." She reached under the counter and gave Anna a handful of change in Canadian coins. "That should do for long distance. And you'll find a toothbrush and some other necessities at the pharmacy—sorry we're out, but we didn't expect such a crowd. Everything's pretty close at hand around here, though. You'll find it all, even in the snow."

Anna kicked out one of her impractical, now snow-ruined high heels. "I can't walk in several feet of snow wearing these . . ."

"No worries, love! We've got tons of extra winter gear—guests are always leaving things behind. Just out by the door. There are parkas on hooks and boots on the shoe rack."

Anna said goodbye to Mr. Dadu, who was now happily watching a Bollywood movie that seemed to revolve around a dorky male lead falling for a beautiful woman wearing a spectacular sari. "Spoiler alert, she turns out to be just as dorky as he is," Mr. Dadu said in a stage whisper, pointing at the screen. Then he waved at her. "Good luck today!"

At the front door, Anna found a roomy, warm parka—and

blushed lightly, remembering how cozy Mysterious Josh's parka had been, how nice it had smelled. This one didn't smell quite as nice, but it was thick and warm. She also found a pair of boots that were a size too big but better than her high heels. *There.* Two problems solved with hardly any worrying.

Soon, she reached the town proper. Shop owners were out shoveling and greeting one another. All of them smiled and waved at Anna and declared "Happy Holidays!" as she passed.

Red brick buildings decorated with lights and garlands were lined up like well-dressed Christmas elves along the snowy street. From where she was standing, she could see a sweet little holiday ornament store called Jingle Bells & Co., a curios shop called Yule Love It, a lingerie shop called Naughty or Nice, Northern Lighting, the Christmas Carol Playhouse, and an entire store dedicated to festive garden gnomes. There was a skating rink with a gazebo in its center, strung with tasteful holiday globe-lanterns twinkling in the understated light of the snowy day. Anna couldn't help but sigh happily. Someone around here had very good taste.

Across the street, Anna spotted the phone booth. She dug in her purse for the change Kath had given her, went inside, closed the door against the swirling snow, took a deep breath, and picked up the receiver. Through some miracle there was a dial tone. She dialed, then put in the requested long-distance amount and waited. *Ring. Ring. Ring.* Nick picked up on the fourth ring, sounding like he had been sleeping.

"Nick! It's me! I'm okay!"

"Well, *I'm* not!" The storminess of his tone surprised Anna.

She had assumed he'd be worried—but instead, he sounded angry with her. "You missed the champagne cocktail gala. You missed dinner. The symphony. Brunch. Now the Christmas market. You didn't even bother to call."

"I did call! We talked yesterday."

"Our call was rushed, and you practically hung up on me!"

"My phone died."

"Where in the world are you?"

"Snow Falls, just east of Ottawa, where my plane diverted. The storm has knocked out phone service—"

"Sounds like there's phone service to me!"

"I'm at a pay phone and—"

"If you're on a pay phone, how is there no service in the rest of the town? And what about your cell?"

"The battery died, and my charger is in my lost luggage. I just thought you might want to know that I'm okay, and—"

"You embarrassed me in front of everyone, Anna. I told them I was bringing someone to every single one of these events!"

Anna could see why Nick was shaken up, of course. They had been planning their first Christmas together for months, practically since they started dating. She was missing so much. Like the festive cocktail party this evening, where she was supposed to get to try a famous Vandergrey martini for the first time. Apparently, the secret ingredient was Goldschläger, not Anna's favorite because she wasn't convinced consuming tiny flecks of gold was actually good for you, but she had been determined to be a good sport. Then there was the trip downtown to watch a candlelit performance of Handel's

Messiah at a well-known church, followed by dinner at a restaurant called Canoe, at the top of one of Toronto's tallest buildings, where his parents, Nick had explained, practically owned a table. Then, for Christmas Eve, the entire family would spend the day volunteering at a soup kitchen—before spending what was likely the soup kitchen's yearly food budget on what Nick had told Anna would be the most special Christmas Eve dinner party of her life, held at the family home in Forest Hill.

And among all these activities, Anna now knew, Nick had something else planned. The proposal. She swallowed hard. "Christmas Eve is in three days. I still have time. I'll get there."

"You really don't sound all that concerned," Nick said.

"I'm trying not to worry, okay? But it's hard. I'm stuck here. If I get all upset about it, that will just make things worse," Anna protested.

"Do you know how stressful this is for me? I need you here, Anna. You *said* you'd be here. I hardly know what to say to you!"

Anna bit her lip—and found she didn't know what to say, either.

Except that all at once, words were in her head, loud and insistent ones, almost shouting to be heard: *I don't want this. This is not me. I need some space.* All those emotions that had been rattled out of her by the turbulence were flying around inside her brain now, like her mind was a snow globe someone had picked up and shaken. Suddenly, Anna found she couldn't help but ask herself: Did Nick Vandergrey know the real Anna Gibson—or did he just see the woman he wanted her to be?

"Anna? Are you still there?"

"I am," she said. "I'm here. In an unfamiliar town during a huge blizzard, with no luggage and no idea how I'm going to get a flight out—"

"What do you mean, without your luggage?"

"My luggage got lost! You'd know that if you had actually listened to me, asked me how I am, rather than just worrying about you and your plans."

"*Our* plans! I just can't believe there isn't something you can do to fix this," he said, sounding petulant. The flare of anger that had risen up inside Anna grew more fierce.

"I'm not in charge of the weather," she retorted.

"No one said you were!" he shot back.

"I need a break," she found herself saying, surprised by the words that came out of her mouth.

"Anna!" Nick sounded shocked, but recovered his composure quickly. "Fine," he said, his tone now cold. "If you're not sure about us at this point, maybe you'll never be."

"That's not what I meant . . ." In her mind's eye, Anna could see the glittering diamond ring. Marriage was a huge decision—and just the day before, she had been convincing herself that saying yes to a proposal was the right thing to do. Because she had grown used to going along with the things Nick wanted. But if they couldn't get through a snag in their holiday plans, should they really be considering spending the rest of their lives together?

But before she could say anything more, Nick blustered out an angry-sounding "Fine! If you need a break, let's take one. Goodbye, Anna." The line went silent.

Anna stared down at the receiver. In the now quiet phone

booth, arguing with Nick suddenly seemed like a huge, terrifying mistake.

It wasn't too late to rectify it, though. Her finger hovered over the buttons that would call him back. She could tell him she was sorry, that she didn't mean any of the things she had just said to him, that she certainly didn't want a break from their relationship.

Or . . . she could let it be. She could take Mr. Dadu's sage advice and *not worry about it right now*. She could decide not to call Janey, either—given that being snowbound in the middle of nowhere was a very good excuse not to check in to work. Anna blew out a sigh so forceful the glass of the phone booth fogged up completely. But her mind felt clearer than ever, decluttered from the debris of her many concerns, like a freshly cleaned and painted room.

She was startled by a tapping on the glass.

"Everything okay in there?"

It was a familiar voice. She opened the door.

"Josh!"

"Sorry, hope I'm not being nosy—but you sounded upset. I wanted to make sure everything was okay . . . ?"

She stepped out of the phone booth and stood in front of him in the falling snow. He wasn't wearing his glasses today, and she found herself suddenly lost in his deeply concerned, warm brown eyes. She also felt that sense of déjà vu she seemed to experience when he was around. "Coming to my rescue, yet again?" she managed to say.

"I'm happy to see that at least today, you've got a coat and boots on," he replied. "But seriously, Anna, are you okay?"

"I am," Anna said, and meant it. "That was just . . . work stuff," she lied. "My boss isn't thrilled that I'm still stuck here."

"I guess all the planes are still grounded," Josh said. "It's snowing again, and it's starting to look like yesterday was just a dress rehearsal for the real storm."

Anna nodded. "I came into town to try to find a few necessities, but to be honest, I have no idea where to find anything."

Josh checked his watch. "I have about half an hour before I have to be back at my . . . work thing. I can help," he said. "Come with me."

Soon, they were passing by a strip of stores and establishments that were nothing like the ones on Main Street. Those had red brick and gingerbread-icing-like trim, all with the same colored lights and decorations. But this area of town was a hodgepodge. There were four old town houses in a row, mini versions of a Brooklyn brownstone, each containing a different kind of shop: Funkytown Cheese, Randy's Rare Manuscripts, Jatinder's Fabrics, and Sanko Japanese Goods. There was also a Turkish coffee shop called Topkapi Café, a Chinese restaurant called Heavenly Hakka, a Jewish deli called Lala Lavine's ("The best smoked-meat sandwiches this side of the forty-ninth parallel!" Josh told her), two *other* Hakka Chinese restaurants called Hav-a-Hakka and Hakka Empire, and a Tandoori House.

"Wow," Anna said as they walked. "This town isn't exactly what I expected."

"Snow Falls contains multitudes," Josh agreed. "That's why I like it here so much. And here we are."

They were standing in front of a pharmacy. Anna found

herself laughing as she read the sign. "Of course it's called Chemis-Tree," she said.

"Naturally. I'll wait out here?"

Anna headed inside and soon emerged with a bag full of toiletries.

"There," Josh said. "That's one problem solved. Now, what's next on your to-do list?"

"I could use some more practical clothes . . ."

"This town isn't exactly the place for buying practical clothing, but I do know a place where you can get a warm sweater. It's just down this way."

He led her to a shop called Don't Sweater It. She pushed open the door and tinkling bells rang out. Inside, the shop looked like the place where the idea for every ugly-Christmas-sweater party in the world had originated. At the front, an older couple wearing matching red, green, and white sweaters that said "Merry Christmas!" in giant block knit lettering were working in tandem on another garish holiday sweater, their knitting needles clicking and clacking as they worked away. "Last Christmas" by Wham! played on the stereo.

"This may not be the high fashion you're used to, Anna," Josh said with a wink. "But you'll definitely find a cozy sweater here."

Side by side, they browsed through the racks. Josh pulled out a royal blue cable knit with the words "I Love You a Latke" in bright yellow. "I think I have to buy this for my mom," he said, folding it over his arm.

It was something Beth would have bought for her dad, and Anna felt a pang of sadness. She distracted herself by pulling out a mint green sweater with a cute little elf on the front. It was tacky, yes, but the wool was soft and the color appealing.

"You don't have anything . . . not holiday-themed?" she asked the knitting couple as she laid her chosen sweater down beside the cash register.

"We don't keep old stock," the woman answered with a smile, never pausing in her knitting. "Everything we knit and don't sell goes to homeless shelters in Ottawa. What you see here is everything we have now." She clacked her knitting needles together for emphasis. "But honey, it's the holidays! December is for . . ." She held up the sweater she was knitting with her partner. "Red, green, gold, silver! It's for . . ." She put down her knitting needles and picked up a bedazzling tool on the counter beside her. As she pointed it at Anna and Josh, they both couldn't help but duck. "Bedazzling! Those sweaters are just what you two need. Sweet of you to buy the 'Love You a Latke' sweater for your man, by the way. *Quite* the catch, that one."

"Oh, he's not my man." Anna found herself suddenly blushing furiously. "We just met."

"Just met?" The woman tilted her head, as if confused. "I could have sworn you two had known each other forever."

"The sweater's for my mom," Josh said—and Anna was almost certain that underneath his close-cropped beard, he was blushing, too.

The man behind the cash register was now looking at Anna closely. He put down his knitting, then reached under the counter. "It's the season of giving," he said. "And I've been searching for the perfect person to gift this to." He was holding a knit toque with not one but *two* pom-poms: one red, one green. Before Anna could protest, the woman had laughed with delight, grabbed the toque, popped out from behind the counter, and placed the hat on Anna's head.

"My hubby is right, it's perfect for you. Now, *that* is festive, isn't it, honey? Try the sweater on, too. You can wear it out of the store."

"You really do look . . . festive," Josh said, gazing at her sidelong as they left.

"Let's be honest, I look like Christmas threw up all over me."

He turned and tweaked one of her poms while gazing into her eyes. "It's cute," Josh said. They were now standing still, facing each other as soft snowflakes fell between them. Anna felt a fluttering in her chest, but it was quickly tamped down by guilt and worry. She and Nick had just had an awful fight and declared themselves to be on a break. Was it okay to be flirting with a stranger in the gently falling snow as if she didn't have a care in the world?

Then Anna thought of Mr. Dadu's advice about abstaining from worry. There was something about Snow Falls—and Josh's fun, easy manner—that made pushing her worries to the side surprisingly simple.

"Okay, we have one more stop to make before I head back to work," Josh said. "I need to show you what the true necessities in Snow Falls are."

They walked along in companionable silence until he said, "Feeling better now? You seemed so upset in the phone booth, I was worried."

As Anna thought about his question, she stopped walking, took a deep breath, and looked around her at the little snowy town she had landed in unexpectedly, then into the inviting brown eyes of Josh Tannenbaum. "I'm not sure," she said truthfully, thinking of the upsetting conversation with Nick. "I have some life stuff I need to deal with, but I think I can handle it."

"If you need anything, just let me know, okay?"

She couldn't help but bask in his genuine concern. "Thanks, Josh," she said. The truth was, she felt very close to *happy*. Almost . . . free. Just as she had the thought, she smelled something absolutely tantalizing. "Oh, my goodness, what *is* that . . . ?"

The corners of Josh's eyes crinkled as he smiled. "Our final stop of the Snow Falls tour. Come on," he said as he led her into a bakeshop called Gingersnaps.

Inside, "O Tannenbaum," one of Anna's all-time favorite Christmas songs, was playing. You couldn't listen to this carol and not have your heart warm several degrees. Nat King Cole's voice was like butter melting luxuriously on a fresh-baked muffin. But, Anna noticed with surprise, this bakery had a lot more to offer than just standard bakeshop favorites like muffins and cookies. "Rugelach!" she exclaimed. There were more flavors than she had ever seen. "And babka!"

"Yes, and check this out! Artisanal dark chocolate gelt." He ducked his head and spoke softly in her ear over the din of happy customers. "On the surface, this looks like a Christmas town through and through—but Hanukkah is well represented here, too."

"I love this place!" A few patrons stood along a live-edge wood bar counter drinking espressos and chatting. All the baked goods were gorgeously displayed in a sparkling-clean glass case. "There are too many choices," Anna groaned. "I have no idea what to try. Christmas cookies? An olive oil donut? Mini Yule logs?"

"Do you trust me?" Josh said, and Anna felt that unexpected flutter yet again. This time she didn't chase it away.

"Yes."

"Then you have to order the upside-down pineapple cake rugelach. It's the best thing you will ever taste, I promise."

"Done. And a cappuccino," Anna added.

"*And* a square of Grandma Jean's prizewinning fudge," Josh added, glancing at her sidelong. "As long as you really do trust me."

"Chocolate fudge is serious business, but I'll try it if you say so."

The countertop was thick as cupcake icing and shiny as cake glaze. She and Josh leaned against it and ate their treats, washing it all down with good coffee. "You were right," she said, her mouth filled with the delicious pastry studded with maraschino cherries and caramelized pineapple. "This is *incredible*." Then she tried the fudge and nearly swooned. "I think I'm in heaven!"

Anna felt she could stand there all day, enjoying the food and the atmosphere—but Josh was looking regretfully at the door. "I'm sorry," he said. "I'm late for work. But you stay here, finish my rugelach, too? And . . ." She couldn't shake the sensation that Josh suddenly looked sad. ". . . I hope I see you later," was all he said. Before she could thank him, he had disappeared into the small crowd in the bakery, and then out the door and into the snowy day.

Anna forced herself not to analyze how bereft his sudden absence made her feel—or to wonder why a lot of the bakery customers seemed to be staring first at Josh as he exited, and then at her, with inexplicable interest. As she finished her coffee and treats, she thought about Maryam instead, and what Mr. Dadu had suggested about a potential friendship between the two young women. Maryam seemed like a tough nut to crack—but wouldn't anyone be softened by trying the delectable baked goods at Gingersnaps, especially after a day of fasting? So, Anna ordered a boxful to bring back to the inn and share, and left the bakery laden with bags from her successful morning of necessity-hunting.

"Now, was that a right and a left and a left, or a left and a right and a right to get back to the inn?" Anna muttered to herself as she walked along. There were worse places to be lost, she decided, slowing her pace and peering through the window of a pet supply store displaying a collection of cute, festive costumes for cats and dogs. Next was an adorable little Italian restaurant, not open yet, the empty tables cloaked in red-and-white-checkered tablecloths and topped with red and green taper candles in empty wine bottles. As Anna peered through the window, she felt a shiver of recognition. Had she been here before? No, impossible. But she could swear she had seen this exact restaurant before, right down to the Botticelli angel prints hung on the exposed-brick walls.

She gasped in delight as she realized what she was seeing: this was Buon Natalie's, the Italian restaurant from *One Night at Christmas*! This was an exact double of the Italian restaurant where Tyler had proposed to Jane!

Anna took a step back from the window—and noticed there now seemed to be a small crowd of people heading toward her. When she spotted a camera and a boom mic, she realized what she was seeing was a film crew. She couldn't be imagining this—it *had* to be true. Snow Falls was the secret location of the much-anticipated film shoot of *Two Nights at Christmas*—and her new friend Mr. Dadu was going to be thrilled. Anna turned on her heel and headed in what she was suddenly certain was the direction of Snow Falls Inn, excited to get back and tell him all about it.

EIGHT

Maryam

December 21

Maryam hadn't been able to do anything to help her sister with the wedding, so she ordered her favorite dinner instead. To her surprise, there was a halal Hakka Chinese restaurant in Snow Falls, and even better, they promised to deliver despite the snow.

When she requested that the food arrive just before sunset, the young woman at the other end of the line paused. "Muslim?" she asked, and Maryam responded in the affirmative. "Ramadan Kareem," the woman said before disconnecting.

Maryam looked at the phone, puzzled by the greeting. As far as she could tell, Snow Falls was a tiny town obsessed with Christmas. The lobby of Snow Falls Inn was smothered with Christmas decorations, including a large tree practically bent double under the weight of ornaments—shining balls and baubles in red, green, silver, and gold; enamel figurines of laughing elves, sleds, reindeer, and Father Christmas; plus strings of popcorn and cranberry, tinsel, and fairy lights in a

cacophonous clashing display, clearly a result of Kath's enthusiastic efforts. Wreaths adorned every door. And yet their
Tasmanian hosts had known it was Ramadan, and what that
entailed.

In her (admittedly limited) experience, small towns weren't
especially known for their diversity. Yet this was the second
time that Ramadan had been acknowledged by the townspeople.
A small part of her was starting to wonder about Snow Falls.

The wedding party spent the day sleeping, watching television in their rooms, and chatting in the front foyer, which
they had started to use as a sort of gathering place. Her parents
and Dadu had grown up in India, spending the majority of
their waking time in communal spaces, and the foyer, with its
central location, comfortable seating, and warm fireplace, served
that purpose well. Plus, Deb and Kath seemed pleased to see
their foyer used and enjoyed by their guests. Dadu had found a
Christmas movie marathon running on the Heartline Channel,
and by the time Maryam joined him, he had already watched
One Night at Christmas while the rest of the wedding party had
caught up on sleep. She was sorry to have missed her favorite
holiday movie, but she was sure it would play again during the
marathon at some point. Dadu was taking a break to pray *zuhr*,
the afternoon prayer, when Farah sidled up to Maryam as she
set up the next movie. Dadu had packed a collection of VHS
tapes and was keen to watch *Kuch Kuch Hota Hai*. The movie
had come out only two years ago, but was already a classic.

"Did you pass along my message to Saif?" Farah asked.

Maryam nodded, trying to keep her story straight. Dadu
was praying nearby, and if it got back to her parents that Saif

had barged into her hotel room, no matter the reason, they would not be impressed, especially given their earlier warning. "Yes . . . I bumped into him. At the . . . ice machine . . . because I needed ice after I . . . bumped into him," she said, improvising. Farah watched her carefully, and actually laughed when Maryam stumbled to the end of her explanation.

"Still a terrible liar," she observed. "Saima and I used to try to get you to lie, just to watch you turn red. It was hilarious."

Maryam swatted playfully at Farah. "If you didn't come to the wedding to be set up with Saif, why are you here?" she asked, genuinely curious.

Farah sighed. "I didn't have anywhere to go for winter break. Adam is celebrating Christmas with his mom and stepfather in Denver, and things are . . . complicated for us right now. I guess I was in the mood for an old-fashioned *desi* wedding. Remember how many of these we went to when we were younger?"

It was true—their childhood had been filled with weddings, ladies-only *mehndi* dance parties, and family dinner parties. South Asian culture was all about family, and weddings were always large-scale affairs. Most people brought their entire families to weddings, which were often held in community centers, mosques, or banquet halls.

Maryam nodded. "Christmas was basically the unofficial start of *desi* wedding season," she joked, and Farah smiled in agreement.

"Are your parents unhappy about Adam?" she asked, after inserting the VHS cassette and making sure the subtitles worked, in case any non-Hindi-speakers wanted to join them.

She thought about Anna, and wondered what her new acquaintance was doing right now. *Not my problem*, she reminded herself.

Farah shrugged. "They want me to marry a *desi* Muslim guy. They think Saima hit the jackpot. A brown doctor from a rich family? Come on."

"The holy grail," Maryam agreed, and the women laughed.

"They think I'm a disappointment. I'm dating a non-Muslim, I teach art to grade school kids—"

"Mom told me you teach physics to middle school geniuses at a charter school!" Maryam interrupted.

Farah rolled her eyes. "I didn't study physics beyond grade nine. I teach eight-year-old kids how to draw lines and sculpt clay. Plus, I have a craft stall at the local flea market. It's called Farah-licious. I mostly draw portraits of my cat."

Maryam laughed. "I'm glad you came to the wedding," she said sincerely. "I hope you find what you're looking for."

Farah looked sly. "You, too. I think Saif is finally opening his eyes."

"What do you mean?" Maryam asked, even as a blush crawled up her neck. Farah was right—her emotions showed too plainly on her face.

"Everyone knows you've had a thing for Saif since we were kids. I'm glad he's finally starting to clue in." Farah hesitated, as if debating whether to continue. "I get that you might be feeling a bit . . . unsure of yourself," she said carefully. "It's normal, after everything you've been through. And if I know your parents, they're cautioning you to stay away from Saif." She went on only after Maryam gave a small, embarrassed nod. "If you'll let an old friend give you some unsolicited advice?

Saif is a good guy. Don't make assumptions, and seize happiness when it's being offered."

Maryam blinked at Farah, who was three years younger than she was and yet seemed, in this moment, as wise as Dadu. "Where is all this coming from?"

The look Farah threw her was sympathetic, and made Maryam feel seen in a way she hadn't in a long time. "You're not the only brown girl who carries her family's hopes and burdens, Maryam. It took me a long time to accept that we deserve our happy endings, too, even if they look a little different from what our family imagined for us."

Before Maryam could respond, Farah squeezed her arm and left, just as Kath, dressed today in sleek gray wool slacks and a black cashmere sweater decorated with embroidered red bells along the collar, walked past, her arms full of clean bedding.

"How're my favorite Muslims?" she asked. Maryam noticed that Kath pronounced it correctly—*Muss-lim*, not *Muzz-lim*—the latter pronunciation that felt like nails on a chalkboard to Maryam.

"We're great. We used the tablecloths for prayer sheets after we ate our morning meal, hope you don't mind."

Kath had been about to bustle off, but she stopped, a look of dismay crossing her face. "We wanted to prepare a special meal for your early-morning breakfast, but we clean forgot! The fasting day ends at sunset, right? Let me ask Deb to rustle up some nibbles and—"

"It's fine," Maryam hastened to assure their host. "I ordered from the Hakka restaurant in town."

"Hav-a-Hakka?" Kath asked.

"No-o," Maryam said.

"Heavenly Hakka? That one's a coffee café, too."

"Hakka Empire, I think."

"Muriel runs that with her daughter. Good choice. Right, then, for tomorrow's breakfast, we'll fix you something."

"Actually, Miss Kath, with your permission?" Dadu had rejoined the women and now interrupted smoothly. "We would be happy to rustle up our own nibbles," he said, repeating Kath's lingo.

"He means, can we use your kitchen?" Maryam said, smiling. The wedding party had already discussed this, in consideration of how busy the innkeepers were. The look of relief on Kath's face confirmed her suspicions.

"Of course, love, we'll set you right up. Can't have my Muslims starve during Ramadan." She paused. "I mean, starve *outside* of daylight hours." Laughing at her joke, she hurried on her errand.

"Dadu," Maryam said, thoughtfully, "have you noticed something strange about Snow Falls?"

"The people are exceptionally kind and also attractive?" Dadu asked. "It must be the good Canadian water."

Maryam shook her head. "I actually meant . . . well, the town is surprising, that's all. Not at all what I expected. I'm going to check on our food delivery—they should be here any minute."

Outside, Maryam walked around to the side street by the inn's parking lot—and immediately ran into Anna.

"Anna! I tried looking for you at the airport, but couldn't find you anywhere!" Maryam said. The smile that sprang to her face, accompanied by the spark of joy at seeing the other woman again, were entirely unexpected.

She took a closer look at Anna's outfit: a wool hat with not one but two pom-poms, plus a bright green knitted wool sweater featuring a jaunty little elf, worn over her blue cocktail dress. She carried a parka over her arm.

Anna shrugged helplessly. "Lost luggage. Remember?"

Maryam did remember, and shivered in sympathy. It was still snowing, and quite chilly outside. "Your sweater is really nice," she said, feeling a twinge over Anna's lack of clothing.

"I think the word you're looking for is 'tacky.' But I found it in town, which has so many cute stores and restaurants. I spent hours exploring, and there are so many shops, not just ones that sell Christmas things—Snow Falls has everything. Plus, the most wonderful bakery." She held up a large box, from which the most delicious, sugary aroma was emanating.

"That smells amazing. How did you know where to go?"

"A new friend showed me around," Anna said, and got a strange look on her face as if there was something she wanted to tell Maryam. "You can have them after you break your fast—and I'll consider them a treat for the form of fasting I did today, at your grandfather's suggestion."

Maryam wasn't sure what Anna meant, but was happy to hear Dadu had had a chance to do his favorite thing: give advice to the younger generation. "That was really nice of you," she said. It was, actually. "Did you say you were fasting today?"

Anna shook her head, looking abashed. "Not fasting, exactly. Mr. Dadu told me that since he is diabetic, he doesn't fast the same way, but makes sure to try to get something out of this special month. I've been dealing with a few things in my life, and he suggested I try to spend the day sort of fasting from worry? I have this idea that fasting is like an act of radical compassion, and I guess I was trying to apply some of that compassion to myself." She seemed flustered at this admission, and Maryam tamped down her initial reaction, which was to tease Anna for her earnestness.

"I've never heard it described that way," Maryam said instead. Then, more gently, "I think it's great that you took Dadu's advice and decided to be kinder to yourself today. I need to practice some of that radical compassion on myself, too."

"I thought you would think it was a dumb idea," Anna admitted, and Maryam felt another twinge. She had made Anna feel small, had made judgments about the woman, when Anna had been nothing but sweet—and, okay, also a bit annoying, but mostly sweet.

"I don't think it's dumb," Maryam said. "Thanks for chatting with my grandfather. That's what 'Dadu' means, by the way. His name is actually Mohamed Ali Mumtaz Aziz, but we call him Dadu."

"Oh," Anna said, looking embarrassed once more. "He never corrected me when I called him Mr. Dadu."

"That's because he wants to be everyone's granddad," Maryam said. They smiled at each other. Which was when two delivery cars pulled up to the curb, and Saif came running out of the front door of the inn, making the women jump.

"Surprise! I ordered Hakka for *iftar!*" he announced.

Maryam looked from the delivery vehicles back to Saif. "*I ordered Hakka for iftar.*"

Anna held up the box of pastries again. "And I have dessert."

Maryam started laughing and gestured for the delivery people to follow her inside.

*I*n the end, there was so much food they ended up sampling only some of it, leaving the rest to share with any hungry guests. With any luck, they would be on their way to Toronto tomorrow—the earlier, the better. Saima had calculated that if by some miracle they made it to Toronto the next day, the wedding could still proceed, though the *mehndi* would have to be canceled. Considering it was still snowing outside, Maryam didn't like their odds, but she was loath to dash her sister's hopes. At least not until they had finished eating, and she had an extra large cup of *chai* in her hands. Somehow, the idea that they would be stuck in Snow Falls for another day wasn't horrifying to Maryam.

While the fire in the massive fireplace popped and crackled, the wedding party, plus Anna, shared dishes of spicy chili beef, black pepper shrimp, chicken Hakka noodles, fried rice, sweet-and-sour momos, and tofu in black bean sauce laid out on the large table in the foyer, plus the treats from the bakery Anna contributed. A contented air settled over the impromptu dinner party, and even Saima seemed more at ease.

Anna took a seat beside the sisters on the couch, and Saima studied Anna's bright Christmas sweater. "Let me guess. Lost luggage?"

Anna nodded.

"Listen, we always overpack," Maryam said. "I think it's a genetic condition. We might all be around the same size, so if you don't mind jeans and sweaters . . ." She trailed off as Saima jumped to her feet, suddenly energized.

"I'll pick out a few outfits for you, Anna. Maryam, you don't mind if I go through your stuff, right?" She moved for the stairs without waiting for an answer, but Maryam was so relieved to see her sister distracted, she didn't object. She would figure out how to get her clothes back from Anna later.

"I really appreciate this," Anna said to Maryam.

"It's fine. This has all been . . . a lot."

"At least you have your family with you. You're so lucky, you know? To have a big family. And a sister . . ." Anna looked wistfully in the direction Saima had rushed off in and sighed. "I've always wanted a sister. Or a sibling at all. And a big family, like yours. It just seems so—"

"Trust me, it is not as fun as it looks from the outside," Maryam said.

At her side, Anna stiffened. "I just meant it must be nice to have people around you for the big things. When things go terribly wrong and you're stuck in a strange town without anyone. Anyways, I should probably"—Anna made to pick up a few stray plates on a table—"get these to the kitchen."

"You're right, I have a wonderful family and I love them very much," Maryam said, smiling ruefully. "But they can also be overwhelming. They depend on me to solve all their problems, and blame me when things don't go right. I guess sometimes I wish I didn't have to always be available."

Anna looked wistful, even as she nodded her understanding. "You're a good sister. And daughter. And granddaughter. I imagine sometimes that must feel like a lot to be, all at once. I think you're handling it beautifully, by the way. Saima appreciates you, and Dadu understands you."

Maryam was touched by Anna's words. She was about to respond, and ask what had happened with Nick and her foiled Christmas plans, when Saima returned with a huge armload of clothes.

"Okay, let's get started here." Saima dropped the pile of clothes on the couch and held a blue blouse against Anna. "Nope! Too dowdy!" She tossed it aside while Maryam muttered, "Hey, that's my favorite . . ."

After just a few minutes, Anna had enough clothes in her arms to get her through an entire week in Snow Falls.

"Thank you so much," she said. "I should get upstairs . . ."

"Stay a bit," Saima implored. "We're going to watch some Bollywood movies. You haven't lived until you've watched Shah Rukh Khan's smolder."

Anna laughed. "I really can't," she said reluctantly. "I don't want to impose, and you've all been so kind already."

She still thinks I don't want her here, Maryam thought. Then: *Do I want her here?* She thought about what Dadu always said: *Reach your hand to others; you never know when you will need the same kindness extended to you.*

"We would love it if you joined us," Maryam said. "It's a holy month—in fact, today is the twenty-seventh night, which is very special—but it's also a month for reconnecting with family and making new friends."

"Okay," Anna said, settling back down on the couch. "So, speaking of movies, when your dadu comes down from his room, I can't wait to tell him this: I think there might be a movie being filmed in Snow Falls—and it's the sequel to *One Night at Christmas*. Mr. Dadu said you liked that one?"

The sisters looked at each other in shock. Saima put a hand to her heart. "No way! Chase Taylor is my celebrity crush," she said. "I've watched that movie ten times, and Maryam watched *Moonshine* twenty times!"

"Not that many," Maryam muttered.

"You referred to Chase as 'Mr. Maryam Aziz' for about a month last year," Saima said, and this time Maryam blushed. "You kept going on about being unable to resist an attractive man who could also write."

From across the room, Saif raised an eyebrow at Maryam, then casually strolled over to join them. "Did I hear you mention celebrity sightings in Snow Falls?" he asked.

"Anna thinks Maryam's future husband, Chase Taylor, is making a movie in town, and we're trying to figure out how to set up the perfect meet-cute," Saima teased. When Saif looked blank, Saima explained. "He starred in a holiday rom-com my family is obsessed with, followed by a stinker of a superhero movie, and then wrote and starred in Maryam's favorite indie movie."

Saif snapped his fingers. "I watched his big flop, *Captain Eagleman*! I actually paid for a movie ticket and walked out halfway through. I think it won the Razzies," he said, referring to the Golden Raspberry Awards, given to the worst movies of the year. "But he showed up for the award ceremony, which was pretty big of him."

Saima was sifting through a pile of magazines beside her, fingers landing on an old *Us Weekly*. "Here it is!" she said, her excitement reaching fever pitch. "I read a few weeks ago that they were filming the sequel to *One Night at Christmas* in some remote Canadian village." She looked up, eyes wide. "They're filming *Two Nights at Christmas* in Snow Falls!" she squealed, and Maryam smiled at her sister's enthusiasm. This was the first time she had seen Saima smile since they landed in the tiny town.

"I walked past the restaurant they used in the film— remember, the cute Italian one? I recognized it after I watched *One Night at Christmas* this morning with your dadu. I bet Josh would think that was hilarious, actually. I should tell him . . ." Anna was blushing, and Maryam wondered at her reaction.

As if reading her mind, Saima perked up. "Oooh, who's Josh?" she asked, picking up on Anna's obvious embarrassment. "Did you meet a cute *boy*, Anna?" she needled, causing the woman in question to squirm in discomfort.

"It's nothing, really, he's just someone I met last night at a sports bar. We're both from Toronto originally, and you know the Maple Leafs are a sore spot for every die-hard Toronto fan. Josh and I were just commiserating, no big deal, really . . ." Anna trailed off. Maryam's sister smiled in delighted amusement.

"And?" Saima encouraged, her instinctive nose for gossip all but twitching.

Anna made a guilty face. "And . . . he might have carried me through the snow because I was wearing those silly heels yesterday, remember?"

The howl of delighted laughter from her sister echoed around them. For someone who didn't flinch at treating severely wounded patients, her sister was helpless when it came to gossip and intrigue. Once Saima had regained her composure, she indicated Anna should continue with her story.

"We bumped into each other again on Main Street this morning, and he showed me around the town. But it was no big deal, obviously."

"Obviously," Maryam said, keeping her face neutral. She gave her sister a look, and Saima took the hint and changed the subject.

"It's settled, we're all going into town tomorrow to check out this film set," Saima said. "You should see if your new friend Josh wants to come along. Right, Maryam?"

"I'm up for a little light celebrity stalking," Maryam said, trying to spare Anna more teasing, because she knew that Anna's romantic situation was more complicated than she was letting on.

"What about you, Saif?" Saima asked, her smile turning mischievous. "I'm sure you'd like to meet Tenisha Barlowe, and I know Maryam could use your company to chase down Chase Taylor."

Maryam nearly groaned at her sister's lack of subtlety. She clearly didn't share their parents' reservations. "Saima," she hissed.

But Saif was gracious. "Since we seem to be snowbound in the Hollywood North Pole, we might as well make the most of it. Maybe one of us will be discovered by a casting director." Eyes twinkling, he wished the women a good night, after making plans to meet in the morning. Maryam watched him go with mixed feelings. She respected her parents' well-meant warning, but Farah's words still ricocheted in her mind: *Saif is a good guy. Don't make assumptions.*

Saima hopped up from the couch. "I need to plan my outfit

for our big trip into town and call Miraj. Hopefully the roads will be clear tomorrow, and we can leave right after I meet Chase and get an autograph. Good night, you two!"

Saima headed upstairs, and Maryam turned to Anna and smiled. "Thank you for distracting Saima. This is the first time she's talked to me all day without scowling."

"If my wedding had been derailed by a snowstorm, I'd be freaking out, too," Anna reassured Maryam. Then, after a delicate pause, she continued in a tentative voice. "Did Saif say anything? About the conversation he might have overheard on the plane?"

Maryam put her head in her hands. Part of her had hoped Anna wouldn't remember, but another part had been waiting for her to bring this up. Maybe it would help to have Anna's perspective. "Yes," she admitted. "He heard everything, but assured me it was no big deal."

The glance between the two women confirmed what they both thought of that statement. The implicit *Men!* only served to cement their new friendship. "He seemed pretty friendly this evening," Anna offered.

"A little too friendly. My parents told me this morning that he has a girlfriend, and he's estranged from his family. Two giant red flags waving in the wind, and I can't afford to make any more mistakes when it comes to love," Maryam said.

Anna must have wondered what Maryam meant, but thankfully didn't probe. "Have you asked Saif about any of this? I guess that would be pretty awkward, considering he knows how you feel, but you don't know anything about him except what you heard from your parents."

Maryam nodded, miserable. "When he used to live in Denver, he was a cute, safe brown boy who was part of my family's social circle. Having a crush on him was so easy, and since we barely spoke, I didn't have to worry about it going anywhere. Then he moved to California and life went on, but now he knows how I felt—or maybe how I feel?—and he's turned into this flirty stranger."

"You think he's toying with your feelings," Anna finished.

"Farah told me I shouldn't judge. My parents felt they had to warn me away. And Saima is obviously on Saif's side."

"What do you think?" Anna asked.

Maryam sighed. "I think I don't have time for any more romantic drama in my life. I've been burned by charming men before."

"Then don't get burned this time," Anna said, thoughtful. "Maybe just enjoy the attention."

Maryam appreciated that Anna hadn't pushed her for more details, but she couldn't help her next question. "Is that what's happening with you and this Josh guy?" she asked. She hadn't meant to bring up Nick, but suddenly, he was the elephant in the room.

Anna bit her lip. "You can probably guess that I've been having some doubts about Nick. Today we had a huge fight, and to be honest, I don't know where we stand. We're taking a break. Because of your dadu's advice, I've been managing not to worry about it too much, but I know I'll have to deal with it at some point. The phones are finally working again, and I keep thinking I should call him. It's just, I have no idea what to say. And meeting Josh—honestly, I don't know what to say about that, either! It's complicated," she finished.

"Sometimes that's all you can say to describe weird relationship dynamics," Maryam joked. Anna looked distressed, so she decided to bring their conversation back to safer waters. "Well, thanks again for distracting Saima. After she told her fiancé to cancel the *mehndi*, I honestly thought she was going to punch me. The *mehndi* is a ladies-only dance party where we apply henna, sing funny songs in Urdu, share stories, and rock out," she explained in response to Anna's puzzled expression.

"I know what a *mehndi* is," Anna said, smiling. "I was just wondering why Saima is mad at you. Are you responsible for the weather now?"

"Haven't you heard? I'm the elder daughter in an immigrant family—I'm responsible for everything."

Anna looked thoughtful for a moment. "Why can't you host Saima's *mehndi* here?" she asked. "I'd be happy to help plan it."

Maryam laughed at the idea. "You need food, decor, henna, all sorts of things for a proper *mehndi*."

"When I was in town with Josh, I noticed so many shops with goods from all over the world. I bet they'll have everything you need in Snow Falls. What else are we going to do tomorrow? With the blizzard still going, I doubt we'll be able to leave. It will be fun!" Anna jumped up and started hopping up and down on one foot, then stuck one hand in the air and made corkscrewing motions with her fingers.

"What are you doing?" Maryam asked, horrified.

"When my college roommate Nadia got married earlier this year, I had to learn how to do this choreographed Indian dance. For one of the moves, they told me to pretend to screw in a lightbulb while hopping up and down. Come on—it's cold outside, we're stranded. I'll even show you some of my

Bollywood moves," Anna said, her excitement palpable. Then her face fell. "I'm interfering again, aren't I?"

Maryam looked at Anna, taking in her hopeful expression and upbeat energy. *We need this*, she thought. *Maybe Anna needs this, too.* "Yup, you're interfering again. It's almost like you're an honorary *desi* girl now."

Anna's smile was wide and delighted in her assent.

"I just have one condition," Maryam said, mock severely. "I'm sure your friend Nadia was trying to help, but you're sorely in need of some proper dance instruction. Friends don't let friends attend a *mehndi* without learning how to *bhangra.*"

NINE

Anna

December 21

Anna was laughing so hard she had to wipe tears from her cheeks. "Come on, please," she begged Maryam. "Just one more time!"

Maryam rolled her eyes in mock annoyance, but she was laughing, too. "I'm telling you, you're a lost cause. Some people just have two left feet."

"I do not have two left feet!" Anna said. "If you must know, I think my rhythm is off because I've been taking ballroom dancing classes with Nick to practice for his family's Christmas ball." Anna felt a small ache as she said this, because it highlighted just how much she and Nick had been putting into their holiday plans—and given what had happened between them earlier, maybe she should feel guilty for being unexpectedly happy, just where she was. But she pushed the thought away, as she was growing used to doing. Clearly, she had decided not to break her worry fast at sunset. She was having fun. "Maybe I can't master *bhangra*—but you should see me do the foxtrot!"

"Oh, this I have got to see," Maryam said, and beside her, Saima laughed. She had returned downstairs after calling Miraj, drawn in by the music. Saima looked happier than she had since she landed, and Anna was glad. They had pushed the couches to the side and were playing the up-tempo *bhangra* beats courtesy of Maryam's CD collection, curated especially for Saima's now canceled Toronto *mehndi*. Anna and Maryam had decided to keep their plans to throw Saima a replacement party the next night a secret—until they were sure they could pull it off—and had told Saima they were just having some fun with the dancing.

Anna grabbed Maryam before she could protest and said, "Well, the foxtrot is not something you can do solo. Just follow my lead. Two walking steps forward. *Walking*, Maryam, not trying to run away. Ow, my toe. Now . . ." Anna paused, wracking her brain for the next directions. "Back, back, side left—no, right. Side, slow . . ." She let go of Maryam and threw her hands in the air. "Never mind! I admit it, I wasn't really paying attention in the classes we took. I'm a terrible dancer!"

At that moment, Saima gasped and sat bolt upright on the couch. Anna followed her startled gaze—straight into Mysterious Josh's eyes. "Ohmigod," she whispered. "That's him."

Saima had jumped up off the couch. Just as Anna whispered, "That's Mysterious Josh!" Saima whisper-shouted, "That's Chase Taylor! And Tenisha Barlowe! I think I'm going to faint!"

Saima gripped both Anna's and Maryam's arms as Anna stared at the scene unfolding in the entranceway: a tall, beautiful woman stood beside Josh, and a small crowd of people were filing into the lobby—one of whom Anna recognized as the director Katrina Wakes.

"I almost didn't recognize him with the beard, but Saima, I think you're right. It's Chase Taylor. What do we do?" Maryam whispered out of the corner of her mouth.

"Stand here and look pretty, of course," Saima whispered back.

Anna felt like she was losing her balance. She clung to the sisters, trying to make sense of her swirling thoughts. Josh's eyes were still on hers. Anna couldn't read his expression, but she thought he looked a combination of embarrassed and guilty. She was sure she was the picture of shock.

"I thought he was a spy," Anna said faintly. "Turns out he's—"

Saima sprang forward, apparently no longer able to contain herself. "Chase Taylor!" she shouted. "Huge fan! And Tenisha Barlowe! Huge, huge, *huge* fan."

"Oh, boy, here we go," Maryam said under her breath. "Prepare to be embarrassed beyond belief. Saima doesn't do subtle."

Saima was pulling Anna and Maryam along toward the crowd of film people, as Anna wished there was a way to escape from the room unnoticed.

"I'm Saima!" She pumped Josh's hand and then Tenisha Barlowe's, before pushing Anna and Maryam forward to do the same. Anna's cheeks felt like they were on fire as she nearly stumbled into Josh's broad chest. Except he wasn't Josh, was he? Now she knew there was a reason she had been convinced she had seen him before. Because she *had*. In magazines, and in the movie she had watched that morning with Mr. Dadu. He really was a good actor—and had done such a great job of pretending to be just a regular guy that she had fallen for it, head over heels.

"Anna, say something," Saima said through a big, clench-teethed smile.

"Um, hi," Anna managed. "It's nice to . . . see you."

"It's nice to see you, too." That *voice*. It made her heart do things it shouldn't. Flutter and swoon. And now she knew why. Because he was a movie star—not the person she had thought he was, not the sweet, slightly mysterious guy who had come to her rescue twice in twenty-four hours.

Beside him, Tenisha's smile was cool. She linked her arm through Josh's—*Chase's?*—and said, "We have lines to run. We should probably head upstairs."

But Saima was grasping Josh's hand again like she wanted to find a way to bronze it and keep it as a souvenir.

"Our dadu—who, sadly, has gone to bed and will be devastated to have missed the pleasure of your company—is truly your *biggest* fan, and in fact, he spent part of today sitting on that very couch, watching *One Night at Christmas* not once, but twice."

"Oh, yeah?" Josh said, beaming his charming smile—one that had been so much more endearing when Anna had not known that he smiled this way at everyone. "Well, listen." He leaned in close to Saima. Maryam put her hand gently on her sister's back, presumably so she didn't swoon and fall right over. "I happen to know the director is looking for some extras for a scene we're shooting tomorrow that requires a bit of a crowd.

We need people of all ages. Would you and your family like to be part of that? Your grandfather included?" Now he looked over at Anna. "You, too?"

"Oh, um, well, thank you, but I actually have things to do tomorrow," Anna managed.

"Things to do in Snow Falls?" Saima said, nudging her.

"That's right. I'm very . . . busy," she trailed off. "I have an extremely important fax to send. For my job."

"Don't you think the fax can wait?" Saima nudged her again, hard, and Anna almost fell into Josh's chest again.

"Well, I—" Anna was almost sure she had never been more confused or embarrassed in her life. She just needed this moment to be over. So much for resolving not to worry. Look where that had gotten her. She had not-worried herself into a situation where she hadn't paid attention to important details, and now she felt like a total fool.

"Chase, darling," Tenisha murmured, moving even closer to him. "We really do need to go."

Josh was looking at Anna as if he had something he wanted to say—but wouldn't in front of an audience. Which, Anna decided, was funny considering he was an *actor*. He shot her a look that was hard to read, then turned to Saima and Maryam. "I'll let the casting director know you'll be there tomorrow, then?"

"Definitely," Saima said with enthusiasm. Josh smiled, then shot one last probing look at Anna. "If you manage to get that important fax sent in time, maybe you'll join in, too. Call time for extras is nine o'clock sharp."

He headed off, Tenisha on his arm. As they climbed the

stairs that presumably led to the rooms on the nice side of the hotel, where all the Hollywood people were staying, he leaned down and said something to her, softly, in her ear. Tenisha glanced over her shoulder at Anna, then said something to Josh in reply—and a moment later, they were gone.

"So, that was Chase Taylor," Maryam said softly.

"Actually," Anna said, turning to the sisters, "that was also Mysterious Josh."

"What?" Saima blustered. "Anna, are you saying . . . ?"

"That he took me for a fool and lied to me about who he was? Yes. But I should have known. I'm so embarrassed!"

"It was an honest mistake," Maryam said. "He didn't have a beard in *One Night at Christmas*." But Maryam's expression was now just as hard to read as Josh's had been. Anna looked naive and foolish—that was all there was to it.

Anna felt suddenly exhausted. "You know what? I need this long, confusing, very strange day to be over. I had fun dancing—"

"Attempting to dance," Maryam interjected with a smile Anna found herself unable to return.

"And thanks so much for loaning me the clothes. I'll see you tomorrow, okay?" She didn't look back as she rushed for the stairs that led to her dismal room, even though she could hear Saima begging Maryam to let her run after Anna and get the full story.

"She's obviously upset," she heard Maryam say. "She just needs to be left alone."

But that wasn't true. Anna had never felt more lonely.

Upstairs in her room, she sorted quickly through the clothes, hanging up anything that would wrinkle, and changing into the jaunty, cupcake-adorned pair of pajamas borrowed from Maryam. *Don't worry, don't worry*, she kept telling herself. But it wasn't working anymore.

As she passed into the bathroom to brush her teeth, she accidentally knocked her handbag to the floor, spilling its contents. Beth's Happy Holiday Missive was right at the top of the pile, and Anna silently cursed Mr. Sandy-Haired Flight Attendant, who had chased her down as she exited the plane and given the letter back. Without giving it a second look, she edged the letter under the bed with her toe, where she hoped it would stay. Then she climbed into bed.

But no matter how hard Anna tried, sleep eluded her. Nothing worked. Not counting sheep. Not counting paint-color names. Not counting her fingers and toes over and over, hoping she'd get so bored she'd finally succumb to slumber. All she could think about were the many worries she had put aside all day, all the things in her life she was simply not dealing with. Was Janey going to fire her because of the Malone Mansion layout? Had she made a huge mistake with Nick? Did they belong together, or were they completely wrong for each other? And why couldn't she stop thinking about *Josh Tannenbaum*—a guy who didn't really exist, who had a beautiful starlet girlfriend, and who had fooled her into thinking he was someone else?

Anna tossed and turned, these thoughts filling her head, all questions without answers and problems without solutions, until finally, she threw the sheets aside and stood, straightening the lapels of the cupcake pajamas and heading for the door. Maybe she'd be able to find some chamomile tea in the kitchen downstairs, something that would settle her down enough to sleep. She opened her hotel room door, glanced up and down the dimly lit hall, then walked down the stairs, through the lobby, and toward the kitchen.

As Anna moved through the cozy, silent inn, she was struck by how homey and charming it was, despite the fact that it was still a work in progress. She couldn't help it; her "work brain" kicked in, and she imagined a "before and after" story: "From Shabby to Chic Just in Time for the Holidays . . ."

Anna paused outside the kitchen door, her thoughts interrupted by something inside, banging and rattling. Was it—she squeezed her eyes shut—a *rat*? A raccoon? Some sort of northern animal that had broken into the kitchen to steal the leftovers from the *iftar* earlier in the evening? Her choices were to run back to her room and spend the rest of the night sleepless, cowering in fear—or to face something head-on for once.

There was a broom beside the doorframe and she grabbed it, then pushed open the door. The broom held aloft, she shouted out, "*Aha*, you nasty little creature! I've got you!"

But it was not a nasty little creature she discovered in the kitchen. It was Josh Tannenbaum—or rather Chase Taylor—looking first startled, then sheepish. "Busted . . ." he said, holding up a fork that contained a deep-fried sweet-and-sour chicken momo. "I was sneaking a midnight snack. Cute pajamas, by the way."

"Oh!" Anna glanced down at the cupcake-embellished flannel material and wished she had stayed in her room. "I thought you were—"

"A nasty little creature," he finished with a smile. "Which I suppose you could say I am, given that I lied to you about who

I was—and then played dumb in the lobby earlier. I'm so sorry, Anna. I wish I could go back in time."

"Why didn't you feel you could trust me with who you were?"

He put down his fork and ran one hand through his hair, mussing it appealingly. "The truth?"

"Of course I want the truth," Anna said.

He thought for a long moment. "I didn't think I was ever going to see you again," he finally said.

At this, she couldn't help but laugh. "Wow, thanks so much."

"No, no, it's not like that—I mean, I *wanted* to see you again. I just figured I wouldn't. I didn't know how serious the storm was. I figured you'd be gone in the morning. That night we met, you made me feel like my old self. The self I was before . . . before Hollywood, I guess. I was able to be really honest with you in a way I haven't been able to be with anyone in a long time."

Anna put one hand on her hip. "I think I would have been willing to forgive you for being dishonest with me once. Maybe. But we met again this morning! You had the chance to come clean. And you didn't. You made me feel, and look, like a fool. Plus, you embarrassed me in front of my new friends."

"Please, believe me, that wasn't my intention. Anna, the thing is . . ." He looked distraught, but she told herself he was just a good actor. "'Josh Tannenbaum' is my real name. 'Chase Taylor' is just my stage name. It felt so nice to be me with someone who knew that. I didn't want it to end." He shook his head. "It was a dumb move, though. And I don't blame you if you never want to speak to me again. But I really enjoyed meeting and spending time with you. Like I said, you made me feel like myself again. I'm really grateful to you for that. I owed you better."

"Why don't you use your real name?" Anna asked, genuinely curious.

"My first agent told me I needed something more . . . I think 'universally appealing' were the words she used. But sometimes it makes me feel like I'm playing a role, not just on-screen but in my life." His expression was far off, and then he seemed to come back to reality. "Sorry. I've lost the right to unload stuff on you by being dishonest."

Anna couldn't help it: she wanted to stay mad at him, but she felt an immediate rush of empathy. "It's okay," she found herself saying. "I think I can understand why you wanted to keep your real—fake?—identity a secret." She thought back to the way Saima had fawned all over him. "Being famous must be so strange."

"To say the least," Josh said with a relieved smile.

"I really do feel silly for not recognizing you. All this could have been avoided if I had. But, I'll admit, I hadn't seen any of your films when we first met. Mr. Dadu really is a huge fan, though, and he showed me *One Night at Christmas* this morning. I don't even watch holiday movies, and I loved it!"

"Really? Who doesn't secretly love holiday movies?"

"Maybe because it's always bugged me that Hanukkah is almost never included in them, too, I just never got into them."

"I hear you on that—I'm Jewish, and I've given up trying to convince writers and directors that a Hanukkah romance is a good idea. They always ask me, what could possibly be romantic about Hanukkah?" Josh rolled his eyes.

Anna gasped. "The candlelight, for one thing! Also, eight days rather than just one—that's a lot of time for a romantic slow burn, right?"

He grinned at her. "Exactly. You're Jewish, too?"

"No, but the stepmother I grew up with was, so we celebrated both Christmas and Hanukkah." She paused. "I miss it." What was it about this guy that always made her tell him exactly what she was thinking and feeling—even now?

"It's hard being stuck away from home over the holidays, isn't it?" he said. "Especially since we have no idea when we're going to be able to travel out of here. And Katrina, our director, wants to take advantage of the cast and crew being marooned here—not to mention all the snow—to shoot what she says is going to be the most authentic Christmas movie ever. Tenisha had me practicing lines all night for some extra scenes. I didn't get the chance to eat—so here I am, sneaking leftovers."

Tenisha. His rumored girlfriend, and the most beautiful woman Anna had ever seen. Anna felt her naive heart plummet all the way down to her fuzzy-socked feet. "Maryam and Saif ordered enough food for about a hundred people," she managed. "We barely made a dent. You're welcome to it."

"Want some?"

"We-ell, I couldn't sleep and was looking for some tea— but maybe what I need is a midnight snack."

They chatted easily as Anna grabbed a plate and filled it with leftovers. If she didn't look at him and focused instead on her food, she found she could get back to feeling almost as relaxed around him as she had when she thought he was just a regular, sweet guy named Josh Tannenbaum. It helped to know that was his real name—made *him* seem more real again, somehow.

"That must be hard for your friends, stuck in an unfamiliar place while trying to celebrate such an important holiday," Josh was saying. "Actually, there are a few Muslims on crew and I heard them talking about a Turkish coffee shop in town that doubles as a mosque. You could try to find that tomorrow."

"That's a good idea. I'm sure Maryam and her family would really appreciate that."

"They're saying the snow is going to slow down around noon tomorrow—so we might all get to go home eventually. I think most of the crew are starting to worry they won't be home in time for the holidays at all." He paused and put down his fork, while Anna tried to hide her involuntary grimace at the idea of leaving Snow Falls—a grimace that surprised even her. "Hey, did I say something wrong?"

"I just . . . really love snow," Anna said. She put down her fork, too, then carried her plate to the sink so he wouldn't see the disappointment on her face any longer. The blizzard was going to end, they were going to clear the snow, flights would start up again, and it was possible she'd be out of Snow Falls and on her way to Toronto by tomorrow. But . . . was she still welcome in Toronto? And if she wasn't, where else was she supposed to go? She had an honorary aunt—she had been her mother's best friend, and had kept in touch with Anna all these years—who lived in Kansas City, but Anna hadn't seen her for a while. Her father had some close friends she knew she could call. But could you just contact people you hadn't seen in ages and say you were coming to stay for the holidays? She had college friends and work friends—but admitting she was alone for the holidays felt like yet another embarrassment. So much of the past few years, Anna had felt alone. But somehow, in Snow Falls, she didn't feel that way. She felt part of something. She didn't want to consider how fast it was all going to end.

"Hey, let me wash these." Josh gently took the plate from her hands and began to wash the dishes himself. When he was done, he stepped close. Anna felt her heart begin to flutter under the cupcake-festooned flannel. That was just the effect he had on people, she reminded herself. He was an actor. It was his job to be charming. He was being friendly with her, that was all. He liked her as a friend because she, regular old Anna, made him feel like a regular guy. Plus, she was wearing flannel pajamas printed all over with giant cupcakes, and he had just spent his night practice-kissing the beautiful Tenisha Barlowe. She looked away from him, back out the window at the snow— but her gaze returned to his face, as if pulled there by a magnet. He was watching her, wearing a half smile that reminded her of the way he looked in almost every scene in *One Night at Christmas* in which he was about to profess his love to his costar, but then ended up losing his nerve.

"I'm really enjoying getting to know you, Anna," he said.

She couldn't help but be honest in return. "I'm enjoying it, too."

"It's nice to know someone here knows my real name. That someone around here is a friend. And I'd really love to see you on set tomorrow. I think you'll have fun. I can get you a plum role. Festive Townsperson number 6?"

"I accept the role," Anna said—and for the first time in a long while, she didn't feel like she was pretending.

TEN

Maryam

December 22

3 days until Christmas
Hanukkah begins
The 27th day of Ramadan

The next day, the wedding party rose early for *suhoor* and worked together to prepare eggs, toast, and fresh fruit in the inn's ample kitchen. Everyone helped, though Maryam, Farah, and Saif took the lead. Afterward, they prayed *fajr* together, before Saima turned on the Weather Network on the large television in the foyer. Incredibly, the forecast called for even more snow today. "I'm going to call the airline and see what I can find out," Saima said, her smile strained. Maryam thought about offering to take this on—but then she saw Anna enter the foyer with dark circles under her eyes as if she'd hardly slept, but also a big smile on her face. She waved Maryam over.

"So, I ran into Josh—Chase . . . well, you know who I mean—again last night, after that awkward meeting here—"

"Last night? When? Last I saw you, you were heading off

to bed." Maryam couldn't help it; even though the last thing she needed was someone else to feel responsible for, she was starting to feel protective of Anna.

"I couldn't sleep. So, I came down looking for tea—and Josh was in the kitchen, and . . ." Anna trailed off and smiled somewhat dreamily. Maryam could swear she saw little cartoon hearts dancing around her friend's head. "He convinced me to join you when you visit the set. I said yes. It'll be fun, right?"

"Actually, I was thinking about not going," Maryam started, nervous. "There's a lot to do, and I should keep my parents company." Plus, despite her bravado about Saif from last night, she wasn't sure if she wanted to be around the full force of his charm.

"Look outside, Maryam. We're not going anywhere today. This is a free day, a gift. You said you feel as if you never have time for yourself—and now you have this precious day to do what you like. Maybe there's a reason all of this is happening." Anna shot her another starry-eyed grin before drifting away to the kitchen, calling out that she'd meet her at the front door at eight a.m.

Anna was right. Maryam couldn't remember the last time she'd had this much unstructured time to do nothing. Maybe when she was in college, during school breaks. No, she had worked every summer. Maybe during high school? No, she had volunteered and worked during high school. Now that she thought about it, Maryam realized the last time she'd just taken a few days to simply . . . *be* had been in middle school.

No wonder Saima called her Bor-yam. Maybe a more accurate description would be "Always-on-yam."

Sigh. Even her nicknames were tragic. It was a good thing

she was a pharmacist and not a writer. Somehow, that thought was the most depressing of all. As if reading her low mood, Saif sidled up to Maryam.

"I recognize that look. You're planning your escape," he said, voice pitched low so the rest of the wedding party chatting in the lobby wouldn't hear.

Despite herself, Maryam smiled. "Have you taken a look outside? There's plenty of snow, and we're still stranded."

"What time are we heading into town for our celebrity-stalking session?" he asked with a smile.

Despite her dark thoughts, Maryam's mouth tilted up, and *oh God*, was her family watching her flirt with a man—during Ramadan—right after praying *fajr*? She subtly glanced around, and just as she had suspected, Dadu was taking a little too long putting on his shoes, while her father glowered at Saif, and Saima gave her a thumbs-up. She would yell at them all later. For now . . .

She turned to Saif. *Snow day*, she thought. "Take-a-chance-yam" was a better nickname, actually. She could always use a new friend, right? "Actually, change of plans and a new development. After you went upstairs, we met Chase Taylor, who not only is staying at the same inn, but turns out to be Anna's new friend! He invited us to be extras on that holiday movie. How do you feel about making your Hollywood debut this morning?"

Saif agreed readily, and Maryam decided on a whim to invite Dadu, too—she knew her grandfather missed his directing days and would enjoy the impromptu field trip.

At the appointed hour, the small party assembled in the lobby. "Come along, come along, we don't want to be late. Film sets are very particular places, *nah*?" her grandfather said, and then hurried out the door. With a huge grin, Saif followed Dadu.

As they walked behind the men, Saima started to sing, off-key: *"Maryam and Saif sitting in a tree. Getting their nikah witnessed by the Imam and a three-hundred-person wedding party!"* Thankfully, the men were far ahead, Dadu setting a fast pace considering he was six inches shorter and forty years older than Saif.

For a moment, Maryam felt pure joy. She linked arms with her sister and Anna and walked faster. No way was she letting her seventy-year-old grandfather beat her into town. Besides, after her conversation with Anna yesterday, she was curious about Snow Falls. She wanted to see this magical town that somehow supported three different Hakka restaurants.

The walk into town was rough going, and if Saif hadn't been hovering close to her grandfather, she would have worried for him. Snow was piled several feet on either side of the skinny path carved down the sidewalk by an intrepid snowblower, requiring the group to walk in single file in some places. Maryam trailed the party, with Anna and Saima chatting amiably in front. It took them nearly half an hour to walk to the town center, mostly because of the snow, and also because they kept stopping to take pictures using the camera Saima had bought for her honeymoon. It was one of those new digital ones, and the ability to scroll through pictures on the tiny screen and delete the ones where someone's eyes were closed (half of them) or that were not suitably flattering, was irresistible to Saima.

Soon the houses—most of them small and cozy-looking, with smoke puffing gently from brick chimneys—changed into a few storefronts, and then the street they were on led to a main thoroughfare of quaint stores dressed up in their holiday finery. Christmas sparkle festooned storefronts, and the women stopped to admire a particularly beautiful display in front of an independent bookstore that featured Nora Roberts, Maeve Binchy, Terry McMillan, Margaret Atwood, Robert Munsch, and other familiar names.

Ahead, Dadu dragged Saif inside a tiny coffee shop called Topkapi Café.

"This must be the café Josh was telling me about," Anna said, excited. "He said there's a prayer space in the basement for the local Muslim community. And amazing coffee and treats." Her face fell. "You're all fasting today and won't be able to try the food."

"We'll take some home for *iftar* and enjoy after sunset," Saima assured Anna. Today really did feel like a snow day, Maryam thought as she followed her sister and Anna inside. A day full of possibilities, when anything could happen. The world felt like a frozen winter wonderland, all the grime and slush wiped out by fresh powder. She raised the camera and took a few more pictures, trying to capture the gentle, if relentless, snowfall before joining the party inside. No wonder the planes were still grounded, Maryam thought. She had never seen weather like this before.

Inside, the café was decorated in reds and bright blues, with enough seating for a dozen people. A large display case dominated the front, and Saima and Anna drooled over luscious desserts: honey-soaked phyllo pastries; baklava bursting with walnuts, pistachios, and almonds; a spongy cake made from semolina and topped with bright orange strands of saffron and sugar-glazed almonds. Delicate glass cups and saucers decorated with gold paint were arranged on the shelf behind the bar, in front of a wall of brilliant turquoise tiles painted with intricate geometric patterns. On the opposite wall, giant prints in ornate gold frames of the Aegean Sea, the Bosphorus Strait, and Islamic calligraphy decorated the space. The moment she stepped through the door, Maryam felt like she belonged. She wasn't Turkish, but she could tell she was among friends. A young woman in a simple white hijab emerged from the back and smiled in welcome.

"*Salam!* I'm Sarah. Welcome to Snow Falls, uncle," she said, addressing her grandfather before turning to the women and Saif. "My sisters, my brother. How can I help you?"

Maryam's heart filled. This subtle acknowledgment of their shared Muslim heritage made her feel instantly at home.

Anna came forward eagerly. "I heard there was a mosque inside this café. Our flight was canceled and we landed here two days ago. I wanted to show my"—she paused as if stumbling over the word—"new friends so they could join you for prayer."

Sarah instantly perked up at this. "Oh, you are the stranded passengers staying at Snow Falls Inn!" she exclaimed. "The fasting Muslims who ordered too much Hakka for dinner last night. Muriel from Hakka Empire is a dear friend, and she told me all about it this morning. You must join my family for *iftar* today."

The group protested, but Sarah was adamant. She only relented when they assured her that they had plenty of leftover food, but that they would join them for tea another time. In the meantime, Dadu, parched from the walk, ordered thick Turkish coffee and settled at a table to enjoy it.

"I'll take mine to go," Anna said. "Since we have a bit of

extra time, there's a shop across the street I want to check out." She shot Maryam a look, and Maryam knew she was off to source some items for the secret *mehndi* party. She gave her a wink.

After Anna slipped out, they continued to chat with Sarah until the doorbell chimed and a new customer walked in. A familiar deep voice said, "One coffee please, Sarah."

"Of course, Chase," Sarah said without missing a beat— and Maryam turned around to admire the actor. The lighting had been dim in the hotel last night, but now she looked her fill. Chase—or should she start thinking of him as Josh?—wasn't the most handsome Hollywood star; he lacked the obvious sexiness of Brad Pitt or the smoldering intensity of George Clooney. But he had a contained energy and charisma that drew the eye and made it linger.

"Hey, did I see Anna come out of here a minute ago?" he asked, and Maryam noticed a dimple in his cheek. Maryam nodded in response to his question and felt the beginnings of a blush when she realized she was staring. *I'm fasting*, she reminded herself. Beside her, she felt Saif stiffen.

Meanwhile, her sister attempted to play it cool, even as she inched closer to the actor.

"Chase—or should we call you Josh?—we met so quickly last night, I didn't get to ask for an autograph," Saima said, sticking a napkin and lip liner into the actor's hands. "I've watched *One Night at Christmas* a dozen times. Maryam, quick, where's the camera?"

"'Josh' is fine," the handsome actor assured the trio. "'Chase' is my professional name."

Saima frantically gestured for Saif to take a picture of her and Maryam posing next to the actor. Frowning, Saif snapped a few photos without warning, then stepped forward to introduce himself.

"Hello, Mr. Taylor, I'm Saif Rasool, attorney-at-law," he said formally, sticking out his hand to shake. "I saw about half of *Captain Eagleman*. You owe me ten bucks." He smiled unconvincingly, and Maryam tried not to laugh. Saif clearly didn't like being overshadowed by a movie star.

"You must meet my grandfather," Maryam said hurriedly, feeling sorry for Josh. "He's a retired Bollywood film director."

Dadu, who had been sipping his coffee and watching the show, got to his feet with a genial smile and shook hands with Josh, who towered over him. "Young man, you flirt on-screen almost as well as Shah Rukh Khan," he said. "If I was still in the business, I would hire you to teach the young actors how to make love to the camera."

Josh laughed, taking the comment in stride. "The key is eye contact, but not so much that you look like a serial killer," he joked.

"I am sure you are putting your acting powers to good use with Ms. Barlowe," Dadu said cryptically, and Josh blinked.

"Um . . . yes," the handsome actor said. He made a show of looking at his watch. "I'll meet you all on set, I just"—he glanced across the street at the same shops Anna was browsing—"have an errand to run."

Maryam felt a surge of protectiveness, but what could she do? She wasn't Anna's minder. Besides, Saima and Dadu were practically running out the door, determined to be early for their call time. They accepted a box of treats that Sarah insisted was a gift, and then headed out into the snow once more, following Josh's directions toward the set.

Saif took the bakery box from Maryam, his eyes trained on the actor, who had just reached the door of Kate's Kurios. "He's not that good-looking in person," he muttered, and Maryam hid her smile.

"Yes, he is," she teased. "And that unfamiliar feeling in the pit of your stomach is jealousy."

"I'm not jealous, I just didn't think you'd be so easily taken in by a guy who clearly has his teeth whitened, and probably travels with his own hairstylist."

This time Maryam didn't bother hiding her amusement—she laughed out loud. "I've never seen a man more obsessed with his hair than you. I watch you fiddle with it every time you spot a shiny surface."

Saif flushed, but relented. "Fine. Mr. Taylor is gorgeous, and maybe I'm a tiny bit jealous because you looked at him like he was a delicious piece of baklava," he grumbled, and this time it was Maryam's turn to flush. Did it really bother him that Maryam found the actor attractive?

"I'm pretty sure he only has eyes for Anna," Maryam allowed, and glanced over her shoulder again, half hoping Anna would be running to catch up.

Saif only shrugged. "Anna is a stunner, but a guy like Chase . . . He might like Anna's company, but I'd hate for her to get hurt. Right now, he has nowhere to go and nothing better to do than flirt with pretty women marooned in the same town as him."

Maryam pondered Saif's words. Maybe he had let on more

than he realized, revealing how he felt about her, too. Was he also being friendly and passing the time before he returned to his regular life, with his regular girlfriend? *Pull yourself together,* she told herself sternly. She wasn't some teenager with a crush. This was a snow day, and the magic of a snow day was not worrying about tomorrow and all the missed homework it would bring.

They approached the outdoor set, which had attracted a small audience. Maryam recognized a few people from the inn, no doubt enjoying this unexpected opportunity. They were all on snow day time, too.

Dadu wandered up to a tall Black woman dressed in an orange puffer vest and oversized glasses, braided hair piled artfully on her head, and Maryam recognized the director Katrina Wakes. He murmured something to her that Maryam couldn't hear, and gestured to the camera. The director glanced over at him, then threw her head back in laughter.

Her grandfather, making friends wherever he went, Maryam thought. After the death of her dadi-ma three years ago, Dadu had been completely lost in a sadness he described as a fog. He slept at odd hours and visited her grave every day with flowers—fresh jasmine when it was in season; otherwise lilies, daffodils, and white carnations. At the grave, he read his late wife Urdu poetry and spent hours updating her on the lives of the family. And of course, Dadu being Dadu, he made friends with everyone who had visited the small section of the cemetery reserved for their Muslim community—fellow grieving spouses, parents, children, each in different stages of their own grieving process. It felt good to see him vibrant once more, taking an active interest in the world of the living.

Except, looking around at the crowd, Maryam felt a sudden case of nerves. She hadn't thought this whole being-an-extra-in-an-actual-film thing through. As much as she enjoyed watching movies, she wasn't sure she wanted to be in front of the camera, even as a background extra. As if sensing her unease, Saima turned to her.

"I'll be okay here with Dadu," her sister volunteered. Saima was avidly absorbing the film set, eyes bright with interest. She gestured toward Saif, who was leaning against a storefront nearby. "Why don't you take your hot lawyer for a stroll around town?" she suggested, eyes dancing. "Take in the sights. Plan your future. Discuss how many babies you intend to have. You know, all the important stuff."

Saif looked over when he felt both sisters' eyes on him. When Maryam told him she was going to walk around Main Street instead of waiting around, he instantly volunteered to accompany her.

"Are you sure you wouldn't rather stay?" Maryam asked.

"I live in California. I'm immune to Hollywood magic," he joked.

"I thought you lived in Sacramento?" Maryam asked innocently, and Saif pretended to be offended.

Together they trudged through three feet of snow, down to the main strip. She spotted the knit shop where Anna had purchased her adorable sweater, as well as places called June's Cauldron and Kate's Kurios, but it wasn't until they ducked into a side street that the fabric of the town began to fully reveal itself.

Snow Falls wasn't only the picture-perfect postcard of a classic Christmas town—it had layers, just like Anna had mentioned. Maryam spied contrasts all around her. A kosher deli beside a halal butcher next to an Afghan bakery advertising fresh-baked naan, which was neighbors with a Sri Lankan grocer. An old-school barbershop alongside a repair shop that advertised services to "send money back home." A Lebanese restaurant beside a Jamaican restaurant next to a Pakistani clothing store beside a Guyanese roti takeout shop. All independently owned stores, she noted, with no chain establishment in sight. Saif and Maryam looked at each other in confusion.

"Is this the UN of small Ontario towns?" she asked out loud, and Saif shrugged. Plus, everyone was so friendly. At the roti shop, Maryam finally broke down and asked the friendly shopkeeper Abdullah about the overwhelmingly warm reception.

"Maybe this is where multicultural Canadian hospitality goes for corporate training?" she asked after he offered to cater dinner for the entire wedding party for free and, when she refused, insisted she take home a dozen *philauri*—pillowy-light deep-fried dough balls—to eat with her tea after breaking fast.

Abdullah, an older man with a pot belly and gray in his beard, laughed at her joke. "Many of us used to live in the big cities. Toronto, Montreal, Vancouver. But we were looking for something different, something else. Yes?"

Maryam nodded, still not understanding. She leaned close, so as not to be overheard. "But aren't small towns a little . . ." She trailed off, raising her eyebrows in unspoken communication: *A little small-minded. A little conservative.*

Abdullah knew what she meant, and he only chuckled. "Snow Falls is different. Most of us, we came from elsewhere. Whether it was from another country or another part of this big country. Maybe that's what has helped us build community."

He winked at Maryam. "Plus, Snow Falls is very popular with movie folk. We film year-round, and that helps all the businesses. They like our small-town energy, but with the food selection and diversity of a big city. Just don't tell anyone in Toronto, or they'll ruin it for everyone."

Maryam promised to keep Snow Falls's secret. Saif chimed in, asking if there were any places they should check out while in town. Abdullah directed them to a historic theater that served as the town's unofficial museum, as well as the local library.

Maryam used the bathroom before they set off, and when she returned, the men were speaking together in low voices. When he spotted her, Saif thanked Abdullah for the food and the information, and they set off.

"Did I miss something?" she asked as they walked in the direction of the theater.

Saif shrugged. "He was just filling me in on some of the town's traditions. Let's get to the theater—Abdullah recommended it highly."

The sun was out, but it was still cold, and their breath fogged as they walked and chatted. He told her about his job as legal counsel for an insurance company in California, and entertained her with funny stories about the awkward CEO, who was obsessed with actuarial tables, and who had predicted the date of Saif's death with supreme confidence as part of the interview process. She shared stories about working alongside her dad at the pharmacy, and their plans to expand beyond the local neighborhood.

"On the plane, you told Anna you wanted to be a writer," Saif said. "You could have moved to LA, set up shop at a café, and lived an artist's life."

Maryam laughed out loud at the thought of herself scribbling in a notebook or writing in a café. "My parents would've loved that," she joked. "They'd never hear the end of it from their friends."

Saif stopped walking. "I wanted to be an actor," he said abruptly.

Maryam blinked. "What?"

"I was a drama kid. I performed in community theater and took every drama class in high school. I even cut class in grade nine to audition for a few commercials. I never got any spots," he said, smiling self-consciously. "I don't think the world was ready for this," he said, gesturing at himself, and Maryam laughed. Saif continued: "When I told my parents, they thought I was nuts. And maybe I was. Have you ever seen a brown kid on TV unless they were holding someone hostage?"

Maryam remembered watching some awful movie a few years ago, where the only brown characters were terrorists, or villains, or the helpless victims. There was a muscly all-American man there to save the good guys, of course.

"I'm so sorry, you're missing your big chance to be part of a movie," Maryam said.

"I'd rather be here, spending time with you," he said. Then, as if realizing what he had just admitted, he smiled crookedly at her. "Besides, I have main-character energy. It's protagonist or bust." She laughed again and decided to take him at his word. Saif was an adult; if he wanted to be an extra on a holiday movie, he would tell her.

And she was enjoying spending time with him too much to encourage him to leave.

"I don't regret going to law school," Saif said now. They

had walked down another side street, and the theater was up ahead, a brown brick building that looked like an old church, complete with spire, steeple, and beautiful stained glass windows. "In the end, I wasn't a very good actor. Still, at least I can say I tried."

Maryam felt the sting of his words. "People who look like me don't get to write stories," she said.

They were on the front steps, and Saif paused before he pulled the large wooden doors open. His look was inscrutable. "And as long as we believe that, we never will," he said.

They walked into the theater, the smell of musty carpet and furniture polish strong. The stained glass main doors opened onto a small foyer, and grand double doors led to the main stage. Maryam admired the prints on the walls as she considered Saif's words.

Around her were framed playbills and group shots of past productions of various community theater troupes going back to the 1960s. A large sign proclaimed a meeting of the theater board in session, and she spied an advertisement for something called the "Snow Falls Holiday Hoopla" on Christmas Day. Maryam smiled at the wording—she had no idea what a Holiday Hoopla was, but knowing Snow Falls, it was sure to be special. She looked around for Saif, but he had disappeared inside the double doors that led to the main stage.

"Saif," she hissed, following him, "they're having a board meeting . . ." Maryam trailed off as she stepped inside the beautiful theater space. Inside, plush red carpet, stadium-style seating for three hundred, wood paneling, and a soaring ceiling with exposed wood arches lent the auditorium an elegant air. In front, on a raised wooden stage framed by heavy red velvet curtains, a trio of people looked up from their table.

"Can we help you?" an older Black man with gray hair and a silk scarf tied around his neck called.

Maryam was about to apologize and drag Saif out, but he was already striding toward the stage. She hurried after him. They weren't supposed to be here. Had Saif lost his mind?

"This is Maryam. She's a writer from Denver, and she wants to help with the holiday play. Abdullah sent us," Saif announced.

Maryam froze. What was Saif talking about?

An older white woman rose from the table and beckoned to Maryam with a smile. Why did she look relieved? "Thank goodness you've arrived! Our play could use your expertise, Maryam."

"I'm not . . . I'm not a writer," Maryam stammered, looking wildly at Saif.

"Don't worry, we aren't writers, either, dear," the older woman said, and introduced herself as Celine. "This year, since Christmas, Hanukkah, and Eid are all falling so close together, we wanted to honor the tri-holidays. Unfortunately, one of our committee members, Abdullah's wife, Salma, is sick with the flu. When Abdullah called to tell us about you, Maryam, we were absolutely thrilled!" The other two people at the table nodded in agreement.

Maryam had caught up to Saif now and pulled him aside. "What did you do?" she said, keeping her voice low. "We're supposed to be extras on the movie set. I know you wanted to be there."

"I'll run back and tell them we got delayed," Saif answered without hesitation. "Why not try something a little different? Maybe it's time we write ourselves into the story."

"But I'm not a writer!" she protested.

"Do you know what writers do?" he asked, gently clasping her hand and pulling her, reluctantly, up the stairs to the stage. She was so nervous, she didn't even register the feel of his hand in hers, but it was a steadying presence. "It's very simple: writers write," he said firmly.

Writers write. It was trite, but somehow the words helped calm her mind. Ever since she landed in Snow Falls, she had felt different from the stressed-out Maryam who herded her family through Denver International Airport. This new Maryam spilled her secret dreams to a stranger, and now her lifelong family friend was helping to make those secret dreams come true. Maryam accepted the seat at the table that Saif pulled out for her. "You should stay on set," Maryam whispered.

He grinned at her. "Not a chance," he said before leaving to inform Saima and Dadu about their change in plans.

The Holiday Hoopla committee introduced themselves: Celine was a retired middle school teacher; Bruce, with the scarf, was a classically trained actor, and beside him was his partner, Teddy, a giant mountain of a man and retired school custodian. Maryam explained that she was a pharmacist and avid reader but had no professional writing experience. They didn't seem bothered in the slightest—this was their first time putting together the holiday pageant, too.

Saif joined them a few minutes later. He must have run to the set and back, but he had barely broken a sweat. "Maryam has always wanted to write something meaningful," Saif said as he took a seat. "It would be great to include some stories about the origins of all three faiths. I bet a lot of the towns-people have no idea about one another's celebrations, beyond the surface level."

"Great idea," Bruce said before turning to Maryam. "Do you think you could come up with something? Teddy's already stretched doing set design, I'm on props and costumes, and Celine is coordinating the choir."

"Help us, Maryam, you're our only hope," Celine said, doing her best Princess Leia impression, and it was that more than anything else that unfroze Maryam and made her laugh. Maybe Saif was right. Nobody knew her here; there was zero expectation; she might even be good at this.

Bismillah. "Tell me what you have so far, and I'll do my best. My friend Anna might be able to help with set design, too." Beside her, Saif gave a thumbs-up. *He's a dork*, she thought with genuine fondness. Then: *No one has ever done anything this nice for me before.*

The group quickly got to work, with Celine, Bruce, and Teddy brainstorming, and Maryam furiously taking notes. An hour flew by, then two, and she didn't even notice. Finally, Celine sat back and stretched.

"Promised I'd take my grandkids sledding, give their parents a break this afternoon," she announced. "Maryam, you're an absolute saint. I think this will be the best Holiday Hoopla yet! Meet back here tomorrow?"

Maryam looked uncertainly back at Saif, who nodded eagerly.

"She'll be here," he said.

She was buoyant on the walk back to the film set, and after

five minutes of nonstop chatter, Maryam realized she was monopolizing the conversation. But Saif only shook his head when she tried to thank him.

"You were meant to do this," he said. "I'm pretty sure writers need a whole lot of hard work and experience to back up any natural talent, but if anyone was meant to be a writer, it's you. I've never seen you smile that hard, or enjoy yourself this much, and I've known you since you were two years old."

Maryam blushed. "Maybe I've been stuck in a tiny bit of a rut," she admitted. "Maybe I've been playing it safe and worrying about what my family expects of me instead of what I want for myself. The one time I did go out on a limb and do something for myself, I got burned. Badly."

Saif looked down. "Sometimes, I wonder if we all drank the Kool-Aid." He continued when Maryam gave him a questioning look. "I know our parents put a lot of pressure on us to excel academically, but I'm starting to realize that a lot of that pressure was internal, you know? We just assumed that our parents were typical *desi* immigrant parents, and that they embodied all these stereotypes, expecting us to become doctors and whatnot."

"They did want us to become doctors," Maryam laughed. "Have you heard the way my parents boast about Saima?"

Saif shook his head. "They wanted us to do better than they did, or at least just as well. They wanted what every parent wants for their kid—to live a safe, happy life. If they saw you were happy, they would come around to everything else. Maybe we never gave our parents enough credit. They packed up and left their homes, their families, their friends, everything they knew, to move to another country and build a new life, all when they were younger than us. I'm pretty sure they could handle it if we decided to forge our own path, too. I bet they won't stop bragging when you write your first play, or movie, or maybe even your first book."

"I think you mean 'if,'" Maryam laughed, but Saif just shook his head again.

"'When,'" he said firmly. "Admit it, Maryam Aziz—there's a wild artist's heart beating beneath that puffer jacket. I'm just happy I get to see it unleashed, right in time for the Holiday Hoopla."

"That name has to go," Maryam vowed, but she was touched by Saif's words. If he thought she could write an inclusive holiday play, then maybe he was right.

Saif's dark eyes softened as they lingered on her face, and her cheeks heated, like a reticent flower unfurling under the attention of the sun.

"You can deflect and joke all you like, but"—Saif cleared his throat—"I feel as if I'm finally getting to see the real you."

Maryam waited, breath stopped in her throat, for him to continue, but he only looked at her intently, leaving her to wonder. Did he like what he saw?

He has a girlfriend, she reminded her treacherous heart. *But Farah said not to make assumptions, to seize happiness when it was offered*, another voice offered. Was that what was happening here? There was only one way to find out. *Snow day*, she thought to herself. *Take-a-chance day*. She took a deep breath.

"Can I ask you something, Saif?" she said, and didn't wait for a reply, afraid she would lose her nerve. "We . . . we're just friends. Right?" she asked, motioning between them. Maybe Snow Falls Maryam could be excused for asking the question out loud.

Saif stopped walking to look at her. He was silent for a long moment, eyes roving her face. "Is that . . . what you want?" he said finally. He looked uncertain, but then firmly said, "In that case, I'd love to be your friend. Friendship with you would be great."

Maryam tried to hide her crushed feelings behind a jaunty everything-is-fine smile. "Got it." She plowed ahead, hoping Saif hadn't noticed her flaming cheeks. That's what she got for putting herself out there.

But Saif called out to her, and when she turned back, the uncertainty had returned to his face. He shook his head, as if shaking it away, and when he spoke, his voice was low and determined. "Before this trip, if anyone had asked me about Maryam Aziz, I would have said: she's quiet and responsible, someone I've known all my life who always does as she's told."

Maryam flinched at his spot-on description. "That Maryam sounds like a ton of fun," she said dryly. "No wonder Saima calls me Bor-yam."

"Your sister has no idea," Saif said. "None of us do." He took a step toward her, and then another, until they stood so close, their breaths puffed and intermingled in the crisp air. "You're not boring or quiet. You're fire and passion hidden behind a perfect face, and you certainly don't do what you're told. If someone asked me about Maryam Aziz right now, I would tell them: I've known her my entire life, but I don't know her at all. I'd like to change that, as soon as possible."

Maryam's heart was beating so fast she thought she would

faint. Saif's eyes had darkened, and heavy flakes of snow swirled, enveloping them in a cold blanket of quiet. She looked down, shifting, the weight of the moment suddenly making her shy. "Is that what you tell all the girls?" she asked softly.

Saif shook his head, eyes never leaving her face. "Only you," he said.

ELEVEN

Anna

December 22

Anna headed out of the Turkish coffee shop toward a storefront across the street that had caught her eye: June's Cauldron. She was drawn to June's glittering window display of crystals, candles in unique glass jars, and essential oils in little brown glass bottles. Maybe she could find something in here for the *mehndi* party *and* something to help deal with the smell in her room.

Inside, Anna was immediately greeted by the scent of incense burning, and a striking woman with blue-black hair, dark lipstick, and a long violet velvet dress that swept the ground as she walked. "Come on in, warm up, have a look around! I'm June. Holler if you need me," she said in a bell-like voice before returning to the ledger she was writing in.

Anna picked up a brown glass spray bottle labeled "Energy-Cleansing Room Spray," which, according to the ingredients list, contained essence of palo santo, rosemary, clary sage, and hyssop.

"That is our strongest, most effective oil blend," said June, glancing at Anna over the rims of her reading glasses.

"You don't know what I'm dealing with here, but I'll try it," Anna said with a good-natured grimace, setting it on the counter.

"Oh, dear, some bad energy?"

"A bad *smell*," Anna said, wrinkling her nose. "Actually, what's your strongest-scented candle, too?"

June showed her the candle display, and Anna chose a pine-and-cedar blend. "Very festive," June said, nodding her approval. Anna browsed around more, finding a box of brightly colored votives and some flower garlands she knew would be perfect for the party later.

As Anna stood at the register, preparing to pay, June looked at her appraisingly for a long moment before reaching under the counter and pulling out a little bottle of perfume oil, much like the one Anna had exploded all over Maryam on the plane. It had the words "Potion #9" scrawled in curlicue writing on a white label. The purple ink matched the inky purple of June's dress.

"A gift for you, it's the last of my batch."

"What is it?"

"My exclusively formulated love potion number 9, but it's also the most divine-smelling perfume oil I have—if you're dealing with bad smells, as you said, it will help. Here." June stood and lifted Anna's hair, rubbed the oil on the back of her neck. Anna had to admit it did smell divine. "It has neroli, golden champa, cinnamon leaf . . . and a few secret ingredients," June said.

Anna tried to pay her for the potion along with everything

else, but June shook her head. "Potion number 9 can only ever be given away. Happy holidays, sweetie. Oh, and you might like the shop next door, too."

Outside, Anna did as June had suggested and headed into Kate's Kurios. Every letter was made of a different found object: teacups and saucers, candlesticks and thimbles, driftwood, netting, mosaic glass. When she pushed open the door of the shop, she saw that the chime that sounded above was made of tarnished old cutlery. Inside, Bing Crosby's voice singing the "Holiday Inn Medley" flowed from the stereo. *Happy holidays*, he crooned over and over. Anna couldn't help but smile at the familiar song.

"Hell-ooo," trilled a voice from somewhere deep within the cluttered store. "Browse around, enjoy! If you need me, just holler an approximate location—as in, 'Kate, I'm standing in front of a display of rude garden gnomes!' or 'I'm just to the left of the macramé giraffe!' And I'll come find you."

"Sounds good," Anna said, and set about the business of browsing through the crowded shelves and items stacked on the floor. As she did, Anna became certain this store had everything, from a set of iridescent glass paperweights shaped like a sweet little peacock-and-peahen couple, which she paused to admire, to cocktail glasses etched with scenes from fairy tales and fables, to boxes of postcards sent from all over the world by strangers possibly long dead who, at the time the cards were sent, only had to address them to the name of their friend or family member and then add "Snow Falls, Ontario" for the card to reach its mark. "Happy Holidays from Banff, Alberta!" "Mele Kalikimaka from Hawaii!"

There were inkwells and antique pens, a stained glass lamp

with a deep blue shade covered in comets and constellations—
and the most beautiful brass menorah Anna had ever seen. It was
shaped like a golden tree, topped with softly blushing pome-
granates, and studded with gentle green leaves. Once Anna
picked it up, she knew she wasn't going to be able to put it down
again. It reminded her of the one Beth used to light during Hanukkah. As she held it, the sadness she had been keeping at bay
returned—but it was okay, she told herself. Even if her life now
was different, and certain people were missing from it—her
dad, and now Beth—that didn't mean she couldn't rebuild in
her own way. So maybe she would buy the menorah, even if she
had been trying to tell herself something like this no longer
had any place in her life.

She turned, looking for a clear path to the cash register—
although she didn't remember seeing a cash register, or ever
making it to the front of the crowded store. Bing Crosby was
now singing about being *careful, it's my heart.* "Kate?" she called
out. "Hello? I'm"—she looked around her—"in front of the life-
sized replica of *Venus de Milo*, across from the display of vintage
brass goblins, and there's a"—she turned to her left to check
what was on her other side—"Josh Tannenbaum to my left."

"Josh Tannenbaum?" Kate called back. "I just saw Chase
Taylor walk in, I don't know about any Josh Tannenbaums . . ."

Kate rounded the corner then. She was a slender woman
with thick red-framed glasses and lime-green garage-style
coveralls with a name tag that read "Biff." "Oh, hello, Chase.
Good to see you. Guess the film crew's back in town?" She held
her finger to her lips. "I won't tell a soul, I promise."

Josh smiled that full-lipped, crinkly-eyed smile and greeted
Kate, then turned to Anna. "Hello, again," he said, his smile

widening. "Fancy meeting you here." Then he looked down and stepped closer. *Swoon. Flutter.* Her traitorous heart was at it again. "That's the most beautiful menorah I've ever seen. And you smell *great*, by the way," Josh said.

"Isn't it?" She held the menorah out to him. Josh turned it over in his hands before giving it back—his hand brushing against hers as he did and sending what felt like a shower of electrical sparks up and down her skin.

"That really makes me think of home." His eyes took on a faraway look. "My mom's latkes are to die for. She uses leeks instead of onions—but don't tell anyone, that's her secret." He winked.

"Sour cream or applesauce?" Anna asked.

"That's *my* secret," Josh said before ducking his head and whispering, "ranch dressing."

Anna gasped.

"And hot sauce."

"Scandalous! What does the rest of your family think of that?"

"I'm an only child, so the best part of the holidays for me was always my huge gang of cousins coming to stay. We'd build these huge forts in our attic, and our parents let us sleep up there. Such great memories . . ."

As he told his story, Anna marveled at how easy it was for them to talk. It felt like they'd known each other forever.

"So," he said to her. "What was *your* favorite part of celebrating Hanukkah? And how does it feel being in the most Christmassy town on the planet at this time of year?"

Anna smiled. "At my house, we had the best of both worlds.

Latkes *and* chocolate cakes shaped like Yule logs. Brisket *and* turkey. Rugelach *and* Christmas cookies. I'm an only child, too, by the way. One year, I insisted on both a Christmas tree and a Hanukkah bush—so my dad and I found the last garden center with any bushes left, and we put a potted bush in the middle of our living room." Josh laughed. "It just felt so special. Like anything was possible. It was the best time of year. I miss it," she admitted. "It's especially poignant this year with Christmas and Hanukkah falling at the same time. That's why I was buying this. I saw it, and it reminded me of old times."

"Haven't been home for a while?"

Anna had been looking down at the menorah but now she looked up at him. "Home doesn't really exist anymore. My dad passed away a couple years ago and everything changed after that." She suddenly felt stricken. It had just been a few sentences and yet she'd unloaded a lot. She couldn't look up at him. "Apologies for the overshare."

"It's not oversharing—I asked. And . . . Well, I know it's not the same, but my zayde died last year. We were really close. It's been hard. So, I'm sorry for your loss, Anna. I really am. I don't like to see you looking so sad."

"Thanks," she said, trying to smile so he wouldn't feel sorry for her. "That must make it even harder for you, that you aren't home for the holidays this year when your family has lost someone."

"My mom wouldn't dream of me missing work for anything, and never makes me feel guilty. But—" He stopped talking and swallowed hard. All at once she wanted to reach out to him, offer an embrace, a shoulder to cry on—except he wasn't really

Josh Tannenbaum, not in the real world. He was the movie star Chase Taylor, and one could not just randomly hug Chase Taylor. Still, Anna reached forward and touched his arm.

"Josh," she said in a low voice, "it's hard to lose anyone. And firsts are always painful. Like the first Hanukkah, which you're going through now. Don't be hard on yourself. It's okay to feel what you're feeling. My dad always used to say, *A day of sorrow is longer than a month of joy.* And it's true, right? It's okay to let yourself feel it."

He nodded. "As usual, you are correct, Yoda."

"I told you, I'm not the wise one, my dad was."

He didn't say anything, just looked at her intently—as she felt her cheeks start to grow warm under his gaze. "I guess I was hoping working through it would make it go away, you know? But it's still there."

She nodded. "Always. Like you're carrying around . . ."

He finished the sentence for her. "Rocks in your chest." He pointed to the base of his sternum. "Right here."

It was a sad topic, but she still laughed with surprise. "Exactly! Right there. But maybe that's okay, you know? If you had a fantastic zayde, then it's going to hurt. That's what I tell myself. My dad was the best, too. I know I wouldn't miss him so much if he hadn't been so wonderful. That's a gift, as painful as it is." It was the first time Anna had been able to speak about her father like this to anyone. Josh held her gaze, and she suddenly felt like he was holding her, too—holding, for just a moment, the grief she had been carrying alone for so long. She couldn't help but wonder what it would feel like to be in his arms again, the way she'd been the night they'd met, when he had held her close and carried her through the snow.

"Anna, there's something I want to talk to you about," Josh began. But just then, a cuckoo clock behind them began its demented chirp and he stepped back. "We're late," he said. "You're coming to set, right?"

"Definitely," Anna said. "But I'd better pay for this first . . ." She looked around, searching for a clear path out of there.

"Kate!" Josh shouted. "We're still in front of the *Venus de Milo*, to the left of the grandfather clock and in front of the brass goblins and . . ." His brow furrowed. "Are those . . . pewter statuettes of NSYNC?"

"They most certainly are! But they're on hold for someone. Take the menorah with you, though! It's yours. Holiday gift from me. Except—" Kate popped her head out from behind the *Venus de Milo*, her hair inexplicably covered in red and green and white feathers, some of which were still raining down around her from some unseen source. "There's one condition. You can't just let it sit. That is a menorah that's meant to be lit—so make good use of it. Better yet, light it together. Happy holidays!" She produced a brown paper bag and some blue and silver tissue paper as if from out of nowhere, tucked the menorah inside, nestled it in the tissue paper. "Oh, and you'll need these." She rummaged around on a shelf and unearthed a box of candles for the menorah. "There you are, all set," she said, and sent them on their way.

"You know," Anna said as they walked together through the falling snow, "that's the third gift I've been given since I got here."

"That's right. Sam and Hope at Don't Sweater It gave you that toque—and it looks very cute on you," Josh said, winking at her before lifting the hood of his parka to protect himself from the still falling snow. "I'm jealous. Think I'd look good in two pom-poms?"

"I think you'd look good in anything," Anna said, then felt mortified that she'd actually said that.

"You said three gifts," he prompted. "The menorah and candles, the hat, and what else?"

"Oh—er, some perfume," Anna said, not about to tell him she was wearing a love potion.

"I noticed that earlier," he said. "I really like it."

"Thanks," Anna said, feeling the blush that had started earlier intensify.

"Hey, Anna?" They had almost reached the set, and they stopped walking now. He appeared thoughtful, like he wasn't quite sure how to say what was on his mind. He just shook his head, and the moment passed. "You're headed over there," he said, pointing to the extras tent. He paused again and swallowed a few times. "So, uh . . . when I get back to the inn this evening, maybe we can light the menorah together? I shouldn't be too long after sundown. And it's the first night of Hanukkah, after all."

Anna felt a rush of happiness, unbidden. She tried to remind herself of the rumors about Josh and Tenisha being a couple. But it was no use; her heart had taken over. As her dad used to say, quoting Descartes, *The heart has its reasons, of which reason knows nothing.* "We probably should, right? We did promise Kate."

He grinned. "A promise is a promise. If you give me your room number, I'll leave a message for you when I get back."

"I'm in room 207."

"Ah, the work-in-progress zone."

"Yes," she said, punching him playfully on the shoulder. "They save the nice rooms for the movie stars."

He laughed. "What can I say? There are a few perks that go with the job. I'll see you tonight, Anna."

"See you tonight, Josh."

As Anna hustled over to join the small crowd of extras, she noted that Maryam and Saif were nowhere to be found.

"I told Maryam to take him on a little walk around the town," Saima explained, waggling her eyebrows. "It might give them some time to get to know each other better."

"I thought they were family friends and have known each other since childhood," Anna said, glancing around. Mr. Dadu was deep in conversation with Katrina Wakes, the film's director. Josh had been whisked off to hair and makeup. Anna tried not to wonder if Tenisha was with him.

Beside her, Saima snorted. "My sister has always been so shy around Saif. It's like she lost the ability to talk around him! I don't know what changed, but she seems to just not care what he thinks anymore. And now *he* can't take his eyes off *her*."

"I noticed that, too," Anna said as a PA with a clipboard approached.

"Looks like we're up. This is so exciting!" Saima said. "Dadu, come on!"

In the few minutes they had left him alone, he had somehow changed into a loud Christmas sweater with a giant embroidered Rudolph, complete with blinking red lightbulb nose.

"I'm staying right where I am. Miss Wakes has kindly asked for my help in perking up the romantic tension between

Mr. Chase and Miss Tenisha. I have suggested inserting a few musical numbers and perhaps a costume change or two. Nothing like dancing to make the love flow faster, *nah*?"

"Your grandfather has a lot of good advice for us," Katrina said with a smile. "I can't believe he directed over a hundred films in Mumbai. He's a living legend! I'm sure he's going to help us amp up the chemistry between our stars."

Anna's heart felt like it was doing a confusing, Bollywood-esque dance at the mention of Chase and Tenisha. Did it mean anything that the romantic tension between them seemed to be lacking?

"Let's go," Saima said, pulling Anna the way the casting director was beckoning. "Take Dadu's advice and don't let your mind pull you in a million directions—just have *fun*!"

The hours on set flew by. Anna mostly only saw Josh from a distance because the scenes she was in were B-roll that would be added in during editing, but a few times, he waved and smiled from across the set, and she tried to tell herself the warmth in her cheeks was just from the hot apple cider or hot chocolate she had in her hands at the time. She found herself fascinated by the intricacies of the set design—how real everything felt, but also the way each object on set was essentially an artifact from a story. She busied herself tallying the items she planned to source for the *mehndi* party, and was excited to share her plans with Maryam.

Before Anna knew it, it was time to head back to the inn. Maryam and Saif were hovering on the edge of the film set, and she couldn't help but notice they seemed to be standing closer to each other, and had a more intimate aura about them. She wondered what they had gotten up to in the past few hours. Catching her eye, Maryam beckoned her close.

"Are you still up for helping with Saima's *mehndi* party tonight?" she asked, keeping her voice low. "I managed to find some things in town, and I even found a few tubes of henna paste. I thought maybe you could think of a few ideas for the decor?"

"I'm totally in," Anna said, and Maryam beamed. "I found some cute decorations in town, too, and a few other things I know you'll be pleased about."

"Let's get Dadu and Saima and we can head back to the inn, and then you can tell me all about it," Maryam said.

As they walked through the set, Anna looked around for Josh, to say goodbye—and found him with Tenisha, sharing an intimate moment, cameras rolling. Mr. Dadu was standing close by. "Maintain eye contact, you two!" he exclaimed.

"Come on, Dadu, this has been a long enough day for you. Why don't we head back now?" Maryam said.

"Oh, yes, absolutely. I am exhausted. But they are having me back tomorrow. So I have to get my rest! Ah, there's Saima."

She was heading toward them, and she was hard to miss because she was now wearing an electric green Christmas sweater emblazoned with all eight reindeer and a giant red sleigh.

"What do you think? Just my style?" She twirled in the snow and curtsied, and they all laughed. But then Saima lifted her face to the falling snowflakes and let out a desolate sigh. "This snow is never going to let up, is it? We might be stuck here all winter. If only I had a reindeer and sleigh to carry us away."

"Oh, *beti*, I am sure we will not be stuck here *all* winter," Mr. Dadu offered as they set off for the inn—but Anna could only imagine how frustrated Saima was feeling. Today was supposed to be her *mehndi*. Anna felt like she could stay in Snow Falls forever because she and Nick weren't speaking—there'd been no messages for her from Nick when she checked with Deb and Kath—and Anna no longer had any holiday plans. But Saima was another story.

"Come on, let's hurry," Maryam said. "*Iftar* is in an hour, and we have a surprise for you that might cheer you up."

Saima perked up at this. "Oooh, what surprise?"

"You'll see," Maryam said mysteriously as they approached the front door of the inn. "Be at the foyer at eight p.m. . . . and wear your green *lengha*."

Saima shrieked. "Are you throwing me a *mehndi* party?!"

Maryam shrugged, but her sister ran up the stairs of the inn, radiating excitement.

"Saima has always loved parties," Maryam said.

"Especially when *she* is the center of attention," Saif added, and winked. "See you two later—and have fun tonight, ladies."

Anna watched as the handsome Saif murmured a quiet goodbye in Maryam's ear and walked away.

"Sooooo . . . what's going on there?" Anna asked.

She was sure Maryam was blushing as she said, "We had a really nice time together. We talked a lot and I think . . ." She looked up at Maryam—but instead of happiness, Maryam looked afraid.

"And you look absolutely terrified because?"

Now Maryam's expression changed even more, as if a door were swinging shut. "It's complicated" was all she said. "Now, we have a lot of work to do. You're sure it's okay I'm throwing this on you last minute?"

Anna waved her words away. "Of course. I love decorating. It's my thing!"

"Even with very little to work with?"

"Especially that! My favorite kind of decorating—it's the most rewarding. Besides, I have lots to work with! Now, if you'll excuse me, I have party decor to set up, and I can't wait."

*W*hen Anna was on set that day, she had found out the producers stored extra textiles and furniture from the film in various places around town—including in the basement of the inn. Unbeknownst to Maryam, she had managed to clear it with sets and staging to borrow a few pieces for the party. She was going with a maharani theme—which she hoped Maryam wouldn't think was too on-the-nose for an Indian wedding, but had a feeling Saima would be thrilled about.

After an *iftar* of leftovers, which Anna was invited to join—Maryam and Saif really had ordered way too much food yesterday—everyone retired to their rooms to prepare for the henna party. The men had decided to make themselves scarce, Maryam explained to Anna, and planned to attend the late-night *taraweeh* prayers at the tiny Topkapi Café and mosque, while the ladies-only *mehndi* took place in the lobby.

When Maryam made her way downstairs, she gasped at the transformation Anna had performed in only a few short hours. "How did you *do* this?"

Anna beamed proudly. She had managed to source half a dozen large screen dividers to section off the open space and provide the women with some privacy for the party. And then she had transformed the sectioned-off space. Luxurious fabric in bright colors was laid on the ground, and the room dividers had been decorated with bright saris, which Anna had borrowed from Maryam's mother and some of the other older ladies from town. She had folded them in pleats, and they hung like streamers. Anna had even cobbled together a small raised platform using various construction materials she found around the inn, creating a place of honor for Saima to sit with colorful decorative pillows and silk flowers. Deb and Kath had also provided candles and strings of holiday lights—Anna tried not to look shocked that even after stringing every available surface with them, indoors and out, Deb and Kath still seemed to have more holiday lights available—and this completed the look.

Soft sitar instrumental music played in the background, and silver trays were heaped with finger foods (Deb and Kath had insisted on taking on the food): cocktail samosas, finger sandwiches, tea in the pretty glass cups they had borrowed from the Turkish café, a decadent chocolate Yule log Kath had baked, with "Merry Mehndi!" piped across the length in brilliant red and green frosting.

Maryam could barely believe her eyes. "This is too much!" she said, looking around. "I can't believe how fast you put this together. Anna, you're a miracle worker!"

Anna ducked her head, shy at the praise. "I thought if it was private, you could take off your hijab and let your hair down without worrying about anybody disturbing us," she said, motioning at the dividers. "Deb and Kath promised no one would bother us for a few hours. I invited Sarah from the café, as well as Muriel from the Hakka restaurant. I hope you don't mind."

Anna was surprised to see Maryam's eyes welling up with tears. "I'm so touched by this," she said, her voice thick with emotion. "All the little details . . . it's just perfect."

"I honestly loved it so much. I adore doing stuff like this."

"Well, you're good at it! You should do this for a living. Oh, speaking of which . . . before I forget—" Maryam subtly wiped the tears at the corners of her eyes and smiled. "Saif talked me into helping out with the holiday pageant earlier. They needed a writer and they weren't too picky about lack of experience. I'm helping to organize the Holiday Hoopla, the annual town pageant. Seeing how great you are at all this, do you think you'd like to help out with set design? I think you have a natural talent for it," Maryam said, gesturing around her. She loosened her hijab and shook out her hair.

"That sounds like *so* much fun," Anna said, feeling a surge of excitement. Having more to do would make it a lot easier not to focus on her worries—and possibly distract her from checking, yet again, to see if Nick had tried to reach her. She was upset with him, but the cold way he had cut off their phone call and his lack of regard for her predicament still stung. Being on set all day, then setting up for the *mehndi* party, had been a nice diversion—and now she would have another rewarding task to occupy her time. A high-pitched squeal announced Saima's arrival. Dressed in the elegant pale green *lengha* she had packed for the now canceled *mehndi* in Toronto, she bounded directly into Anna's arms.

"You're officially an Aziz sister, now!" Saima exclaimed, looking around. "I can't believe you did all this for me!"

Now it was Anna's turn to be overcome by emotion. She buried her head in Saima's shoulder for a moment so no one would see her sudden tears, which she blinked away, fast. Weddings—and the holidays—really were all about family, and Anna had been feeling like she had none. But now a burst of warmth filled her. When she was released from Saima's embrace, Maryam even gave her a slightly awkward, one-armed hug.

"Truly, thank you," she whispered, and Anna nodded.

"My pleasure," she said—and she meant it.

Anna had never had henna applied, so Maryam set to work with one of the plastic cones from the Sri Lankan grocer. She carefully drew a large mandala design on the back of Anna's hand, with delicate paisley and flower patterns brushed within. Anna watched her work, wondering at her easy talent.

"It tickles, and I didn't realize henna would feel so cold," she said.

"Women use henna as an adornment, but it's also a way to cool the body during hot weather," Maryam explained, keeping her hand steady as she worked the henna applicator. "It's basically just crushed henna leaves, ground into a paste. After the henna dries and flakes off, it will leave a beautiful dark red dye on your hands that usually lasts a couple weeks."

The rest of the wedding party started to trickle in, and everyone admired Maryam's handiwork. Farah settled to work on Saima's *mehndi* design—Maryam explained she had always been the best among them at applying henna, with the steadiest hand. Around them, the older women chatted, nibbling on samosas and enjoying the light tea. Anna felt the warmth inside her increase. This really had all come together so well.

She watched as Maryam applied henna on Sarah, the woman who owned the Turkish coffee shop, and then listened as Maryam's mother sang a traditional Urdu song.

"The lyrics are full of jokes teasing the bride, and making fun of her future in-laws," Maryam explained, and Anna wished she could understand. A few other women joined in with the well-known folk songs, while other women clapped along to the beat and laughed.

"Oh, hey, I have more music!" Anna said once the singing was over. "Borrowed from Mr. Dadu!" She popped a Bollywood mix CD into the stereo and pulled Maryam up to dance to the first song, "Mehndi Hai Rachne Wali."

When the next song—a fast-paced *bhangra* tune—started, all the women rose at once and started to dance, even Maryam's mother. They pulled Saima to the middle of the space and moved to the beat around her, careful not to smear her henna, which was mostly dry by now. Anna made Maryam laugh, dancing her funny one-foot hop despite the lessons from the night before. She eventually gave up, shimmying her hips and tossing her hair instead. The next half dozen songs passed by in a blur of laughter, dancing, breaks to drink tea, followed by more dancing. After nearly an hour, the group collapsed in a heap, sprawling on the comfortable carpet or across cushions.

"How long have you known your fiancé? What's his name again?" Anna asked, trying to catch her breath as she lay on the carpet in front of the platform where Saima sat in happy exhaustion. Maryam sat beside her, leaning against her sister. Her hair spilled over her shoulders, and her cheeks were pink from dancing, and from happiness.

"His name is Miraj, and I've known him for just a few months," Saima said. "I knew he was the one from the moment I saw him, though."

Anna suddenly thought of Nick, and her heart plummeted.

She sat up, fanning herself. "You've only known Miraj for a few months and you're already getting *married*?" she asked, incredulous.

Saima laughed, but Anna noticed Maryam look away. "We're observant Muslims," Saima explained. "We don't date for years before moving in together. We jump straight into marriage."

"But . . . what if you're making a mistake?" Anna asked.

Saima shrugged. "Sometimes people get it wrong. Or they're happy for a while, but not happy forever."

Anna looked at Maryam, but she was still gazing at the floor.

"I love Miraj," Saima continued to Anna, not seeming to notice her sister's suddenly morose expression. "I think we'll be really happy together. But if it doesn't work out, we'll just get divorced, and the world will keep turning." Then, as if realizing what she had just said, Saima clapped a hand over her mouth. Beside them, Azizah had grown still, and a sudden embarrassed silence descended.

"Saima, we don't talk of such things in front of guests," Azizah said stiffly.

Anna was mystified, and beside her Maryam, looking more uncomfortable than ever, reached for her hijab. She carefully wrapped it, avoiding Anna's frankly curious stare, and slipped beyond the dividers to the main foyer.

"Excuse me," Anna said, following her friend.

Outside, there was so much snow. The sheer amount of powdery precipitation heaped around the inn felt overwhelming, even in the dark quiet. Maybe Saima was right and they would be stuck here all winter, Anna ruminated. She had truly never seen so much snow, and it was still falling. But the air was crisp, and the cold felt good after the delirious heat from dancing. Anna inhaled deeply and looked around in the darkness before spotting Maryam, leaning against the rough brick wall of the inn.

"I'm sorry if I sounded judgmental about your marriage customs," she started, but Maryam shook her head.

"It's not that. That had nothing to do with you. I'm just . . ." She shook her head again. "I'm sure it feels sort of strange to you, the idea of marrying someone so quickly. Before you know who they really are, or who you are together."

"It's not what I'm used to," Anna said. "But I also think it's quite hopeful. It takes a lot of courage to take that sort of plunge. I admire the faith Saima has that things will work out. I don't have that. It's partly why I was so unsure about Nick. I just didn't feel sure I could take a chance. I still don't. But maybe, with the right person . . ." Suddenly, Josh's image was in her mind. She had been trying not to think of him all night, to get her feelings in perspective, to not glance at the door to the inn every time it opened, hoping it was him. It was getting late and he hadn't shown up. For all she knew, he was somewhere with Tenisha—and had forgotten all about his suggestion that they light the menorah together. And that was fine, she told herself, turning back to Maryam.

As if reading her thoughts, Maryam cleared her throat. "Listen, about Josh," she began. She looked lost in thought for a moment, but then her expression cleared. "Just be careful, okay? I know what I'm talking about."

"Is that why you looked so upset earlier?" Anna asked. "It seems like something Saima said about marriage struck a chord. What's going on, Maryam?"

Her friend sighed. "I know you wish you had a big family like I do, but sometimes, having a sister like Saima isn't always easy. I love her with all my heart, but she has a habit of sticking her foot in her mouth, especially when she's excited. She brought up something from my past I don't like to talk about— it only makes everyone uncomfortable and ruins the mood."

Anna wanted to push Maryam, but she could tell this was a topic Maryam really didn't want to revisit. "I'm sorry you've had difficulty in your past," was all Anna said. "And I'm here to talk if you ever need to."

"Thanks," Maryam said. "Maybe sometime."

In the silence of the night, Anna couldn't help but feel like she was waiting—and she knew exactly who she was waiting for. Despite Maryam's words of warning, she was looking into the dark, snowy night, willing Josh to appear and keep his promise of lighting the menorah with her. But the sidewalk stayed empty, and she and Maryam stood there staring into the darkness, together but alone with their thoughts.

The door to the inn opened, startling them both.

"Saima, I'm fine, I'll be right in," Maryam said.

But it wasn't Saima; it was Kath. "There you are, Anna. I thought I saw you head out here. I have a call for you. Someone who says his name is Josh?"

Anna blushed as Maryam caught her eye. "I'll be right there," she said to Kath, then turned to her friend. "You're sure you're okay?"

"I'm really fine," Maryam assured her—but Anna could tell that wasn't quite true. She put her hand on Maryam's arm.

"I meant it. I'm always here to talk. Anytime. Okay?"

"You, too," Maryam said, shooting her a meaningful look as she headed inside to take the call.

"Hey, Anna," came Josh's deep voice on the phone line. "Hope you don't mind I used my code name. The one only you and your friends know."

"You mean your *real* name." Anna tried to keep her tone light, even though the sound of his voice—and the fact that he had called her—was causing those now familiar flutters he always seemed to provoke. *Be careful*, Maryam had warned her. But where Josh was concerned, Anna was having a difficult time keeping a level head.

"I'm calling to apologize," he said. "I stood you up for lighting the menorah tonight—sorry, hang on a second." She heard some muffled voices, then he returned. "And I'm afraid I'm not going to be back for a few more hours. Rain check? Or should I say, snow check?"

"Sure, of course," Anna said. "It was a busy night around here anyway. I hardly even noticed." This was *almost* true.

A pause, and then he said, "Well, *I* noticed. I was really hoping I'd get out of here on time so we could spend time together. But there's always tomorrow. Good night, Anna."

"Good night, Josh."

Anna was smiling as she hung up the phone and returned to the sitting area—but then she saw Maryam's grim expression. She was trying to keep it to herself, but Anna was observant enough to tell her friend had once had her heart seriously broken. Maryam's somber eyes should be a reminder to stay grounded and realistic, Anna told herself. The problem was, her heart didn't want to listen to reason. It took just a few seconds for the dreamy smile to return to Anna's face as she drifted around the room, cleaning up after the party—still hearing Josh's voice in her mind, telling her they always had tomorrow.

TWELVE

Maryam

December 23

2 days until Christmas
The 2nd night of Hanukkah
The 28th day of Ramadan

Maryam waited for Anna and Dadu downstairs the next morning; they had made plans to walk into town together. She was early—restlessness had pushed her out of bed an hour after falling asleep following *suhoor*—and now she paced inside the small recessed alcove-slash-cloakroom beside the main entrance, her mind racing.

It was silly to feel hurt, but Maryam couldn't help it. She had organized Saima's *mehndi* party—with Anna's help—and how had her sister reacted? By declaring Anna an Aziz sister and humiliating her actual sister. As usual, Maryam had said nothing. Why had she kept silent? Maybe for the same reason she had remained silent after Saif's confession outside the playhouse yesterday: because she was afraid. She had been too hurt to confront Saima, and she had been terrified to respond to

Saif's confession. *Only you*, he had said, and the words had thrilled her at first. Until overthinking had set in. Because his words weren't true, not for either of them.

According to her parents, Saif had a girlfriend, even though he hadn't mentioned her at all. She should just ask him; he would tell her the truth. But a part of her didn't want to know the truth because then she'd have to do something about it. Her heart had been battered badly once, and she wasn't sure she was ready to take a chance again with someone new, even if that person was Saif.

Maryam was so lost in these thoughts, she almost didn't notice Josh and Tenisha walking toward the front door. She was about to step out and greet them with a smile, when something made her pause. They were an attractive couple; Tenisha's warm brown skin glowed beneath the soft lights of the inn, her elegance matched by Josh's more casual charm. Their heads were close together, bodies angled close. Her eyes widened as she realized they were holding hands. The actors walked straight past Maryam without stopping, and she caught a blinding flash just as the main door shut behind them, as if someone had been waiting to snap a photograph.

Maryam emerged from the alcove to find Anna waiting for her by the fireplace; she must have just arrived, and missed Josh and Tenisha's dramatic exit by a minute.

"How are you doing this morning? Still tired from last night?" Anna asked.

"It was a late night, and we were up early for *suhoor*," Maryam said, debating how to bring up what she had just witnessed. "Are you disappointed Josh didn't show up last night?" she asked.

Anna shrugged. "He had to keep filming, and the day ran long. It was nice of him to call and let me know."

Maryam didn't respond; then, unable to keep what she had seen to herself, blurted: "Actually, you just missed Josh. With Tenisha. They just walked past me, but I think they were in a hurry or something. They were holding hands. Someone snapped a picture of them as they left the inn together," she finished. "I'm so sorry."

"Oh. Wow. Well, I heard Snow Falls has their very own paparazzo," Anna said faintly. Then, catching Maryam's eye, she smiled. "It's fine. They're rumored to be in a relationship. We knew that already, right?"

"Right," Maryam echoed, still worried. "You know what? I think helping the Holiday Hoopla will be a good distraction. For both of us," she said.

"Will Saif be joining us today?" Anna asked, attempting to change the subject with a smile, but Maryam only shook her head. Thankfully, Anna didn't push for more information. If Saima had been here, she would have demanded to know every detail, and then forced Maryam to hear her judgment. Maryam was grateful for this time to sit with her thoughts and figure out what she wanted to do, without anyone else's input.

Once Dadu joined the women in the lobby, they made their way into town together, separating once they had reached Main Street—Anna and Maryam to the playhouse to help with the Holiday Hoopla, Dadu to the film set. They agreed to meet in the late afternoon to walk back to the inn together.

They arrived at the theater, and Maryam felt a leap of excitement as she pulled open the door. Inside this old brick building, with the fading carpet and cast photos on the walls, she wasn't Bor-yam, dull older sister, dutiful daughter, and nerdy pharmacist. She could be something else, someone more: a writer of stories, a spinner of tales. Saif had seen that in her. He had listened to her confession on the plane and then helped her take a chance on an old dream. Maybe she was being foolish, not jumping on the rest of the dream he had offered. Yet when she thought about beginning a relationship with Saif, her heart flooded with panic, not joy.

This is not the time, she thought, and forced herself to focus on the job at hand. If there was one thing Maryam Aziz was good at, it was pushing her emotions to the bottom of her to-do list.

Inside, dozens of people milled around, Celine presiding over the organized chaos. Beside her, a woman in a fluffy white sweater and flared jeans sorted costumes into piles while an adorable blond-haired boy helped. Celine introduced her family—her daughter Hannah and grandson Shane—before waving Anna toward the stage, where a small crew were being lectured by a steely-eyed Teddy in full-on general mode.

"Don't let his bark scare you," Celine cautioned. "He really does live up to his name. Maryam can introduce you before she gets to work. We've set up a desk in a quiet corner backstage so you can start on that play," she said, nodding at Maryam. "Where's your handsome fella today?" When Maryam shrugged, Celine smirked. "I'm sure he'll be along shortly. Couldn't keep his eyes off you yesterday, that one."

Trying not to blush, Maryam led Anna to the stage and introduced her to Teddy, who welcomed Anna warmly.

"Always happy to have another designer on hand," Teddy

said. "These young ones can't tell a jacquard silk from a linen blend. Have you done any set design in the past?"

"She's a natural," Maryam assured Teddy. Anna seemed slightly overwhelmed by the chaos, but based on the miracle she had worked at Saima's *mehndi* last night with just a few room dividers, borrowed textiles, and cushions, she would be a welcome addition at the playhouse.

Backstage was quiet, with only a few people wandering through the halls in search of supplies. The desk set up for her looked like it had been scavenged from the local school, complete with squeaky drawers that still held scrap paper and chewing gum. Maryam took a seat on the metal folding chair and looked over the outline Celine had put together, her notes neatly handwritten on lined paper. There wasn't much, which meant Maryam would have total creative freedom. She had spent a few hours last night, when she couldn't fall asleep, thinking up ideas for the play, and as she gripped her ballpoint pen, she felt the unfamiliar rush of focusing on a creative task. It had been so long, but as she shook off the cobwebs, she felt a glowing ember of happiness ignite in her chest, and she bent her head over the paper. Before she knew it, the morning had flown by. She couldn't remember the last time she had felt this energized by work. Except this wasn't work—it was a brief break from reality.

Someone tugged on her sleeve, and she looked away from her notes, to meet the inquisitive gaze of Celine's grandson, who looked to be about four years old. He shyly pointed to her papers.

"What's that?" Shane asked.

"I'm writing a play for the Holiday Hoopla," she said. "Would you like to hear what I've come up with so far?"

Shane nodded soberly, sticking a finger in his mouth. Maryam set up a folding chair for him, then went through her plans, explaining them as if he were a colleague with the power to weigh in, and not a four-year-old with a limited attention span. Shane listened to her ideas and, after she was done, removed his finger from his mouth to chime in. "I like Christmas songs. My favorite is 'Rudolph the Red-Nosed Reindeer.' What's your favorite?"

"Definitely 'Silent Night,'" Maryam said gravely.

Shane nodded. "Will Santa Claus be at the Howl-iday Hope-la?" he asked, the mispronunciation making her smile. "And Mrs. Claus? She'll be sad if she's not invited," he added.

"Santa wouldn't miss it for the world," Maryam assured him, making a mental note to ask about the availability of a local Mr. and Mrs. Claus.

"There you are, you little scamp," Celine said, sticking her head around the corner. "This one took off the minute his mom mentioned nap time. I hope Shane was behaving himself?"

"Shane is a vital member of the team," Maryam assured the older woman. "He thinks my ideas show great promise."

The young man in question ran off without so much as a backward glance, eliciting a fond chuckle from his grandmother. "My daughter and son-in-law took their time giving me grandchildren," she confided. "One of life's great blessings, now that they're finally here. But they sure are exhausting. Do you have kids?"

Maryam shook her head. "Not yet," she said.

"I bet that Saif fella would make a wonderful father," Celine said.

"You're as bad as the aunties back home, with their match-making," Maryam teased.

"Plenty of auntie types in Snow Falls, too, and I'm proud to be among their number. I couldn't help but notice you seem a bit down today. Is everything all right?" Celine said. Maryam was surprised to find herself wanting to confide about her bewildering feelings for Saif.

"Saif isn't my 'fella,'" Maryam started. "He's a family friend. Someone I've known my entire life—and someone I've had a crush on for more years than I'd like to admit. Yesterday, after he brought me here, he said that he'd like to get to know me better. And I didn't know how to answer him."

"That scared you, I take it?" Celine asked.

"I might have changed the subject and avoided him since," Maryam admitted.

Celine huffed out a laugh. "I'm old enough to know that even when people say they want advice, what they really want is absolution for their mistakes. So here it is: you're allowed to react however you like. But take it from someone who's been there, done that, and had to live with the consequences—letting the ghosts from your past haunt your present is a recipe for disaster. Don't you remember what those spirits did to old Scrooge?"

Maryam laughed at that. "I'm no Scrooge," she assured the older woman.

Celine patted Maryam's arm. "I know you're not, dear. In fact, I suspect you might be the opposite. Unlike old Ebenezer,

I think you wear your heart entirely on your sleeve, and you've had it lacerated a time or two, which makes one wary. A good strategy, that, if you want to keep your heart safe. But I've found the key to happiness is to figure out who will cherish your heart, not trample it. Keep that person close." Celine straightened. "Enough philosophizing. I actually came by to insist you stop for the day. I know you're fasting, but I think your friend Anna could use a snack. You're both welcome to come back tomorrow, but no more work today."

Summarily dismissed, Maryam bent to gather her papers, then paused. She had always enjoyed "A Christmas Carol" as a child, but Celine's comment had shaken something loose in her subconscious, and she lunged for her pen and started writing. A few minutes later, she had the beginnings of an idea, one that would lend itself well to including the three faiths in the Holiday Hoopla. She couldn't help thinking that Saif would be the perfect person to play a major role in her play. Pleased with her progress, she made her way to Anna, who was deep in conversation with Teddy and Bruce, who sported another brightly colored scarf knotted around his neck.

"I'm thrilled we didn't scare you off yesterday," Bruce boomed. "Where have you been hiding this treasure? Anna, you were made to work for the stage, my lady."

Anna blushed and thanked the men before following Maryam outside. Anna looked sheepish. "Would it be okay if we stopped by Main Street for something to eat?" she asked. "I didn't really feel up to breakfast this morning. I know I shouldn't complain, since you haven't eaten since dawn, but I'm really hungry. Only if it won't bother you."

"Watching you eat won't bother me at all," Maryam said. "In fact, I insist on it. That way you can tell me what's good, and I can bring it back to share for *iftar*."

"Maybe we should clear it with the group first, or you'll end up with leftovers for another two days," Anna joked, linking arms with Maryam.

On Main Street, Anna ordered a pastrami on rye bread with extra pickles and hot mustard from the deli. She sipped her cherry cola as they sat outside on a bench. It was cold, but not freezing, the snow finally tapered off, the sun warm on their faces while Anna ate and Maryam kept up a stream of light chatter.

Once Anna was done, Maryam stood up, stretching. "I should go check on Dadu at the set," she said casually. "Come with me?"

Anna got a funny look on her face. "Actually, I'm feeling pretty tired. I'm going to head back to the inn. See you later!" Without waiting for Maryam to respond, Anna took off, walking as fast as her oversized boots would allow through the foot-high snow. Josh had some explaining to do, Maryam thought as she turned in the direction of the filming.

On set, she found her grandfather perched on his own folding chair beside the director, chatting while sipping a steaming-hot tea from a cup and saucer. Maryam wondered at Dadu's ability to make himself at home anywhere, even on the set of a holiday rom-com. Her smile vanished when she recognized the tall form hovering by her grandfather's elbow. What was Saif doing here? He looked up and met Maryam's gaze. Tentatively, he raised a hand in greeting, which she returned.

"Having fun?" she called out. Dadu turned in his seat, slopping tea onto the saucer.

"I was sharing stories working with the Bollywood greats, like Amitabh Bachchan, his lovely wife, Jaya Bachchan, and of course Shah Rukh Khan," Dadu explained eagerly.

Maryam smiled at Katrina, who this morning wore oversized pink fuzzy earmuffs. "Dadu has plenty of war stories from his trenches in the Bollywood machine," she joked, but her grandfather shook his head.

"I miss that life, but my place is in Denver, with my family," he said, smile never wavering. "You should go back to the inn, *beta*, and take Saif with you. He has been hanging around for my sake only."

"I think it's time we all headed back," Maryam suggested. "I could use a nap, and Mom and Dad will be upset if I return without you." She included Saif with a nod; no doubt he had been roped into keeping her grandfather company.

With some reluctance, Dadu agreed. "Could you pick up my bag? I left it in Josh's trailer, behind craft services."

Saif accompanied Maryam to the trailer, and an awkward silence descended as they walked. "Thanks for keeping Dadu company. He has a tendency to throw himself into things," she said, and Saif nodded.

"Your dadu is my dadu," he said, smiling. "I was so sad to hear your dadi passed away a few years ago."

Maryam kept her eyes on her feet. Even now, whenever she thought about her dadi-ma, she had to blink back tears. Her grandmother's death hadn't been sudden, but there also hadn't been a lot of time between her diagnosis and palliative care. Three years later, it still felt like a fresh, open wound for the whole family. "I still miss her," she admitted. "I think about her all the time, but especially in December. She loved Christmas, loved having everyone at home together." Maryam laughed. "Actually, I think she just loved my gingerbread cookies."

Saif gently bumped her shoulders. "I bet my chocolate cookies could take your gingerbread anytime."

Maryam's eyes met his. "Bring it, Saif Rasool."

"Gladly, Ms. Aziz."

Not for the first time, Maryam marveled at the ease of their banter, their effortless chemistry. If only she hadn't been so shy around Saif when she was younger. Maybe things would have been different, for both of them. On impulse, she turned to Saif and filled him in on her epiphany at the playhouse. His eyes lit up when she explained her idea to use "A Christmas Carol" to celebrate the tri-holidays.

"You never got a chance to make your film debut because you were helping me," Maryam said shyly. "But you do know that serious actors consider the stage superior to the screen?"

"I had no idea you were such an acting expert," Saif teased. "And here I thought your talents were limited to writing. Do you have an in with the production team?"

Maryam laughed. He was such a dork. "Let's just say that when it comes to the Holiday Hoopla, all casting decisions go through me. I was wondering if you'd consider playing the Ramadan Host—instead of Christmas Ghost, get it? As a favor to me," she added, in case he thought she was offering the part out of guilt.

But Saif seemed flattered at her request, and his delighted smile warmed her. "I'd like nothing better."

———————

There was only one trailer behind craft services, "Chase Taylor" printed on a card above the aluminum door. Saif brushed off the snow on the steps before gesturing for Maryam to climb ahead. She grasped the door handle and entered the trailer.

Inside, on the small couch facing the door, Chase passionately kissed Tenisha. His hand cradled her face, caressing her long hair, her dark brown skin rich and lush beneath the bright lights inside the trailer. "Oh!" Maryam said, shocked. She averted her gaze, aware that Saif had frozen behind her. "I'm sorry, Dadu sent me to pick up his bag, I'll come back when you're . . . um . . . finished—" she babbled, and urged Saif down the stairs.

In front of the trailer, Maryam and Saif looked at each other, speechless.

"Tell Dadu we'll grab his bag later, when Josh's trailer is less . . . occupied," Saif said. "Poor Anna. I think she really likes him, and from the way Josh behaved yesterday, he's encouraging those feelings."

"Anna isn't naive," Maryam said, defending her friend, even though she privately feared the same thing. "Besides, she has a boyfriend waiting for her in Toronto." *Who seems like a bit of a jerk, but that's none of my business*, Maryam silently added.

"Well then, they both know the score," Saif said smoothly. "That's always important in a relationship, don't you think?" Before Maryam could ask what he meant, Saif walked ahead.

They picked up Dadu and the trio set off for the inn. Her grandfather was in an exceptionally good mood as they walked through the snow, Saif clearing the path and Maryam bringing up the rear. They still had to walk single file, but Dadu kept them entertained by sharing amusing anecdotes from the set that morning. Apparently, Josh kept messing up his lines, exasperating both Katrina and Tenisha.

"What would you do when that happened on one of your sets, Dadu?" Maryam asked.

Her grandfather chuckled. "Actors are professionals, so if they keep forgetting their lines, there must be a reason. Perhaps they have something on their mind. Actors often lead colorful lives, you see. Always falling in and out of love."

"Or trying to keep track of their new *friends*, right, Maryam?" Saif called back, his eyes twinkling as he turned to look at her.

Her grandfather noticed the glance but said nothing. "I understood, of course," Dadu continued. "Some people fall in love again and again, but others only have one true love. It was that way with me and your dadi-ma."

"Did you have a romantic meet-cute, too?" Saif asked Dadu. He was teasing, but there was genuine curiosity in his voice, too. She smiled to herself; Dadu loved to share his favorite love story—how he met his wife.

"Kulsoom was my neighbors' cousin, and she lived in the countryside with her family," Dadu started, his voice clear in the crisp winter air, the words taking on the cadence of a burnished tale. "During summer holidays, her parents would send her into town to visit. All of my friends would look forward to the summer break to escape school, but I would wait all year to see Kulsoom. She was tall, with beautiful clear skin, and the prettiest dark eyes. Everyone thought her sister was the real beauty because her skin was fair, but Kulsoom took my breath away from the very first. Her hair was thick, tied in a thick plait that hung to her waist, and she always smelled of jasmine flowers."

"It's true," Maryam confirmed. "Jasmine was her favorite Yardley powder, but she also kept the flowers in her hair whenever she could get them. Tell Saif what happened when you asked for Kulsoom's hand in marriage."

Her grandfather smiled, delighted to remember his adventurous youth. "I was the mischievous one in the neighborhood, always playing pranks. None of the adults took me seriously. It was my neighbor who was the golden child. Kulsoom's parents had already arranged a match with him, her own cousin. Marrying your cousin is quite normal, you see, in many parts of the world. Except neither of them really wanted the match, but what to do? The elders had decided."

"If Kulsoom or your neighbor didn't want the marriage, why didn't they just say something?" Saif asked. "Marriage without consent is forbidden in Islam."

Dadu only laughed and shook his head. "Young people, you always think everything is so simple and clear-cut. It wasn't like that, not in the 1950s. Anyways, I decided to take matters into my own hands. I convinced her to elope with me."

Saif's shock was clear in his voice. "You didn't!"

"She packed a bag, made her sister promise she wouldn't say anything until the next morning, and we ran away in the night. Together, we took the train to Mumbai, where we were married in a small *musallah*. My *mehr* gift to her was a simple gold bangle my mother gave me. My ammi and her sister were the only ones who knew about our plans."

"Wasn't your mother upset?" Saif asked.

"Ammi was a romantic," Dadu said. "Also, she thought Kulsoom was better off with me. The neighbor boy had a bad temper and was stingy. Still, she knew my father would lose face if it turned out his wife knew all along, so she had to pretend for years that she was shocked about our elopement. When I brought Kulsoom back to visit my parents, Ammi gave her the rest of the gold set: a ring, necklace, and earrings. She wore that gold set every day until she passed, even though over the years I made enough money to shower her with diamonds."

The crisp air was silent as the trio trudged through the snow, and Maryam thought about the improbable lifetimes her dadu had lived: first as a young dreamer in Hyderabad; then as a new husband, his beloved wife taking the biggest risk of all by leaving her family and trusting in him, even as he forged ahead in a precarious and notoriously closed-off industry; and then, decades later, joining his children in a new country. Today he was in another country yet again, experiencing the type of weather that would have seemed impossible to a young man in southern India. No matter how many times Maryam heard this story, it always made her tear up. Her grandfather's grand romantic gesture, her sweet-tempered grandmother's steadfast love, and their willingness to take a chance on each other always felt like a fairy tale—and, after everything that had happened to Maryam, almost impossible.

"So you moved to Mumbai, made your way in the film business, and spent the rest of your life directing love stories," Saif said, impressed.

"Allah has been generous," Dadu said. He looked back at his

granddaughter, and the twinkle in his eye took on a knowing glint. "My Kulsoom and I were young when love found us, but it can strike at any time. You just have to stand ready."

Walking behind her grandfather, Maryam flushed. Dadu wasn't being subtle. "Oh, look, we're at the inn already," she said. At the front entrance, they stamped their feet and brushed snow from their hats and jackets. Saif lingered in the foyer, while Dadu made a beeline for the giant fireplace.

"I'm sorry if I made you uncomfortable yesterday," Saif said, his voice low. Something tightened in Maryam's stomach. She had avoided this conversation for nearly twenty-four hours, but in such close quarters it was impossible to maintain her silence. She indicated he should follow her outside to the porch, where they could have some privacy. The massive evergreen tree in the yard, branches still burdened with snow, faced her, and she took courage from its resilience. She turned to Saif and looked into his warm, intense eyes. He was so attractive it was almost a distraction. She swept the snow from a bench on the porch and motioned for him to take a seat. This way they were nearly at eye level, which somehow only made things worse. Staring over his shoulder at the tree behind him, Maryam tried to organize her jumbled thoughts.

"You want more from me than I can give right now," Maryam started, and her words clearly took Saif by surprise. His lips twitched before he schooled his expression back into what she was starting to think of as his "lawyer face": neutral, unemotional.

"What is it that you think I want?" Saif asked, his voice calm and curious, and it was this tone more than anything else that pushed her over the edge.

"A holiday flirtation," Maryam said, her voice sharper than she intended. "Though I wonder what your girlfriend would think about you propositioning another woman while you're stuck in Snow Falls." The words slipped out so easily, Maryam realized she had wanted to know—badly—all this time.

Saif's eyes widened, and she noted that his neutral mask had vanished entirely. "What are you talking about?"

He hadn't denied it, she noted with a simmering anger. Maryam started to pace the porch. "You think just because you overheard my deepest secrets on the plane that you know me. But how can you? We haven't spoken in five years. We barely spoke even when we saw each other regularly. You didn't tell me about your girlfriend, you're way too charming—"

"Maryam, stop," Saif said, his voice clipped, and she stopped her pacing to glance at him. There was an anger in his eyes that she had never seen before, and a deep well of hurt. *I put that there*, Maryam thought. Then: *Maybe now he'll see what sort of person I am. The kind that burns down any relationship I'm part of.*

As if confirming her thoughts, Saif's next words stopped her short. "Don't blame me for your past."

"What do you mean?" she asked. Blood roared in her veins now. "You've been pestering me since we landed, talking about that winter cottage trip we took with our parents, encouraging me to write, but I see you for who you are, Saif. A charmer. An opportunist, an—"

"Enough," Saif said quietly. He was standing, and now he took one step back, his retreat leaving her cold. Maryam stared defiantly into his dark eyes. How could she have ever thought of them as unfathomable? There were depths there, but she couldn't trust him. He spoke with difficulty. "It's not fair, what happened to you. I'm sorry your ex-husband was a jerk. I'm sorry he cheated on you."

She flinched. Of course Saif had known the truth about her past; everyone in her community knew. Her failure was writ large for all to see, judge, and hold up as an example to others. Even her own mother thought her an embarrassment. Hadn't she said as much at the *mehndi*? Shame clawed at her throat.

Saif wasn't done. "But I'm not him. I'm not Yusuf. I said I know who you are because I've been watching you since we landed. You're strong and funny. Beautiful and generous. Even when everything is going wrong, you somehow manage to perform miracles. You think of everyone but yourself. So, I know you, Maryam Aziz. I also know you're scared, and it's that fear that's driving you to push me away."

Maryam stared at her feet, encased in her sensible boots and wool socks. She didn't want to hear Saif's words. He was right, but hearing it all out loud made her itchy, as if new skin had grown on top of old scars, and she wasn't used to their new texture.

Saif wasn't done. "You've made yourself smaller to fit into how you think your family wants you to be, but you're wrong. They love you and support you. Don't blame everyone else for being trapped. You hold the key, Maryam." His eyes never left hers, and every word he spoke was the simple, unvarnished truth. "Maybe this feels fast for you, but I've learned to go after what I want. And I want you." He paused, breathing hard. "And I don't have a girlfriend. You of all people should know better than to believe idle gossip."

Maryam turned to stare at the giant evergreen in the yard;

behind her, the door to the inn closed softly after Saif, and then she was alone on the porch. As she watched, a pile of snow gracefully fell from the lower branches, and the tree swayed as if in relief. *Lucky tree*, Maryam thought. Then she sat on the bench and cried.

THIRTEEN

Anna

December 23

Anna was in her room, staring out her window at the now lazily falling flakes drifting outside. Contrary to the weather report, the snow hadn't stopped that day—but the blizzard's end was getting close, Anna could feel it. If she were in Toronto right now, she'd be having an intimate preholiday dinner with Nick's father's closest business associates before heading to the opera. But Toronto felt like it was in another universe, not just a short plane ride away. She was so lost in her thoughts she almost didn't register the light tapping at her door.

It was Josh, holding a white box tied with twine. She couldn't help but notice how handsome he looked in his jeans and a white T-shirt that was just fitted enough to reveal his toned chest and abs, with sleeves that strained slightly over his biceps. She had been trying so hard not to think of him as she attempted to reconcile in her mind the reality that he and Tenisha were probably very much a thing, not just a rumor— but now here he was at her door. All her reason and rationales flew right out the window and into the snowy night. "Hi, there," she said.

"I brought you a nighttime snack," he said, holding up the box.

"If those aren't pineapple upside-down rugelach, I'm closing the door." She was trying to be flippant, but could hear her heart beating in her ears. *Boom, boom, boom.*

"Of course it's the rugelach," he said with a smile. "Can I come in?"

She stood aside.

"I'm going to need to go into the bakery and ask for the recipe. I'll be a hit at every holiday party for the rest of my life."

"Oh, I've tried. Family secret, and Ginger is not giving it up—not even to me, with my many charms." He waggled his eyebrows, and Anna couldn't help but laugh.

"Well, you *are* very charming, you know," Anna said.

"It's all an act," Josh replied. He was joking, but Anna still felt a pang and her laughter fell silent.

"So," he said, tilting his head and looking into her eyes. "I'm not just here bearing treats. We never did light the menorah together. And we promised Kate from the store we would . . ."

"Oh, right," Anna said, as if she had completely forgotten about it. She felt a surge of joy that he had remembered. *Slow down, Anna.* She reminded herself that he was possibly deep in a relationship with Tenisha Barlowe. Whereas she had just broken things off with Nick. Her life was in disarray—and the complications of someone like Josh Tannenbaum, or Chase Taylor, or whoever he was, were not needed. She was trying to *de*-crease her worries, not *in*-crease them.

"Anna, are you okay?"

She'd been standing in front of him in silence for an awkwardly long time while her thoughts swirled like the wind outside.

"We should do it," Anna blurted. "I mean, not *it*." Her cheeks immediately flamed with embarrassment. "We should *light* it. The menorah. Together. In here. Right now."

"Thought you'd never ask," he said.

"Maybe the candlelight will improve things in here. You know I'm not in the fancy section of the inn where all the movie stars get to stay."

"Hey, it's really nice in here, what are you talking about? And it smells—" He spun a slow circle and sniffed the air. "It smells *amazing*. I mean, *you* always smell amazing, so I guess I shouldn't be surprised."

He walked across the room to the table where the menorah sat. The room spray she had purchased from June's was on the table, too, along with the little bottle of perfume oil "potion." He picked it up.

"Is this your secret?" he asked, removing the lid and taking a deep sniff. "Ahh. Yes. It is." He read the label. "Potion number 9, the key to Anna Gibson's irresistibility."

Anna was blushing furiously now. Was he going to figure out that she'd been wearing a love potion? Was that why he was in here? Had she somehow charmed him?

No. That was ridiculous. Totally absurd. She smelled nice; that was all. June's perfume oil had a pleasant smell.

He was watching her intensely, the way he often seemed to. "You have that look on your face again."

"Which look is that?"

"The one where I feel sure you have at least a dozen thoughts in your head, all at once, and I don't have a hope of knowing what you're thinking."

"I'm just—I realized we don't have a lighter or matches," she ad-libbed.

"Thought of that already." He reached into the pocket of his jeans and pulled out a lighter. It was red with little miniature Santas all over it. "Obviously, I borrowed this from Kath," he said. "Perhaps not the most Jewish lighter in the world, but it will do."

"A lighter is a lighter," Anna said with a smile. "Thanks for planning ahead." She felt a little buzz inside her chest at the idea that he had been thinking of this—of her, and the promise they had made.

"I'm really grateful to you for this, Anna. It can be so hard to feel grounded when I'm always traveling, always working, these days. This year has been so busy. I've started to feel like I'm floating above myself sometimes . . ." He trailed off and looked embarrassed. "Sorry. That sounds weird. I don't mean to sound ungrateful. There are a lot of people who would kill for the life I have."

"You don't have to edit yourself with me. It actually doesn't sound weird at all," Anna said. "I completely understand. I'm not a movie star, as my hotel room will attest, but my life has changed recently, too. A lot of things have happened that I think are supposed to feel like dreams coming true. But mostly I just feel . . ." She stared up into his dark eyes. So much for reining in her racing heart; it was out of the gate now and going for broke, and it clearly had lost the plot on the "just friends" concept now that she was alone in a hotel room with

Josh. "A little lost," she concluded. *Though not when I'm with you*, she wanted to add.

Instead, he said it for her. His voice was husky. "I don't feel that way when I'm with you. I feel like I can be myself."

Anna blushed and tried to change the subject. "So, I guess we should . . ."

"Right. The menorah." He held up the lighter "Care to do the honors tonight?"

"Are you sure?"

"Absolutely," he said. "I can light it tomorrow."

Tomorrow. Anna turned to the small menorah on the table and tried to stay in the moment rather than wondering if it could ever be possible that she and Josh could have a tomorrow.

"When you were a kid, did you think these candles were magic?" Josh asked softly. "They never went out accidentally, we always allowed them to burn down. And that meant we had to arrange our schedules around them. When my cousins and I got old enough to stay home alone, our parents would tell us, if they had to go out somewhere after they'd lit the menorah, that we were in charge of staying home and 'watching the light.' This felt like such an important task. I took it so seriously."

Anna smiled at the idea of Josh as a serious little boy in charge of an important task. "I love that," she said. "And yes, I totally thought it was all magic. Then my stepmom got tired of my millions of questions about it, so she took me to the synagogue and let me ask the rabbi myself. I remember he said" —she turned the lighter over in her palm, trying to get the memory right—"that it was about the miracle of the light, yes, but it was also about hope. Hope that in the world we live in, light will triumph over darkness. Good over bad. I found that really comforting because I was—and still am—a bit of a worrier. So, knowing there was this whole holiday that was about light and good—in addition to the one I already celebrated, which, at least in our interpretation of it, was all about giving and generosity, about family and love—just made me feel really good about the world. And celebrating both together made me feel so happy and secure. It was all about family and togetherness. Being with the people you loved." She felt her mouth go dry as she stared into his eyes. "Okay, are you ready?"

He stood close beside her, his shoulder grazing hers as she lit the *shamash*—the raised candle in the center of the menorah—then breathed in deeply before she began to recite the blessing. "*Baruch atah, Adonai Eloheinu, Melech haolam.*" Josh's deeper voice joined hers. "*She-asah nisim la'avoteinu bayamim hahem bazman hazeh.*"

She then used the shamash to light two of the candles from left to right, leaving the rest unlit because it was the second night of Hanukkah. Six more to go. She tried not to wonder where she and Josh would be when it was time to light the final candle. All this would be a memory—and that was going to have to be enough.

She gazed down at the little pinpoints of light, then turned to Josh. His eyes were on her. He stepped closer.

"This feels like home," he said. The candlelight danced across his cheekbones and jaw and made his eyes even more beautiful than they already were. She felt a sense of calm—as if she was exactly where she was meant to be. Home. He was right.

"I'm glad we met, Josh."

"I like it so much when you call me by my real name. It

makes this all seem more real." He was very, very close to her now. "I really like you, Anna," he said. "I liked you from the moment I laid eyes on you. It sort of felt like—like I was actually living in and not just *acting* in one of my movies. It almost felt too good to be true, to have you just . . . fall into my life."

Anna's mind was racing. By all appearances, he had a girlfriend, and she had just taken a break from Nick. They should definitely not be standing as close to each other as they were—and yet she felt as if she had no choice. She had to be close to him. It was a requirement of her existence. *He's going to kiss me,* she realized. *And I want him to. I've wanted him to since the moment we met.*

Josh put his hand on her cheek and tilted his face to hers. Their lips were now inches away. "All day, on set, I kept messing up my lines," he said. "All I could think about was"—he moved his lips a millimeter closer to hers—"doing this."

The kiss was soft and exciting, sweet and delicious. Even with closed eyes, she could see the flickering of the candles, warm and inviting, as perfect in memory as they were in the reality she knew would wait for her in this room when she opened her eyes again. Josh had his arms around her, and she had her hands on the back of his neck, touching his hair, drawing him closer.

Knock, knock, knock!

A sharp rap at her hotel room door startled them both. They jumped away from each other, and Anna felt abruptly cold, as if she had suddenly been pushed outside into the snow. She crossed the room to open the door and was surprised to see Tenisha Barlowe standing in the hall.

"Oh. Hi . . . um." Anna was mortified. What had gotten into her? How could she have done this? Judging from the look on Tenisha's face, she was more than just a rumored girlfriend.

"I was told Chase was in here," she said. "I really need to speak with him."

Josh went to the door and started talking to Tenisha in a low voice. Anna tried not to eavesdrop, but she was sure she heard Tenisha say, "I need you." Anna's heart now pounded not with the excited rush of a first kiss—but with embarrassment, disappointment, and a harsh understanding. Just moments before, Anna had felt as though Josh belonged to her, somehow. But he didn't. He wasn't just some guy she had developed feelings for who liked her back. She had become caught up in a fantasy world—and it was time to wake up.

"Okay," she heard Josh say. "I'm coming. I'll meet you in your room."

He turned to Anna, his tall body framed by the door. Tenisha was still standing in the shadows—and when her eyes met Anna's, she felt sure her expression was sympathetic. As if Tenisha felt sorry for Anna. As she should, Anna realized. What a fool she had been.

"Tenisha and I have some lines we need to work on. But . . . Anna, there's something I need to explain to you." He closed the door. "Tenisha and I . . . it's complicated," he began. Just then, Anna's room phone started ringing. "And I feel like I owe you a proper explanation, because—" *Ring. Ring. Ring.* Whoever it was wasn't giving up.

"I should get that," Anna said. She crossed the room and picked up the phone. "Hello, Anna here."

"Anna! Thank goodness! I've been frantic!"

"Nick!" She glanced across the room at Josh. "Can you just hang on for one minute?" She hit the hold button and put the phone down.

"Nick?" Josh repeated the name as if weighing it. And it felt heavy.

"Yes," Anna said. "He's my . . . well, he's . . . up until a few days ago, he was my boyfriend. It's complicated, too. We're on a break."

"Was he your boyfriend when I met you at It's the Most Wonderful Time for a Beer?"

Anna nodded, feeling sick at heart.

"And he's the reason you were heading to Toronto for the holidays?"

"Yes, but—then we had an argument. And we haven't spoken since."

"But that's him, calling to make up."

Anna didn't know why Nick was calling. All she knew was her emotions were a confusing, boiling inferno inside her. "I . . ." she began. But the words didn't come, and what did words matter? Josh was shaking his head and backing away.

"It's okay. You don't have to explain yourself. All this, it went too far. We both have complicated lives and other obligations. I should go. I *have* to go." His eyes were on the blinking hold light on the phone. "You need to talk to him," he said. "I'm sorry, Anna. You don't need me in your life, making things more difficult than they should be."

He left, clicking the door shut decisively behind him. The blinking light on the phone was now a harsh accusation in the dim room. Anna stood still, watching the flickering candles that had given her so much joy moments before now slowly lose their appealing gleam as cold reality set in.

She crossed the room to pick up the phone again. "Hi, Nick, I'm here." As she spoke to him, she looked out the window. The snow was slowing down now. And less snow made the world out there look different, less like a fairy-tale snow globe and more . . . real. She had been suspended in time here in Snow Falls—but there was another world out there, and that world wasn't about kissing movie stars in hotel rooms. She shook her head as if to dispel the dreamlike state she had allowed herself to fall into. It had all really happened, at least. She really had been an extra in the sequel to her favorite holiday movie. And how many people could say they had kissed Chase Taylor, the new Hollywood It boy? It was a secret she would keep forever, but it was still hers. She touched her lips, where his had just been, and tried to tell herself it was okay. That she could forgive herself a few errors in judgment. Then she focused on Nick.

"Anna, answer me! Are you all right?"

"I think so . . ." she began, but he rushed over her words.

"I'm so sorry the last time we talked I made it seem like I didn't care about your well-being. These past few days have been torture. Have they been torture for you?"

She wanted to be as honest as possible. "Well, it's been a busy few days. I've actually made a few friends. This is a really sweet little town, and there's a—"

But again Nick interrupted. "I'm sending my father's plane, now that the snow has stopped. It can't leave until morning, but it will be there first thing to pick you up and bring you here. You won't have to be alone for Christmas."

"*Oh.*" Anna hadn't been considering the fact that if she didn't get out of Snow Falls, she was going to be "alone." In fact, Snow Falls was a pretty difficult place to get a moment alone in. She opened her mouth to try to explain this to Nick—but couldn't find the right words. You had to see Snow Falls to believe it. She started again. "Thank you, but I'm not sure if I—"

"I know what you said, Anna. That you wanted time. A break. But I don't accept that. I know you, and I know you sometimes create emotional problems for yourself."

"Wait—"

"It's okay. We don't have to get into it now. Just suffice it to say I *know* you. I love you. We are *going* to be together. We are *going* to have our perfect Christmas. Can you get yourself to the Rockport Airport by nine o'clock tomorrow morning? A plane will be waiting for you. That's what matters, right? Being with the one you love on Christmas? My family is expecting you. You have to come. We have to give ourselves a chance. We owe this to ourselves. We've been planning for so long."

Anna's head was spinning and swirling with thoughts. She wasn't sure *what* mattered anymore. Nick kept repeating the word "Christmas," but here in Snow Falls there was so much more than just *Christmas*. It was Christmas, Hanukkah, and Ramadan all wrapped into one chaotic, sparkling, festive package. It was light and laughter and fun. It was . . . everything she had been searching for, always. It wasn't easy and it wasn't perfect—but was she ready to leave it behind already?

"Anna, please, let me come to your rescue. Don't push me away. You need me."

Now Anna frowned. Was that what she had always wanted,

to be rescued? Hadn't that been what she liked about Josh—that he was always coming to her rescue? Maybe it was time to stand on her own.

"Well, it's just I've already told Maryam I'd help with the set decoration for the play. I can't just bail on that."

"The set decoration? For what play? What are you talking about? Who's Maryam?"

Anna tried to explain her new friends, the Holiday Hoopla, her role in set decorating, to Nick, but none of her explanations about Snow Falls were coming out right.

"You sound strange," Nick said, his voice even heavier with concern. "Like you have Stockholm syndrome or something."

She couldn't help but laugh at the ridiculousness of that statement. "I haven't been kidnapped, just snowbound."

"But admit it, it's all very traumatic. And it's almost over. I have to go now, I'm going out shopping with Mother, but I'll see you in the morning."

He hung up before she could respond. She sat still, watching the candles on the menorah burn down. Even when they were reduced to stubs, she still didn't know what she was going to do.

But she had an idea about who she could turn to.

*A*nna tapped on Maryam's door, and seconds later her friend answered, her eyes red-rimmed and watery.

"Anna, are you okay?" Maryam asked, just as Anna said, "You look like you've been crying." They both laughed ruefully.

"Come on in," Maryam said, moving aside to let Anna into the room she shared with Saima, which was bigger than Anna's but also faced out the front of the inn. She could see the sweet, twinkling lights of the town in the distance, and briefly wondered where Saima could be.

"You're upset—please tell me what's going on," Anna said.

"You go first. What's wrong, Anna?"

Anna sighed and flopped down on the bed.

"I kissed Josh. It was such a mistake. And then Nick called, and it was so awkward, and . . ."

It all came out in a rush, the intense moment in Anna's room, Tenisha's abrupt arrival, the ringing phone, Josh's hurt expression. "But does he have a right to be hurt? He has a girlfriend, too! He's stringing me along!"

Maryam looked even more stricken than she had when she answered her hotel room door. "I saw him kissing Tenisha today on set, and I didn't want to hurt you, so I didn't tell you. I had no idea things were getting so serious. I'm so sorry!"

"You don't have to be sorry. This isn't your fault, it's mine. I knew there was probably something going on between Josh and Tenisha—I just didn't want to believe it. I got caught up in a fantasy."

"No one could blame you," Maryam said softly, and Anna turned to her.

"What's going on with you? You seemed so shaken up when you came to the door."

"It's . . . Saif."

"But I thought things were going well with you two!"

"Maybe that's the thing about Snow Falls. It's only a break from reality, but the real world is always there. Saif and I have no chance in the real world, and that's just the way it is. Case closed." She folded her arms and let out a loud, frustrated sigh.

"Honestly, sometimes I think men are just more trouble than they're worth."

Anna nodded in miserable agreement. "Nick's sending his father's plane," she said morosely. "Tomorrow morning. And he thinks I'm going to get on it and come to Toronto."

"A plane," Maryam repeated. "Wow, he's that rich."

"His family is, yes. And he really wants me there with his family for Christmas."

"What did you say when he asked?"

"He didn't exactly ask, I guess. It's just . . . happening. Should I be happy? It's a grand gesture, right? He's showing me how he really feels. And at least he's being honest."

"It's a big thing to do. Very cinematic, actually. Someone in one of Dadu's movies would probably send a plane. But . . . are you able to see through all that to how you really feel? Are you happy about this?"

Anna started to fiddle with the bedspread. "Yes," she finally said. "Nick deserves another chance. He didn't do anything wrong except get upset when our plans got ruined. How could I fault him for that? As you said, Snow Falls is not real life. I owe it to Nick to get on that plane and deal with things. I owe it to *myself*."

Maryam reached out and gently pulled the bedspread from Anna's hands. "You're going to rip that thing in two," she said. "Take a deep breath. Look at me, Anna. You're not as calm as you're pretending. And that's okay." Anna did as her friend suggested and felt Maryam's level gaze bring her chaotic thoughts back down to earth. "Take it from someone who's been there and has the therapy bills to prove it," Maryam continued. "When you're trying to convince yourself that you're happy, all you're doing is ignoring the part of you that knows things aren't working."

Anna knew Maryam was probably right, and it made her feel stricken. "I don't know what to do," she whispered.

"The last few days have been pretty crazy. Maybe the best thing to do is give it a little time," Maryam suggested. "I think that's what Dadu would suggest. But really think about all this carefully. A long time ago, I was caught up in a relationship that looked perfect from the outside, but it didn't make me happy. I had to figure that out for myself."

"Is that what you were upset about last night?"

"Yes," Maryam said. "I was married once, but it fell apart. When he left, my world imploded, and I haven't trusted anyone since. It still hurts, to this day."

Impulsively, Anna leaned over to hug Maryam. "No matter what I decide to do, I know this: meeting you has been the best thing to happen to me in a very long time." She felt a lump form in her throat when she said the words, and when she pulled away, Maryam's eyes were shiny.

"Thank you," Maryam managed, looking a bit flustered by the sudden outpouring of emotion—but Anna knew she felt the same.

Maryam stood and walked to the window.

"It stopped snowing," she said, turning.

"A holiday miracle," Anna said. She joined Maryam at the window to gaze out at the now clear night. It was strange not to see falling snow. "Maybe I need to do a pro-con list," she said reflectively. "If I leave, I get to experience the Vandergrey family Christmas—"

"I predict sugarplums and fancy gifts," Maryam said with a laugh.

"But then I also miss the Holiday Hoopla. I haven't been to a real Christmas pageant since I was in school. Now that you're writing the play, I know it will be something really special. And I'm not quite done with the set decor. I'd be letting you down."

"I'm sure it will be fine, you've given the volunteers so much to work with—much more than we had before you came along. Don't let the Hoopla influence your decision."

They had been speaking so intently they hadn't noticed the hotel room door had opened. Saima was standing in the doorframe, her face a dark thundercloud.

"You're writing a *Christmas* play?" Saima demanded. Her voice was loud and accusing, pink splotches high on her cheeks, her usually neat hair in disarray, as if she had been running her hands through it in frustration. "My wedding is falling apart, and you're getting cozy with the locals and putting together a holiday pageant?"

Maryam crossed the room and tried to reach out a conciliatory arm toward her sister, but Saima jerked back. "Don't touch me!"

Saima was normally so good-natured, if impetuous. It was a shock to Anna to see her livid. Maybe having a sister really wasn't as wonderful as Anna had always dreamed.

"I've been on the phone for hours, calling the airline, calling cab companies, the weather bureau," Saima said, heated. "I tried to book a helicopter today, Maryam. A *helicopter* to get me out of this godforsaken town and back to my fiancé so I can actually get married now that it has finally stopped snowing."

"My boyfriend has a plane coming to get me tomorrow," Anna said. "Maybe I can figure out a way to help you, too."

Saima turned to her. "*A plane?*" she shrieked. "You get a plane and I get . . . to be stuck here?"

Anna took a nervous step back.

Saima's eyes were wild, fists clenched tight at her side. "This is all your fault," she hissed to Maryam. "We never should have left the airport. And now all you care about is . . . some sort of hoopla?!"

"Saima, calm down. The Holiday Hoopla is just a bit of fun," Maryam said, conciliatory.

"Fun would be nice! All I can think about is my wedding and how it's ruined!"

"Listen, I know how stressful this has all been for you," Maryam said, her tone soothing. Unfortunately, her words were having the opposite effect. The calmer Maryam was, the more agitated Saima became.

"You've been so busy flirting with Saif and running after some stupid dream of being a writer, you have no idea what's been going on," Saima spat, and Anna was sure she saw Maryam flinch when her sister spoke Saif's name. "It's like you've forgotten all about your family. Well, I hope you're happy—I just got off the phone with Miraj. We had to cancel the wedding." Anna gasped quietly as Saima's shoulders now heaved with emotion. "You have five minutes to grab your stuff and find somewhere else to sleep tonight. I don't want to see you."

She slammed the door hard as she left the room, and Anna stared at Maryam in shock. Her friend looked stricken.

"You know how you've always wished to have a bigger family?" Maryam said bitterly. "Maybe you're the lucky one."

She turned and started opening drawers and throwing clothes into a bag. "I'm going to go stay with my parents—see if I can convince them to talk some sense into Saima," Maryam said wearily. She walked Anna to the door and patted her shoulder. "Good luck with your decision," she said—and Anna couldn't help it; she felt a wave of loneliness. Maryam was her friend, but family came first, which Anna really did understand. Anna wasn't family.

As she said good night to Maryam and turned away, she knew there was really only one decision for her to make. She needed to go where she was wanted, and try to make a go of it with the people who might turn out to be the only family she really had.

FOURTEEN

Maryam

December 23

Maryam sat on the bed after Anna left and stared at nothing, her overnight bag half filled. Irritated, she threw it to the floor. She knew Anna was disappointed that she had shown her the door, but the truth was, Maryam was just so tired. Her sister was—rightfully—furious. The wedding Maryam had spent so much time and energy organizing on behalf of her family was canceled. They were still stuck in Snow Falls. Yet despite all the little disasters piled on top of one another, it was Saif's harsh words she couldn't shake. In truth, they hadn't stopped ricocheting in her mind all evening.

Saif was right. She *was* scared. He had recognized her outburst as just another coping mechanism. She had buried the pain of her failed marriage so deeply, she had convinced herself it didn't exist. Instead, she had made herself indispensable to her family and refused to think about any of her old ambitions, making it impossible to move forward—all so she could protect her wounded heart, save face, and feel like less of a failure.

She needed to get out of here. A restlessness drove her downstairs. While the rest of the wedding party had dispersed, Dadu was settled in his favorite spot in front of the fire. As she claimed the spot beside him on the couch, she realized he was the person she wanted most to see right now. Dadu would understand.

"Ah, my favorite granddaughter," Dadu said, twinkling at her. "Don't tell Saima. Though I suspect she already knows." His gaze was perceptive, but as usual, he waited for Maryam to open up. They sat in silence, watching the fire, and slowly Maryam felt her body ease. He smelled faintly of starch and the attar he favored, a comforting potpourri of cloves, cinnamon, and *oud*.

"Everything is such a mess," she said in a low voice.

Dadu reached over and took her hand. "And yet we are still here. *Beta*, you do too much, for all of us. You work too hard to make sure everyone else is happy. It makes *me* happy to see you run after your dreams as well. Tell me, how did it feel when you were put in charge of the writing?" he asked. The knowing look in Dadu's eyes made her flush.

"It felt like . . . I was doing exactly what I was put here on earth to do," she admitted, feeling slightly foolish but also sure her grandfather would understand.

Dadu sat back and sipped on his tea with more than a hint of satisfaction. "Remember that when you start to feel guilty for running after your dreams. You and I, we have creative souls. If we don't create, something inside of us dies. Yes?"

Maryam leaned into the cushions, thinking. Somehow, talking with her dadu had always had a way of centering her. Now his words sparked a memory of the notebooks she used to carry around everywhere. She had dropped the habit when her marriage unraveled. Yusuf had never encouraged her writing anyway.

Dadu had probably overheard her disagreement with Saima, Maryam realized—her sister's voice traveled. Knowing his natural inquisitive tendencies, he likely suspected what had happened with Saif as well. But as usual, he was offering help in discreet ways. He tended to stay out of family disagreements. Her grandfather was a big believer in conflict. *Conflict serves your story*, he would always tell her or Saima when they complained to him. *Let us blue-sky some ways this conflict can help develop your character.* It really was a wonder she hadn't dived into writing earlier, Maryam thought wryly.

Dadu rose to his feet and, after wishing her a good night, headed upstairs to his room, leaving Maryam in front of the fire to consider her options. She could go in search of Saif. Or she could try to find her sister, or Anna. Instead, she sat and did nothing. She must have remained completely motionless because when Josh strode into the foyer and slumped into the first armchair he spotted, across from her, he seemed to jump when he noticed her.

She was shocked at his appearance. He seemed exhausted and rumpled in a way she had never seen the put-together movie star before. Maybe the long days of nonstop work were starting to get to him.

"Should I stay, or would you like to be alone?" Maryam asked. She didn't know him that well, but he looked so sad and weary, she thought he could use a friend.

"Did you know Anna had a boyfriend?" he asked abruptly. *Uh-oh*, Maryam thought.

"I wasn't sure what the status of their relationship was . . ." she started, but trailed off at his hurt expression. "Yes, I knew," she finished. "I also know that I caught *you* kissing Tenisha Barlowe in your trailer today."

"We were practicing for the movie," Josh said. "Katrina was getting annoyed at me messing up my lines, so she told us to take five and nail the kissing scene."

Maryam considered his words. Dadu had mentioned something about Josh's distraction when they had walked home from the set. "Okay, what about this morning, when you strolled out of the inn holding Tenisha's hand?" she asked. "You know Anna doesn't have any family, and this is a difficult time of year for her. She doesn't need a Hollywood movie star playing with her heart."

Josh seemed surprised at the vehemence in Maryam's voice. She suspected that most people didn't push back or question him very often, and she felt her hackles rise. Anna needed to be protected from this guy. She opened her mouth to warn him off, when he surprised her.

"You're a good friend. Anna's lucky to have you in her life."

She snapped her mouth closed. "Actually, I met Anna for the first time at the airport," she admitted.

"I never would have guessed. I assumed you two have been friends for years."

"Three days and counting," Maryam said. Then, relenting: "I guess we both haven't known her for very long."

Josh, now slumped backward on the couch, stared at his hands. "I really like her," he said in a low voice. "She's funny and sweet. Kind. Generous. Beautiful—inside and out. She's authentic, and you don't meet people you can say that about every day in Hollywood. Plus, I can talk to her about things without it ever feeling like . . . I'm talking to a fan. Or a coworker. We just immediately connected. You know?"

He sounded so sincere, Maryam was pretty sure he wasn't acting. "She feels the same way about you, too," she found herself saying.

"Then why didn't she tell me she had a boyfriend?" Josh asked.

"I get the sense that Nick has been putting a lot of pressure on her, and things have been rocky for a while. But technically, they are on a break right now."

"'On a break'?" he echoed in disbelief. "Like on *Friends*?"

Maryam narrowed her eyes at him. "She can't be on a break from her boyfriend, but it's okay that you're dating one of the most famous movie stars in the world?"

At that, Josh's face seemed to crumple. "You don't understand," he said. "Dating isn't easy when you're an actor. This is a brutal industry. When you're first starting out, you're so desperate to make it, sometimes you agree to things that you later regret . . ." He shook his head. "I wanted to explain this to Anna, but she didn't give me a chance."

"Explain what, exactly? Have you made a deal with the devil and your heart belongs to another for ninety-nine years?" Maryam asked.

Josh gave a bark of laughter. "No. But I did agree to pretend to date Tenisha Barlowe while we filmed *Two Nights at Christmas*." The moment the words were out of his mouth, his face turned red, just as Maryam's jaw dropped. "I wasn't supposed to say that," he said. "I'm exhausted and upset. Ignore me."

"But . . . you were holding hands this morning," Maryam sputtered.

"Because her publicist tipped her off that Jerome, the town paparazzo, was waiting for us outside. We try to throw him a few pictures he can sell to the gossip magazines. It's Christmas and he has kids."

Maryam blinked, trying to absorb this information. She wasn't sure what to say, but that didn't seem to matter. Now that the truth was out, Josh couldn't stop talking. Maybe it was a relief to finally tell someone. "Tenisha cooked it up. The buzz around her career has been massive—and she wanted to protect her personal life. She also thought pretending to be a couple as we shot *Two Nights at Christmas* might help me out. We've been good friends for years, but I guess our dreams have grown and changed, and we just never talked about it. Tenisha thinks I want one thing, while I know she wants another." He put his head in his hands again. "Fame is just so intense, when it comes for you, and her solution is to try to protect our-selves, while growing our 'brand'—but it turns out that even though I'm a pretty good actor, I hate pretending. Especially now, having met Anna. It's all such a mess."

"So you and Tenisha Barlowe aren't *really* a couple?" Maryam asked, still trying to absorb the news. They had looked so casual and intimate this morning. The pictures in the mag-azine Saima shared had felt so *real*. Her mind was still reeling. No wonder Josh was so upset about Nick. This changed every-thing.

Josh shook his head. "There have always been rumors about us. *One Night at Christmas* was supposed to be this little network holiday movie, but somehow it became a huge ratings hit. When Nora signed on to write the screenplay for the sequel"—that was Nora Ephron, Maryam assumed—"everyone wanted a piece of us. We were invited to all the late-night talk shows, and they all had one question: What was the story with our real-life romance? Our agents thought—and Tenisha agreed—that us dating would play better than the truth, which is that I am hopelessly single, and Tenisha has been with her boyfriend since high school. No one needs to know that, and it's not a very interesting story."

"Tenisha has a high school sweetheart?" Maryam asked.

"His name is Matt, and he's great," Josh confirmed. "Tenisha worries about what effect the spotlight could have on them, so she wants to keep it a secret. I was going to tell Anna everything, but then I found out about *Nick*—" He made a face.

Maryam contemplated Josh, all of her opinions readjusting in light of this new information. He wasn't cheating on Tenisha with Anna. In fact, he seemed just as smitten with Anna as she was with him. "I think you should come to the playhouse tomorrow," Maryam said.

"What?" Josh asked, blinking at this abrupt change in topic.

"Have you heard of the Holiday Hoopla? I think it's a silly name, but that's what they call the holiday pageant. This year the town is putting on a tri-holiday event, to commemorate Eid, Hanukkah, and Christmas all happening at the same time. I think it's caused a bit of an uproar in some parts of Snow Falls, actually."

Josh and Maryam shared a single, wordless glance. For the first time since she had taken a seat, she felt as if they were on the same wavelength. Despite their vastly different life experiences and backgrounds, they both understood what it felt like to be perpetually on the outside looking in, and how special it felt to be welcomed with a seat at the table.

"I can imagine the pearl-clutching," he said. "But why do you need me?"

"Have you heard of *A Christmas Carol*?" Maryam asked.

"You mean the most famous Christmas story of all time? Yes, I've heard of it," Josh said dryly, but he seemed intrigued.

"I've been put in charge of writing the play, and I'm writing a tri-holiday take on Scrooge's journey, except instead of ghosts, I'm including 'Holiday Hosts' to share the magic of the three holidays. I could really use a Hanukkah Host. Having Chase Taylor act in the Snow Falls Holiday Hoopla would be a great way to give back to a town that has treated you well."

She could see he was thinking it over, and decided to reveal her hand. "I see this going one of two ways," Maryam said, all business now. "If Anna decides not to rush off to Nick and shows up tomorrow to help with the decor, she'll see you on stage and have a lot to consider. And if she doesn't show up, you end up making some good press by helping out a hometown play, and start building a reputation that doesn't depend on who you happen to be dating. Either way, see you at ten a.m.?"

Josh blinked, and a slow smile suffused his face. He really did have that Hollywood charm; she could see why Anna had fallen for him so quickly. "Maryam, you are diabolical," he said, standing up, and he seemed lighter, happier. Telling the truth had set him free. "And a good friend. I'll find a way to get a few hours off tomorrow, even if I have to fake getting buried in a snowbank. See you at the playhouse."

———

Maryam made her way to her parents' room after Josh left. She was sure Saima hadn't bothered to fill them in about the canceled wedding, leaving it to her. As usual. She paused. No, not as usual. Saif was right, and so was Dadu. She had to take some responsibility for the way she had simply accepted her role as the family problem-solver. Things needed to change, and that change would have to start with her.

Her parents were preparing for bed when she knocked. She briefly explained the situation.

"I don't understand. Is the wedding postponed, or has Miraj called the whole thing off?" Ghulam asked.

"I'm pretty sure the wedding is on, but it won't be happening over the holidays like Saima wanted."

Azizah let out a breath. "I didn't want her to get married during Ramadan, but she must be so upset."

"Very," Maryam agreed, before asking if she could bunk with her parents. Their room had two double beds, and while Ghulam cleared the second bed—they had been using it to store their many suitcases after Dadu snagged a room to himself after their first night at the inn—Maryam updated her parents on what else was going on, namely that she had been put in charge of the Snow Falls Christmas play.

"But you have never celebrated Christmas in your life," Azizah said.

"The town is putting together a tri-holiday celebration, to honor Eid, Christmas, and Hanukkah," Maryam explained. "Saif talked me into volunteering, and the committee put me in charge of writing the play." She waited for their reaction to hearing that Saif had encouraged her.

"Maryam *beta*, I told you to be careful around that boy," Ghulam said, immediately protective. "The stories we have heard—"

"I'm sure lots of people have said things about me, too, things that aren't true," Maryam responded, surprising herself. Was she actually sticking up for Saif? But her parents had the grace to look abashed at her gentle reminder of the gossip that still continued to swirl around their family, even years after her divorce.

"We don't want you to be hurt again," Azizah said. "It was hard to watch, the first time." Maryam nodded, not trusting herself to speak, and her mother went on. "But about this holiday play. They want you to write something? Did you tell them you are a pharmacist?"

Maryam wanted to laugh. Her parents knew she enjoyed writing and had always loved to read. They had indulged this interest when she was younger. Yet despite Dadu's encouragement, their goals for their own children had been clear: to enter a professional field.

"I'm a pharmacist, but lately I've been feeling like I'm missing something. I want to write, to work on something creative."

Her parents looked at each other. She could see they were trying to understand. "I've been thinking about putting together a newsletter for the pharmacy," Ghulam said. "Perhaps you could write that?"

Maryam smothered her smile. "I mean, write for myself.

Maybe a book, or essays, or short stories. I'm not sure yet. In the meantime, I want to work on this play. We're stranded here, probably for another few days. The people in Snow Falls have been so kind. I'd like to repay their generosity."

Maryam could feel her parents thawing. "The residents have been very hospitable," Azizah agreed. "I still do not understand why you must work on a Christmas . . . *tri-holiday*," she amended, "play, but I suppose it will not hurt. Except what are we going to do about Saima? A delayed wedding might turn into a canceled one."

"Maybe that's not a bad thing," Maryam said. The abrupt silence in the room had the feel of a record scratch.

"*Beta*, do you think your sister is making a mistake?" Ghulam asked gently.

Her sister's wedding plans had been so sudden, her parents so thrilled their younger daughter, with her nomadic tendencies, was marrying a doctor, that Maryam had put aside all fears and worries. But they were still there; they had simply been lying in wait.

She didn't approve of her sister's mad dash into matrimony, she realized. She had never approved, and the few times she had tried to bring it up with Saima, or with her parents or even with Dadu, they had waved aside her objections. And she had shut up, fearful they would think her jealous. Maybe she was, but she was also concerned about the marriage for all sorts of normal big-sister reasons: it was too rushed; they barely knew Miraj; his family seemed stuck-up and not welcoming of Saima.

Maybe the Storm of the Century had actually been divine intervention.

Maryam felt guilty at the thought, and made a *dua*: Dear

God, she thought, *if this wedding is the right path for my sister, then make it easy for her and Miraj. Let the wedding take place, and help them build a happy life together. But if it is not good for Saima, then . . . let it snow, let it snow, let it snow!*

Now Maryam fiddled with the tiny side table. It was rickety and wobbled. "Don't you think Saima is making a mistake?" she asked, getting up, restless now. She needed a piece of cardboard or napkin to level the table.

"No," Azizah said firmly.

"Because Miraj is a doctor? Because his family is wealthy? Saima has known this guy for five minutes and she thinks she should marry him?" Maryam found a small notepad on the console table and ripped off a piece of paper, leaving behind a jagged tear. She started to fold the paper into a tiny square, fingers clumsy in her sudden fury.

Azizah reached out and took the paper from her daughter's hand. "Sometimes, no matter how long you have known someone or how prepared you think you are, it will not work out. We must simply accept Allah's *qadr.*"

Fate. Had it been her fate to meet and marry a liar? She had known her ex-husband, Yusuf, for four years before they married. Maryam still remembered when they met, on the first day of pharmacy school. She had been sitting outside the building after a stultifying two-hour seminar when she pulled out a bag of *bhel puri,* puffed rice mixed with spicy, salted peanuts.

"I remember eating that when I was on a beach in Mumbai," a voice said behind her. She turned to meet the amused gaze of a cute guy—dark eyes, brown skin, curly hair.

"My dadi-ma makes it at home using Rice Krispies. She

roasts the peanuts herself," Maryam offered. "You can't buy this stuff in Denver." He was the only other brown guy she had seen so far in the program, and she wondered who he was.

"I'm Yusuf," he said, holding out his hand. Misinterpreting, she offered him her bag of snacks instead. Laughing, he helped himself.

"Now we have to be friends, if you're already feeding me," he had joked. "Who are you, beautiful, mysterious woman?"

"Maryam Aziz," she had said, blushing.

The next day, Yusuf showed up for their morning Medicinal Chemistry class with a Ziploc bag full of roasted, salted *moong dal*—whole lentils—and offered them to her. After that, they were friends. When he confessed he had feelings for her in second year, it was the natural progression of their relationship. She was twenty-four years old, and it had felt like the right time for this to happen.

Her parents hadn't approved of the match. They thought they were both too young; that Yusuf, in particular, was not ready. In hindsight, their objections likely made the relationship feel more romantic, the stakes even higher. When Yusuf told her he loved her, she hadn't stopped to ask herself if she felt the same, too swept up in the moment.

In the end, her parents had reluctantly given the couple their blessing and paid for a lavish wedding. By then, the cracks in their relationship were obvious: Yusuf wanted to move out of state while Maryam was content to live in Denver; he wasn't especially close with his family and didn't understand why Maryam wanted to spend so much time with hers; he was dismissive of her dream to pursue writing and subtly put her down in front of their friends. She made excuses for him, and thought things would improve once they married and moved in together. They didn't.

"You spent all that money on my wedding, even though you didn't approve, and we ended up divorced in the end. Aren't you angry at me? Everyone still talks about what happened as if it were my fault Yusuf left," Maryam said in a small voice.

The first few months after her divorce, when she moved back in with her parents, she had felt too raw and in shock to discuss any of this. Later, after friends urged her to go to therapy, she had talked it all through with an insightful Chinese woman who understood the complexities of first- and second-generation immigrant identity. But she had never had this conversation with her parents.

"You have always been so mature. You want to take on all our burdens because you have a good heart," Ghulam started. "When you brought Yusuf for us to meet, we knew he was wrong for you, but what could we do? We made our opinions clear, but we love you, *beta*, and even if you make decisions we don't agree with, we will never abandon you. You are our child, no matter what you do or who you choose to love. Even if he is a selfish *ullu*."

Maryam laughed at the epitaph. Yusuf did look a bit like an owl, actually. "How did you know he wasn't right for me?" she asked through her tears.

"You laughed at his jokes with your mouth closed," Ghulam said, shrugging.

"We thought: better you should love, better you should try, rather than do nothing at all. You have to fight for your future, even if it doesn't turn out exactly as planned," Azizah said.

Divorce was still relatively rare in their mostly immigrant

community. For years, Maryam had felt like she wore a scarlet letter *D* on her chest whenever she went to a party or event. She knew she was held up as a cautionary tale among young single girls: *See what happens when you don't keep your husband happy? You get left behind, and your family is shamed.*

Except her family had never made her feel like that, or blamed her for any of it. She had done the blaming all by herself. It was beyond time for her to forgive herself, to accept what had happened, and to move on. Impulsively, she hugged her parents, squeezing hard. They hugged her back; they weren't normally a very physically affectionate family, preferring to show their love through kind acts, but the embrace was appreciated, and returned. Her mother had tears in her eyes when Maryam let her go, and she wiped them away with a smile.

"You know, Saif said that maybe we don't give our parents enough credit," Maryam said. "You came to a new country and ran after your own dreams. He said that if I had insisted on pursuing writing when I was younger, you would have supported me. Is that true?"

Her parents looked at each other, conducting one of those lightning-fast, entirely silent conversations that only people who have lived together for decades can do. "Don't be ridiculous, Maryam," Azizah said. "Writing won't pay your bills. What would people say?" But she smiled as she said it.

"Perhaps this Saif boy is not as bad as we had been led to believe," Ghulam added.

As she cuddled into the blanket on her bed, Maryam felt lighter than she had in years. No matter what tomorrow brought, she knew that her family would face it together.

FIFTEEN

Anna

December 24

Christmas Eve
The 3rd night of Hanukkah
The 29th day of Ramadan

Anna opened the window to let some fresh air into her room and clear her head as she gathered her things, making a little pile of the items she needed to return or planned to give as gifts, and a pile of the things she was taking with her. The Happy Holiday Missive, still unopened, sat near her handbag. She placed it on the windowsill and turned away. Then she took one last look around her room. Even with the funny smell and the stained ceiling, she felt an ache at leaving it behind. But, she told herself, she was making the right choice. She had to give things a last chance with Nick. Because he was her shot at the life she had always wanted. The life she *needed*.

Anna had written notes to Maryam, Saima, and Dadu, and chosen little gifts for each of them: she was giving her loud Christmas sweater to Mr. Dadu, her love potion to Maryam, and her double-pom hat to Saima, hoping it would cheer her up. She was also leaving the menorah for Deb and Kath, in case they ever had guests who wanted to light the menorah during the holidays. It had been a hard decision, to leave all this stuff behind rather than taking mementos with her, but Anna had decided it felt right to seal her new friendships with gifts, and it was definitely in keeping with the spirit of the holiday season. She had decided against saying goodbye in person, however. It would just be too painful—and potentially impossible. It had been an intense few days, emotions were heightened—and Anna didn't want anything to stop her from walking out the door of the inn, toward Nick. She *had* to do this. She had faith that this would not be the last she saw of the Aziz family, and that had to be enough.

After distributing her gifts at various hotel room doors, Anna ducked out the back exit of the inn, avoiding being seen by anyone, and went around front to wait for the taxi she had called. The snow had stopped and the world was muffled and silent, as though wrapped gently in a layer of cotton. Anna breathed in deeply; the cold air tickled her nostrils and almost made her sneeze. Then a sudden gust of wind startled her, blowing the snow around her into a little cyclone that covered her with feather-like snowflakes.

As she dusted off, she saw something in the snow at her feet.

Beth's Happy Holiday Missive.

She looked up at the inn and realized she had left her window open—and the letter must have blown outside. She

picked it up and stared down at it. This letter had been following her around for days. Maybe it was time to just open it
and get it over with.

The first thing she saw inside the envelope was a small
stack of photos. She sifted through them. They weren't of Beth,
in her current new life—instead, there was one photo from
every year of their lives together, right up until the last one,
two holidays previous. Anna's breath caught in her chest, her
eyes filled with tears, and she swallowed over a huge lump in
her throat as she saw the photos of herself at seven, eight, nine,
ten. There she was, sitting between Beth and Jack beside the
Christmas tree and the Hanukkah bush. There they were,
walking home from the Christmas Eve service with candles in
their hands. There were Anna, Beth, and her dad, grinning
over a platter of latkes. There was the disastrous time Anna
and Beth had decided to make their own applesauce for the
latkes, but forgotten to close the lid of the food processor
properly. They found little bits of applesauce on the tops of the
kitchen cupboards for years. Anna found she was deeply happy
to see these photos, to sift through these memories. It wasn't
sadness she felt, but joy—and sudden gratitude.

She took a deep breath and teased the letter out of the envelope. The header across the top read, "Anna's Personal Happy
Holiday Missive."

Dear Anna,

*I only did one holiday mailing this year: to you. I hope
you enjoy looking at these photos of our holidays past as
much as I enjoyed compiling them. Seeing all these years
we had together made me feel sad, of course, for all that*

*has been lost. But also happy, for all the many joys we
experienced together—for all the joy your father brought
into my life.*

*First things first, just in case you stop reading. I'm
writing to let you know that I came across an investment
your father made on your behalf when we first got
together and he sold his home in Toronto to move in
with me in Denver and start our life together as a
family. It was a conservative investment, so it hasn't
appreciated a staggering amount—but it has
appreciated, and I certainly hope it's enough to make a
difference in your life in some way.*

Anna took in the amount Beth had written down. It wasn't
huge. For someone else, it probably wouldn't be life-changing.
But it was enough to get her out of the debt she was in and to
start fresh—without the pressure of a job she hated. Suddenly,
and for the first time in a long while, Anna felt like she could
breathe again. She felt as if a weight had been lifted from her
shoulders. She kept reading.

*I know it's hard for you to understand how I could
move on and marry Rick. I also understand why the fact
that I now have another stepdaughter is painful to you. I
need you to know that no one will ever replace your father
in my life—just as no one will ever replace you. I will
never be "over" your dad. I knew that the moment he
died—and Rick is well aware of this, too. He's also
widowed, and his previous wife, and my previous
husband, are a part of our relationship in a personal way I*

will not explain to you—but believe me, it's true. It's wonderful, and healing, and sad sometimes. We are doing our best. Yes, we moved quickly when we met. Only time will tell if it was too quickly. But we are people who have a good understanding of how fast life moves and how short it can be. We knew we wanted to make a life together, so we did. It was not my intention to make you feel you had no place in that life. On the contrary, I very much want you to be a part of my life—and perhaps, when you're ready, our life. I know Rose could use someone like you to talk to as she navigates the loss of a parent, a heartache you have also experienced. No pressure, okay? But your friendship would be a gift to anyone.

Anna, I have missed you fiercely. I will never stop calling, and sending you letters, and inviting you back into my life. I hope someday you will accept the invitation, but know this: it will never be withdrawn. I love you unconditionally, the way your father did. You were a wonderful daughter to us both. You are a wonderful daughter to me still.

I know you have struggled with your grief these past few years, and I know you feel alone. I want to remind you of who you are, through these photos of a little girl at seven, with the bravery and maturity to open her heart to me the way she did. That young lady you were at twelve, on the cusp of teenagehood—you switched schools that year because we moved neighborhoods. I remember how worried you were about making new friends. And how quickly it happened for you, once you revealed your kind, generous, honest soul to others. The year you graduated high school and went to college across the country. We missed you so much, but we were so very proud. And you learned so much, and bravely and openly made more new friends. This is something else about you that has always made me proud: the way you are able to make friends and open yourself to others—but also the way you are able to feel comfortable being alone. That's a skill you're better at than I am, I'm afraid. I hate being alone; it makes me too sad. You have an inner strength I don't think I have. Your dad would say your still waters run deep—and that is so true. You are more than you appear, and I envy the people who get to know you for the first time. What a treat they're in for.

You're going to be fine, Anna. Better than fine. You have all the resources you need inside you to find your way in this life, and I hope that if you don't already know that, this letter serves as a reminder. I love you very much, and my door is open to you, always and forever.

I do hope we can start fresh, one of these days.

Happy holidays, Anna.

With love,

Beth

xx

Anna was startled by the honk of a car's horn. She picked up her handbag and put the letter and photos inside it. She was going to reread the letter later and think more about moving forward with Beth, when she was ready. But for now, she felt very certain of two things.

She couldn't get in that taxi.

And she didn't want to go to Toronto for the holidays. She wanted to stay right where she was. Even if it meant being alone. Because this was something she now realized she was strong enough for—thanks to a person from her past she knew she was not ready to leave behind.

Later in the morning, once she had rechecked herself into the Snow Falls Inn (Deb and Kath had informed her that no, they had not given her room away) and called Nick (he didn't answer, so she left a message explaining she wasn't coming), Anna pushed open the door of the playhouse and stepped inside. Maryam was sitting near the door, reading something on a clipboard. She looked up, and her face registered surprise, then delight. "You stayed!" She hopped off her stool and threw her arms around her friend. "Somehow I had a feeling you would."

"Wow," Anna said, laughing. "This is more the sort of greeting I'd expect from Saima!"

"Sorry, sorry, too much? I'm just so happy to see you."

"Not too much at all. I'm flattered to get a hug from you. And yes, I decided to stay. For myself. Because it's what *I* wanted to do. And because of a letter I got from my stepmother, Beth." She wasn't ready to share the contents of the letter with anyone, but she explained to Maryam that she had received an important message from her former stepmother, and that it had helped her make the decision to stay.

"Okay, so now that you're staying, I really need to talk to you. There are some things I think you should know about—"

As Maryam spoke, a familiar voice boomed across the stage. Anna looked up. Bathed in the floodlights was Josh.

"What is he doing here?"

"Well, he's helping me out, actually. He's doing a bit of

writing for me, and I've asked him to play a role, too. Everyone says this year is going to be the best Hoopla ever, and I can't help but agree, given there's an actual movie star in the cast now."

"But . . . I thought you said he was nothing but a charmer, a liar, and . . ."

Maryam looked sheepish. "I may have judged him a bit harshly. We had a talk last night, and I learned a bit more about who he really is—the way you have. He's really torn up about you two. I think he developed some real feelings, and I owe you an apology for warning you off him so fiercely. I was just worried about you—but I was probably also projecting my past onto you. Just because something bad happened to me doesn't mean it's going to happen to someone else. And Josh . . . well, it turns out he's different."

Anna listened to him deliver his monologue for another moment, then turned back to Maryam. "Is he? He *does* have a girlfriend—you were probably right to warn me."

"That's the thing . . ."

Maryam pulled Anna back into the shadows and relayed what Josh had told her about his relationship with Tenisha just being a PR stunt—and a way for them to keep their private lives more private.

"It's all so complicated," Anna said when Maryam was done. "And he was so hurt when he found out about Nick. The night we met at It's the Most Wonderful Time for a Beer, it all seemed so simple—but it really wasn't at all. We had chemistry, sure. It was exciting. But we never truly understood who the other was. And I'm afraid now it might be too late."

"But you two get along so well. There's just . . . something *right* about the two of you together. Chemistry, yes. I'm a pharmacist, and I want you to know chemistry is *important*." Maryam smiled.

"But it's not everything. I was just in a relationship where I didn't think it all through. I don't want to do that again." Anna couldn't help it, though. The chemistry was still there. Almost against her will, her gaze was drawn across the dim theater to Josh again. He was watching her, too. But she wasn't able to read his expression. Was he surprised to see her? Happy? Still hurt that she had never explained about Nick? Most likely a combination of all of these things. Anna took a deep breath. "Maybe we'll get a chance to talk and try to put all this behind us, somehow. But for now, Josh or no Josh, it doesn't change anything for me." She turned back to Maryam. "I really like him, don't get me wrong. How could I not? He's . . ." She trailed off and Maryam nodded.

"He's a dreamboat," Maryam supplied. "That's all there is to it."

"Just looking at him and hearing his voice . . . Maybe the way I react to him will never change. But I came to some realizations this morning, and those are the reasons I'm sticking around. It's not because of my feelings for Josh, or for Nick, or for anyone. It's just about me—and what *I* need."

"It doesn't change anything for you, though, knowing he's not really with Tenisha?"

Anna watched Josh's handsome face again as he continued to read from the script, turning the tri-holiday take on "A Christmas Carol" into something special.

"In a world that can feel so full of darkness," Josh was

saying in his deep, appealing voice, "Hanukkah is a holiday that provides light and hope for the future. Hope that maybe things can be better . . . that happy endings are possible for anyone."

She did feel an emotional tug toward him, and an attachment to the connections they had shared—but she wasn't going to let that dictate the choices she made. "I'm just not sure how I feel" was all she could say to Maryam. "But I know I want to stay. So, please, let's get to the reason I came. Set design. I'm back. And I want to get to work again and make this the best Holiday Hoopla in Snow Falls history!"

Maryam directed Anna side stage, where the other volunteers were working away on various set design projects. Anna noticed Saif was at the playhouse, too, enthusiastically playing the role of the Ramadan Host, and she paused to watch his performance. For an amateur thespian, Saif had impressive range—he did a wonderful job with his lines, and had an excellent command of the stage. Anna couldn't help but notice the way Maryam gazed at him when he read his lines, pulling herself together with obvious effort in time to deliver his stage directions. Anna made a mental note to ask for an update on that front. But soon, she was lost in the buzz of activity and excitement, buoyed by her sense of purpose—and full of the satisfaction that comes from doing something that you love doing and you're really good at.

Hours later, she was in such a reverie Bruce had to tell her twice that someone had come to the backstage door looking for her.

"For me? Are you sure?" She stood and brushed some tinsel from her jeans—and couldn't help but feel a tiny thrill, despite having told herself earlier she was going to leave Josh out of the equation for a while. Was he waiting backstage to talk to her?

"He seems to feel it's quite urgent," Bruce said, and he sounded a little put out. "Used a lot of big words."

Oh, no. Anna felt a sudden sense of doom.

When she stepped backstage, Nick was standing near the door, arms crossed, a storm cloud expression on his handsome face. "Anna!"

She waited to feel something, seeing him standing there. But she didn't feel anything except an urgent wish that he had not come to find her in Snow Falls. "Nick, what are you doing here?"

"I came to get you, of course. I had always planned to be on the plane. It was going to be a nice Christmas Eve surprise. Until you didn't show up."

"I tried to call you. You didn't answer, so I left you a message telling you I wasn't coming to the airport."

He shook his head. "I don't accept it. I can't. We had plans. Everything was all in place."

"But *I* wasn't in place. I told you I needed time, and that's still true. I didn't think spending Christmas together was a good idea, so I made the decision to stay here."

"Just a few days ago, you were an entirely different person!"

Anna stepped closer and put her hand on his arm. "Maybe that's because you never really knew who I was. I don't blame you for that. I don't think I ever really showed my true self to you because I wanted you to believe I was the perfect woman you thought I was. I'm not. There's so much you don't know."

"Like what?"

"Like, I didn't go backpacking around Europe, the year

before we met. I got fired from my job for taking too many sick days—because I was so grief-stricken over my dad, I couldn't get out of bed—"

"You always make such a big deal out of things, I'm sure it wasn't as bad as that—"

"And I never went backpacking. Once I'd lost my job, I decided to take the trip, but I only made it to Paris. I stayed there for a month, eating croissants and crying in a hotel room. I thought that was something to be ashamed of . . . but I've been starting to realize that it's okay to fall apart sometimes, and you should be with someone . . . someone who gives you the space to share that sort of thing."

"So you hit a bad patch and didn't tell me, okay. Do we really need to talk about it? So unpleasant. Please, Anna. I just need you to come back with me. We don't have much time, the plane has to leave—" He stepped toward her—and then, in one swift move, dropped to one knee. Anna gasped as he pulled a ring box out of his pocket and popped it open.

Inside was a radiant-cut solitaire on a white gold band. Anna peered down at it. "Wait a minute . . ."

"I love you, Anna Gibson. We've had our problems, but I'm sure we can surmount them. Please, say you'll marry me—and then come back to Toronto as my fiancée. Say yes. *Please.*"

Anna stared down at a ring that was unfamiliar to her. "What happened to the other one?" she found herself asking in a daze.

"The other one?"

"The other ring. I found it, by accident, when I was leaving a gift for you in your suitcase."

She watched his cheeks flood with color. He straightened

up and looked sheepish. "Oh, *that* ring." She waited for an explanation. "That one was for someone else."

"*What?*"

"My ex-girlfriend, Elsa, the woman I dated before you. We were supposed to get engaged last Christmas, but we broke up just before we could. I was taking it back to Toronto to return it and get another one for you. Which I did." He shook the ring box at her. "This one."

"I . . . really don't know what to say."

"I'm telling you the truth, at least!" he blustered. "I could have lied, the way you have about your past, but I didn't—because honesty is important. We're making a fresh start here, aren't we?"

"But you had a ring for someone else!"

"Which I exchanged for this one, the perfect ring for *you*."

"No." Anna shook her head. "Not everything can be perfect just because you say it is. I'm not just . . . a placeholder for you. It feels like you want to marry someone—and so it might as well be me."

"I want to marry you. Truly. You're perfect for me."

"What exactly is it that you love about me? Can you give me one reason why you think we should spend our entire lives together?"

"You're beautiful, you're classy. You look great in the clothes I buy you. We'll have a perfect life, I'll make sure of it . . ."

On one hand, Anna was disappointed—in Nick, yes, for his lackluster response, but also in herself for having allowed this charade of a relationship to go on at all. Even six months seemed too long for such a sham. On the other hand, she was relieved she had come to these conclusions before she ended up saying yes for the wrong reasons. Forever was a very long time—and she knew she could not spend the rest of her life with Nick.

"I can't say yes," she said firmly. "It doesn't feel right, and I'm sure if you really think about it, it doesn't feel right to you, either."

"Please." He was sounding increasingly desperate now. "Just come back with me. Put the ring on and say we're engaged. At least long enough for the society pages to take a snap and Elsa to see."

"For Elsa to see? Don't you think forcing someone into an engagement just for optics is not the right solution to your problems?"

"Anna, this is just a misunderstanding. Forget I said that."

"Oh, Nick." He looked so sad, and she felt a wave of compassion for him. He was confused—and probably still heartbroken over someone he had never allowed himself the time and space to get over. "I care about you, and I know you care about me. We had some good times together. I was going through a hard time in my life when we met—and you made my life so much better, helped me take some steps past my grief over my dad, just by being you. I'll always appreciate that. But I'm no one's second choice, and I can't get engaged to you. Not under these circumstances, and not at all."

"You're not my second choice! I never asked Elsa! I never got the chance!"

Anna thought for a long moment and decided to be brutally honest. "Maybe the truth is you'd be my second choice if I said yes. I met someone this week. It's not the right timing and is unlikely to work—but it felt so easy, with this person. So natural. If nothing else, it made me realize what's possible. The kind of relationship I want, that I deserve. One day. When I'm ready. I've made my decision. And I wish you all the best. That's all I can say. Goodbye, Nick."

Nick said nothing. He crammed the ring back in his pocket and stormed out the door, slamming it hard behind him. Anna wasn't sorry to see him go—even if it meant she was standing all alone in the darkness.

SIXTEEN

Maryam

December 24

Maryam burst out of the theater, Anna's words to Nick chasing her: *It's not the right timing . . . but it felt so easy, with this person. If nothing else, it made me realize what's possible. The kind of relationship that I deserve.* Anna had been describing her feelings for Josh, but they aligned so closely with what Maryam felt for Saif, her breath had stopped. Not wanting to add to the drama in the playhouse, she had slipped out, coming to a stop in front of a bench piled high with snow. She collapsed, and the frozen powder cooled her instantly, her long jacket insulating her from the wet.

So much snow surrounding them, everywhere, all at once. She was suddenly sick of this frozen precipitation that refused to budge. Didn't the weather understand how *inconvenient* it was? Snow, snow, everywhere, and nowhere to go, nothing to do, except think and feel, worry and fight.

Maryam stared up at the sky, blinking against the brilliant blue, and quietly resented the crisp, fresh Canadian air.

She heard a loud slam, and then a furious Nick stormed down the steps of the playhouse, his face comically thunderous. So Anna had made her choice—good for her. That was one problem solved, at least.

Snow crunched underfoot, and Maryam spotted Saif making his way toward her. She sprang to her feet, the urge to run away overwhelming, but he stopped her with a single query.

"Are you all right?"

They hadn't spoken since their confrontation at the inn yesterday, yet his first words to her weren't accusatory or demanding, only kind. He had even shown up today because he had promised to play a role in the play. Saif was always so kind.

She nodded, wiping her eyes. "I'm fine."

"Why don't you tell me what's going on? I'd like to help."

Maryam shook her head, not meeting his eyes, and she heard his soft sigh. Part of her wanted to step into his arms. She had a feeling his embrace would be warm, his arms around her a relief—not just from the cold, but from her fear and sadness. Saif would be a safe harbor from her own churning thoughts.

"Are you angry with me?" she asked in a small voice.

"Because you called me a charming opportunist? I'm a lawyer, Maryam. I've been called a lot worse. You should hear what my enemies have to say."

Maryam snorted. "I refuse to believe you have enemies."

Saif settled onto the seat beside her. "My next-door neighbor is nursing a long-running vendetta, just because her cat likes me better than her."

"Cats like food, not people," Maryam countered.

Saif grinned at her. "Which is why I spend a fortune on tuna steak."

Maryam shook her head. This was the problem, right here. This easy conversation, the banter, the . . . rightness of their every interaction. Just like Anna had said: bad timing, unlikely to work, but the relationship she wanted. She had been here before, after all. "I know what you're doing."

"A good lawyer tries to remain transparent in all their dealings," Saif answered smoothly. Then, shifting to face her, concern on his face clear, he reached for her hand, stopping short of her mittens. "Did you leave because you were afraid you were about to punch Nick? I don't know what Anna ever saw in that guy."

"I mean, he does have access to a private jet," Maryam said.

Saif grinned at her, but then his smile faded. "I'm sorry. What I said to you, on the porch . . . I was out of line."

"I got a few digs in there, too," Maryam reminded him. "And you weren't wrong." Her gaze, as always, was drawn to him. His face really was distracting, all smooth brown skin and beautiful brown eyes that saw too much. "Maybe we should just leave it here. What happens at Snow Falls and all that. This is a fantasy, a snow day, a time-out from reality. Right?"

Saif looked away, and she took the silence to mean he was agreeing, but his next words brought her up short.

"You were a beautiful bride."

She blinked at him. Of course he had been at her wedding. His entire family had been invited. "Thank you," she said quietly. "You looked nice, too. I think you wore something . . . gray?"

Saif laughed softly. "Navy blue suit. I know men's suits pretty much all look the same. You were wearing that red-and-gold *lengha* dress, with the thing here—" He gestured to his forehead.

"A *tika*," she said, using the word for the jewel-encrusted forehead ornament worn by *desi* brides.

"Right, *tika*. I don't have any sisters, so I never learned the lingo," he said, smiling in remembrance.

"How is Raihan?" she asked. His older brother, the one who had always been friendly with the other kids, and who had helped Maryam and Saima build snow people and snow animals during their winter cottage vacation all those years ago. Right before Saif ambushed them with a snowball fight.

"Still lives in Denver. Still the favorite son. His son, Muneer, just turned two and is really into Thomas the Train."

"Who isn't?" Maryam said, and they smiled at each other.

"You seemed so happy at your wedding," Saif continued. "I remember thinking, that Yusuf is one lucky guy."

Maryam felt her cheeks warm. "You did not," she admonished. "You barely noticed me." When he didn't say anything, she continued, more quietly. "My marriage didn't even last a year. Two months before our first anniversary, Yusuf told me he was in love with one of the prescribing doctors at his pharmacy. They have a daughter now."

"That must have been devastating," Saif said. "If you like, I can fly to Denver and punch him for you."

Maryam laughed. "He would certainly deserve it, but no thanks. It's been almost four years. I don't like to think about that time in my life."

"You know, I didn't even know you weren't with Yusuf until a few weeks ago," Saif said, almost conversationally.

"Wh-what? Everyone knew! It was the gossip of the decade!" Maryam exclaimed. The news of her short-lived marriage had made the rounds among her parents, their friends, and the wider community. Everyone wanted to know what had led to the split. A few people she barely knew had even called her up and demanded to know the details "so the same thing wouldn't happen" in their marriages. They had been quite put out when she told them to mind their own business.

Beside her, Saif ran a hand over his face. "You know I'm not that close to my family," he said. Ever since Saif had moved to California after law school, his visits home had been sporadic, she knew. "I could have tried harder. I was a restless teen, maybe a bit self-absorbed. Not like you and your sister, or my perfect brother, Raihan."

"Sounds like you might have been jealous, too," Maryam said, teasing gently.

Saif smiled sheepishly. "I pretended that I couldn't be bothered. The truth is, my parents used to compare me to the other kids constantly, and especially to my older brother. It pretty much ruined our relationship. I couldn't wait to move away and start my own life, somewhere they wouldn't be able to comment and judge."

"My ex wasn't close to his family, either," Maryam said. "He never understood why I always wanted to spend time with my parents and Dadu and Dadi-ma."

Understanding flashed in Saif's eyes. "Yusuf is an idiot. We've already established that. If my family were more like yours, I never would have moved to California. Who wouldn't want to be related to Dadu?"

"He is pretty amazing. Especially when he starts to spill some serious *filmy* gossip," she said, using Bollywood slang for the movie business.

"Your sister's wedding would have been the first time I met

my family in a year," Saif said. "Our phone calls usually last about five minutes. They refuse to pay for long distance, which means I always have to call them, and then my mom worries about the cost of the call and sets a timer."

Maryam tried to hide her surprise; her parents called her several times a day, and she lived with them. "That sounds . . . lonely," she said.

Saif considered. "It can be. I work a lot." He paused as if weighing his next words. "And you weren't wrong. I did have a girlfriend, but we broke up late last year."

Maryam knew her parents might be shocked to learn that Saif dated. Observant Muslims were expected to remain single until they married, though some hid relationships from their family until they became more serious. Maryam and Yusuf had been open with their families from the start because their end goal was marriage. That Saif at one point had had a serious girlfriend came as no surprise to her; she knew there were many paths to love. "Thanks for being honest," Maryam said. Her curiosity forced out the next question: "What happened?"

"Lisa and I met at law school. We made sense in a lot of ways, but in the end, she broke up with me," he said. "The truth is, we'd been drifting apart for a while."

"I was glad when Yusuf left," Maryam said impulsively. She had never admitted this to anyone before, but sitting beside Saif on this bench on a hill, high above the village of Snow Falls, somehow she knew he wouldn't judge her. "I mean, I hated him for cheating on me, but I was also sort of . . . relieved? We weren't good together, we never had been, but I was too scared to call time of death on our marriage."

Saif nodded as if that made perfect sense.

"I'm just glad my parents never said 'I told you so,'" Maryam said, and Saif laughed, standing up and dusting snow from his pants.

"My parents said 'I told you so' when Lisa and I broke up," he offered. "The first words out of my dad's mouth."

"No wonder your phone calls home only last five minutes," Maryam said.

Saif laughed again. "You always surprise me," he said, shaking his head. "At your wedding, you seemed like this beautiful, unreachable woman, but you're so much more." The look he sent her was open and still so kind. He turned to face her, hands spread wide. All cards on the table now. "You know how I feel about you, but I also know there isn't really a timeline for recovering from the harm Yusuf caused your heart. I like you, Maryam Aziz. I like you more and more every time we talk. I don't want you to choose me because your parents don't approve, or because I'm this incredibly hot lawyer from California—" Maryam laughed, and he flashed her a cheeky smile. "Or because, once upon a time, twelve-year-old Maryam had a crush on me," he continued. "I want you to choose me for yourself. Because I choose you—the woman you are today, the woman I'm starting to fall for. That's the one I want."

His words were beautiful and sincere. This man could truly break her, Maryam thought as she looked up at Saif. She knew that if Saif left her, her heart would never, ever recover. "I can't—" she stammered, hating herself for not being as brave as he was.

Saif didn't say anything, only gave her a small, understanding smile before turning to walk down the hill without another word.

Maryam wasn't sure how long she sat on the bench by herself. Somehow, she pulled herself together and returned to the playhouse, to make her excuses to Celine and the others. By the time she stumbled back to the inn, it was late afternoon and her parents and Dadu were gathered in the foyer, their expressions grim.

"What's wrong?" she asked. Somehow, she knew the other shoe was about to drop.

"It is your sister," a grave-looking Dadu said. "Saima has disappeared."

SEVENTEEN

Anna

December 24

Anna put down the sewing needle and stretched her arms over her head. After Maryam's abrupt departure—followed by Nick's angry one—she had poked her head out the back door of the theater and seen her friend deep in conversation with Saif. Their heads had been close together; Anna had been unable to see their faces, but hoped they were having the heart-to-heart they needed to have, and that whatever had upset Maryam, she'd come talk to Anna about it if she needed her. When Maryam hadn't returned, Anna had decided to keep on working. It was Christmas Eve, and they were running out of time to finish the play. She knew she could help Maryam in a way that would make a difference to something important to her: staying the course and getting things ready for the Hoopla the next day.

It had amazed Anna how many of the volunteers stayed all day, too, even though it was Christmas Eve. No one in Snow

Falls did last-minute shopping, Bruce had explained, given that you could shop for the holidays year-round in their town. It turned out the Hoopla didn't take people away from their homes and families during the holidays. On the contrary, it gave them all something to work toward—and this year, thanks to Maryam, it was even more special because everyone felt included.

Now Anna surveyed her set design efforts.

"This is amazing, Anna," said Celine, approaching from the side stage. "Absolutely gorgeous. We got so much done today, we're practically ready for the big production. It's all going to look incredible. This is going to be the best Hoopla we've ever had!"

"It does look great," Anna said. "But it wasn't all me. I couldn't have done any of this without all of you. Look what we accomplished together!"

They had constructed several interchangeable sets, each one on a rolling screen. There was the town exterior, which a group of high school students had painted to look just like Snow Falls; the interior of main character Elvira Scrooge's bedroom, complete with an elaborately curtained four-poster bed on wheels that Kate had managed to have moved over to the theater; and then the seasonal-decoration-festooned sets that would be used for the visits from the Holiday Hosts: Hanukkah, Christmas, and Eid. There was a huge menorah Bruce and the rest of the crew had constructed, with soft glowing lightbulbs shaped like flames; an enormous Christmas tree from a tree farm on the outskirts of town, covered in beautiful decorations and lights; and a giant crescent moon for Ramadan that would light up along with the menorah and Christmas tree lights at the end of the play. The ceiling above the stage had been transformed into a spectacular night sky, complete with twinkling strings of starry lights and one large star for Christmas. Plus all the costumes and accessories, which Anna and the volunteer crew had also been busy gathering, sourcing, and altering to perfection.

"There," said Celine's daughter, laying a vivid blue-and-gold robe across the table before them. "Chase Taylor's costume is done. I can't believe I'm saying that." She pretended to swoon, then leaned against the table. "Do you think he's coming back here today?"

Anna checked her watch. "It's getting a bit late, so I doubt it," she said, and felt the ache of disappointment in her chest. It was going to take time to sort through her feelings for Josh. "You should probably all get going. Get back to your loved ones for Christmas Eve. As Celine said, we're very nearly done here, and all the little details can be taken care of when we meet here tomorrow a few hours before the play starts."

But Anna found she wasn't quite ready to leave. She continued to work once she was alone, and soon the stage's transformation was complete, the various scenes perfect. Anna knew she had managed to bring to life what Maryam had been imagining when she wrote the play, and that seeing all this done would bring a smile to her friend's face. Anna's stomach growled. It was time for her to get going. She knew she could always count on finding *iftar* leftovers at the inn. She'd head back, get something to eat, then look for Maryam and find out what had happened between her and Saif—and tell her friend everything that had happened with Nick.

As she tidied up her workstation, Anna was startled by a voice behind her.

"*Wow.*"

She turned to see a young woman with dark curly hair, a puffy jacket, and an orange woolen toque, taking in her surroundings. "This place looks incredible."

"Thanks." She stepped down from the stage. "Can I help you?"

"Are you Anna? Chase Taylor sent me over to grab his costume. He's stuck on set and said he still needed to try it on and make sure it fit for tomorrow, so . . ." She extended her hand. "Sorry. Hi, I'm Samantha. I'm the set design assistant for *Two Nights at Christmas*. And I just have to tell you, this set is amazing! We were in here during location scouting, so I saw what this stage looked like before. Did you do this?"

"Well, I have a team of volunteers . . ."

"But the concept, this is yours?"

Anna tried to be humble when she said yes. Samantha was now looking at her with great interest. "Do you mind if I bring my boss by to see this sometime?"

"Of course. You're welcome to come see the play tomorrow, if you're still in town. I'm not sure how well everyone on the crew is doing with their plans to travel out of here in time for Christmas tomorrow—it sounds like commercial flights are really backed up. But if you need something to do . . ."

Samantha nodded. "Absolutely, travel is a mess."

"Well, feel free to come to the show. Bring as many crew members as you want. We have tons of chairs."

"Sure. I just might do that. A lot of us work so much that the crew is like family—so a bunch of us are just staying put, I think. And, of course, we'll definitely want to come out and support Chase." She reached out and took the costume from Anna. "Sometimes home is wherever your friends are, right?"

Anna found herself nodding. "That's true." She cleared her throat and looked down at the costume now in Samantha's arms. "So, um, tell Chase . . ." She looked back up and shook her head. "Just let him know if it fits, he can keep it with him. And if it doesn't, just come back for an adjustment tomorrow at least an hour before showtime."

"Will do! Thanks, Anna. And great job!"

When Anna was alone again, she surveyed the stage. It really did look wonderful and had been one of the most fun and rewarding jobs she'd ever done in her life. Samantha had said she was a set design assistant—and oddly, up until that moment, Anna hadn't even considered that that could be a career path anywhere outside of community theater. Perhaps if she really did show up to the pageant with her boss, Anna could ask them some questions about set design. She filed that away to think about later as she shut off lights and then locked the theater doors.

Outside, Snow Falls was as pretty as a picture on the front of a holiday card. Anna wandered slowly along Main Street, taking it all in, trying to imprint it in her memory. No set designer in the world could create what happened so naturally here. Snow Falls *was* the holidays—and Anna knew she was never going to forget it. She was glad she had decided to stay, even if she did feel a little lonely. *Sometimes home is wherever your friends are*, Samantha had said. Anna was going to try to remember that.

She continued to trudge along the snowy street toward the

inn. Soon, Buon Natalie's, the Italian restaurant that had been part of the movie set, came into view. She saw that the lights were on, but when she looked in the windows as she passed, she didn't see anyone inside. Perhaps they were setting it up for another shoot, although Anna hoped the director of *Two Nights at Christmas* had finally decided to give the cast and crew a holiday break. She kept walking, increasing her pace because, despite how picturesque her trek through the town was, it was a cold night and she could feel her empty stomach grumbling beneath the winter jacket she had borrowed from the inn.

"Anna?"

She turned.

Josh was standing in the doorway of Buon Natalie's, wearing an apron splattered with various stains. He was smiling shyly, looking a bit disheveled—and as handsome as ever. Her heart did a few somersaults.

"Hi," she said, returning his shy smile.

"Heading anywhere important?"

"Just back to the inn to try to scrounge up something to eat."

"Would you care to join me for dinner?"

"Oh . . . well . . ."

He stepped out into the snowy street and came toward her. When he was a few feet away, he stopped. "Listen, Anna, I know things got really complicated with us and that we didn't start off on the right foot. But the thing is . . . I really like you. I can't stop thinking about you. The first time I saw you, it felt like I'd known you forever. That hasn't changed. You're kind, you're generous, you're sweet and funny—plus, you're smart, a good friend, and an even better person, and honestly, I could go on all night. I've never met anyone like you. When I heard you talking to Nick earlier, I couldn't help but think you deserved so much more than what he had to offer you. And when I heard you mention me . . . I realized I couldn't let you go without trying to give us one more chance. So say you'll have dinner with me? An official first date, a fresh start, and maybe a new beginning?"

Anna stood stock-still, every rational thought flown out of her brain. She opened and closed her mouth, painfully aware that she probably looked like a confused goldfish in what was otherwise the most romantic moment of her life.

"Now that you know who I am, and I know who you are . . . what if we took a night to be us, together?" He tilted his head and smiled the adorable, crinkly-eyed smile she liked so very much, and she began to come to her senses. "Plus, I made brisket. And latkes. And once I get my mom on the line and ask her for her recipe, I'm pretty sure I'm going to be able to whip up a chocolate Yule log cake, too."

"Who in their right mind would turn an offer like that down?" Anna managed, walking with him into the restaurant. He took her coat and hung it up as she surveyed the scene: the lights were low, and a table in the center of the room was set with plates, cutlery, and wineglasses, and lit with candles. "Just as long as you don't serve ranch dressing with the latkes!"

He laughed. "Hey—don't knock it until you've tried it!"

Josh told Anna he didn't need help cooking—that she should just sit on a barstool at the large kitchen-pass window, chatting with him and watching him work while enjoying a glass of rich, spicy Italian Syrah. The wine went to Anna's head immediately—and she let it, feeling deeply at ease as she took bites of pillowy, salty, soft sourdough bread dipped in olive oil and balsamic vinegar between sips while watching Josh prepare their feast.

Anna smiled as she watched him drag the phone around the kitchen after calling his mom for baking advice—her name, he said, was Reggie. The phone was attached to the wall by a long curly cord, and he twisted it around the kitchen as he held the receiver to his ear and listened intently to her instructions. "Yeah, Mom," Anna heard him say quietly, his body angled away from Anna. "It is someone special. No, you're right, I've never cooked for anyone before. Yes. I hope so, too. I'll talk to you tomorrow. Love you, too. Say hi to everyone for me. See you soon. Bye."

He brought the brisket out of the oven to rest—it smelled divine, like so many of Anna's holiday memories—popped in the Yule-log-shaped cake, and set to work frying the latkes. Soon the smell of crispy golden potatoes and onions filled the air, and Anna pushed away the bread, wanting to save room.

When all was prepared, Josh set the platters of food along the kitchen window, then handed Anna an empty plate. "Go ahead, you first," he said, touching her waist as he moved past her. His touch sent shivers up and down her body.

He brought the wine bottle to the table and refilled her glass, then sat across from her, plate piled as high as hers. Anna took a bite of the brisket first, and moaned. "This is incredible," she said before dipping a latke in sour cream and bringing it to her lips. She couldn't help but think of all the meals out she had had with Nick—most of them haute cuisine, with foams

and essences and various and sundry forms of molecular gas-
tronomy. The meals had always left her hungry enough to eat
a cheeseburger afterward. She knew that wasn't going to be the
case tonight.

Josh put down his fork and lifted his glass. She lifted hers,
too, and looked into his eyes. "To fresh starts," he said. "And
second chances." She tapped her glass against his and smiled.

"So, should we start right from the beginning?" Anna
asked. "Who exactly do I find myself dining with here tonight
at this fine establishment? Tell me about yourself . . ."

"Josh," he said, staring into her eyes. "My real name is
Josh." He put down his glass and reached across the table to
squeeze her hand. Again, she felt a pleasant tingle from his
touch and squeezed back, feeling like a current was running
back and forth between them. "I was born up in Toronto—ever
heard of it?"

"Sure have," Anna said, nodding enthusiastically. "What
was young Josh Tannenbaum like?"

"I don't remember telling you my last name . . . Are you a
spy?" He winked.

"Lucky guess. So go on, answer my question."

"I was the shyest, dorkiest kid in my class, always had my
head in a book, and I wanted to be a writer—but once I got
contact lenses, I was spotted by a casting director at a mall and
got my first commercial."

"I cannot imagine you as nerdy. And by the way, I think
you look great in glasses."

"How would you know?" He raised an eyebrow. "Have we
met before?"

"We-ell, I did see you in that great movie you did, *One Night at Christmas?*"

"Oh, right. That was my first big break—or so I thought. A nice Jewish boy doing a Heartline Channel Christmas romance. Once I started doing commercials, I decided I wanted to be a serious actor, but the roles I was getting . . . weren't exactly serious. So I decided to act the hell out of *One Night at Christmas.* And it did get me noticed—I got a few other roles, most notably *Captain Eagleman,* which perhaps I should have foreseen was going to be the worst Hollywood flop ever—"

At this Anna held up her hand. "No, wait—it was not as bad as *Howard the Duck.*"

"Okay, fine, *Howard the Duck* being the only other flop of the same stature." He sighed and leaned back. "So, anyway, one bad movie led to a few other mediocre roles, led to me deciding to work my ass off trying to get taken seriously as a true 'artist.' All the while, I had a feeling something wasn't right—like maybe I wasn't on the right path. Then I decided to go back to my original dream: writing. I wrote *Moonlight* and it did well—but I started being really hard on myself and thinking that in order to be truly successful, I had to be good at *everything,* as if I could make everyone forget all about any of my failures by somehow becoming this perfect version of a movie star. Things became a real whirlwind after that, and I was on the wrong path. I finally got the spotlight I thought I had been craving to shine on me. Only, once that happened, I realized I hadn't ever really focused on what was right for me— I had just focused on trying to be the best at what I was doing in every moment, and never on being real."

"Is that so bad?" Anna asked. "Trying to be the best at what you do? I still think you're being a bit hard on yourself."

He put down his fork and thought for a moment. "Maybe not. I think ambition is great. But ambition for the sake of ambition—just to tick off boxes? Well, it can come at a cost. Fame is no joke. Even the small taste of it I've had has proven that. I'm just not sure I'm cut out for it. I miss writing."

"Wow," Anna said, sipping her wine. "This is a deep dive for a first date."

"There's just something about you that makes me feel like I know you. Sure we haven't met before?"

Anna shook her head. "Never. I have one of those faces, though. People think they know me."

He rewarded her with his warm, rumbly familiar laugh. "Actually, you have the most unforgettable face I've ever seen." He looked into her eyes for a long time, and she gazed back at him, feeling perfectly and utterly happy. "Now, how about you? I've been going on about myself, when meanwhile, I know nothing about you. And I want to know everything." He reached across the table and laced his fingers with hers. "Absolutely everything. No stone left unturned." He made that sound so impossibly sexy, all the hairs on Anna's arms stood on end.

"Right," she said, trying to focus, even as his touch had made her body feel like fireworks were going off inside her veins. "Well, I'm Anna Gibson. Also born in Toronto, but I moved to Denver when I was seven."

"And what was young Anna Gibson like?"

"Home-decor-obsessed? The youngest person on the planet to learn the entire Benjamin Moore paint-color lexicon by heart? Also, a die-hard Toronto Maple Leafs fan, even after

I moved from Toronto—and eventually realized they were probably never going to win the Stanley Cup again."

He laughed and squeezed her fingers.

"Something you should know about me is . . . I'm unemployed. And I think I may now know exactly what you mean about ambition for the sake of it—or doing a job just because you feel like you have to, for the wrong reasons."

"You quit a job you hated?"

"Well, technically no, but I'm almost sure I'm fired—and even if I'm not, I don't think I can go back. It's not what I want to do."

"And what *do* you want to do?"

"For one thing, I want more of those latkes!"

He hopped up and grabbed the platter and brought it over to the table. "For another," she said as she helped herself to the delicious shredded potato pancakes with extra sour cream, "I want to enjoy tonight. And get to know you more. And—"

The shrieking sound of an alarm interrupted her, and they both ran to the kitchen to find smoke billowing out of the oven. Anna waved around a dish towel while Josh pulled a smoldering chocolate Yule log out of the oven. "Well," he said sorrowfully, "I guess I really did lean into the spirit of the Yule log."

"Not everything can be perfect," Anna said.

"Not even you?"

"Especially not me. Please, don't ever call me perfect."

He put down the smoking pan and turned to her, pulling her close and looking down at her. "Anna, you are perfectly imperfect—and I like you exactly the way you are."

Anna smiled up at him. "I feel the same about you," she

murmured as he leaned down and kissed her softly, then with more intensity—until the room melted away and they almost forgot where they were. Eventually, he led her back to the table and poured out the last of the wine instead of dessert. In the candlelight, Anna told Josh about Beth's letter, and how it had made her feel—about her hopes and dreams for the future, and how maybe they included finding a way to let Beth back into her life. They carried the plates into the kitchen together and washed up—laughing as they threw the entire burned Yule log straight into the garbage. Later, as Anna dried the last dish, she had to stifle a yawn. They had been too deep in conversation—and deep into each other—to notice how late it was getting. "You're tired," Josh said. "I should get you back to the inn."

But Anna felt dismayed. "I don't want this night to be over."

He pulled her parka down from the hook he had hung it on earlier and bundled her inside it, then kissed her nose. "If you want it to be, this is the first of many nights like this with me."

"You mean, the first of many nights when you borrow a restaurant that's also a rom-com movie set and make me a perfect Hanukkah meal on Christmas Eve?"

"Well, maybe not exactly this," he said with another deep and inviting laugh. He kissed her for a long moment, then smoothed her hair away from her face and looked down at her. "Especially if I'm going to be doing more writing, I may not always be so close to movie sets—but I can promise to always make our time together interesting."

"I'd expect nothing less from a spy," she said, standing on her tiptoes and kissing him again as he wrapped his arms around her and made her feel right at home—even if she was in the last place she'd ever imagined she'd end up on Christmas Eve.

Outside, Josh shot Anna a mischievous look. "Would you like me to carry you home again?" he said, and held out his arms as she laughed.

"No, thank you. This time, I'm wearing much more practical footwear—although I must say, I never thought I'd go on a first date wearing borrowed, enormous snow boots."

"First date, huh?" Josh smiled and reached for her hand. "We really did this, didn't we?"

"We did," Anna said, smiling into the holiday-lit glow of the night, the lights strung across every surface in Snow Falls shining like little red, green, silver, and gold stars.

"It didn't really feel like a first date." He squeezed her hand as they walked.

Anna murmured her agreement but then slowed her pace. Josh stopped walking and looked down at her. "Hey, you okay?"

She hesitated. "I am, but I want to be very honest with you. As you know, I just ended a relationship where things moved very quickly. I never really felt I had time to catch my breath until it was almost too late. I don't want that to happen again. Because I really like you, and also . . . well, I don't want this to end. But I also don't want us to get ahead of ourselves. Am I making sense here?"

"You're making perfect sense to me. You always do. And Anna, please know there is no pressure here." Josh lifted his hand and touched her cheek, then put his thumb under her chin and gently raised her face so they were eye to eye once more. "I understand you. And while what's happening between us feels like it's straight out of the pages of some romance-movie script, it's real. And it's important to me. We will take things slow, and we will do things right. I promise." Then he kissed her and she forgot about everything else but the warmth of his lips in the cold December night.

EIGHTEEN

Maryam

December 24

Back at the inn, Maryam paced her parents' room, thoughts churning furiously while her parents and Dadu watched, concerned. They had gathered away from the others to figure out what to do about Saima's disappearance.

"When was the last time anyone saw her?" Maryam demanded, and her parents looked at each other. Saima hadn't come downstairs for *suhoor* this morning, and Azizah had taken her up a plate.

"She was still upset this morning," Azizah said now. "I told her not to worry about the lost deposits, that we would work something out. I reminded her that this is all the *qadr* of Allah, and that things happen for many reasons, but we must be patient. She promised she would come downstairs later, and that we would come up with a plan together."

"I guess she got tired of waiting and decided to do something on her own. But where did she go, and why didn't she leave a note?" Maryam asked out loud, running her hands through her hair in frustration. She had ransacked their shared room as soon as she heard Saima had vanished, but except for a missing toothbrush and Saima's purse, her sister had left everything else behind. She had tried to track down Anna, but she wasn't in her room, either. Maryam could have used Anna's calm, cheerful optimism right now.

"Have we asked our hosts if they have seen Saima today?" Dadu asked.

Maryam and her parents looked at one another. No one had bothered to ask Deb or Kath; Maryam hastily donned her hijab and ran downstairs to the reception desk.

"Oh, sure, Saima told me she was on her way to the airport," Kath said casually, sorting through a pile of paperwork before her. "Didn't she tell you?"

Maryam gritted her teeth. "She left without a word to anyone."

"Oh, dear. I wondered what was going on," Kath said, looking up from what looked like a bill. "Deb talked to her for a bit, let me ask her." She called her partner out from the back office, and Deb emerged, dressed in another bright Christmas sweater, this one featuring a large gold bow. Deb frowned, thinking, after Kath explained the situation.

"She seemed to be in a right rush," Deb said. "I told her the two taxis that service Snow Falls were tied up, but we just had word that things were starting to open back up. Apparently, Toronto finally dug themselves out, though they had to call in the army reserve to help." Deb and Kath exchanged amused glances. "Snooty Toronto won't live this down anytime soon," she said, laughing. She sobered in the face of Maryam's worried expression. "Sorry, love, I wish I could tell you more. Saima seemed determined, and she didn't really listen when I told her all the planes were booked up."

"I thought she mentioned something about a . . . private plane, was it, Deb?" Kath said, and Maryam closed her eyes.

Nick's plane. Of course. Saima must have been stewing all night over the fact that Anna's rich boyfriend—or, rather, her ex-boyfriend—had sent a plane to rescue her. Maybe her desperate sister thought she could talk herself into a ride, or might be able to stow away somehow. It sounded like something Saima might do.

"When did she leave?" Maryam asked, her worry mounting.

"Shortly after you all left for Main Street," Deb confirmed.

Which meant Saima had been gone for hours. There was nothing else to do but try to retrace her sister's steps. A sudden thought chilled Maryam: What if Saima had gotten lost? What if she had never made it to the airport?

"I'm going after her," Maryam said. "Please, can you tell my parents to stay here, in case she returns?"

"The streets still aren't passable, I'm afraid," Deb said, clearly dismayed at this plan. "Our snowmobile is out on a supplies run right now. If you wait, it will be back soon and maybe you could borrow it? Have you ever driven one before?"

But Maryam shook her head. "My sister might be stranded and all alone. She never had a great sense of direction, and now everything is covered in snow." Plus, after what happened to Nick at the playhouse, she doubted he would be in the mood to give a random person a ride back to Toronto. She had a sudden vision of Saima trudging through snow, frozen, cold, lost. Fear gripped her heart. Her sister was in danger.

"I'm leaving right now," she said. She tugged on the jacket she had brought from her room.

"I don't know if that's a good idea, love," Kath said, still dubious, and Maryam opened her mouth to argue.

"She'll be safe. I'm going with her," Saif said from behind them.

Maryam turned to meet his gaze. She hadn't even noticed him standing there. "You don't have to—" she started, but he was already walking toward the door.

"Come on, Saima had a head start," he called back.

She followed, a small part of her relieved to have company, even as another part couldn't help but notice that he hadn't looked at her. He must be hurt and embarrassed, but he was too polite and kind not to offer his assistance. Wonderful, frustrating man.

Outside, Saif walked ahead, clearing a path, while Maryam trudged behind, and they turned south instead of the usual north to the downtown core. Saima had said it was a ten-mile walk to the airport. In this snow, that would take hours. Worry over her sister hastened her steps, and soon she was dogging Saif's heels, urging him forward.

"What if she—" Maryam started.

"She's fine," Saif said.

"Okay, but what if—"

"Your sister practices medicine in war-torn countries. She fell in love while working in a bomb shelter. A little Canadian snow won't stop her. In fact, I bet it only fueled her fury." Even though his back was to her, she could hear the smile in his voice.

"Saima is good at fury," Maryam agreed, and Saif chuckled, a warm sound.

As they marched through the snow, Maryam blurted: "She blames me. She thinks we should have stayed in the airport that first night we landed."

"If she blames you, it's because she can, because you won't hold it against her. Saima knows none of this is your fault. She and Miraj made the mistake of assuming the Canadian winter would cooperate with their hastily planned wedding."

Saif's words made sense. Her sister had been angry at the one person who wouldn't escalate a fight, the one person in the family who considered it her job to stay calm. It wasn't fair, but it was how things were. Or, rather, how they had been. Maryam knew that when she eventually found Saima, and after she made sure her sister was safe, they needed to really talk: about their relationship, and about how Maryam often felt taken for granted. She needed to be more open and honest about what she wanted. She looked at Saif clearing the path in front of her and wondered why he was still single. Perhaps he was still heartbroken over his ex. "Did you and Lisa plan to get married?" Maryam asked. She was glad the path hadn't widened. It was easier to talk to him this way.

He must have felt the same because he answered readily. "We talked about it, but I think both of us knew we weren't going to end up together." He laughed softly, and she resisted the urge to lean forward to catch the sound, cup it in her hands. His laugh was magnetic. "She realized, in the end, that she wanted to marry someone who knew who she was and where she came from."

"I'm sorry," Maryam said.

"Don't be. She's happier with Brendan. They met at church, but their families have been friends for years. It was a better fit."

Every relationship had its challenges; Maryam was intimately aware of that fact. Some couples started off on the same page, but grew apart. Others appeared wildly different at first glance, but had enough in common to grow together. She and Yusuf had been the former, but the more she interacted with Saif, the more she dared to believe that things could be different with him. *He could break you*, a small voice reminded her. *What if it's worth it?* another voice asked.

"Why did you want to come with me, Saif? Aren't you sick of me by now?" The faint neediness in that last question was humbling.

"It seemed a better option than staying back at the inn and worrying." He glanced back at her, finally. "And no, I'm not sick of you yet. Strangely, it's the exact opposite."

The path widened, and she stepped beside him. Maryam looked at Saif in profile. A handsome face: sharp nose, strong jaw covered in dark stubble. He hadn't shaved, and Maryam wondered what he'd look like with a beard. Saif had always been clean-shaven, but now her fingers itched to run along the bristle.

"I can take care of myself," she said.

"And yet I would still worry," he answered, not quite catching her eye.

"I'm glad you're here," Maryam said quietly, and beside her Saif was silent.

"We'll find Saima," he said. No mention of their earlier conversation outside the playhouse, or the pain it must have caused him. His openness and kindness repaid by her cowardice.

She felt awful about her reaction; he kept offering his hand, and she kept skittering away. "Why aren't you happy?" Maryam asked. "You told me you weren't, during that first *suhoor*." Maybe she wasn't ready to have that other talk, the one that involved her heart, but she could give him this. A listening ear. "Is it because of your breakup with Lisa?"

Saif's lips quirked, as if amused by the trace of jealousy in her voice, but he shook his head.

"Are you tired of being a lawyer?" Maryam guessed, but he shook his head again. "Have you secretly recorded a death metal album, and you're afraid your parents will disown you?" she tried again, and Saif burst out laughing.

"It's like you can see directly into my heart," he said, smiling at her. They had reached the town limits now and were making good time, despite the snow. At this rate, Maryam guessed they would be at the airport by . . . sometime tomorrow morning. She tried not to sigh, and focused on Saif.

"Tell me the real reason you're not happy," she said now. "I'm not just asking you because my toes are numb and I need a distraction. I'm asking because . . . you're my friend."

She held her breath, wondering if he would push back against the label. But if she was starting to think of Anna, a woman she had met four days ago, as a friend, then surely her longtime family friend and equally longtime hopeless crush could also be something friend-shaped? *And maybe something more*, that new voice piped up.

"When I brought this up last time, you told me to keep my problems to myself," he teased.

"That was when I assumed you were a self-absorbed boy looking for validation."

"And now?" There was a hint of vulnerability in his voice, as if he needed to know her answer.

"Now I know who you really are," she said softly. "Tell me why you're not happy, Saif."

His eyes darkened as he looked at her, before focusing on the landscape around them. Snow was everywhere—on the road, sidewalk, empty fields. Yet beneath, life teemed, even if it was momentarily in stasis. A few weeks of warmth and sunshine, and leaves would grow, flowers bloom, fields and grass grow green and then heavy with their harvest. The world was a miracle, at all times of the year.

"I told you that I felt stuck, but I'm starting to realize it's more than that. I thought maybe I was missing my family, but now that I've had some time to think"—he smiled grimly at this; the last few days they had had nothing but time—"I'm starting to wonder if it's not my circumstances. Maybe there's just something wrong with *me*."

Part of her wanted to assure Saif there was nothing wrong with him; that in her mind, he was perfect. But another part realized that what he needed right now was to be heard. After a brief pause, he continued, gaze staring straight ahead as he spoke.

"Remember when I told you that I thought we hadn't given our parents enough credit? That we made decisions based on an assumed anger without solid evidence? I think that applies to us, too. To me. I wanted to be an actor, and when that dream fell apart, I just . . . gave up. And now that I am what I set out to be—a *very* successful lawyer"—his eyebrows waggled at this self-aggrandizement, and Maryam chuckled—"part of me is angry at that other, younger Saif. For giving up and running away. For not taking failure on the chin and fighting. For not persisting. I don't know if any of this makes sense."

He was mourning his younger self in the shadow of the successful person he had become. Maryam knew how he felt, maybe better than anyone. Hadn't she done the same thing? Beside him, she nodded. "It makes perfect sense to me," she said.

"I feel it more during certain times of the year. Don't get me wrong, I love California. It's beautiful and sunny, and I've made so many good friends. I like where I work. But sometimes, especially during Ramadan, I get this intense pang of . . . homesickness. It sounds strange, I know."

"You're missing your people, being around the ones who know you best," Maryam said.

Saif nodded. "Every Ramadan when I fast, or when I drive to the nearest mosque, I think about how things were when we were young. Being here in Snow Falls—with you and your family—brought that all back. I guess I miss who I was before I became who I am right now."

Maryam was moved by his words. "I like who you are right now," she admitted. "Not just who you were back then."

Saif stopped walking and turned to look at her. "I like who you are, too."

Maryam's heart sped up at his words. How did Saif always know exactly what to say? She wanted to return his trust. To tell him something she had barely admitted to herself because she knew he would understand. "Sometimes I resent Saima. She got to leave home while I stayed behind. I'm happy in Denver," she hurried to say. "But sometimes I wish I had lived a more adventurous life, like you. I love my sister, but she's always taken it for granted that I'll stay at home to take care of things.

When I stopped doing that over the course of our . . . snow day, I think it shocked her."

"Snow day," Saif mused. "Is that what this is? Do you think things will be different once we get back to our regular lives?"

"I think that depends on us," Maryam said. They had stopped walking again. At this rate, they wouldn't reach the airport until tomorrow afternoon, but Maryam couldn't seem to force herself to take another step forward, suddenly lost in Saif's dark brown eyes. His expression softened, and he reached out a hand—

A piercing honk startled them apart. A large truck with an enormous bright orange plow attached to the front sped toward them, horn honking a few more times. The truck stopped beside them, and the passenger-side window rolled down to reveal a worried Deb.

"There you are! We were afraid you'd freeze out here. Jerry offered to give us a lift when we explained the situation."

"What situation?" Maryam asked, nodding at Jerry, an older white man with a thick gray beard. *He'd make a good Santa*, she thought, filing the information away for later.

"Saima didn't head to the airport like we thought. She went into town. She's at that little mosque right now. We came to fetch you, soon as we heard." Deb moved over to make space. "It's a tight squeeze, but can't leave you behind, Saif. The temperature plunges at night."

Saif helped Maryam up, his hand warm even through her wool mitten, before hauling himself inside the cab. Deb wasn't lying—it was a tight fit. Maryam was wedged against Saif. They both tried to ignore the close quarters, but when she hazarded a glance, she could see his cheeks had pinked at the proximity, even as he tried to shift, to give her more room. Impulsively, she laid a hand on his arm.

"It's okay," she whispered. Then: "Thank you for coming with me tonight."

Saif met her gaze. "There's nowhere else I'd rather be," he said. They both looked straight ahead, and Maryam felt her arm tingling where it was pressed against his hard chest. Saif shifted to lay his arm over the top of the bench seat, to give her more room, but the movement had the opposite effect and—briefly unbalanced—she toppled against his side. They both froze at this more intimate position before cautiously relaxing. Maryam closed her eyes and inhaled his scent: pine needles, citrus, and a hint of coffee from his *suhoor.*

"I'm sorry if I stink," he said, trying to joke, though his voice was hoarse.

She turned her face up to his. They were so close her head was tucked right below his chin, and she fought the urge to burrow into the hollow of his throat and inhale deeply. Their physical intimacy was nearly overpowering.

"You always smell good," she said instead, and he huffed out an embarrassed laugh.

Saif had been there for her during this entire trip, Maryam thought. He had helped her cook *suhoor,* ordered food that first night, kept Dadu company, and been unfailingly generous. Plus, he had helped her realize her own dreams. What was happening between them was getting harder for her to ignore—though another, deeper part of her still had doubts, still resisted the pull of a new relationship.

"Sarah from Topkapi Café called the inn after you all left,"

Deb said, interrupting her train of thoughts. They were headed toward Main Street; Maryam had been so wrapped up in Saif she had barely noticed. "Saima had been there for a while, but it was hard to get a word out of her, she was crying so much. Once Sarah got her settled, she let us know, and luckily Jerry was round doing the roads and offered a lift. We came straight after you."

"I'm not sure Saima will want to talk to me," Maryam said, trying not to focus on her galloping emotions. "She's pretty upset with all of us."

"She's your sister; you'll fight and you'll squabble, but in the end, you're all you've got. I've three sisters back in Tasmania. We'd scream and yell in the morning, but then be all cuddled in a heap on the couch by evening. Wildcats, our mum called us. I miss them every day."

Maryam stared out the window, at the pretty shops they slowly passed. Thanks to the oversized tires and snowplow, she could actually see some of the street in front of her as they drove. She straightened as they approached an adorable Italian restaurant.

"Isn't that—" she started.

"Buon Natalie's, yes, excellent meatballs," Deb said.

"It's where they shot the movie my wife loves, *One Night at Christmas*," Jerry rumbled. He even sounded like Santa Claus, Maryam thought.

As they drove past the restaurant, Maryam recognized a familiar couple in the window—Josh and Anna, holding hands and staring into each other's eyes. Her heart melted at the sight of her new friends sharing a beautiful moment together.

Beside her, she felt Saif shift. "I'm glad I was wrong about

Chase," he said, so only she could hear. "He really likes Anna. I bet they will make it work, even if it's long distance."

"Nothing a good long-distance phone plan can't help," she said lightly.

"I was thinking of getting one of those for Eid," he said, and caught her eye. The moment stretched between them.

This is it, she thought, heart pounding. *Time to tell him how you feel. Do it, Maryam! Take a chance!*

Instead, she abruptly turned her head away and blurted, "Jerry, would you like to play Santa in the pageant? I'm in charge of the script, and I think you'd be perfect."

"Glad to," Jerry said. "I'll ask the missus to dust off the costumes."

Beside her, she heard Saif sigh and shift in his seat so his arm lay between them now, creating distance. She instantly missed his warmth.

They pulled up to Topkapi Café, and Saif jumped down before turning to help her out.

"Give us a ring if you need a ride back," Deb called from the window. Maryam turned to face Saif reluctantly; he wouldn't meet her eye.

"Yusuf must have really hurt you," he said. It wasn't a question.

Maryam's hands trembled as she adjusted her mittens. "I think a part of me has been broken ever since."

"We're all broken," Saif said. "We just make beautiful new things with our broken pieces. I hope you can do that, too, one day." He shoved his hands in his pockets. "Take your time talking to Saima," he said, still not meeting her gaze. "It's time for the truth now."

Sarah rushed up to Maryam when she entered the café, Saif following slowly. "Your sister is downstairs in the *musallah*," she said, indicating the prayer room.

Maryam took the stairs at the back, which opened to a large room with a low ceiling. The space was immaculately clean, with bright lighting despite the deeply recessed windows. The floor was ceramic tile, walls painted a sage green. A makeshift wooden *mimbar* had been constructed at the back, the pulpit where the Imam would give sermons during Friday prayers. Neatly folded prayer rugs were stacked next to a bookcase crammed with religious texts. Saima sat cross-legged on a bright red prayer rug, her dark hair covered with a cotton scarf she must have borrowed from Sarah. Her sister's head was bent low over palms cupped in *dua*, prayer. Maryam removed her shoes, and Saima looked up at the approaching footsteps. Her sister scrambled to her feet, and for a moment the two women stared at each other. Then, with a cry, Saima launched herself into Maryam's arms and started to sob. Holding her sister close, Maryam allowed herself to let go, too.

*T*hey ended up sitting on the *mimbar*, the small wooden staircase with three steps and an elevated platform, their arms around each other, Saima's head on Maryam's shoulder.

"I thought about heading to the airport, but it was too cold; plus, I knew there was no way Anna's ex-boyfriend would let me on his stupid plane," Saima sniffed. "I wandered around Main Street instead, feeling sorry for myself. Sarah saw me and brought me here. I sort of broke down again when I came down to the mosque." Tears filled Saima's eyes as Maryam rubbed soothing circles on her sister's back. "I'm sorry I've been so terrible to you lately," Saima said, her voice trembling. "I blamed you for everything, but I know it's not your fault. This is all my fault."

"It's okay, honestly," Maryam said, hugging her sister. "I'm relieved you're safe and warm. I kept having visions of finding you half frozen on the way to the airport. Thank God you didn't throw yourself on the kindness of Nicholas Vandergrey!"

They both chuckled at that before settling into silence. Finally, Saima pushed away from Maryam and, wiping her eyes, sat up straight. "This really is all my fault," she repeated.

"Are you responsible for the weather now?" Maryam teased. "I know doctors have god complexes, but this is too much, even for you."

Saima threw her sister an annoyed glance. "Not the weather. For insisting on getting married in Ramadan, during the winter. For throwing all the organizing into your lap." She took a deep breath. "The truth is, I did it on purpose."

"You fell in love with Miraj and decided you wanted to get married, all on purpose? Wow, I'm shocked."

Saima huffed out a chuckle. "I meant, about the wedding, about insisting it take place so quickly. I did it for *you*."

Maryam blinked, confused. Whatever she had been expecting from Saima—recriminations, passionate arguments, tear-soaked pleas that they rent a jet immediately—it had not been this. "You do realize I'm not the one getting married, right? How is this all for me?" she asked, bewildered.

Saima shook her head impatiently. "I did it because . . . because . . . you were in a rut! I wanted to snap you out of it!"

Maryam stared at her sister. "What?"

Saima fiddled with the borrowed hijab, her movements restless and jerky. "You haven't been yourself in so long. Ever since you and Yusuf broke up, it's like you forgot how to be happy."

"And you thought foisting your last-minute wedding in my lap would bring me back to life?" Maryam asked, slowly starting to piece together what her sister was saying. "How would that work exactly?"

Saima shook her head. "Miraj and I really did want to get married, but I might have made up the part about needing it to happen during the holidays. Mom and Dad and Dadu, they were always telling me how worried they were about you. How quiet and withdrawn you'd become, that you never went out anymore, even when they encouraged you. I thought, maybe if I forced you out of your funk by giving you a big project, it would remind you of everything you were missing out on. It was a stupid plan," Saima finished, looking anywhere but at her sister's face.

Maryam was stunned, too shocked, for a moment, to feel anything. Her sister didn't have to get married in Ramadan, after all. It had always seemed fishy to her, but then Saima's impulsiveness was legendary. Maryam thought about the stressful weeks of planning and harried organizing, the last-minute stress of packing for a wedding that didn't need to occur during the tri-holidays after all, and felt a wave of rage bubble up her throat.

"Do you know how many *hours* I spent on the phone, calling long distance to *Canada*, talking to your *insufferable* Canadian in-laws about food and decor?" Maryam asked, her tone deadly calm.

Beside her, Saima paled. Maryam rarely lost her cool, but when it did happen, it was best to take cover. She started looking around the room for places to hide.

Maryam continued. "We spent two hours debating the merits of Hyderabadi biryani versus Pakistani biryani. *Two hours!*" Maryam scrambled off the *mimbar* and stood on the cold tile floor, glaring at her sister, fists clenched at her sides.

"Who could possibly debate that?" Saima said weakly. "Obviously, Hyderabadi biryani is the best."

"Are you kidding me right now!" Maryam yelled.

"I mean, the wedding has been postponed, so I guess none of us got what we wanted," Saima said, some of the sulkiness returning to her voice. "I really was looking out for you, though. Why do you think I invited Saif? He hasn't stopped staring at you since we landed."

Maryam closed her eyes and tried to steady her breathing by slowly counting to ten. It was Ramadan, and murdering your sister during the holy month was generally frowned upon. Luckily, Ramadan was almost over.

As if catching the drift of her older sibling's thoughts, Saima hurriedly made to gather her things. "We should get back to the inn. I'm sure everyone is wondering where we are," she started, but Maryam held out her hand, slowly shaking her head. They needed to talk. Now.

"Did you really make me plan your wedding to shake me out of a rut? Or did you do it because you're used to having your big sister clean up the messes you make?" she asked Saima.

Saima sat back down on the *mimbar* but said nothing.

"You were furious with me for leaving the airport, for participating in the Holiday Hoopla, but did you ever stop to consider whether I wanted to spend my Ramadan planning your wedding? Whether I enjoy being responsible for picking up the slack and solving everyone's problems all the time? Or would I rather be doing something—anything—else? You claim you're worried about me, that Mom and Dad and Dadu worry about me, but when you found out about the Holiday Hoopla, you freaked out. Don't you realize that the only reason you can run after your dreams is because of the sacrifices I've made? I stayed in Denver so you could do what you wanted with your life."

Saima veered back, blindsided by Maryam's words. "I had no idea you felt that way. You said you wanted to be a pharmacist. I thought you were unhappy because of what Yusuf did."

Maryam sank to the cold tile. "I was. I am. But I had dreams for myself, too, Saima. I always wanted to be a writer."

"Saif knew that about you," Saima said as if working through something. "That's why he took you to the playhouse in the first place." Her face filled with remorse. "I've been selfish every step of the way, haven't I?"

Maryam shrugged, but then nodded. She needed Saima to acknowledge her actions. It was the first step toward repentance, and maybe even reconciliation. She missed her sister, and she didn't want to feel secretly resentful of her anymore. "I think I've just gone along with what I thought everyone else expected from me," she started carefully. "I did it in my marriage; I do it with you, and with Mom and Dad. I'm not sure where I got the idea that in order to be a good *desi* daughter, I had to put myself last, but I'm done with that way of thinking. I'm going to do better from now on, and I want you to do better, too."

Saima stepped off the *mimbar* and joined her sister on the floor, putting her arms around her. "I love you, Maryam," she said. "I'm sorry I've been a terrible sister."

Maryam laughed and hugged Saima back. "That's all right. I've already asked Santa for a better model for Christmas."

Saima smacked her on the arm. They put on their shoes, and Maryam looked around the prayer space, noting the homey details—built-in shelving for shoes, pretty hand-painted Islamic calligraphy adorning the walls, even a corner at the back with low benches, presumably for children to gather for classes. It all felt well-kept and loved.

"I was worried you were rushing into things with Miraj," Maryam said abruptly. Might as well get it all out now. "I don't want you to make the same mistake I did."

Saima squeezed her hand. "It's never a mistake to love someone, or to try to build a life with them. I knew the moment I met Miraj that he was the one for me." She bumped her sister on the shoulder. "Just like you knew with Saif, even at age twelve."

Maryam looked at her feet. "I don't know anything."

Saima raised her eyebrow. "You're the smartest person I know, and you always know everything. That boy is so gone over you. When are you going to put him out of his misery and admit you still have feelings for him?"

Maryam shook her head. "It's too soon. We barely know each other. He lives in California."

"It's not too soon, you've known him all your life, and people can move," Saima countered. "You're afraid. But you can't be anymore, because the new and improved Maryam is better than that. Right?"

Maryam looked away. "What if it doesn't work out?" she said, finally giving voice to her fear.

"Then at least you tried," Saima said. "That's all any of us can do, in the end. Say *bismillah*, and try. You deserve to be happy." Saima started to climb the stairs but turned around. "What time is the Holiday Hoopla tomorrow?" she asked. "I'd like to watch my big sister's script-writing debut."

"What about the wedding?" Maryam asked, following Saima upstairs, where Sarah and Saif waited inside the café.

"My *nikah* should have happened tomorrow. But today is over, and I need to accept reality. The wedding is postponed, and there's nothing we can do about it," Saima said matter-of-factly. "Luckily the snow has finally stopped. We'll leave Snow Falls after the Hoopla tomorrow and head back to Denver. Miraj and I can have a small *nikah* whenever we both have time off. Come on, we should head back. It's already so late."

Her sister's attempt to stay positive and be mature made Maryam's heart drop. Saima had always wanted a big wedding. Anything else would seem wrong, somehow, for her loud, outgoing sister.

But there was nothing Maryam could do about it. Saif had already called for a ride, and the three of them climbed into Jerry's truck for the short drive back. In the truck, Saima dozed, her head on Maryam's shoulder. Beside her, Saif was quiet in the dark of the cab, and the silence between them grew.

"Thanks for coming with me," Maryam said, needing to fill the void. She floundered, searching for the words that would bridge the gulf between them.

"What are friends for," Saif said, flashing her a strained smile, and Maryam's heart plummeted. "Since the roads are clear, I'll probably leave tomorrow for California, right after the show. It's time to get back to my real life."

Maryam stared straight ahead, trying not to flinch at the finality of his words. Part of her wanted to ask him to change his plans, to stay in Snow Falls or maybe fly home with her to Denver. Maybe they could talk, or spend more time together. Except she knew she wouldn't ask him to do any of those things. Her shoulders slumped. "If I don't see you after the Hoopla, have a safe flight," she said, and the words sounded hollow to her ears. This was what she wanted—so then why did her heart feel like it was breaking, all over again?

*B*ack at the Snow Falls Inn, her parents and Dadu were relieved to have Saima back, and kept the women company while they ate a late dinner. The wedding party stayed in the foyer long enough to catch the news. Usually on the twenty-ninth of Ramadan, everyone would anxiously wait to hear if the new moon had been sighted. If it was, Eid-ul-Fitr—the celebration after the holy month—would be the next day. If not, they would all fast one more day and celebrate the following day. Her family would receive news about the moon sighting from their community phone tree. In Snow Falls, they heard it on the news—due to the tri-holidays this year, people were more interested in the mechanics of all three faiths. It turned out that the new moon hadn't been sighted in North America, which meant Eid would be observed on December 26.

After everyone returned to their rooms, Maryam stayed back in the foyer, sipping tea and staring into the fireplace, grateful for the quiet. A part of her was still coming to terms with Saima's postponed wedding—the wedding that she had spent the last six weeks furiously planning—and she couldn't help feeling dejected. Anna and Josh entered the inn, and Maryam smiled when she saw they were holding hands as they walked up to her.

"Hey, friend, are you okay?" Anna asked, the glow on her face dimming somewhat when she caught sight of Maryam's downcast face.

"Sure, I'm fine," Maryam said, trying to muster some animation in her voice.

"What if I go make some tea," Josh offered, and Anna nodded before taking a seat beside Maryam.

"I'm sorry," Maryam said. "I should be asking how your night with Josh went, although I think I know the answer." She smiled, and Anna leaned her head against Maryam's shoulder for a second.

"Things are good. We can talk about all that later. Tell me what's going on."

Maryam was halfway through explaining the drama of the evening when Josh emerged from the kitchen with two steaming mugs, one of which he handed to Anna, before hesitating. Maryam indicated he should stay, and he sat beside Anna, immediately reaching for her hand.

Maryam finished her story, and the couple were quiet, thinking over the events of the night—so different from what had happened to them.

"Well, that's great that Saima was found safe and sound. But what's getting you so down?" Anna asked.

With an embarrassed glance at Josh, Maryam explained:

"It's Saif. And Saima. I mean not both at once, but sort of . . . concurrently?"

Anna nodded in understanding. Maryam continued, her unhappiness spilling out in a rush. "Saif has put himself out there, again and again. He wants to get to know me. He's been nothing but sweet and generous. And every time, I panic and run away. What is *wrong* with me?" Maryam put her head in her hands.

Anna placed gentle hands on Maryam's shoulders. "There is nothing wrong with you," she said so firmly Maryam almost believed her. "You were hurt, badly, by someone you trusted. I guess the question you have to ask yourself is, are you willing to take a chance on Saif? And it's fine if you're not, by the way."

"Is Saif the tall lawyer guy who didn't like *Captain Eagleman*?" Josh asked. Maryam lowered her hands to stare at him, and he smiled sheepishly. "Sorry, I'm not great with names. And I'm not good with this relationship stuff. I mean, I agreed to be in a fake relationship because I'm so bad at it. So . . . whatever Anna said."

The women laughed, and Maryam felt better. "I do want to take a chance on him. But he's basically declared himself three times now, and each time I just . . . froze."

"Maybe that's the problem," Anna said thoughtfully. "Maybe *you* need to make the declaration, the grand gesture. So *you* know you're ready for love again."

Josh beamed at Anna. "You're beautiful, smart, *and* wise. How did I get so lucky?" he asked.

Maryam turned Anna's words over. "The Holiday Hoopla is tomorrow, and everyone will be leaving soon after. I'm not sure I have time to plan a grand gesture."

"I'll help," Anna said instantly. "Just remember, it has to come from the heart and be personal. It should mean something to both of you."

"Wow, I think I might be a little jealous," Josh groused, his eyes crinkling adorably. Maryam hugged Anna, but her second worry—Saima's canceled wedding—rose like a specter before her, and she frowned. As if reading her thoughts, Anna squeezed Maryam's hand.

"You're worried about Saima?" she asked, sympathetic.

"I'm happy that she's accepted that the wedding is postponed, but I wish I could fix this for her. I know how much this means to Saima, and to my parents, even Dadu. I don't want to fail."

"You have not failed," Josh said firmly. "And I'm sure not a single member of your family feels that way."

"No, of course not. I know they don't," Maryam said. "But I feel like I'm failing myself. Like this is something I want to be able to do for my family, for my sister. This isn't just a day—it's a memory she's going to have for the rest of her life. But no matter how hard I try, I just can't think of a solution."

"I might be able to help." Saif approached the trio cautiously, only acknowledging Anna and Josh. "'Tis the season— Ramadan, I mean—for reconciliation. I figured I should probably take my own advice about talking to family. I called my brother, Raihan." He finally glanced at Maryam, but the expression in his eyes remained aloof.

Still, Maryam couldn't help the smile that stole across her face. "I'm so glad, Saif. I bet he was happy to hear from you."

Saif nodded stiffly. "He was mostly surprised, but seemed

on firmer ground when I asked him for a favor. My brother just started working for a company that charters planes."

Maryam's eyes widened. "What did you say?"

"When you first asked me if I knew anyone who had a plane, I didn't even think about Raihan. I offered to do some free legal work for his new boss in exchange for a discount on an emergency flight to Snow Falls."

For a moment, Maryam was speechless. But then her face fell. "The wedding would have been tomorrow. They canceled all the venues, the catering, everything. Even if we made it to Toronto, it would be too late. This wedding can't happen."

"I know," Saif said, and his eyes finally softened as he looked at Maryam. "That's why I told Raihan to charter a plane *from* Toronto."

Anna was the first to catch on; she clapped her hands and jumped to her feet in excitement. "Which means we can have Saima's dream wedding here, in Snow Falls!"

NINETEEN

Anna

December 25

Christmas Day!
The 4th night of Hanukkah
The last day of Ramadan—Eid tomorrow!

A knock at Anna's door woke her from the dream she'd been having about Santa delivering gifts on Christmas Eve while riding on a giant menorah pulled by several reindeer with brightly glowing crescent moons for ears.

She stood and padded over to the door, rubbing the sleep from her eyes.

"Room service," said a familiar voice. She smiled and opened the door, not caring that she had bed head and was wearing the cupcake-festooned flannel pajamas again.

"Good morning, beautiful," Josh said. He was holding a teetering stack of prettily wrapped gifts. "Mind if I come in? I wanted to be the first to wish you a Merry Christmas."

He deposited the gifts on the table and turned to take her in his arms. They shared a sweet kiss.

"There's one more thing I have to bring in," he said, breaking away from their embrace and ducking out into the hall. He returned seconds later carrying a tray with a coffee carafe and a white bakery box.

"Is that what I think it is?"

"You know it. I figured since we'll be leaving Snow Falls soon, our upside-down pineapple rugelach days will be coming to a close for a while. We need to enjoy these while we can."

Anna knew he hadn't meant for those words to make her sad. And that she had absolutely no reason to feel morose right now. It was Christmas morning, and she was spending it in a place she loved, with a person she cared deeply about—who cared back. She needed to stay in the moment and not worry about the future. "So did you buy gifts for everyone at the hotel?" Anna asked, inclining her head toward the stack of gifts.

"Nope, all for you."

"*All* for me? But that's too much!"

"It is Chrisma-Hanukkah, after all. Which means you need eight gifts, plus one extra."

"Really? I've never heard of this Chrisma-Hanukkah holiday. And I only got you one gift." She took a wrapped package from her closet and added it to the pile of gifts.

"Well," he said, taking her in his arms again, "I can think of about eight or nine ways you could make it up to me . . . starting with a kiss?"

Between all the kissing, chatting, coffee drinking, and pastry eating, it took them a few hours to get through the gifts—and it felt, Anna marveled to herself, just as homey and warm as many of the holiday mornings in her past. Josh had bought her winter boots and a parka—"so you don't have to borrow from the inn anymore," he had said, "and because I'm still not convinced you actually own any proper winter gear." He had also given her a pair of Toronto Maple Leafs mittens, rose quartz crystal earrings from June's Cauldron, a knit scarf from the knit shop, the peacock and peahen paperweights from Kate's Kurios, artisanal dark chocolate Hanukkah gelt from Ginger's bakery—and, finally, an open-ended plane ticket—which certainly helped with some of the melancholy Anna had been feeling earlier, when he mentioned their time in Snow Falls coming to a close.

"I just wanted to make sure you knew beyond a shadow of doubt that even though we're taking things slow, I want to see you whenever you think you can get out to LA," Josh said as Anna stared down at the plane ticket, a range of emotions burbling inside her. "And I'll come visit you in Denver, of course. I mean, if you want?"

"Of course I want," Anna said, placing the plane ticket carefully on the end table, then nestling into his arms. "I guess I'm just not sure what my life is going to look like, or where I'm going to be. But I know I want you to be a part of it."

Josh ran his hands through her hair, then gently brought her face to his.

"I will be," he said, kissing her. "You don't have to worry." He kissed her again. "We can support each other." The third kiss was even deeper, and Anna felt her body melt into his. He pulled back to stare into her eyes, then stroked her cheek. "I'm not going anywhere, Anna."

Their faces were still close. She whispered against his lips. "But don't you have plans?"

"I'm going to take some time, just like you. I've got a few screenplay ideas percolating, and if there's anything this week has taught me, it's that I need to pursue the things that I'm passionate about." He ran his hands down her back, and she felt sparks and shivers all over. "I definitely need to get home for a few weeks. Then I'll be heading back to LA to see if I can approach things there a little differently. But right now . . ." His arms were tight around her. "I kinda just wanna stay in the present, you know?" She lost herself in his kisses once more, but the word "present" was a reminder.

"I have something for you," she said, suddenly shy. What if he didn't like it? What if it was too presumptuous? What if it interfered with his plans to head home and see his mom?

She reluctantly disentangled herself from his arms, then stood to fetch the gift, which was in a slender envelope wrapped in gold foil paper. He reached for her and pulled her back into his lap, encircling her within his arms. With her back pressed to his chest and his arms around her, he propped his chin on her shoulder, his breath huffing lightly against her ear and sending shivers down her spine as he opened the envelope.

Out fell two tickets. "Leafs versus Senators in Ottawa on the twenty-seventh!" he exclaimed.

"I'm sorry, maybe I shouldn't have," Anna said. "I was in It's the Most Wonderful Time for a Beer picking something up, and heard Ron and Don talking about their Senators season tickets, so I impulsively asked if I could buy a pair. But . . . that would mean staying around here until then. And you need to get home to see your mom, so you're probably wanting to get out of Snow Falls as soon as possible—"

He silenced her with a firm kiss. She let herself relax

against the warmth of his body. "Anna, my mom loves me and wants me to be happy." He traced the shape of her lips with one finger. "She already knows how much I care about you and would be annoyed with me if I said no to a few extra days and a hockey game with you. I can't think of any place I'd rather be—and I'm more than happy to stay here a few days longer. With you." The next thing Anna knew, they were kissing passionately again, wrapping paper and ribbons scattered around them and all other thoughts forgotten.

Regretfully, Anna pulled away. "I'd love nothing more than to stay here with you all day, but it's getting late and we have to get to the playhouse."

"Oh, right," Josh said, but he kept on kissing her as she playfully swatted at him. "We definitely couldn't just stay here and let Maryam and the rest of the group down. That would be so wrong . . ." He kissed her again. "But wouldn't it feel so right . . . ?"

"Now, come on, I know you don't really mean that. And we'll have plenty of time for more of this later. But maybe I could just spare a few more minutes . . ."

*A*fter Anna was dressed, she headed downstairs to wait for the rest of the group, who had planned to head to the playhouse together. The first person she saw was Mr. Dadu, waiting by the fire.

"Mr. Dadu! Merry Christmas," she called out, heading over to join him.

"Merry Christmas to you, my dear! You look awfully happy today."

"It's a happy day, isn't it? There's so much to celebrate."

"There certainly is, there certainly is. Can I pour you a coffee?"

"I've already had some today, but sure, why not? It's going to be a busy afternoon." She sat down beside him and he poured her a steaming mug.

"I received my gift from you, Miss Anna, and it is very much appreciated. But I also must say, I am even more pleased to see you still here. I was rather disappointed to hear you were planning to leave. Seems you had an awful lot of unfinished business?" He raised an eyebrow.

"I did, you're right. And I'm happy I made a different decision."

"Sometimes you just need to give yourself a little time to think," he said. "Even if it seems difficult in the moment."

She nodded her agreement. "My dad used to say, *No wind, no waves.* I'm grateful for all the tumult of the past week because it taught me a lot. Like that I wasn't really stranded at all."

Mr. Dadu smiled. "None of us really were, were we?"

Anna gazed into the fire, suddenly lost in thought. "There's still one situation I need to figure out," she said. She explained to Mr. Dadu about her stepmother's letter and her invitation to connect. "It's just I've held on to my bitterness for so long, it feels . . . almost scary to let it go, you know?"

Mr. Dadu nodded and stared into the fire, too. "But surely your father, who was so good at giving you advice that would stick with you, told you the truth about bitterness? That it's like drinking poison and waiting for the other person to die?"

Anna laughed. "You know, I'm pretty sure he did tell me

that one. Or that hanging on to resentment is like holding a knife the wrong way around. The thing about resentment is that it only lets you see one side of things—*your* side. After reading Beth's letter, I realize I've been holding on to my resentment so tightly that I couldn't feel just how much I miss her presence in my life. No matter how I try, I don't know if I'll ever understand how she could have married again so quickly after my dad died, but I do know no one deserves to go through what she did. She lost the love of her life."

Mr. Dadu tended to the fire for a moment with a poker, then leaned it back against the hearth and turned to Anna. "I make no secret of the fact that I am a widower and that I miss my wife very much. Not a day goes by that I don't miss her and wish she were still here with us. I imagine Beth feels the same way about your father."

"I know, but I still wonder, if that's true, how could she have just moved on?"

"Did it ever occur to you that she hasn't moved on? That when you truly love someone and share a life with them and then you lose them, you never move on, not really?"

"But she *did*. She remarried." Anna was a bit embarrassed to hear how much she sounded like a petulant child, but Mr. Dadu just smiled indulgently.

Then his eyes took on a faraway look. "My wife died three years ago this winter. About a year after she passed, I reconnected with an old friend of our family who had also lost her husband around the same time. We went for a few walks, shared a few coffees, and I began to realize that perhaps it was possible something could blossom between us." He sighed. "So, I pushed her away. I was convinced that allowing those feelings to bloom would dishonor my wife's memory, and that it would not be fair to her. My friend understood. She did not want to rush me, and she herself was dealing with her own grief over her dear husband. The next time I saw her, I realized something— that I was never going to get over my wife, but that my dear Kulsoom would have wanted me to be happy. I had realized moving on did not mean what I thought it meant, that I could still care for another person and hold my wife's memory dear at the same time. But unfortunately, my friend, she had already remarried another rather lucky man." He tilted his head and smiled a somewhat sad smile. "I have never told that story to anyone, Anna. You will have to keep my secret. I do not have many regrets in my life, but if I am being honest, that is one of them. I wish I had taken the opportunity for love and happiness when it was presented to me, instead of believing that it was the wrong time. When you lose someone, a 'right time' never really comes. You have to take happiness as it comes to you, while accepting that grief will always live with you, too."

Anna felt a lump rise to her throat. "You're so right, Mr. Dadu. I really needed to hear that. Thank you. You always know exactly what to say. And I'm really sorry about you and your friend."

He smiled, and now it wasn't such a sad smile anymore. "Oh, no need to feel sorry for me. I have a wonderful family, as you know, and a very happy life. But I must admit I admire someone like Beth, who it appears has figured out something about grief that many do not. It had nothing to do with you, Anna, and I am sure she did not set out to hurt you. It sounds like she really does want you in her life. You should give her a chance, and keep an open heart."

"Thank you, Mr. Dadu," Anna said. "I will."

"It is the right decision. Another one." He winked. "You are on a roll!"

"What am I going to do without you and your daily advice?"

He reached over and squeezed her hand. "Miss Anna, I am always here for you, just a phone call away. Just because we are going to be leaving Snow Falls soon does not mean we will be gone from each other's lives. You have made yourself an honorary Aziz family member this week with the generous kindness you have extended to us all—and that will not be forgotten. This is a promise."

*A*nna had intended to watch the play from backstage so she could make herself available in case anything went wrong with any of the set decorations—but Bruce insisted she sit in the front row and enjoy the play as an audience member.

"You've worked so hard and made this the best set we've ever had," he said. "Even if something does go wrong, I'm sure it will be nothing we can't handle. You deserve to enjoy the play like one of our guests. Please, I insist."

So, Anna found herself sitting in a comfy "VIP" front-row seat as the curtains rose on the Snow Falls Holiday Hoopla's first-ever presentation of *A Holiday Carol*, written by Maryam Aziz. She leapt to her feet and cheered when they said her friend's name, then quickly sat back down so the play could begin.

Maryam had written her own take on the classic Dickens tale "A Christmas Carol," with a multi-celebration spin. The story centered around a woman named Elvira Scrooge, who was too caught up in her job as the manager of a large corporation that employed all the members of a small town to remember the true spirit of the holidays. Over the course of three acts, she was visited by three "Holiday Hosts": the Host of Ramadan, as played by Saif; the Host of Hanukkah, played by Josh; and the Host of Christmas, played by Celine. Then, much to Mr. Dadu's and the rest of the crowd's delight, the play ended with a rousing Bollywood sing-along to A. R. Rahman's 1998 classic "Chaiyya Chaiyya," the lyrics projected via overhead projector. The audience did their best to join in; the repetitive refrain helped. Soon people were improvising Bollywood dance moves in the aisles, much to Dadu's and Anna's amusement.

As the curtain fell, Anna's voice was hoarse from singing, her hands ached from clapping, and her feet were sore from dancing. It had been a truly superb performance—and she had especially enjoyed watching handsome Josh play the Hanukkah Host, sharing his love of a holiday she held dear, too.

Afterward, the party spilled out into the town square, where Ron and Don had set up booths serving their mulled wine and cider. Ginger was serving baked goods, too, and the owner of Buon Natalie's was handing out delicious plates of turkey and stuffing, and meatballs with cranberry sauce. Josh was still inside with the rest of the play's cast, but Anna anticipated he would be out soon and she'd get to congratulate him for a job well done in person. She wandered around the square, sampling the food and drink and greeting all the familiar faces.

Then she saw Maryam, surrounded by her jubilant family. They beckoned for Anna to join them.

"Maryam! Congratulations! That was amazing. You did

such a great job! I'm so proud of you. You're a writer now, it's official."

"Thanks," Maryam said. She was glowing. "It really did go well, didn't it? I had so much fun." But then her face fell, and her family backed away to a discreet distance, giving the friends a moment to talk. "Oh, Anna. I'm going to miss it. I'm going to miss a lot of stuff about this place, the last place I ever thought I'd end up celebrating Eid tomorrow. And yet . . . it felt really right."

"It will feel even better after we surprise Saima with the news that her wedding is back on. And, of course, after your special surprise for Saif," Anna said.

Maryam looked around to make sure no one from the wedding party was around, and tapped her nose conspiratorially.

"Excuse me, I'm looking for Anna Gibson," said an unfamiliar voice.

Anna turned and saw a woman with bleached-blond hair and a bright red toque. Standing behind her was Samantha, the assistant set designer Anna had met the other day at the playhouse who had come to pick up Chase's uniform. "That's her," Samantha whispered, nudging the other woman forward.

"Anna Gibson?" the woman repeated.

"Yes, that's me," Anna said uncertainly.

"Hi, I'm Kiki Andrade, head set designer for the movie being shot here in town. It is *such* a pleasure to meet you. Were you the person behind the wonderful set for tonight's play?"

"Well, I mean, I had a team," Anna said humbly, but Maryam interjected, "She had a team of volunteers helping, but the concept was all her. She is a set design genius!" She pushed Anna forward to accept the compliment while Anna blushed.

"She certainly is," Kiki said, looking at Anna admiringly. "You captured the spirit of all three holidays perfectly with your design—not an easy thing to do, and I heard you only had a few days. I'm so impressed. I'd love to get the chance to work with you, if you're not otherwise engaged."

"Oh," Anna said with surprise. "Do you mean—"

"I mean I want you to call me, as soon as possible," Kiki said, taking a business card out of her pocket and handing it to Anna. "I'd love to meet and talk about future projects, see what might interest you. Do you by any chance plan to be in Los Angeles soon?"

Anna thought of the open plane ticket back in her hotel room. "You know, I actually do have plans to go to LA very soon . . ."

Kiki grasped her hand and shook it. "*Please*, call me first before you talk to any other production companies. We would *love* to work with you."

Anna was walking toward the cider booth for a refill when someone slid his arms around her from behind and kissed her neck. She turned and found herself in one of her favorite places on earth: Josh's arms. "Hello, Hanukkah Host! You were fantastic!"

He looked bashful and sweet as he smiled and accepted the compliment. "Thank you. You really think so?"

"I really think so. You helped make the play something special."

"It helped that there was a certain special woman in the front row of the audience, cheering me on. Not to mention the beautiful set she designed, which made *all* of us look good."

"About that . . ." Anna began. She felt nervous, all of a sudden, about her news to do with her conversation with Kiki. What if Josh thought she was trying to move things too fast, suggesting she might have a potential job in Los Angeles, where he lived? He had given her an open-ended plane ticket to come for a visit, but that ticket had been round-trip.

"Hey, you okay?"

She explained about the conversation with Kiki in a rush.

"Oh, *wow*, Anna, that is amazing. Kiki is the real deal, and she does not dole out compliments or job offers if she doesn't really mean them. I'm so proud of you! You really are incredibly talented, and I'm so glad someone noticed. I was going to suggest you talk to her, actually, when you were trying to figure out what your future held—but it looks like she got to you first."

"You're sure you don't think it's . . . too much?"

He looked puzzled. "Too much, how?"

"Because we agreed to take things slow. Taking things slow was my idea. But suddenly I'm going to be taking a meeting in LA, and maybe considering a new job there. It's a lot, isn't it?"

He shook his head and smiled even bigger than he already was. "I don't want this to make you nervous, or for you to think I'm getting ahead of myself—ahead of us—but Anna, you need to know, I want you in my life. I know you want to take things slow, and I respect that completely. But I feel like I've been sure about you from the moment I saw you. If you want to move to LA, I'm certainly not going to complain about it. In fact, I'd be *thrilled.* I couldn't think of a happier turn of events than to be near you as we both follow our dreams."

Josh stared deeply into Anna's eyes as music, laughter, and love swirled around them—and downtown Snow Falls glowed with the light and hope of three beloved holidays.

TWENTY

Maryam

December 26

The 5th night of Hanukkah
Eid-ul-Fitr—the feast after the month of Ramadan
Saima's wedding day in Snow Falls!

It was amazing the difference a plan made to Maryam's mood. For the first time in days, she felt practically effervescent, lit up with happiness like a Christmas tree. Or maybe a Hanukkah menorah. Or maybe a Ramadan crescent moon. Something that glowed, at any rate.

Her play had turned out even better than she had imagined, and Maryam could tell that people weren't just being polite—it was an actual hit. A beaming Dadu handed her an enormous bouquet of flowers after the performance, with a smaller bouquet for Saif, who had been buzzing following the play. Azizah and Ghulam hadn't stopped raving for the rest of the night, much to her bemusement. If her multi-faith take on "A Christmas Carol" had the power to impress her *desi* Muslim parents, there really was no higher compliment.

Plus, in addition to the success of the Holiday Hoopla, she had two more delicious secrets: Saima's wedding was back on; plus, her grand gesture was ready to launch.

The next day, her family slept in until seven a.m., which felt downright luxurious after getting up before dawn for the past month. It was Eid today, the feast after the month of Ramadan, and it felt extra special considering all they had been through.

Usually on Eid day, her family would prepare special treats, attend prayer at the mosque, and then go to the cemetery to visit their grandmother's grave. They would usually spend the evening at one of their friends' homes, sharing a potluck or catered dinner. When Maryam was younger, her parents would give her and her sister gifts, and all the adults would give them envelopes of money, called *Eidy*.

Maryam remembered when they first landed in Snow Falls, her family had worried about keeping their fast in this strange town. Now that they had spent nearly a week in the most magical, welcoming town in Canada, part of her was glad they would get to celebrate Eid with the local Muslim community. It felt right.

Azizah put the finishing touches on a meat *nihari* stew she had cooked overnight, while her father cut up fruit. Maryam had already prepared the *shier korma*, the sweet, milky vermicelli pudding made with plenty of cream, sugar, and cardamom, and loaded with pistachios, almonds, and dates. It never felt like Eid unless she had a bowl of the fragrant dessert. The food was for after the early-morning Eid prayer—her family had decided to prepare this feast as a treat for the wedding party, and had extended the invitation to their new friends, as well as their hosts at the inn.

Maryam planned to announce her special surprise at the end of the meal. She couldn't wait to see Saima's face.

Eid prayers were held at Topkapi Café at nine a.m., and the small crowd of about three dozen people mingled and chatted in the basement *musallah*. Sarah generously provided sweet Turkish tea and honey-drizzled baklava afterward.

"Your play was very touching, Maryam," Farah said, coming up to her after the prayer service and hugging her warmly. "It felt really special to see Saif on stage, too, playing the Ramadan Host. That was the first time I really felt like I was part of a holiday pageant."

"You don't know what you're missing until you're included in the story, too," Maryam agreed.

"Chase Taylor did a great job as the Hanukkah Host, and he's so good-looking. Are he and Anna . . ." She trailed off, raising her eyebrows in a question. No one was immune to the lure of celebrity gossip, but Maryam wouldn't be drawn in.

The wedding party walked back to the inn in buoyant spirits and settled around the table that had become their de facto meeting space, joined by Anna, Josh, Deb, Kath, and, sur-prisingly, Tenisha. They passed dishes around family style, and once they had all eaten, Maryam stood up to make her big an-nouncement.

"When we first arrived at Snow Falls, I think it's safe to say we had no idea what we were in for," she began, looking around the table. "The worst snowstorm in a century had us all worried and far from home. We were fasting, and my sister was about to get married in Toronto. Nobody was happy when we had to make an emergency landing in a town we had never heard of."

Smiles and nods as the breakfast party relived those hectic first few days. To her right, Anna twinkled at her, resplendent in a black velvet holiday dress, her hair piled high.

"Remember our first *suhoor* meal? All we had was junk food from the vending machine," Saima called out.

"Those ketchup chips were pretty good, actually. I bought a box to take back home," Saif answered, and everyone laughed.

Looking around the group, Maryam felt her heart swell. They had all been through something difficult together, but they had made the best of it, had made new friends, and rekindled old relationships. In that moment, she knew this was where they were meant to be, and where Saima was meant to have the wedding of her dreams.

"Saima, I know you're the most disappointed of all of us. Your wedding to Miraj was derailed, and no matter how hard we tried, there was nothing we could do about it. In the end, you had to cancel the whole thing."

"I'll drag him to the Imam yet," Saima said loudly, all bravado. Everyone laughed.

"He might be the one dragging you," Maryam said. Saima stopped laughing and looked at her sister.

"What do you mean?" she asked, a thread of something that sounded like hope creeping into her voice.

"How would you like to be married today, in Snow Falls?" Maryam asked.

Saima jumped to her feet, face transformed into a bubbling cauldron of excitement. "What. Do. You. Mean!" she asked, this time nearly dancing. With a subtle nod at Saif, Maryam turned to her sister.

"Saif's older brother, Raihan, works for a company that

charters planes. Miraj and his family are on their way to Snow Falls as we speak. Saima, the wedding is back on."

For a moment, there was nothing but stunned silence around the table, and then pandemonium reigned as everyone jumped to their feet, cheering. Saima ran around the table to hug her sister, lifting her bodily off her feet. Overwhelmed, Maryam called for silence, eager to explain the plan. It would take all hands on deck to make it a reality, and they had no time to waste.

Maryam explained that Snow Falls Inn had generously offered to host the *nikah* ceremony, while the reception would be held in the playhouse and town square.

"We only have a few hours to make this happen," she said, getting down to business. Saima raised her hand.

"Are you sure we can organize a big *desi* wedding in"—she checked her watch—"six hours? It's not as if we have a crew to help us."

Maryam looked at Saif, and then at Josh and Anna, and smiled. "Don't worry, Saima, we've got this," she said, and started handing out the clipboards.

*I*f being a pharmacist doesn't work out for you, you could always give party planning a try," Anna said fifteen minutes later, after Maryam had marshaled her troops and given them their orders. Everyone in the wedding party—including Saima, because brides didn't get off easy when planning a last-minute wedding—had been given a specific to-do list, along with a rundown of events for tonight. They were to report to Command

Central—aka the dining table in Snow Falls Inn—in three hours. Anna had generously offered to execute the wedding theme Maryam had dreamed up, a cross between one of Dadu's Bollywood wedding scenes and a Christmas gala. Either way, there would be a lot of gold tinsel and red velvet.

"I never realized how much overlap there is between South Asian fashion and Christmas decor," Anna mused as she ran her finger down the list Maryam had handed her. "Both use a lot of candles, gold and silver, red and green."

"Do you really think we can pull this off?" Maryam asked, suddenly nervous. It had seemed important to appear confident at breakfast, but now that everyone had dispersed, her anxiety was spiking.

"I have absolute faith in us. Look what we accomplished in just five days! We saved the Holiday Hoopla, survived the Storm of the Century, and made friends with Hollywood stars." Anna clasped Maryam's hand and squeezed affectionately. "You and I are unstoppable. Now, don't you have somewhere you need to be? I found everything on your list and dropped it off. Good luck."

It was hard to leave her post at the dining table, but Anna promised to make sure things ran smoothly and to deal with any problems that cropped up. The old Maryam would have worried, but the new Snow Falls Maryam only thanked her friend, and rushed to prepare her surprise for Saif. She returned to the inn a few hours later, just in time to check on the progress of the wedding planning. Her troops had worked miracles—the flowers had been arranged, and the restaurants on the list enthusiastically agreed to contribute a feast. Anna had managed to source most of the supplies, and her family had sorted out music for Saima's entrance, and accommodations at Snow Falls Inn for Miraj and his family.

At Rockport Airport, Saima anxiously waited for her fiancé and his parents, older sister, and brother-in-law.

"They're going to love you," Maryam whispered in her sister's ear. "You got them a ride on a private jet!"

Saima was too nervous to respond, but when the guests finally disembarked, she ran straight toward a short, handsome man with light brown skin, hazel eyes hidden behind chunky dark glasses, and a beaming smile. They hugged, before trailing up to Maryam and the rest of the family. Introductions were quickly made, and she studied her sister's new family.

"I can't believe we're here," Miraj said, gazing adoringly at Saima. "I thought our plans were snowed under that storm. I was so worried about you." This comment endeared him to Maryam immediately.

The jury was still out on the rest of his family, though. Maryam couldn't forget how snooty they had been when she was coordinating the wedding from Denver, and their current aloof expressions fit her initial judgment. Miraj's parents were fashionably dressed, as if they traveled by private jet regularly, his father in a smart dark suit, and his mother, her features haughty, dressed in a floral silk *salwar kameez* suit completely inappropriate for the wintry weather.

"How fortunate the wedding can proceed," Miraj's mother, Mausam, offered through pursed lips, but her son's clear delight was enough to vanish any lingering worries Maryam might have had. Difficult in-laws were such a common stereotype among South Asian families, they had practically inspired the entire movie and drama industry. What really mattered was that Miraj was clearly besotted with Saima, and the feeling was very much mutual. This wedding was happening, one way or another.

The streets were finally clear after nearly a week, and the ride from the airport into town took less than fifteen minutes. When the cab pulled up in front of Snow Falls Inn, Maryam told everyone to be ready in two hours for the *nikah*.

In the meantime, she had a grand gesture to make.

*A*fter much discussion yesterday, Anna and Maryam had decided that the playhouse, where the Holiday Hoopla had taken place the night before, would be the perfect spot for her surprise. Or, rather, the snow-covered field behind the playhouse, which happened to border a frozen pond. Now all she had to do was wait. And worry that Saif wouldn't get the reference, or wouldn't find it romantic, or that he would run away.

She turned to the snowman beside her, complete with carrot nose, coffee bean eyes, scarlet scarf, and woolen toque. "This will work, right?" she asked. The snowman's curved grin—also made with coffee beans—did nothing to reassure her. A second snowman, two snow cats, and the snow dog she had constructed earlier refused to chime in, so she busied herself by arranging the halal marshmallows Anna had sourced on a platter, and set them in front of the portable stove on the ground.

Just then, a flustered Saif came running up to her, breath

visible in the cold. He frowned at the snow army surrounding Maryam. "Anna said you had an emergency, that I had to get here right away . . ." He trailed off, taking in the scene more carefully. "What's going on, Maryam? This looks just like that frozen lake beside the winter cottage, from when we were kids. Did you make all these yourself?"

Maryam took a deep breath and nodded. "I made them for you."

Saif still seemed confused. "Why?"

"That first morning in Snow Falls, after *suhoor*, you told me you kept dreaming about a place like this: a quiet town, away from everyone, covered in snow. A place that reminded you of the family cottage trip."

"You remembered," Saif said softly. He looked around the scene she had created with Anna's help, seeming to take in every detail: the carefully decorated snowmen and snow animals, marshmallows ready to be roasted over the portable stove, even a stack of neatly rounded snowballs ready for a playful battle. It was a re-creation of a cherished memory, back before their lives had grown complicated.

"I remember it all," Maryam said now. "Every conversation, all the things I said, every sweet thing you did." She stepped closer to Saif; part of her was terrified, but another part sensed that she was on the brink of a glorious fall. Anna had been right—it was Maryam who had to decide to take that leap. "You're right that I'm still broken over my past. But when I look at you, all I see is my future. Saif, when I crushed on you as a child, it was because you were my Muslim Prince Charming. But the man you've grown into is so much more than that. You're strong, funny, supportive, and so kind. You give to others, even when they—I—give nothing back. All because of your beautiful, generous heart."

Saif's eyes were intent on hers as if he were memorizing this moment, as if he couldn't believe it was really happening. Maryam could hardly believe it, either, but the exhilaration of finally telling Saif how she felt—how, on some level, she had always felt about him—was a joyful rush. "I choose you, for who you are," she said. "If you let me, I promise to choose you, again and again."

Saif closed the distance between them and pulled her into his strong arms. "I was willing to wait," he said, his voice muffled. "I wasn't going to give up." He pulled back, and his face was haloed by the sun.

"I think we've both waited long enough," Maryam said.

They walked back to the inn holding hands.

They settled on a few things during their too-brief walk: First, upon returning to California, Saif would immediately get a long-distance phone plan. Then, Saif decided, he would give notice at his company.

"I've been thinking about moving back to Denver for a while," he reassured her when she protested. "You would just be an added inducement. I want to work on my relationship with my parents. I want to get to know Raihan and his wife, spend time with my nephew."

Maryam had some changes to make as well. First, she planned to scale back at the pharmacy—her father could hire help, and she wanted time to work on making her writing dreams come true.

As for the dreams Maryam and Saif had for their future, they decided to keep their news quiet for now. Saima deserved to have her big day—though Maryam thought her blissful happiness might be obvious from the beaming smile on her face.

Once in her room, Maryam quickly changed into the outfit she had originally packed for Saima's wedding in Toronto. She had been particularly excited about the cream-colored *lengha* she had sourced from one of the few Indian boutiques in Denver, and now she admired the long-sleeved tunic and voluminous skirt, both made from flowing satin and embroidered with delicate paisley patterns in black, blue, and red thread. The outfit was elegant and flattering, and also completely wrinkled; with a sigh she plugged in the iron and got to work. Once she was dressed, her matching cream hijab secured, makeup applied, and the last bangle fastened, she went in search of her sister, who was getting ready in their parents' room.

Anna was already there, putting the finishing touches on Saima's bridal makeup, and Maryam gasped when she saw her sister.

Saima had chosen to wear traditional red, and her *lengha* mirrored her sister's in design, except the lavish *zari* embroidery work was hammered gold, inlaid with crystal and tiny mirrors, the red a deep maroon that matched her lipstick. Anna had subtly highlighted her sister's cheekbones with an iridescent blush, shaded her eyelids a darker gold, and outlined her eyes with black kohl. Her jewelry was lavish—a pearl choker necklace paired with a heavy gold chain, gold bangles on her arms with matching rings. The oversized nose ring, with its single pearl and ruby, traditional among Hyderabadi brides, and matching *tika* forehead ornament completed the look. With a luxuriously embroidered gold silk *dupatta* pinned to her hair, Saima looked every inch the *desi* bride, and Maryam pressed her hands to her mouth in admiration, even as tears filled her eyes.

Anna wore an off-the-shoulder royal blue dress that skimmed her knees and hugged her curves that she had found in one of the stores on Main Street. Compared to the two Aziz sisters in their *desi* finery, her dress was simple, but it suited her. The one nod to the season was a festive crystal-encrusted star pinned near her waist, her dark hair arranged in an elegant chignon with a matching star-shaped ornament.

Saima rose when Maryam entered the room and swiftly came to her side. "You made this happen," she said, kissing Maryam on the cheek. "How can I ever pay you back?"

"Don't start crying now. You'll ruin your makeup," Maryam said, wiping her eyes.

"Weddings are for happy tears," Anna said. "Don't worry, we can always reapply the makeup."

Behind them, their mother, Azizah, beamed. She was dressed in a dark green sari heavily embroidered with silver, with an ornate lace-filigree silver necklace and matching ear bobs. "Let's not keep our guests waiting," she said.

As Saima descended the stairs into the reception area of the inn, where the *nikah* would be performed, she was supported by her mother on one side and Maryam on the other, with Farah and Anna bringing up the rear. The chatting crowd quieted as the strains of a wedding song from one of Dadu's Bollywood movies started. The beat started slow, but then picked up as Saima came into view, and the appreciative crowd burst into raucous applause. Her sister, noticing all eyes on her, spontaneously did a few *bhangra*-style dance steps, much to the crowd's delight. Maryam grinned, nodding at Deb and Kath, Josh and Tenisha, before her gaze landed on Saif—and her breath caught in her throat.

He had changed into a formal black *salwar kameez* suit that emphasized his broad shoulders, silver embroidery around the starched collar. His hair had been neatly combed, and she noted with some disappointment that he had shaved. He was the best-looking person in the room, and his eyes were focused entirely on her. He winked, before schooling his expression into a serious one.

The Muslim marriage ceremony was simple—all it required was the consent of both parties, the giving away of the bride by her *wali* (in this case by her father, Ghulam), a short sermon by the local Imam, followed by signing the legal marriage contract, which Miraj had brought with him. Afterward, they all posed for pictures. Saima glowed beside her new husband, and Miraj looked as if he couldn't believe his luck, which made up for the shallow smiles from his parents. When Maryam hugged Saima and whispered her *duas* and well-wishes in her ear, Saima gripped her extra tight. Nothing could dim the happiness of this moment. Her sister was married, in the last place any of them would have expected.

Maryam looked around at the decorations. The walls of the inn were strung with fairy lights and streamers, and Anna had done a superb job setting up a makeshift stage for the happy couple, festooned with potted poinsettias, and covered with rich tapestries borrowed from the film crew.

Saif was at her side the moment the ceremony concluded, warm fingers grazing her waist. "*Mubarak*," he said softly. "I think we should hire Anna to decorate and plan our wedding, too. What do you think?"

"Actually, I was planning to dump the planning in Saima's lap," Maryam said, smiling up at him. She was so happy.

"Seems only fair. Make sure you only give her six weeks' notice," Saif said, nodding thoughtfully. "And then, last minute, we should elope. I know running away is a family tradition."

Maryam laughed, the sound brimming with joy. "My running-away days are over," she vowed. "From now on, I'll only be running toward you."

Saif bumped her with his shoulder. "I knew you were a romantic all along. You just needed to meet the right sort of charming opportunist." He leaned closer. "Or maybe you just needed to meet me again."

She stood up on tiptoe to bridge the distance between them. "Eid Mubarak, Saif."

"And many more, Maryam."

Once the pictures were taken, they all walked over to the playhouse, where the reception would be held in a larger venue to accommodate the crowd. Nobody in Snow Falls could resist a day-after-Christmas, Eid-day, Hanukkah, and wedding celebration, and it felt like the entire town had turned out. The restaurants Saif had contacted had not disappointed, and banquet tables onstage groaned with treats from all their favorites—brisket, latkes, tandoori chicken, naan, and enough Hakka for several days' worth of leftovers—plus hot chocolate and cider and pop for everyone, and an entire table full of desserts—baklava, pastries, even *mithai*.

The happy couple posed for photos with everyone who asked—and they all did. Dadu was surrounded by a circle of admiring film folk who hung on his every word and laughed at every joke. Ghulam and Azizah made small talk with Miraj's parents, and Maryam thought she saw them smile at one point. The playhouse was filled to capacity, and the party continued outside, where groups of revelers broke out in Christmas carols, and even a traditional *nasheed* song.

Anna found Maryam by the stage, poking through what was left of the paneer kebabs. "Happy?" she asked, and Maryam grinned.

"So happy," she replied. They both turned to look down at the audience pit, where Josh and Saif were deep in conversation. The women exchanged bemused glances.

"Josh and I are going to spend some time together in Ottawa, and then . . . I've got a shot at working in set design. In LA," Anna said shyly.

Maryam nearly dropped her glass in her excitement, and threw her arms around Anna in a big hug. "I'm so proud of you!"

"What about you?" Anna asked.

Maryam shared the plans she and Saif were already making for their future. Anna squeezed Maryam's hand, and the women turned to look at the guests, chatting, laughing, enjoying one another's company, wrapped in a happy cocoon of joy.

"I don't want it to end," Anna said. She turned to Maryam. "Maybe we could meet back here in Snow Falls again?"

Maryam could see it now, in a way she hadn't before: the future would contain challenges, but it would also be filled with blessings and grace, so long as she surrounded herself with the people who truly mattered, who supported one another's dreams, provided comfort during difficulty, and urged one another to take chances. "I can't wait."

Acknowledgments

First off, we are so very grateful and delighted to be writing the acknowledgments for this meant-to-be book! All the stars for a collaboration that was written in the stars, and has been a joyful experience from start to finish. We're sad to say goodbye to Snow Falls, Maryam, Anna, and the rest of the gang, so we'll only say farewell, *for now.* In the meantime, we have many people to thank!

Thank you to our editors, Tara Singh Carlson and Deborah Sun de la Cruz, whose wisdom and kindness made the editorial process a joy; our teams at Putnam and Penguin Random House Canada, including Ashley Di Dio, Katie McKee, Molly Pieper, Samantha Bryant, Dan French, Beth Cockeram, Mary Beth Constant, Andrea St. Aubin, Maija Baldauf, Emily Mileham, Hannah Dragone, Elke Sigal, and Tiffany Estreicher. And a huge thank-you to Sanny Chiu for the fantastic cover.

Uzma: Thank you to my agent, Ann Collette, for always being in my corner and for the invaluable advice and cheerleading. Thanks also to my large extended family, but a few special stars to the following: to my husband, Imtiaz, for your support, love, and for always making space for my dreams; to my children, Ibrahim and Mustafa, for always getting into the spirit of Ramadan and Eid; to my parents, Mohamed and Azmat, for teaching me to fast, and to value the importance of community; and to my mother-in-law, Fouzia, for the support and good wishes. Thanks in particular to my mom and mother-in-law for the special treats: it isn't Ramadan or Eid without your patties, homemade samosas, palada, kichri, coconut chutney, and sheer khurma.

Marissa: I'm grateful for my agent, my constant, Samantha Haywood, and her dedicated, supportive team at Transatlantic Agency; and Dana Spector at CAA, who makes magic in the background. I couldn't do any of this without my family—especially: my dad, Bruce Stapley, for always cheering me on, believing in me, and driving around with copies of my books on his back dash; Joe Sr. and Joyce Ponikowski for being my biggest fans; my stepdad, James Clubine, for the Christmas Eve pageants, candlelit services, and steady guidance; Su Scrimgeour, for being a first reader, and for the gift of the most beautiful, fated menorah; and my mother, Valerie, always, forever—my work brings me such joy because I feel you in the details. Finally, thank you to my children, Joseph and Maia, for being my proudest accomplishments; and to the Toronto Maple Leafs for making it into the playoffs that one fateful year so I could meet and marry Joe, the love of my life.

Three Holidays and a Wedding

Uzma Jalaluddin and Marissa Stapley

A Conversation with the Authors

Discussion Guide

BOOK
ENDS

PUTNAM
—EST. 1838—

A Conversation with the Authors

What was it like to co-write this book?

Marissa: Without a hint of hyperbole, this book was probably the most fun I've ever had writing anything. Not only did I laugh a lot, but I also learned a lot—which I always find invigorating. Ramadan fell in the month before we started our first draft and Uzma suggested I fast for a day as research for the book. We could probably turn the texts we sent between dawn and sunset that day into a comedy routine. The Hakka Chinese place I ordered *Gilmore Girls*–gluttony levels of takeout from that night still have me on their list of best customers. I was that person who says, "But not even water?!" over and over. (And I did end up drinking water, I just couldn't do it.) In the end, though, the experience was beautifully profound. Writing with a co-author of a different background from my own made the process even more of a collaboration. It was a constant conversation, from the moment the idea was born—involving compromise, generosity, open-mindedness, and faith—to the moment the book was finished.

Uzma: This was my first co-authored book and I wasn't really sure what to expect. Writing a novel is an inherently isolating process—it's just you and your characters most of the time. When Marissa first approached me about this project, I had just finished a draft of my third novel. After spending so much time in my head, I was ready to share the reins with someone else! The resulting partnership went even better than I expected. I think we did a great job communicating and compromising. We also did a great job outlining, which is the key to any happy author collab!

What was your co-writing process like?

Marissa: There are a few keys to successful co-writing: a fully developed outline, a willingness to compromise, the wisdom to know when to let things go or stand your ground, and a sense of humor. Writing books is normally a solitary endeavor, which is why co-writing can be such a joy, but it's also a major change in process for any author. Our particular process was that we outlined the book first and made sure that outline was as detailed as possible. Dividing up the chapters was easy because we were each writing a different character. We wrote the first half of the novel before having a check-in with our agents and our editors, then carried on with the rest of it. We wrote mostly in tandem and would read each other's chapters as we went, which also makes the process a lot smoother.

Uzma: I also really enjoyed getting immediate feedback. The fun little comments, texts, and reactions we shared were so encouraging and galvanizing to read. We made each other laugh, and cry. Usually I'm a little shy to share my work with anyone in the early stages, but since we were writing partners, it felt natural. From the outset it was clear that we were creating something really special and unique.

How did you think of this original and heartwarming idea?

Marissa: A few years ago, we were having a phone chat about some film/TV options we had respectively signed for past projects and confessed our mutual desire to one day write a screenplay.

Uzma: Like most writers, I always have a dozen story ideas and prompts in my head, each fighting for attention. I love holiday movies like *The Holiday*, *It's a Wonderful Life*, *Home Alone*, *Die Hard* (yes, it's a Christmas movie, fight me) and *Love Actually*. The idea of writing a multi-faith holiday movie popped into my mind. Some readers might not know that Muslims traditionally follow the lunar calendar, which is 354 or 355 days long. So our calendar jumps back ten days every year. Over the decades, I've observed Ramadan in December, as well as July (I much prefer December, in case you were wondering). The last time Ramadan was in December was in the early 2000s, and I remember there was an extra festive magic in the air, as three holidays—Christmas, Hanukkah, and Ramadan—all fell within days of each other. I thought it might be neat to use this situation to spin a fun holiday story that encompassed the joyful aspects of each holiday. I even had a working title for the holiday movie—*Happy, Merry, Eid Mubarak*! I mentioned this to Marissa during our call.

Marissa: I couldn't stop thinking about the concept, though at the time, neither of us had the space in our schedules to take on a new project. Then the stars aligned and, suddenly, we both did—and it made sense for us to turn this screenplay idea into a novel. I remember calling Uzma to ask her if she wanted to write a novel with me. She was so surprised! (And, I like to think, delighted.)

Uzma: I would say it was initial surprise—I had never even thought about co-writing a book before—followed by excitement.

Marissa: She told me she needed two weeks to think it over—which impressed me. I'm impulsive and jump right into things, which is sometimes great and sometimes not so much, but Uzma is very thoughtful about her decisions.

Uzma: Actually, I just truly believe in a pro-con list, plus I was in the middle of marking essays for my high school classes. I needed to schedule some time to think it over!

Marissa: It meant a lot to me to know how deeply she had considered it before saying a wholehearted *yes*.

Did these three holidays really coincide in the year 2000?

Yes! We took a bit of liberty with the exact timing, though. In the year 2000, Eid ul-Fitr (the celebration after the month of Ramadan) was actually celebrated on December 28. Hanukkah started on December 21, 2000, and ended on December 29.

Do either of you see any aspects of yourselves in either Maryam or Anna?

Marissa: As we were writing, Uzma would write to me and say, "That's you, isn't it?" (A semblance of the scene on the airplane where Anna explodes a bottle of perfume actually happened to me once. I'm also a very nervous flyer so I have engaged in all sorts of nervous and ridiculous in-flight behavior.) And, like Anna, I was raised in a multifaith home—my stepmother was Jewish, my stepdad a Christian minister; I have Jewish half-siblings—so many of her emotions and experiences come from my own life too. When I had children, my daughter in particular was very curious about Hannukah's role in the holiday season.

Uzma: I'm the eldest daughter of South Asian immigrants, so I can relate to some of the expectations placed on Maryam, though my parents are way more relaxed. I'm also not quite as dutiful as

Maryam! And while I've been known to put my foot in my mouth, I haven't managed to embarrass myself quite like Maryam did on the plane, thankfully. Other than that, most of my characters feel entirely separate from me, but I'm sure they're all composite quilts of all the interesting people I've met in my life.

The Rumi quote at the start of the book is beautiful. How do you think it informs the story you've written?

Marissa: It perfectly encapsulates what we are trying to express with this book and, which I in particular, having been raised in first a Christian household and then a multifaith one, have always suspected to be true: that all faiths are predicated on some universal tenets and truths about God, faith, charity, kindness, goodness . . . it really is all the same light, even if it hits a little differently in certain places. There's so much fear and unrest in the world and I think a lot of it comes down to lack of education about what all these other faiths center around. Being able to come together with another author and write a beautiful story that honors all three traditions in a way that also entertains and delivers joy and inclusion feels like one of the most important creative projects I've ever been involved with.

Uzma: Ditto.

Was there a real-life inspiration for the town of Snow Falls?

There's a real town outside Ottawa called Almonte that practically doubles as a holiday romance movie set. After reading about it in a *New York Times* article, it seemed like the perfect location to turn to for Snow Falls inspiration. But really, it's also supposed to be the kind of town you'd read about in other holiday rom-com novels or see in your favorite holiday movie, because part of the beauty of these books and films is that the places they're set in feel familiar—almost like they're all set in the same little town. There's such comfort and familiarity in that. And then, of course, we put our own spin on the typical holiday rom-com town by making it diverse in a way that surprises everyone who looks beyond the snowy, festive surface.

This book often compares the families we are born with and the families we choose for ourselves. What do you think a found family can provide that a family of origin might not be able to?

Marissa: I'm very close with my family—but it's also an unconventional family with step-parents and ex-step-parents and half siblings, and friends who are family. None of it is textbook, and that's perfectly fine with me. While a chosen family can provide many of the things perhaps your blood family already does, one thing a chosen family can give you that traditional family cannot is a vision of you outside of the context of your background. Anna is able to see Maryam as someone other than the responsible, in-charge person in her family—but she also admires that about her new friend, and makes Maryam value the qualities in herself she may have been overlooking. And for Anna, who has a smaller family circle, the Aziz family provides her with a chosen family.

Uzma: I'm fortunate to have a large extended family—aunts, uncles, cousins, nieces, nephews, all of whom live in Canada, the United States, India, and the Middle East. We keep in touch through Zoom calls, WhatsApp chat groups, and visits when we can, and I get together with my family in Toronto often. Yet I also have a large network of friends who have become found family. I think this is common for immigrant families. When my parents first moved to Canada from India, they didn't have any family living here. And so they made good friends through the mosque or cultural events. Growing up, I had a lot of "aunties" and "uncles" who weren't blood-related, but they were all supportive, and in many cases, surrogates for family who lived thousands of miles away. I'm still very close to the friends I met through my mosque, and I consider them my sisters.

Uzma, you mention several Ramadan dishes in your acknowledgments. Which is your favorite dish, how is it prepared, and why is it your favorite?

I truly can't pick one! Ironically, while Muslims fast during Ramadan from dawn to sunset, there is a lot of emphasis on food the rest of the time. You eat the early morning meal together with family and break fast with family. In this context, food feels especially nourishing to both the body and the soul. When we break our fast at sunset, we usually eat a small appetizer meal before dinner that consists of delicious snacks and fruit and drinks. For instance, my mom makes amazing *dahi vada*, which is fried dumpling fritters made from ground lentils soaked in yoghurt and drizzled with tamarind chutney. I also love my mother-in-law's *palaada*, a crepe made with rice or wheat flour and filled with sweetened, shredded coconut. This past Ramadan, I became addicted to mango milkshakes. And for Eid, we make a sweet pudding called *shier khurma*, with vermicelli noodles, nuts, dates, and cream. I'm craving it right now!

Marissa, what is your favorite holiday dish, how do you like to prepare it, and why is it your favorite?

I love latkes but have only ever made them once. They were so much work! So now, I just really appreciate it when people make them for me. (I've never tried them with Ranch dressing, by the way, but am a Ranch Dressing Enthusiast, so maybe I should. #ranchdressingoneverything!) At my family holiday dinners, I'm always in charge of the turkey and dressing, which I learned how to make from my beloved late mom, Valerie. It was one of our favorite "no-recipe recipes." She was an interior designer and we used to play "No Room, No Budget!" too. When rooms in my 1920s Toronto fixer-upper needed an upgrade but I'd already spent all my money on rewiring or a new roof, I knew just who to call. I loved being able to put that in the book.

I like to think my turkey dressing is one of my "famous" dishes. I can never replicate it year over year, but it's always a hit. The main ingredients are good bread, sausage, celery, onions, plenty of fresh herbs, and lots of creativity. I'm also a big fan of any sort of holiday fudge. My Grandma Jean made traditional chocolate fudge around the holidays, but also the kind that has peanut butter, caramel, and multi-colored marshmallows. It should be disgusting and maybe empirically it is, but it's my absolute favorite holiday treat. It takes me right back to my childhood.

What does the "holiday season" mean to each of you?

Marissa: It means a break from the regular schedule, time with family, friends, and time spent giving back to the community. It means Christmas Eve church services, always an important tradition for our family (those candlelit services Anna so fondly remembers come from my own experiences at my stepdad's church), and lighting menorahs while thinking about ways to spread light in the coming new year. I live in Ontario, so the holiday season definitely always means snow, too—and, hopefully, a good old-fashioned blizzard (perhaps without the need to call in the army for a rescue!) and a few cozy snow days. It really is the most wonderful time of the year, no matter what you celebrate.

Uzma: I've always loved the holiday season. For one, I got married during the holidays. Saima isn't alone in thinking Christmas is a good time to tie the knot—for Muslims and people of other faiths, getting married during the holiday season just makes sense. Everyone is off work and school anyway! It's also a time to reset and relax. I always return to work feeling refreshed and eager to jump into the new year. Since my family doesn't celebrate Christmas in the traditional sense, we have learned to make the holiday meaningful for us. We have a *Lord of the Rings* marathon and sleepovers with my nieces and nephew. I bake way too many gingerbread and shortbread cookies and decorate them very badly. Seriously, no one should allow me near royal icing. My extended family usually plans a big get-together on Christmas or Boxing Day. It's truly become a special time of year.

Which was your favorite scene to write for this book, and why? No spoilers, please!

Marissa: The plane scene always made us laugh, even the umpteenth time we read it. It was a pleasure to lend some of my own absurd behavior to this character and have Uzma not just find it funny, but still want to be my friend.

She did say she will never get on a plane with me, though . . .

Uzma: We will definitely be travelling in separate planes. Though you like the window seat and I prefer the aisle, so maybe we can make it work after all! For myself, I enjoyed writing the early interactions between Maryam and Saif—meet-cutes are always fun. And of course, Dadu's antics put a smile on my face. He stole the show every chance he got, and I love him for it!

If you could cast Anna or Maryam in a movie or TV series, who would play them? How about Nick, Saif, or Josh?

Marissa: With Anna, I have never been so clear on my muse for a character: she has always been Lily Collins. And, Josh? Justin Baldoni. Except when I told Uzma that, she said she imagined Saif as Justin Baldoni, too! I think it's safe to say we both find him rather swoon-worthy. Josh could also be a Justin Guarini type. And if we could time travel, Nick would be played by a '90s Ian Ziering (as Steve Saunders in Beverley Hills, 90210), or Scott Foley in the late '90s and early aughts, when he played Noel Crane on Felicity.

Uzma: I'm so bad at dream casting! Justin Baldoni aside, I'd love to see some wonderful up-and-coming actors play the roles of Maryam and Saif!

What do you most want readers to take away from *Three Holidays and a Wedding*?

First and foremost, we want this book to entertain our readers and make them happy—but there is of course a deeper desire here too, and it's twofold: we hope to either show readers a side of the holiday season they've never considered or perhaps have even been misinformed about, and to make other cultures and faiths feel included. As fans of holiday movies, and holiday traditions, we know how important it is to feel seen and included. Being able to write this adorable, joyful holiday romance that respects and values three different faiths has been so personally meaningful for both of us. I hope this book is as fun for you to read as it has been a delight to write! And no matter what holiday you celebrate, may you always be surrounded by love, kindness, and empathy. Happy all the holidays!

Discussion Guide

1. What does the holiday season mean to you? Did this book change the way you think about the holidays?

2. Like Anna discovering Nick's engagement ring, have you ever been overwhelmed or confused by news that ought to be "good"?

3. Were you surprised by the contrast between how Maryam and Anna saw themselves and the way they saw each other? What do you think they eventually learn from seeing themselves through each other's perspectives?

4. Have you ever had a meaningful interaction with a total stranger? If so, describe it.

5. What might you confess to a total stranger during a moment of extreme turbulence on a plane?

6. How do you think Maryam's and Anna's lives would have turned out if there hadn't been a snowstorm?

7. Dadu suggests that Anna take a "fast from worrying so

much." What do you think you might need to take a one-day fast from? How do you think the fast might affect you?

8. This book has several instances of hidden or overlooked identities. What do you think the book is trying to say about what it means to really know someone?

9. What roles do snow and winter play in creating romantic chemistry in the novel?

10. Which character would you most want to be stuck in Snow Falls with, and why?

11. What was your favorite scene in the novel, and why?

12. What did you think of the ending? What do you think will happen to Anna and Maryam after the story's end?

Photo credit: Andrea Stenson Photography

Uzma Jalaluddin is the internationally bestselling author of *Ayesha at Last, Hana Khan Carries On,* and *Much Ado About Nada.* A high school teacher, she has also written a regular column for the *Toronto Star* and contributed to *The Atlantic.* Her first novel was optioned for film by Pascal Pictures, and her second novel was optioned for film by Kaling International and Amazon Studios. She lives with her family just outside Toronto, where she also teaches high school.

VISIT UZMA JALALUDDIN ONLINE

UzmaJalaluddin.com
🐦 UzmaWrites
📷 UzmaJalaluddin

Marissa Stapley is the *New York Times* bestselling author of the Reese's Book Club pick *Lucky*, as well as international bestsellers *Mating for Life*, *Things to Do When It's Raining*, *The Last Resort*, and *The Lightning Bottles*. She has also cowritten *The Holiday Swap* and *All I Want for Christmas* under the pen name Maggie Knox. Many of her novels have been optioned for television, and her journalism has appeared in publications across North America. She lives in Toronto with her family.

VISIT MARISSA STAPLEY ONLINE

MarissaStapley.com
MarissaStapleyAuthor
MarissaStapley